A Psalm for Cock Robin

⁋ A Harp and His (*Dead*) Mother Mystery ⁋

E.E. "Doc" Murdock

H.O.T. Press

Published by
H.O.T. Press
Los Angeles
www.hotpresspublishing.com
Established 1983

ISBN: 0-923178-21-X
ISBN-13: 978-0-923178-21-5

Acknowledgments

I am indebted to the members of the Ojai Writing Workshop who provided valuable feedback as I worked through the many drafts of this book. And of course, without the help of Zoe, this book would not exist.

*Who saw him die? I, said the Fly, with my little eye, I saw him die.
Who caught his blood? I, said the Fish, with my little dish, I
caught his blood.*

From "Who Killed Cock Robin?"
In the earliest known book of nursery rhymes,
Tommy Thumb's (Pretty) Song Book, London, 1744

There once was a boy named Harp

The court-appointed attorney admitted that Harp was a little odd. But he loved his mother. He wouldn't hurt her, let alone kill her. He said Harp was a nice lad, gentle and soft-spoken. He'd had a rough childhood, but he wasn't a bad kid at heart.

The prosecutor said the evidence proved the fire was not an accident. It was arson. Harp must have done it.

So the judge took the two attorneys to his chambers and they sat in big comfortable chairs to talk about what to do with this strange young man who had no family and nowhere to go. They had a little bourbon in their coffee and they talked for a while about whether Tennessee whiskey was as good as Kentucky whiskey. Then they agreed on a compromise: Harp should be locked up in the East Aurora State Mental Hospital. Forever.

Part 1
Who Killed Little Hilly?

A trainee was on the ward last night. After he left, there was a little notebook on the aide's desk and nobody else noticed so I grabbed it. I'm going to start a diary. This is it. I'll hide it inside the hole in my mattress so nobody can ever find it. First I'll write my name. Harp. Then I'll write the place I'm in. It's called Ward D-4 and there are 19 men here, not counting me because they say I'm not really an adult yet. Mitch is the name of the aide who is in charge of the ward. He makes me eat pills so I won't hear things.

1-1

Auguries in the Fog

*W*ake up.

Harp wakes up.

Is someone there?

He listens.

He doesn't hear anything except the sound of his own breathing. Maybe it was just a bad dream.

He smells the sharp, tarry smell of the old wood and knows that means he's safe in his secret little hole up under the pier, like the boy who got away by hiding in the witch's hut in the deep, dark forest. Nobody can hurt you if they can't find you.

It's me. I'll be with you now, always.

No, no, no, not her again. I can't let this happen, not again. I have to get away from her.

Harp hurriedly pushes the piled-up sand away and crawls out. It's dark. It must still be the middle of the night. It's cold, and the fog is so thick and scary it makes the dark seem even darker, as dark as the King's black forest that never gets sun, the forest where the magic tree was hidden.

Harp pushes some sand back up to hide the entrance to his secret place, then he slides down to the flat part of the beach. He dusts off his pants and spins around, looking in all directions, trying to see through the fog. But it's no use, he can't see anything. The fog is blocking his eyes. It's like it's closing in on him, clinging to him, trying to make everything look really spooky and bad. Tonight, even the old pier above him looks scary, like . . . like the dark skeleton of the evil giant in the story about the boy who had the magic sword. He wishes he had a magic sword like that so nobody could hurt him. All he'd have to do is yell, All heads off but mine, and the giants would all be lying dead, right there on the ground with no heads on any of them.

Stop that nonsense and listen to me. The Lord heard my prayer and let me come back to be with you.

Oh no, it really *is* her, and she's talking again, just like she did after the funeral. I have to get away fast before she gets stuck in my head again. I should . . . run away, that's it. I'll be like the boy who could run as fast as the wind after the magic water had turned him into a roebuck. Harp laughs to himself. She'll never catch me. I'm too fast. Nobody will ever catch me again.

He starts to run, but before he can get going really fast, he trips over something and falls down. He sits on the sand and rubs his hurt knee. Why do I always have to be the one who falls down and gets hurt? Why can't I be quick and nimble like . . . like that roebuck. Harp remembers that story well. It was one of his favorites. When the boy got thirsty, he had to drink water from the brook. The wicked stepmother was secretly a witch and had seen him sneak away into the forest so she crept after him, like sneaky witches do, and she knew he would get thirsty sooner or later, so she bewitched all the brooks in the forest so when the boy drank the water he was turned into a roebuck. But Mother said it was okay because a roebuck was a cute little deer that could run fast like the wind.

Hey! Listen to me. Am I talking to a brick wall? Pay attention. Look what's right next to you.

Next to me? She's right, I did trip over something. What was it?

Harp looks back, trying to see through the fog. But the fog is too thick. It's like she brought the fog with her, closing it in on him, making it so he can't see and can't think and almost can't breathe. It's almost as bad as when the young huntsman couldn't breathe when the seven-headed dragon found him with the king's daughter and got mad and roared, What business hast thou here on my hill? And then the dragon breathed fire all over the boy so he could hardly breathe at all.

Stop that! Pay attention to what you are supposed to be doing.

"But what am I supposed to be doing?"

Are your ears full of wax? Look at what's next to you.

Harp leans forward and tries to see through the fog. There *is* something lying on the sand. Is that what I tripped over? It looks like . . . a dark shape. Could it be the shape of a person?

Oh, no. That would be bad. Harp says, "Oh, I'm sorry. I didn't mean to step on you."

The shape doesn't answer. The shape doesn't even move.

Harp crawls a little closer. The shape *is* a person. It looks like a man, all curled up, close to the water's edge. Harp realizes it must be somebody else without a home to go to, somebody else who slept under the pier last night. Maybe the man is drunk. Harp has seen some of the men who don't have a home get so drunk you'd think they were dead. Maybe this one is so drunk he doesn't even realize he's lying too close to the water. The whispering waves slide in and out, lapping around the man's feet, almost as if they are trying to say, "Wake up! Wake up!"

Harp decides he'd better wake the man up. He cautiously puts his hand on the man's back and leans close to whisper, "Wake up, mister. You'll get all wet."

The man still doesn't move.

Harp pulls away his hand and feels wetness between his fingers. But it doesn't feel like regular water wetness, it feels thick and . . . sticky.

You know it isn't water. It's blood.

Oh no, Harp doesn't want it to be blood. Blood is bad. Blood is like when the evil mother cut off the toes of her daughter to try to force her foot into the glass slipper and then there was blood all over the place and the two pigeons sat upon the hazel-tree above the graveyard and cried:

> *Turn and peep,*
> *turn and peep,*
> *there's blood within the shoe,*
> *it is too small for her,*
> *your true bride still waits for you.*

But this isn't like that. Harp is almost sure this can't be blood. There's no reason for it to be blood. He wipes his hand on the front of his jacket until he can't feel the wetness anymore.

Suit yourself, but you know I'm right.

"No, you're not right. Besides, I told you I'm not listening to you anymore." He puts his fingers in his ears. That's how to stop her. I'll shut her out. I'll shut everything out, like when the witch stopped up the ears of the white maiden so she couldn't hear anything but her own crying.

He sits on the sand and rocks forward and back, keeping his fingers tight in his ears, listening to the roaring inside his head, waiting for his heart to slow down.

Is she gone?

Silence.

He cautiously takes his fingers out of his ears.

Who killed Cock Robin? Who saw him die?

"Stop that. I don't want to think about that old Cock Robin rhyme anymore. I hate that one. That one makes the bad dreams come."

If you have bad dreams it's your own fault.

"My fault? I didn't do anything."

Well then, do something.

"What should I do?"

Get out of here. That's what you should do.

"But shouldn't I do something for him?"

There's nothing you can do for a dead person. Think about yourself for a change.

Dead? No, no, no, Harp doesn't want to think about the person being dead. This can't be happening, not really. Maybe he's dreaming. Maybe he'll wake up and it will be morning. The fog will be gone. The sun will be up, and it'll be a nice warm sun, and there won't be any dead people lying on the sand.

Silly boy. Always pretending.

Harp looks out of the corner of his eye. Is it still there? Or did I wake up, and the not-dream reality is gone?

Oh, no, the dark shape *is* still there. Harp has the very bad feeling that he may not be able to stop this reality. Mother always said reality works like walking on a carpet that's unrolling out in front of you. As it unrolls, you begin to see the patterns. And when you see the whole pattern, it's too late to change it because it's already happened. Harp is beginning to think this is one of those. This may be real.

It's real all right. And you know who it is.

"I do?" Harp looks closer. From the person's small size, it could be . . . Is it Little Hilly?

You know it is.

But it can't be Little Hilly. He had been talking to Little Hilly only yesterday. Little Hilly'd found a broken crutch in the trash and said he was going to pretend to be crippled so he could do some panhandling down at Venice Beach. Little Hilly'd said the crutch would make people want to give him money. He borrowed Harp's hat to hold out to the people that passed by on the strand sidewalk.

Harp quickly crawls back up to his secret hiding place under the pier and digs his backpack out of the sand. Then he slides back down and feels around inside the backpack until he finds his little flashlight. He shines the light on the body. Oh no. It *is* Little Hilly. And his eyes are open.

Look out! If a dead person's eyes are open, he's trying to find someone to take down to hell with him.

Harp jumps back. He quickly turns around in a circle, then he turns back the other way. It's the only thing that will confuse Little Hilly's ghost and stop him from dragging him down to hell. Harp doesn't want to go to hell, or wherever Little Hilly is going. Harp knows all about that look of eyes staring at nothing, eyes trying to take you. When he was back on Ward D-4, he woke up one morning and saw Bacon Benny in his cot across the aisle, staring right at him. He soon found out Benny wasn't really staring at him. He was dead.

He shines his flashlight on the back of Little Hilly's old coat. It's wet with dark red blood, and there are long tears in the cloth. Somebody must have stabbed poor Little Hilly with a knife, and then did it some more. It's like they didn't want to stop stabbing.

But why would somebody want to kill Little Hilly? He didn't have anything to steal. Nobody who lives on the beach has anything worth stealing.

But wait a minute, where's Big Hilly? Big Hilly and Little Hilly were always together. That's why they were called Big Hilly and Little Hilly. Big Hilly was tall with a big chest. Little Hilly was kind of . . . little.

If you want to think about something, think about this. He was the same size as you. And it was dark.

"So what? Why should that matter?"

You know. Think.

"I don't need to think about him being the same size as me. That's not important."

Listen to me. I'm telling you--

"No, it's not important. I'm not going to listen to you anymore. What's important is Big Hilly's missing. Maybe he did it."

All right, fine. Don't listen then, but you'll see.

Harp stares at Little Hilly's body, wondering what he should do. I liked Little Hilly, didn't I? One time, Little Hilly found some pizza in the dumpster and shared it with me. It must mean Little Hilly wanted to be my friend. Nobody else on the beach ever shared anything. And nobody on Ward D-4 ever shared anything either. Sharing that dumpster pizza had to mean Little Hilly wanted to be my friend.

While they ate the pizza, Little Hilly asked him questions. Nobody else ever did that either. Little Hilly asked him if he was happy. Harp wasn't sure how to answer that question, so he just said, "I don't know. Are you happy?" Little Hilly didn't look up at first. He stared at his piece of pizza for a long time, then he said, "I've never once been happy in my whole life." Then he took a bite of his pizza and shook his head. He looked up, right into Harp's eyes, and said, "Why don't we get to be happy like other people? It's not fair. If we can't be happy, we might as well be dead."

Ever since that day, Harp often thought about what Little Hilly'd said. Now he wonders if Little Hilly was right. Is it really better to be dead if you aren't happy? Harp remembers being unhappy all the time when he was little.

You were just a naturally unhappy child. It wasn't my fault.

But now Harp is not sure whether he's unhappy or not. Maybe being happy isn't important anyway. Not really. What's important is staying warm, and finding things to eat.

And being careful.

Yes, and being careful. If you aren't careful, you could end up dead, like Little Hilly.

Harp snaps off his flashlight and stares down at the dark shape of Little Hilly's body.

Forget him. No use crying over spilt milk.

That's right. Maybe there isn't anything I can do for Little Hilly. He's already dead. That's real. And once something is really, really real, there's no way to make it not real again. Like Mother said, once the milk is already spilt there's no use crying about it. Maybe I should just go away before somebody finds out and blames me.

Yes. Run away.

Harp puts his backpack on and hurries down the beach, heading away from the pier. Yes, it's better to just go away. And it's better to not think about bad things. He doesn't want to think about Little Hilly's staring eyes anymore.

Stop! Go back.

Harp stops. "What? Why should I go back?"

You know.

"But I don't want to go back there. It's too scary back there."

You have to go back. There's one more thing you have to do.

Maybe she's right. Maybe I should check one more time. Maybe I forgot something.

He goes back under the pier and creeps close to Little Hilly, staying behind him to make sure those staring eyes can't get him. "Now, why did I come back? What was I looking for?"

Do I have to remind you of everything? The money. Get the money!

Money? Oh, that's right. The money.

He sits down on the sand and searches through Little Hilly's coat pocket. Some string. Two plastic buttons, one of them cracked almost in two. A rubber band. Nothing much here.

Keep looking.

In Little Hilly's other coat pocket he finds a broken plastic hospital bracelet. He shines his flashlight on the writing. It says, *Santa Monica General Hospital Emergency Room. John Doe. February 11, 1986.*

Who is John Doe? And when was February the eleventh? Yesterday? Maybe. But why had Little Hilly been in the emergency room? Was he sick?

That's not important. What's important is the money. Does

everything I say to you go in one ear and out the other?

"But there isn't any money."

Keep looking. Look in his pants pockets.

"Do I have to? I mean, do I have to touch him?"

He can't hurt you. He's dead. Get to it.

Harp carefully squeezes his hand under Little Hilly and feels inside his pants pocket. Money! He feels money in there.

Harp pulls the money out. Three one-dollar bills, all crumpled up. They're wet. Why are they wet? Harp slides his hand under Little Hilly and feels inside his other pocket. This time he feels coins. He pulls out his hand and opens it. Three quarters and a dime. It must be money Little Hilly got from yesterday's panhandling. So if he made some money from panhandling, why didn't he share it like he said he would?

Take the money. It should have been yours in the first place.

Harp stuffs the money and the hospital bracelet into his pocket. No reason to leave good money behind. Little Hilly can't use it now. And, besides, he shouldn't have kept the money all for himself when he said he would share it.

Harp gets up and stands over Little Hilly's body. "What are you supposed to do when you find a dead person? Aren't you supposed to tell somebody? The police?"

Are you crazy? Get out of here. Right now!

Right, right, better not tell the police. Even if I tell them I didn't do it, they might not believe me. They might look up my record and find out the judge said I had to be locked up on Ward D-4 in that bad place, and then they'd find out when they closed it down I wasn't supposed to be let out with the others to go live in the Half-Way house.

Am I talking to a deaf person? Move!

Maybe it is better to go somewhere else. A lot of people will come to the beach as soon as the sun comes up and the fog goes away. They'll find Little Hilly. They'll know what to do. He turns to go.

Wait! Where's your hat? Don't leave until you find your hat.

He turns back and shines his flashlight on Little Hilly's head. No hat.

You have to find that hat.

Harp frantically shines his flashlight everywhere under the pier. There's no sign of it. He rolls Little Hilly over to look under him. "It's not here."

It's gone. You lost it.

"It's not my fault. Little Hilly lost it. It's his fault."

1-2

The Hunger

Harp grabs his backpack and heads down the beach away from the pier, staying close to the water. The fog still clings to him, like it's following him. It's cold and it's wet and it makes him shiver. If only the fog could be a magic fog, like the wonderful magic fog in the story about the amazing juniper tree that lived and breathed like a person whenever the bones of a dead person were gathered together under the tree. Then the tree would began to stir itself and come alive and begin clapping its branches like they were hands to turn the fog into a wonderful warm fire and then the beautiful bird would spring out of the fire and everything would be nice again with no fog and no dead bodies lying on the wet sand or anything bad like that and the bird in the tree would begin to sing:

> *My mother she killed me,*
> *My father he ate me,*
> *My sister, little Marlinchen,*
> *Gathered together all my bones,*
> *Tied them in a silken handkerchief,*
> *Laid them beneath the juniper-tree,*
> *Kywitt, kywitt, what a beautiful bird am I.*

Stop that. Somebody's coming.

A shape in the fog is coming toward him, moving fast.

Run! Hide!

Before Harp can run away and hide, the fast-moving shape almost runs right into him. It's a tall thin man, running. The man dodges around him and says, "Morning."

It's only a runner. Nothing to worry about. Harp sees those runners all the time. They come to the beach early every morning. For some reason they like to run back and forth on the beach.

The runner disappears into the fog, heading toward the pier.

When that runner finds the body, you're in for it. He saw you. He'll call the police.

Harp hurries on. Maybe she's wrong. Maybe that runner didn't hardly notice me.

Ha! You wish.

Harp goes even faster. There's not a sound, and walking inside the thick fog makes it seem like everything else is gone away. He wonders what it would be like if all the people and all the cars and all the buildings and everything else was gone. Then he'd be all alone, like when the Virgin Mary left the golden child all alone in Heaven to be tempted to open the secret thirteenth door that she hardly opened more than a crack so it didn't seem fair that she got cast down out of Heaven into the wilderness just for that.

But then, from somewhere farther down the beach, hidden by the fog, Harp hears a sound.

It's a dog.

She's right. It is a dog. It's howling. Why is it howling?

Then it suddenly stops.

A dog howling in the night. It's a sign of death.

Using his left hand, Harp makes the secret sign of the upside-down sacred cross like Mother taught him. It will fool death into passing on by. He repeats the magic sign twice more, just to make sure.

He hurries on, still shivering. He wishes he didn't always have to be so cold.

He pulls his thin little jacket tighter around himself. He wishes they would have given him a warmer coat at the Half-Way house, one that had a zipper that worked.

He turns up the collar in back and tries to bury his nose down deeper into the front. Why is the sun taking so long to come up? He whispers, "This night is going on too long. It's like the long, long nights in my closet."

Your closet was safe. I put you in there for your own good.

"That closet didn't feel safe. It was scary."

No, you're wrong, as usual. It couldn't have been all that scary. It was a nice safe place for you to be while I went out. You're just a scaredy cat.

Harp knows that closet was dark and scary and lonely, no matter what she says.

He walks faster, trying to get warm. He hopes the sun will come up soon. Then somebody will find poor Little Hilly and take care of him.

Don't think about that. Think about this, he was the same size as you. And it was dark. Maybe he was wearing your hat.

"No, no, no, I don't want to think about that." Harp shakes off that bad thought. He wonders if maybe he's too hungry. When you get too hungry sometimes your brain makes up bad things.

He stops and looks back toward the pier. I should go find something to eat. Then I'll feel better. Then I'll get warm.

Are you ignoring me?

Harp knows the best place to find food is in the dumpsters back on the pier. "I'm going to go find some food."

Are you out of your mind? That pier is the one place you should stay away from.

"But I have to go there. The pier is the only good place to find food."

I can't believe this. You're going back to the one place you should stay far away from.

Harp knows there's almost always something good to eat in those dumpsters. Maybe even pizza. Compared to everything else in the garbage, pizza is the best. When it's still in it's nice cardboard box it means it's hardly been touched by anybody. But to find pizza, you have to get there before anyone else.

Harp hurries across the soft dry sand toward the lights of the strand sidewalk.

When he gets there, he heads back toward the pier as fast as he can, walking head-down against the cold breeze that's coming straight from the north. He softly sings the little song Mother taught him about the north wind:

The north wind doth blow,
and we shall have snow,
and what will poor Cock Robin do then?
Poor thing. He'll sit in a barn, and keep himself warm,
and hide his head under his wing.

That bad north wind is picking up newspapers from the sidewalk and pushing them along right at him. Maybe he should stop and read one of those newspapers. Maybe there will be a story about Little Hilly and why somebody killed him.

No. Stay away from them.

"But why? Maybe a newspaper can explain things to me, explain why Little Hilly had to die."

How many times do I have to tell you not to read anything? You have to stay away from newspapers, and books too. They hold the sins of the world.

Harp sees a blowing newspaper coming and jumps to the side to make sure it doesn't touch him.

Two young girls walking the other way laugh out loud. One of them hides some words behind her hand, and they both laugh again and hurry on.

They're laughing at you. Why can't you act normal?

Harp looks away. Let them laugh. I don't care. Someday they'll be sorry they laughed. He remembers a story Mother read to him about Simpleton, the king's youngest son. They all laughed at that boy too, just because he believed in magic toads. But in the end Simpleton showed them. The toads brought out their magic box and gave him gold and silver and jewels and everything he ever wanted. Harp hurries on, whispering a good rhyme from that story:

Little green toad,
hopping hither and thither.
Hop to the door and see who is there.

Harp soon sees why there were so many papers blowing: the trash cans along the sidewalk are overflowing. There's not only newspapers, there's paper food wrappers and beer bottles and paper cups and plastic bags lying all around the trash cans. Harp realizes what it means. It means it must be a weekend. On the weekends a lot more people come to the beach, and they aren't careful.

Harp hurries on and when he gets to the pier, he goes up the steps and heads straight for the dumpsters. But before he can get there, he sees some people lined up at the railing along the side of the pier. They're all leaning out, looking down. Are they looking down at Little Hilly? Is he still lying down there on the wet sand?

Harp wants to go find out what they're looking at, but the lights are too bright out there on that part of the pier. He worries about what regular people might think of him.

He looks down at his clothes. They're all worn out, and they're dirty. He worries that maybe he even smells funny. He sniffs under his arm. Is that bad smell me? How long has it been since it was warm enough to get under the outdoor beach showers to get clean? He can't remember.

He looks down at his old jacket. It's not only worn out, it has something dark all over the front of it. What is it?

You know what it is. It's blood.

He whispers, "Blood? Oh no. What should I do?"

Think about the rhyme: Who caught his blood? I, said the Fish, with my little dish, I caught his blood.

"No, stop that. I told you I don't want to hear that bad old Cock Robin rhyme anymore."

Who saw him die? You saw him die.

"I'm not lis-en-ing." If all she can say is that stupid old rhyme, he is determined not to listen to her. Besides, he thinks, it can't be blood on my jacket. There is no way I could have got that much blood all over myself. His throat is starting to feel the old tightness again.

So, hide the evidence. Quick!

Harp looks around to see if anybody is watching him. Luckily, they're all too busy looking over the railing. He quickly takes off his jacket and stuffs it into his backpack. Without his jacket on, it feels even colder. When is that sun going to come up? He looks up at the sky. There *is* a slight glow out over the city, a bit of orange light coming through the dirty smog. It means the sun is out there somewhere. If only it would come up, right now!

Stop that! Pay attention to what you're supposed to be doing.

He turns away from the glow in the sky. He knows the sun will take even longer to come up if he wants it too much. He won't be like the silly boy who was so afraid of the dark he wished the sun would never go down. Well, that boy got his wish all right. The sun got stuck up in the sky so nobody could ever go to sleep anymore.

Harp looks back at the people out by the railing. A man in a cap that says "Dodgers" on the front of it, has climbed over the railing and is leaning way out, hanging onto a light pole.

Harp goes a little closer to listen.

The man yells, "A guy in a suit just went under the pier. I bet it's the coroner."

"Did they say who the dead man is?" says a woman who's dressed in a big brown coat that has lots of pockets. That tells Harp she's one of the fisherpeople who come out early every morning to try to catch fish off the end of the pier.

The Dodgers-hat man looks back at her and shrugs. "Probably just another homeless guy. Got drunk and froze down there, I bet."

It was cold last night," says the fisherwoman," but it wasn't *that* cold. He couldn't have froze."

Another man with no hair except for a little bit on the sides shakes his head. "I was down there before they put up the yellow tape. It was a little guy. I think he got shot."

"Who says he got shot?" says the Dodgers-hat guy, climbing back over the railing. "I bet he just got drunk and froze."

"It wasn't that cold," insists the fisherwoman.

"He had blood all over his back," says the little-bit-of-hair man. "I saw it."

The Dodgers-hat man and the fisherwoman look at each other and shrug. Everyone goes back to leaning over the railing, looking down.

Well, don't just stand there gawking. Run away!

Harp decides he'd better forget about finding something to eat and go to the outdoor wash-basins by the Pavilion restrooms and give his jacket a good washing. People might get suspicious of somebody who has blood all over the front of their jacket.

1-3

Suspicion

Before Harp can get off the pier, he sees Detective Olivera coming up the stairs from the beach. The policeman has on his usual brown suit, but this time he's got his badge pinned onto his front pocket. Everybody on the beach knows Detective Olivera. His black car with the silver spotlight on it is the only car that's allowed to drive on the strand sidewalk.

Harp looks the other way and keeps going.

But it's too late. Olivera spots him and yells, "Hey, wait up, kid. I got to ask you something."

Harp slows, but he doesn't turn to face the detective. All of a sudden he's worried that maybe he got some of Little Hilly's blood on him somewhere besides his jacket. Maybe on his hands. He puts his hands in his pants pockets and keeps on walking.

"Come on now, kid, stop. I'm not gonna hurt you."

Harp has a moment's hope that maybe Detective Olivera is going to ask him about something else. Maybe it's not about Little Hilly. He stops and turns around.

Olivera stares at him, frowning. "I know you, don't I? Haven't I seen you around here before?"

Harp shrugs and tries not to look at Olivera's square face and his funny little mustache. That thin little mustache is so silly it makes Harp want to laugh.

Careful, careful.

But then Harp remembers about maybe having blood on his hands and the funny thought goes away.

"You live around here? You got a home?"

Harp shakes his head.

The policeman gets his face close to Harp's face. His breath smells like beans and onions. "No home, eh? You live on the beach?"

Harp doesn't like to answer questions because he never knows how people want you to answer. They might even ask you questions when they don't really want an answer. When he was little and went to school, one teacher said, Now Harper, we don't just get up and walk out of class anytime we want to, now do we? Those kinds of questions were not real questions. Mother used to ask those kinds of questions too. Like, Harp, why don't you listen when I tell you something? Why are you always daydreaming? Mother didn't really want an answer to those questions either.

It feels like Olivera's dark eyes are drilling into his head. It makes it hard to look away.

"Are you listening to me, kid? Wake up. What's your name?"

"Uh, Harp."

"Okay, Harp, now listen close. This is important. You know the guy they call Big Hilly? Big guy. Bout this tall." Olivera holds his hand up higher than his own head.

Harp shrugs.

"Damn it, gimme a yes or no. Getting anything out of you guys is like pullin' teeth. Do you know where I might find this Big Hilly guy or not?"

They think Big Hilly did it. That's good.

Harp shakes his head.

"Out loud."

"Uh, no, sir. I mean, yes, sir. I know him, but I don't know where he is."

"Did you see him yesterday? He was probably with a little guy, the one you people call Little Hilly."

Harp nods.

"Where were they?"

"By Papa Pan's."

"Papa Pan's? Oh, you mean Papa's Pan Pizza. Down on the Venice Beach strand?"

"Uh huh."

"What were they doing down there? Panhandling as usual?"

"I guess so."

The detective pokes at the weathered wood of the pier with the front of his shoe. Harp notices that most of the policeman's black shoes are all scuffed and dirty, but the front parts are very shiny. Harp wonders why the policeman doesn't make all of his shoes shine instead of just the front parts.

"Let me tell you somethin', Harp. We found the little guy, Little Hilly, down there under the pier. Dead. He got stabbed. Buncha times. You wouldn't know anything about that, would you?"

He's suspicious of you. Be careful.

Harp shakes his head and tries not to change the expression on his face. He stares over the detective's shoulder and tries not to think about Little Hilly lying there with his eyes staring and never closing. He tries to think about beans and onions, even though he doesn't like them. His stomach complains out loud.

"Are you hungry, Harp? We could go up to Denny's and talk. I'll buy you some bacon and eggs."

Harp's stomach thinks bacon and eggs sounds very good.

No! Don't even think about it.

Harp shakes his head.

"Not hungry, eh? I'll bet you are, but have it your way. What I need to know is what the guys around here are saying about Little Hilly. You get me?"

Harp nods and starts to turn away, but the policeman gets ahold of his sleeve. "Wait a minute, kid. How old are you?"

Harp shrugs.

"What does that mean? You don't know? Or you won't tell me."

"Eighteen?"

Olivera stares at him.

Act your age. Stand up straight. God wanted you to grow up big and strong, even though you didn't.

Harp stands up taller and shrugs. He grins at the policeman and tries to keep an innocent, but older, look on his face.

"Yeah, well, maybe you're eighteen and maybe you're not. Little guy like you, hard to say. One of these days I may have to see if we've got anything written up on you downtown."

Olivera seems to be trying to look inside of Harp's eyes. Harp doesn't want the detective to see inside his head so he looks down at the old dark wood of the pier. On Ward D-4, you learned not to look authority in the eye. You got punished for that. You got put on Mitch's shit-list for that, and getting on Mitch's shit-list meant you were in big trouble. As soon as Harp got put on Ward D-4 he learned fast: don't look anyone in the eye, do what you're told, pay attention.

"Hey, listen to what I'm sayin', kid. Where did you sleep last night? Around here?"

Don't say a word.

Harp shakes his head.

"No? Well, let's forget where you slept, for now. You see anything funny going on last night?"

Harp shrugs and looks down at his own shoes. They're all scuffed up and they're very dirty. They need a good cleaning. He hears something and he looks up to see that a few of the fisherpeople have come up behind the policeman to find out what's going on. They're whispering among themselves and pointing at Harp.

They saw something. I saw him die, said the Fly, with my little eye.

Detective Olivera notices Harp is looking past him and turns around. He waves his hands to make the people go away. "All right, all right, move it along. We're just talking here."

"Is he the one who did it, officer?" It's the fisherwoman in the brown coat with all the big pockets. She's looking at Harp like she's just caught some kind of bad fish she doesn't like the looks of.

The policeman waves his hands again. "Like I said, we're just having a little chat. Get out of here. All of you!"

The fisherwoman shrugs and walks away. The others slowly drift off too.

Olivera turns back to Harp. Harp smells the beans and onions again and tries to turn away. But the policeman grabs his chin and says, "Don't look away when I'm talking to you, kid."

He has such a tight grip on Harp's chin, it hurts. But then he lets go and smiles. He puts his arm over Harp's shoulders and leads him to the railing. "Let's have a little talk, Harp. I got a proposition for you."

Watch out. He's trying to trick you.

Harp doesn't like being out there by the edge of the pier where everybody can see him talking to Olivera. If some of the other homeless men come by and see us together like this they won't like it.

Nobody on the beach likes it when the police come around, especially if it's Detective Olivera. He's always snooping around, stopping homeless people to ask them questions, even though nobody ever tells him anything. Harp hasn't been on the beach all that long, but he's been there long enough to know you aren't supposed to talk to the police because people might think you're telling on them.

"Okay, Harp, here's the deal. You help me and I'll help you. I don't know where you came from or what it was made you end up down here on the beach, but I can forget to check on that if you help me out with this little situation we got here. You get along with me and things will go a lot easier for you here. Ask anybody about that. They'll tell you. But get on my wrong side and it'll be a different story. You get my meaning?"

Harp looks past Detective Olivera and tries to think what to say. Out over the water, he sees two seagulls dancing together in the air. They swoop and dive and rise up again to circle around each other. Gosh, it looks like they are really having fun. If only I could be a bird like that and fly away above everybody. I would . . .

"Hey, kid, are you listening to me? I'm giving you a break here. All you got to do is ask around a bit, let me know what your homeless pals are saying about this Little Hilly thing. You and me can be friends, get it? Tight, like this." Olivera crosses one of fingers over and holds his hand up in front of Harp's face. "You be my eyes and ears down here on the beach and maybe sometime I'll be in a position to do you a little favor or two in return. You get my drift?"

"Yes, sir."

"On the other hand, you give me trouble and maybe I'll just have to take you downtown and see what we got on you. A young fellow like you, hangin' out down here on the beach. It ain't right. Gotta be some reason for it. You wouldn't like that would you, goin' downtown with me?"

If they find out, you'll never see the light of day again.

"No, sir."

"All right. That's better. Gimme your hand." Olivera takes a pen out of his pocket.

"My hand?" Harp puts his hands behind him.

"I said hold out your damn hand."

No! Thou hadst blood on thy hands.

Harp doesn't want to hold out his hand. What if he sees the blood? Olivera's waiting, frowning at him. Harp knows he has to do something.

Run away!

Then he has an idea. If there *is* blood on his hands, maybe it will be mostly on his right hand, the one he touched Little Hilly with. He holds out his left hand and tries to keep it from shaking. He looks past the policeman, but the two dancing seagulls are gone.

Olivera grabs Harp's fingers really tight and writes a number on the back of his hand.

Harp looks at the number.

"That's my phone number down at the station. You hear anything, you go to a pay phone and call this number. Got it?"

Harp nods. "Yes, sir, but . . ."

Olivera frowns. "But what?"

Don't you know when to keep your mouth shut?

"Never mind."

"Come on, kid, out with it. I got things to do."

"But what if . . . Big Hilly . . . didn't do it?"

Olivera puts the end of his pen in his mouth and chews on it, looking into Harp's eyes. "Do you know something about this? What aren't you telling me?"

"Nothing, sir. Really. It's just that . . . Big Hilly . . . really liked his little buddy."

Olivera takes the pen out of his mouth and taps Harp on the chest with it. "So maybe they had a lover's quarrel. Ever think of that?"

Harp shakes his head. "I didn't think they are . . . were . . . like that."

"Oh no? You think not? I hear things too, you know."

Didn't I tell you to keep your big mouth shut?

Now Harp isn't so sure about the Hillys. Maybe Detective Olivera does know something. But Harp never saw Big Hilly kissing Little Hilly, or doing anything to Little Hilly with hands inside pants like he's seen the ones who are like that do.

He shrugs.

"Well, that doesn't matter anyhow," says Olivera. "I'm pretty sure one of you people did it. I'll find out which one sooner or later. You know, if you don't help me, maybe I'll get suspicious of you. You wouldn't like that, would you?"

I warned you. Didn't I warn you?

"No, sir."

"Well then, your job is to find out who really did it. Let me know anything you hear. If people are saying somebody besides Big Hilly did it, then I want to know about it. You understand?"

"Yes, sir."

"And don't tell anybody you talked to me. Just ask around like you're curious or something. You know, nose around, act like you're trying to solve the case yourself. Okay?"

"Yes, sir, but . . ."

"Now what?"

"How do I . . . I mean, how do you . . . solve a . . . case?"

"Like I said, use your eyes and ears. Ask people questions. Look for clues. First thing I'd do is find out who had it in for this Little Hilly character. That'll lead you to the main suspects. You with me?"

"I guess so."

"Right. Now get goin'." Olivera waves him away and Harp hurries off the pier without looking back.

Now you've done it. He's on to you. He'll lock you up and throw away the key.

Harp feels a sense of doom. It's like in the story about the king's youngest son who could only stay out of prison by bringing back the golden bird. Except now he has to bring back Little Hilly's killer, instead of only a golden bird. He wishes he had the magic fox to help him like that boy did.

The magic fox can't help you now. They'll lock you up again and this time you'll never get out.

"Why did Olivera pick on me? Why do I have to be Olivera's eyes and ears?"

You brought this on yourself. If you'd have just listened to me, you wouldn't be in this mess.

Harp chews at the inside of his cheek. What if Olivera does go downtown to look up my record?

It'll be the end for you, my son. I'll be sorry to see you go.

1-4

Of Mice and Mammals

*H*arp doesn't want to think about scary things like getting locked up again. He decides to just think about walking and not think about anything else. If he can only walk the right way, with every step exactly the same, everything will be fine.

As he walks, he whispers an old rhyme, "As I walked by myself and talked to myself, myself said to me." He stamps his left foot, right on time with the last word. "Look to thyself, take care of thyself, for nobody cares for thee but me." He stamps again.

Stop that. People are staring.

Harp looks up. A man sitting on a bench is watching him. The man only has one leg and two crutches are lying on the bench next to him. The man is smiling, like he's happy about something.

Harp keeps his eyes on the ground and goes on past. He knows people had better quit staring at him or else they might end up like the wicked step-sisters and get their eyes pecked out by the fairy godmother's pigeons and be punished with blindness for as long as they live.

Harp glances up at the sky. The sun has finally decided to come out from behind the fog and it's starting to get nice and warm. That makes him smile. He figures if that man on the bench with one leg can smile, then he can too. Normally, Harp doesn't like to let his face show what he's feeling, but Little Hilly said he should try to be happier, so maybe he should. He wonders if he could learn to smile more, maybe he would feel happier inside.

You only smile when something's going on in your head. Are you keeping secrets from me again?

Harp decides to ignore her, but maybe he'd better stop smiling in case it might give away his secrets.

He suddenly notices there are a lot more people on the sidewalk than usual. Is it because the sun has finally come out? He stays to the side, keeping out of their way, but he keeps his eyes on them. Are any of them looking at him? Do they suspect him? He knows he'd better hurry to get to the outdoor wash basins and get his jacket washed up before anybody finds out what's on it.

Aren't you forgetting something?

He stops. "What?"

The story of yesterday.

Oh no, she's right. He completely forgot to write in his diary that morning. A mistake. Break the pattern and the carpet of reality might start to unravel.

He hurries to the nearest bench, ignoring the people passing by. He takes his diary out of his backpack and opens it to where he left off writing yesterday's story. He rereads it. It tells about walking, looking at people, searching for food. He can see right away the writing is no good, as if he wasn't caring enough when he wrote that story. To make it right, he'll have to do it all over again. He crosses out all of yesterday's words and turns to a new page. He stares at it, waiting.

Don't forget the prayer.

Oh, that's right. He almost forgot to start with the morning prayer. He writes:

Thank you Lord for letting me live today. Let others die instead of me,
this I pray.

Now for yesterday's story. He closes his eyes and waits for the words to come. He knows the words won't come until they are ready. Then, they'll fly down out of the sky and jump right into his head. If he tries to make the words talk when they're not ready, they'll just cause trouble.

Get to it.

"No, I have to wait for the words."

Well, hurry up.

He waits. He knows he has to be patient, no matter what she says.

Come on, come on, we haven't got all day.

"But the words aren't coming."

Just tell what happened.

He opens his eyes. Maybe I shouldn't waste time writing yesterday's story. Nothing happened yesterday anyhow except Little Hilly borrowed my hat. Better to write what happened today.

He licks the tip of his pencil and begins:

> I woke up. It was still dark. It was cold. I couldn't remember how I got to the pier last night. I got up and I tripped over Little Hilly who was lying on

He stops writing and reads the words. They're no good. It's not a story, it's only words. The words say what happened, but they don't *feel* like what happened. When I read it again later, how will I remember how it *felt*?

Harp looks up at the sky, hoping to see the right words, but all he sees are the last wisps of fog swirling around up there. He worries that maybe the thick fog of the night got inside his brain and made everything all cloudy and evil. Or maybe it's because of what happened to Little Hilly. Maybe his brain has got all filled up with thinking about those slashes in the back of Little Hilly's coat, or with thinking about Little Hilly's staring eyes. It makes Harp very sad, remembering Little Hilly's staring eyes. He wonders if the words aren't coming because he's too sad this morning.

There's no reason to be sad. It didn't happen to you. Just write.

"But shouldn't I at least write down what happened, even if I can't get the feeling right? If I don't write down everything that happens every single day, how will I know it really happened, and I didn't make it up?"

Suit yourself, but hurry it up.

He begins to write again:

> 1. Little Hilly got stabbed. Lots of times. Was somebody mad at him?
> 2. Hospital bracelet in his pocket. February 11. Who is

John Doe?
3. Where is Big Hilly? Why wasn't he there to protect his little buddy?
Cain and Abel?

You're forgetting the most important part.

Harp looks up from his writing. "Like what?"

Your hat.

"My hat? Should I write something about Little Hilly borrowing my hat?"

It was dark.

"So what? Why should I write that down?"

Don't you get it? The killer wasn't trying to kill Little Hilly, he was trying to kill you!

"No, no, no, I already said I didn't want to write that. So what if it was dark? So what if Little Hilly was wearing my hat?"

Hey, quit talking out loud to me. Do you want people to think you're crazy?

Harp looks around. The people are just passing by, like usual. Everybody is looking the other way like they don't want to look at him.

"It's a mistake to write down bad things," he whispers. "It might make the bad things really happen."

It doesn't matter if you believe it or not, somebody is trying to kill you.

"No, they're not. Nobody would want to kill me. And I'm not crazy. You're the one who's crazy."

Kill you. Kill you.

He puts his fingers in his ears. No, it's not true. Who would want to hurt me? No, and no again. It's not true and that's final. The carpet of that reality is still rolled up tight. It's Little Hilly who's dead, not me, and that's all there is to it. It's too bad somebody had to die, but there's nothing I can do about it now. Now it's time for me to put away the diary and stop thinking bad thoughts. It's still cold so I have to go back to walking. And I have to find something to eat.

He slaps his diary closed. He's written enough. Everything is going to be all right now. The sun is coming out and everything will be nice.

He puts his diary away in his backpack and stands up. Now, what's next?

The blood. You caught his blood.

"Oh, that's right. I have to go get the blood washed off of my jacket."

He starts walking again, keeping his head down, being careful not to look at anybody. That way nobody can use their eyes to cast a spell on him. Mother always warned him that some people's eyes were like cat's eyes; they could mesmerize you and make you do things you didn't want to do. And she said there are some people who have eyes like mirrors that can make you hate yourself. And mirrors can be bad too. Mother only allowed one mirror in the house, the one she had in her room, and that one was always covered with a special black cloth so no light could get through to it.

What were you doing in my room?

Now that he thinks about it, he hardly ever went into Mother's room. Honest.

To keep away from the people's eyes, Harp concentrates on looking down at the sidewalk.

Watch out for the night forces.

That's right, the night forces. I have to be careful to stay away from them. In the months he's been on the beach, Harp has learned a secret about the strand sidewalk. There are night forces hidden under there, bad things that are trying to break free and get out. In the night, when nobody is looking, the night forces make cracks in the sidewalk to try to get out and the cracks look like terrible pictures. One time, in the middle of the night, the entire world shook and it woke him up. To calm himself after the world stopped shaking, he went to walking and found a bunch of new cracks in the strand sidewalk that looked like pictures of crazy animals, mean pictures of things with big eyes in the wrong places and upside down noses and mouths big enough to swallow you. And some of those mouths had sharp-looking teeth and a lot of those teeth had fallen out and were scattered all over the place, little points and angles of sidewalk pieces that might never find their way back into the evil mouths again.

That's right. Evil is all around you.

Harp decides not to think about the scary pictures in the sidewalk anymore. He should be looking for clues. Detective Olivera said he should nose around and act like he was trying to solve the case himself. But how do you nose around? Does it mean I should go up and down the strand asking people questions like Olivera does?

No! If you talk to people, they will suspect you.

Okay, maybe it's better not to talk to people. Maybe it would be better to just stop thinking about who killed Little Hilly. Maybe it would be better to only think more important things, like . . . like being hungry. "That's right, I never did find anything to eat back at the pier, did I?"

So what? You think I never went hungry? All you ever think about is yourself.

As Harp passes the little wooden stand where the man in the white hat stirs the caramel corn around and around in his great big metal pot with his big wooden paddle, Harp's stomach complains out loud. He looks around to see if anybody heard, but the people are still going right on by like they don't even notice him. His stomach is telling him he's got to find something to eat soon. Where to look? Then his brain remembers a place. What about the big stack of garbage where people throw stuff behind the sea wall on their way off the beach? Sometimes there's food left over from their beach picnics. There might even be some pizza in there. Harp's stomach grumbles again and urges him to go take a look.

What about the blood on your coat? Remember the rhyme. Who saw his blood?

"This will only take a minute, then I'll go take care of the blood."

He cuts through the parking lot and when he gets to the pile of garbage, he's happy to see that the pile is really big this time. His stomach aches with hope.

Don't go near it. Who knows who might have touched that stuff.

Harp knows he shouldn't eat things that have been touched by strangers, but how else is he going to take care of his complaining stomach?

He starts to paw through the pile, but it's mostly the regular stuff, dirty paper plates and paper cups and plastic bags and deflated balloons with words printed on them and wadded-up paper napkins and really icky smelly plastic baby diapers. He sees an old tennis shoe, but it looks too big for him. Besides, he can't see the other one. He spots a bottle, but after he digs it out, he sees that it's only a beer bottle, not returnable for money. He throws it down and digs deeper into the pile. Wet newspapers. Cardboard. Somebody's dirty underpants. What are they doing here?

Filthy things. Don't touch them.

He holds them up for a better look. The back part is all stained and icky and smelly. How could somebody lose their underpants? It's suspicious, but he can't think why it would have anything to do with killing Little Hilly so he throws them aside.

Then he sees the corner of a fairly clean looking pizza box, way out in the middle of the pile. The pile is really stinky, but he holds his nose and wades in, kicking aside bags and cups and bottles and cans and newspapers and sticky paper plates and a single sandy sock that's no good because it has a hole in the toe part.

When he finally makes it to the pizza box and opens it, it's a big disappointment. It's empty, except for a little bit of cheese stuck to the sides. He smells the inside of the box. It smells like pepperoni. His stomach aches at the yummy smell of it. He realizes he shouldn't have smelled it because it only makes him hungrier. He drops the pizza box and digs down deeper. Soon he finds another pizza box, buried way down deep in the pile. He pulls it out. The outside doesn't look too dirty. This may be it. He takes a second to hope: "Help me, Lord, for I am really hungry." He opens the lid just a little bit and peeks in. There *is* something in there. Is it pizza? He looks closer. Yes, it is pizza, a whole piece. But there's something else in there too. Harp slam the pizza box lid down. Something moved in there. What was it? He opens the lid a crack and peeks in again. Whatever it is, it's moving around in there. Then Harp realizes what it is: it's a mouse, a little teeny mouse. He opens up the box, expecting the mouse to run away, but it doesn't. It just looks up at him, wiggling its whiskers. Then, suddenly, it runs right across the back of Harp's hand and jumps away into the pile. It scares him so much he drops the box and the piece of pizza lands upside down right on top of all the dirty garbage. He quickly picks it up and tries to blow the dirt off of it. Maybe it's still clean enough to eat.

No! It's unclean, polluted by the world. Drop it.

Harp puts down the piece of pizza, being careful to place it on top of a fairly clean-looking newspaper, just in case he doesn't find anything else. But then the mouse pops out from under the garbage and heads straight for the piece of pizza. Harp tries to shoo the little fellow away, but it bites the pizza and won't let go. The mouse starts to drag the piece of pizza away and Harp hesitates just a second too long before he makes a grab for it. The mouse pulls the pizza out of sight under a stained white sack that says "Coffee Crazy" on it. It peeks back out, wiggles its whiskers once, and then it's gone.

Harp carefully moves the white sack aside, ready to grab the pizza. But it's not there. There's nothing but a hole. Harp peers down into the hole. It's dark down there and there's a strong smell of mouse coming out. The mouse must have a secret hiding place down there. Maybe there are hundreds and hundreds of mice down under the garbage pile, a kind of mouse city. Do they come out at night to eat the garbage, just like the homeless do?

That little mouse reminds him of what his teacher said that one time the man came and said he had to go to school. The teacher told the class that mice and humans had evolved from a common ancestor.

She was wrong, dead wrong. I warned her.

When Harp told Mother about it, she got mad and said it wasn't true. She said God had created Adam and then made woman out of one of Adam's ribs. The next day, Harp went to the library to find out what was true and what wasn't true. He found a book that said mice were mammals, just like man, but all mammals had originally been fish. The book said the fish crawled up on the land and eventually turned into monkeys. The book said it was an easy step from there to becoming human beings.

Just because such blaspheme gets printed in a book doesn't mean it's true.

So, the book had disagreed with Mother. When Harp went home and told her what he'd read in the book, she wasn't happy about being a fish, or even a mammal. She got really mad and hit Harp a whole bunch of times.

You needed to be taught what was right. 'Spare the rod and spoil the child.' That's what the Good Book says.

Harp remembers he had to stay locked up in the closet all that night and it was soon after that when they moved and Mother said he couldn't go to school anymore. She said he had to stay home and help her because she was sick and needed him there with her all the time.

From then on, Harp kept things he read to himself.

Yes, but I knew you were up to something. God knew you were reading books in secret. God sees everything you do, and He knows what you're thinking too.

Harp tries to turn off those bad old thoughts. He looks up at the sky. The sun is getting warm. He should just think about the warm sun and nice things like that. But it got him starting to wonder if there were other things in books that disagreed with what Mother said.

I warned you about books, but did you listen? No. Those books put bad ideas into your head.

Harp remembers how nice and quiet it was at the library. Almost nobody else went there. At the library, he could read as much as he wanted. He could even look at the big books full of famous paintings and some of them had pictures of women with no clothes on. He could look at those pictures all he wanted to and nobody could stop him.

What? I won't have this. Proverbs 30 says, 'The ravens of the valley shall peck out and eat the eyes of the boy who dare mocketh his mother.'

Harp looks up at the sky, thinking about those pictures. Some of them even showed paintings of women and men who . . .

Stop that!

Harp suddenly realizes he's still standing up to his knees in the middle of a big stinky pile of garbage. How long has he been there? He'd better keep track of where he is, or who knows what could happen.

That's right. You'd better pay attention when I'm talking to you.

He must have been daydreaming again. Mother always said daydreaming was bad for him.

Get out of that filth. How many times do I have to tell you things?

He struggles out of the garbage pile and looks around. No food. Now what should I do?.

I can't believe you. Have you forgotten all about the blood?

Harp decides she is right. He's still very hungry, but maybe he'd better get that blood washed off of his jacket.

You're always getting distracted. What would you do without me?

Harp knows he shouldn't keep on letting himself get distracted. Now he's going to really concentrate. Right now, getting that blood washed off before anybody finds out is the most important thing in the world.

1-5

Balance

*H*arp hurries toward the public wash-basins, but he doesn't get far before he notices a lot of people gathered on the sidewalk in front of Billy Goat's Emporium. Billy's store is never open this early. So what are all those people doing there?

He goes closer and sees that it's only Bailey the Balancing Man. He's walking around with a chair balanced on his chin and it's drawing a crowd, like it always does.

There you go again. Getting distracted. Remember the blood. Who saw the blood?

Harp knows he really doesn't have time to stop and watch. There's that blood on his coat that has to be taken care of. But I should at least wait until Bailey's cute little wife comes out in her bikini swimming suit.

So that's what you're waiting for. I might have known.

The people watch as Bailey staggers around. He's pretending the chair is really heavy against his chin, but Harp knows Bailey balances that same chair up there every day.

Harp wonders why nobody is putting money in Bailey's jar today. Maybe they're waiting for Bailey's cute little wife to come out. Harp hopes she'll come out soon.

Bailey keeps on balancing the chair until his wife finally comes dancing out, smiling and bowing and spinning around. Harp is always amazed at how tiny she is. She's really pretty in her little bikini swimming suit and some of the men whistle at her as she dances around. Today, she has on her red sparkly bikini. Harp likes that one the best.

God knowest thy foolishness. Your sins are not hid from Him.

Harp knows he shouldn't be watching her when she's dressed so skimpy like that, but she seems like a nice person. She seems to like it when the men whistle at her. She puts her hand behind her head and smiles at them.

God will punish you for the lust that hides in your heart.

I'll just wait until she's up in the air. Then I'll go wash up my coat.

Carnal pleasures are the meat of the lustful heart.

Harp concentrates on watching her and tries not to hear anything else.

Go ahead, pursue your low pleasures of the flesh. But you'll be sorry. Mark my words.

Harp thinks it's funny that Bailey's wife never pays any attention to Bailey. When he finally puts his balancing chair down, she goes right over and sits on it. Bailey acts like he's surprised to see somebody sitting in his balancing chair. He scratches his head and circles around her. She crosses her legs and folds her arms. She won't look at him. Bailey walks around and around her, until suddenly, he grabs the chair and lifts it right up into the air with her still sitting in it. He staggers around like he's about to drop her. She pretends to look really scared with her eyes opened up wide and her hands up to her mouth. Just when it looks like he can't hold her up much longer, he puts the chair leg on top of his chin and balances her there.

Everybody claps, but Harp is worried. Something's wrong. Bailey really does seem to be having trouble holding her up this time. He's shaking and his face is getting red. He doesn't usually act like that. Is he only pretending?

Then it happens, just like Harp was afraid it would: the chair slips off of Bailey's chin and his little wife goes tumbling. Oh no, is she hurt?

Now look what you've done. It's your fault.

Harp doesn't think everything should have to be his fault. He can't always keep the worried thoughts out of his head, but he didn't mean to make her fall down and get hurt.

She jumps right up, rubbing her bottom. She doesn't seem to be hurt very bad. She looks at Bailey and says, "What the hell's the matter with you today, Fred?"

Bailey shrugs and says, "I told you you were putting on weight."

She turns away from him and goes back to smiling and dancing and spinning around in front of all the people. Bailey grabs up his jar and goes to the people to try to get them to put money in it. But a lot of the people just walk away.

Well, what are you waiting for? You've had your fun.

Harp decides he'd better not wait for the part where Bailey's wife stands on top of Bailey's head while he staggers around and acts like he's about to fall down. He might have more of those worried feelings and make her fall off again. But he waits until she comes dancing by with the jar to try to get money from the people. He smiles at her and she smiles back, just a little.

Quit that! The Lord sayeth, depart from this evil.

But maybe she wasn't really smiling at him. Maybe she was just smiling at everybody. He'd better just walk away. No reason to look back, he decides. Let her smile at the other people, I don't care. But if she's not careful, she might end up like the witch's beautiful daughter who tricked the huntsman boy into lying down with her just so she could steal his magic wishing-cloak. She got hers in the end when he dyed his face brown so even his own mother wouldn't recognize him and pretended to be the king's messenger so he could trick the old witch and the beautiful daughter into eating the magic cabbage so they were both tuned into ugly donkeys. Served them right.

Harp hurries on down the sidewalk. Now he's really determined. He isn't going to stop anymore, not for anything. He'll keep right on going until he gets to the outdoor wash sinks, and he'll get his jacket-washing and hand-washing taken care of. He'll be like the boy in the story who pushed the ghost down the stairs and just walked away without looking back.

In that story, the boy was a silly blockhead.

"I don't think he was a silly blockhead, not really. In fact, he was pretty smart. In the end he got the princess and the three chests full of gold, didn't he?"

It was the Devil inside him that made him do those things, just like the Devil is inside you, making you want to watch half-naked women.

"Well, maybe the devil *was* inside that boy, but he's not inside of me. No way. I'd feel him in there." Harp puts his fingers in his ears and walks on. He tries to think about other things, good things. Like all that money Bailey's cute little wife gets by holding the jar out to the people after Bailey finishes balancing her. Harp wishes he could balance things so he could get some of that money. As he walks, he holds his hands out wide like Bailey does and pretends to balance Bailey's cute little wife on top of his head. He can almost feel the weight of her up there. She's not very heavy, not really. He balances her very carefully, and then sneaks a peek up between her legs at . . .

Stop those sinful thoughts! Besides, just look around. You're making a spectacle of yourself.

Harp looks around. A young boy is pointing at him. The little boy is holding a silver balloon that says, "Happy Birthday" on it. Harp smiles at the little boy, but his mother takes him by the hand and quickly pulls him away.

Harp goes on down the strand, thinking about that silver birthday balloon. "Why didn't I ever get to have a nice birthday balloon like that?"

Childish nonsense. Pay attention to what you're supposed to be doing.

Harp stops thinking about silly old things. He's got to focus on what he's supposed to be doing. He's supposed to be trying to find something to eat. If only he could get some of Bailey's money he could buy himself something good to eat.

Food? Is that all you ever think about? Stop thinking selfish thoughts and think about the blood. You caught his blood.

Harp doesn't want to think about blood. He wants to think about good things to eat.

Listen to me. You are in danger. Who got Cock Robin's blood all over himself?

But Harp doesn't want to think about dead things anymore. He especially doesn't want to think about that blood all over Little Hilly's back. But wait a minute, what about that money he found in Little Hilly's pocket, the money Little Hilly made from panhandling and forgot to share? Little Hilly is dead now, so he doesn't need that money anymore. If he wanted to, he could use Little Hilly's money to buy something to eat. His stomach murmurs that it likes that idea. He's almost to the Sunnysidewalk Café. If he wanted to, he could walk right in there and get something good to eat just like a regular person.

No! People will be suspicious of you.

That's true. Somebody in that restaurant might start to wonder where he got the money. And what if the money has some of Little Hilly's blood on it? Better not take a chance.

He goes on down the strand, but now that the sun is completely out a lot more people are filling up the sidewalk. It's getting hard to stay out of their way.

Don't let them touch you. They're unclean, tainted by the Devil's filth.

Harp knows he has to be very, very careful to not let anybody touch his body. You never know where those peoples' hands have been. He has to weave through the people like he's a snake, always watching their hands. It's scary because any one of them might sneak up and touch him when he's not looking and that might let them come into his dreams at night and make him do things he doesn't want to. And there are roller skaters too. They're the worst. They come at you so fast you have to be ready to jump out of their way or else they might crash right into you. And not only that, now that it's getting warmer and sunnier there are people with cameras taking pictures.

For they intended evil against thee and imagined a mischievous device to perform against thee.

That's right. I have to be especially watchful for those people with cameras. Mother said they might take my picture and sell my soul to the Devil.

But that thought stops him. Who are all those people with cameras, and why are they taking pictures around here? It's suspicious. Detective Olivera told him to look for suspects. Some of those people with cameras could be suspects. But how were you supposed to tell who is a suspect and who isn't? Are there certain clues that tell you which people are suspects?

You're his main suspect. Didn't you see the way he looked at you?

Harp remembers Olivera's eyes. Those eyes were looking him over, trying to see inside his head. Good thing he already hid his jacket in his backpack. If Olivera would have seen that blood on the front of his jacket he might have got suspicious and locked him up and thrown away the key. Harp knows about that. When he got put on Ward D-4, the first thing Mitch told him was if he didn't mind his Ps and Qs the Growler would lock him in the Time-Out Closet. Mitch said he might throw away the key and leave him locked in that closet forever. Harp promised never to be bad, but Mitch locked him in that closet for a while anyhow, just to show him what it was like. Harp found out what it was like. The Time-Out Closet was very small and dark.

Your closet at home was safe and warm.

But Harp didn't mind the dark in Mitch's closet. The thing he didn't like about Mitch's closet was that it was cold. And it was too small to move around, so that made it feel even colder. Harp didn't like being cold and not able to move around, so from then on he made sure he did everything exactly the way Mitch wanted it. After a while, there was nobody on Ward D-4 who was better at doing things perfect than Harp. He was so good at doing everything exactly the right way, he never once got put into the Time-Out Closet again.

The real reason you didn't get put in was because I was there protecting you.

"No, it was because I did things right. The other men did things wrong. That's why they got put in there." Harp remembers the sound of them screaming inside that little closet and clawing at the door. When they finally got out, most of them were even crazier than they were when they went in. "I'll just have to learn what Detective Olivera wants me to do, just like I learned what Mitch wanted me to do."

Fat chance of that.

But what if he can't figure out what Olivera wants? He might have to run away from the beach and go somewhere else. But where could he go? The thought of leaving the beach is really scary. What if he went somewhere else and they thought he acted funny and sent him back to that bad place? Maybe Mitch would be there, waiting to get revenge on him.

Don't be silly. Mitch is in prison. You're getting yourself all worked up over nothing.

Harp shakes off that scary thought. She's right. That can't happen. They took Mitch away, and after that the bad place was closed down. Carl the Older said the President of the United States closed down all the other places like that too. But if that's true, where did all those other crazy men from Ward D-4 go? He's never seen a single one of them on the beach.

Good thing.

Yes, that is a good thing. If anybody from that place saw him, they'd know where he came from. On the beach nobody knows who anybody used to be, or where they came from, or what they did that was so wrong.

That's right. Nobody knows. Nobody can ever know.

"But maybe I don't have to worry. Maybe Olivera doesn't really suspect me. He said he suspected Big Hilly. Hey, maybe that's why Big Hilly went away. Maybe he found out Detective Olivera suspected him so he just ran away. "

But where would he go? He and Little Hilly never left the beach, did they?

Harp remembers something he found in Little Hilly's pocket. A broken plastic bracelet.

He takes it out to look at it. The writing on the bracelet says, "*Santa Monica General Hospital – Emergency.*" Why was Little Hilly in the emergency room? Does it have something to do with why he was killed?

Don't let anybody see you with that. Throw it away quick!

But Harp can't throw it away. Detective Olivera said he was supposed to look for clues, and so far this is the only clue he has. Maybe he should go to that emergency room and ask questions like Detective Olivera said he should. Where is the Santa Monica General Hospital? Maybe it's a long ways from the beach. It makes Harp nervous even to think about going very far away from the beach.

Harp puts the hospital bracelet back in his pocket. It's so hard to know what's an important clue and what isn't. Maybe everything is a clue, and you just have to figure out what each thing means.

Don't be stupid. Everything can't be a clue because then it wouldn't be a clue.

No really, it makes sense that a person who watches everything could see a lot of important clues. It would be like in the story when the grinning skull in the tower window watched everybody go by on the road below.

That's wrong. It was the girl who saw everything, watching through her little window.

Oh, that's right. She was a brave little girl. She watched, and she was the one who brought her sisters back to life after they'd been hacked to pieces by the Devil. That little girl watched the Devil through her little window and saw how to trick him. Harp whispers the girl's words softly to himself.

I am looking through my little window.
I see what you are doing.

1-6

Cleanliness is Next to Godliness

Harp goes on down the strand sidewalk, determined to be the watcher who sees everything. He knows he can't let himself get confused by things that don't matter, but he still has to watch for the things that do. Yesterday Little Hilly was alive, and today he isn't. When one thing changes, other things have to change too. It's only logical. Some other things must have changed since yesterday. All he has to do is keep on looking until he sees what's changed.

I can't believe you. Did you already forget what you're supposed to be doing? You'd forget your head if it wasn't attached.

What?

The blood. Who caught his blood?

Oh, that's right. The blood on my coat. I have to go to the outdoor sinks.

Harp puts his head down and walks as fast as he can. First things first. He's not going to even look for any more suspects until he gets that blood washed off.

When he gets to the outdoor sinks, some surfer boys are already there washing off their rubber clothes. Harp hangs back until they're finished, then he goes to the sink that's farthest away from the sidewalk. Now to get that blood off.

First wash that phone number off your hand before somebody sees it.

"Oh, right." He quickly washes Detective Olivera's phone number off of his hand. With that taken care of, he pulls his jacket out of his backpack. He's surprised to see how much blood is on it. How did that happen?

The shroud, the bloody shroud.

Well, no time now to worry about how it got on there, the important thing is to get it off. He frantically scrubs away at it. But it's stubborn. He gets the darkest blood washed off, but the outline of it is still there. He needs something to scrub with. He gets an idea. He takes off a shoe and sock and uses the sock to scrub the jacket.

I can't believe this.

Harp scrubs at the jacket, really hard, keeping the water running all the time.

He holds it up to look. That scrubbing worked pretty good. I've got most of the blood off.

But then he's not so sure. Now that part of the jacket looks *too* clean. It might make people notice it even more. What to do? Maybe he should make that part of the jacket really dirty so nobody will notice the blood underneath the dirt.

That's about the most stupid idea I've heard yet.

"No, it's a good idea, really it is."

Harp leaves his shoe on the sink and limps over to the grass. He finds a place where the grass has been worn thin by all the kids playing on it and he rubs the wet part of the jacket into the dirt.

Stop that. You're attracting attention to yourself.

He looks around to see if anybody's watching. Some kids are playing in the sand nearby, digging a big hole with plastic red shovels. One of them has stopped digging and is staring at him. Harp waves to him, but the boy turns away and goes back to digging. That digging in the sand looks like fun. Harp tries to remember if Mother ever took him to the beach to dig in the sand.

Childish nonsense. Pay attention to what you're doing.

Oh well, no time to think about that now. He picks up his jacket and inspects it. It's very dirty. Now nobody can see the blood underneath the dirt.

Are you kidding? Just look at it.

Harp stares at the big brown spot on the front of his jacket and he begins to have doubts. "Do you think people will wonder why I have mud all over the front of my jacket?"

Do you do these things just to annoy me?

Maybe the dirt wasn't such a good idea after all.

Now he thinks it wasn't such a good idea.

Harp limps back over to the sink and washes the dirt off. But some of the dirt doesn't go away. Oh well, maybe there's just enough dirt to cover up the blood stain. "See there, it was a good idea after all."

You think you're so smart. You think you're going to get away with it? You're not even paying attention to who might be watching you.

Just in time, Harp looks up to see the two beach bicycle cops coming down the sidewalk. They're riding slow, looking in his direction.

Now you're in for it. Get out of here!

Harp rolls up his wet jacket, grabs his sock and his shoe, and runs around to the front of the restroom building. He ducks inside and hides inside one of the stalls to wait until they go by.

If they come in they'll catch you red-handed.

She's right. If they come in they might ask why his jacket is all wet. And they might say, Why do you only have one shoe on? Harp holds his breath and listens. Voices. Somebody is coming in.

"Did you see the knockers on that chick?"

"Which one?"

"The one with the knockers. You didn't see her?"

It's not the bicycle cops, it's two boys. They go on saying bad things about girls while they pee, their voices echoing inside the small room. Harp stays perfectly still, not making a sound.

When the two boys finally go out, Harp sits down on the toilet and puts his wet sock back on. He looks at his old beat-up shoes. They are really dirty. He hates to put them back on without giving them a good washing too, but he'd better get away from there if those two bicycle cops are nosing around. Before he leaves, he takes out the three dollar bills and looks at them. They're still a little damp and there's some brown spots on them. Is that blood? It's not red like blood, but maybe blood changes color when it's on money. He decides to look again later, when he's out in the sunshine.

He puts the dollars back in his pocket and puts his jacket back on. The wet jacket soaks through and gets his shirt wet too. It feels cold against his skin.

You should have dried it in the sun before you put it on. Can't you do anything right?

Harp doesn't mind having a wet jacket and a wet shirt, not really. They'll dry eventually.

When he gets back outside, he peeks around the edge of the restroom building. The two bicycle cops are bicycling away down the sidewalk.

You got lucky that time. Better go the other way.

He hurries away in the opposite direction. His wet sock squishes inside his shoe as he walks, but he knows from experience that walking is the fastest way to get a wet sock dry. But what if the bottom of his shoe is so worn out the wet sock soaks through and leaves behind a wet footprint? That would make it easy for somebody to follow him. He whispers one of Mother's favorite Bible prayers to make sure they don't: "Dear Lord, save me from all them that persecute me lest they tear me apart like a lion. Diggeth them a pit and maketh them to fall into it so their mischief may falleth upon their own heads. Amen."

Look out! Servants of the Devil ahead.

Harp sees them and quickly turns away, his hands over his eyes. That was close. I almost didn't see them in time. It's the Devil Boys with their shaved heads and their big sign that says "Hare Krishna." The Devil Boys always wait for him in front of the cotton candy stand. They're wearing their magic yellowish-orange clothes, trying to fool him into thinking they're not devils by wearing funny-looking pajamas.

The Devil comes in many disguises.

Harp isn't fooled by their magic clothes. He knows to stay away from them. If you get too close to the Devil Boys, they'll try to touch you and make you take their Devil Papers. They try to put their evil thoughts inside your mind.

Harp makes the magic sign of the sacred upside-down cross to ward off their eyes and walks seven steps backward so they won't be able to see him anymore. He counts each step, counting back from seven down to one.

It works. They don't notice him. But they're still there on the sidewalk, passing out their Devil Papers to the off-beacher people. Harp gets off the sidewalk and goes around to the other side of the palm trees. He continues to walk backwards until he's way past them.

Luckily, he's able to get past without them noticing. Thank goodness. Once he's far enough away to be safe, he gets back onto the sidewalk and hurries away, hoping the Devil Boys won't try to follow him, even if he is leaving a wet footprint on the sidewalk.

The Lord shall swallow them up in his wrath, and His fire shall devour them.

That's right. The devil worshippers should be swallowed up by the Lord's fire. But that makes Harp think of something else. What if those devil worshipers did it? Maybe they caught Little Hilly in the night and killed him.

That's right, maybe the police will blame it on them. Remember, who caught his blood?

Harp whispers that part of the rhyme:

Who caught his blood?
I, said the Fish, with my little dish,
I caught his blood.

Could that be the answer? Did the Devil Boys want Little Hilly's blood?

Yes, we'll say it was some kind of Devil ritual. They needed blood.

That's right, the Devil Boys could have killed Little Hilly to get his blood. Maybe he should call Detective Olivera and tell him.

No! Stay away from that cop. Do you hear me?

But maybe Detective Olivera would want proof. Harp decides it would be better to find the killer by myself, then, once he's sure, he could tell Olivera. He tells himself to keep his eye on those Devil Worshipers until he gets some evidence on them. And he'll watch everybody else too. He'll be like the watcher king who watched all night to see who was eating the fruit from his magic pear tree. That king watched and watched until he caught the girl whose hands had been cut off by her father so the Devil wouldn't want her.

But the Devil has more tricks up his sleeve than you will ever know. Didn't he trick the king into having the poor girl's eyes and tongue cut out?

Harp decides he doesn't really want to be like that bad king. Instead, he'll be like . . . like the smart boy who learned what the dogs were saying when they barked, what the frogs were saying when they croaked, and what the birds were saying when they sang. If he was like that smart boy he could ask the dogs and the frogs and the birds to help him find out who killed Little Hilly.

That'll be about the only way you'll ever figure it out.

Harp puts his fingers in his ears. He doesn't want to hear what she's saying. He whispers to himself, "I will too figure it out. All I have to do is watch for clues, like Detective Olivera said I should. I'll figure out who did it. I will. I really will."

1-7

Secret Messages

*H*arp decides the first step to finding out who killed Little Hilly is to pay close attention to everything until he spots the clues that will lead him to the killer.

This I've got to see.

The next place he comes to is Sally's Sunglasses Hut. He looks at everything very carefully. Are there any clues? Sally's two worn-out flags are out in front of her store, flapping in the wind, same as always. But then he sees something wrong: the red flag still has the same silly dog wearing dark sunglasses, and the white flag still has the big red lips on it, but there's a little picture drawn on the white flag. Harp goes closer and sees right away what it is: somebody drew a dirty picture. It's a drawing of a little man with his great big privates thing sticking right between the red lips on the white flag. Sally is going to be really mad when she sees that.

Harp looks around. Who could have drawn that dirty picture? He was afraid something like this was going to happen. Things that used to be nice before Little Hilly got killed are changing now. Bad things are starting to happen.

So, what else has changed? What other bad things are starting to happen? He turns around in a complete circle, looking at everything.

You're attracting attention to yourself again.

Harp stops turning. A woman with a scarf over her head has stopped to stare at him. But as soon as Harp looks at her, she quickly turns away and goes on down the sidewalk.

See there. People are staring. Didn't I tell you?

So what if people stare? He's looking for clues, and that's

important. He goes back to turning around in a circle, watching everything spin around him. He spins so fast everything starts to look blurry.

Stop that! Do you want people to think you're crazy?

He hears someone laugh, so he stops spinning. A very tall black man with a very tall white turban hat is smiling at him and nodding his head. He says, "Groovy, man."

Harp hurries away. He's seen that man on the strand before. He spends all day roller skating up and down the strand playing his guitar. He does it to try to get people to give him money. "Why was that man watching me? And what does 'groovy' mean?"

It means he thought you were a nut.

Harp decides to act very normal, but he'll keep on looking for clues. He's sure other things must have changed besides that dirty picture on Sally's red-lips flag.

What about the off-beacher people? Are they suspects? Harp stops to watch them, but they just look like the usual weekend off-beachers in their usual flowery shirts and white shorts. No clues there.

Who else? There must be *some* suspects.

The red-faced old man in the funny little plaid hat is sitting on his usual bench, like he always does. Nothing unusual about that. But wait, there *is* something different about him today. The man stands up and looks around, and then he sits back down again. He normally doesn't do that. What is he looking for?

Soon Harp figures it out: where is the little white dog that's usually hiding underneath the old man's bench?

Harp hurries over and asks, "Where's your little dog?" He's surprised at himself for being so quick to talk to the old man. He's never before said a word to the old man in all the time he's been on the beach. This asking questions could get to be a habit.

The man holds up his hand to shield his eyes from the sun. "Have you seen him, son? He's gone missing. I can't find him anywhere." He looks very sad about it and his face seems even redder than usual.

"No, I haven't seen him," says Harp. "Did he run away?" There it was again, another question. It just slipped out. Once you startasking people questions, it gets easier and easier.

"No, no, he wouldn't run away. He's never run away before. I let him out last night to go poop, and he just didn't come back. You haven't seen him, have you?"

He suspects you. Don't let on.

Harp shakes his head.

You don't even like dogs.

"Could you look for him?" The old man's voice is very shaky. "I'll pay you if you find him."

Harp tries to figure it out. First Little Hilly is killed, and then the red-lips flag has a dirty picture drawn on it, and now the little dog has disappeared. All on the same night. It's a pattern. It all adds up.

What adds up? You don't know what you're talking about.

No, now he's sure of it. Things are beginning to fall into place. It's true, no matter what anybody else thinks.

The old man is staring at him, waiting for him to say something.

"I'm . . . uh, investigating something else right now." Harp feels like he's hearing somebody else talk, somebody who isn't himself. Maybe asking all these questions is changing him. "But if I see your little dog, I'll bring him back to you."

"Oh, would you? It would be wonderful if you could find him. His name is Teddy. He'll come if you call him. He's very friendly to . . . you people."

So the old man thinks I might be good at finding the dog, just like Olivera thought I'd be good at finding out who killed Little Hilly. Maybe I *could* be good at finding things. Maybe I could make money doing it.

You? Don't make me laugh.

But Harp knows he is good at noticing things, no matter what anybody thinks. He knows exactly how many light poles there are between the pier and the weight-lifter's pen. And he knows every crack in the sidewalk. So why wouldn't I be good at finding things too? If he finds the dog and the old man pays him a lot of money, maybe he should start looking for other things too.

Are you kidding? You, find things?

All I have to do is look around.

"Are you listening to me, son?"

"Oh, yes. I was just . . . thinking."

This isn't getting us anywhere. A waste of time.

"Well, I sure hope you find him. Teddy must be getting very hungry by now."

Harp wishes the old man hadn't mentioned anything about being hungry. His stomach doesn't need to be reminded of that. But the old man's words make him feel proud. If the old man thinks he can find the little dog, maybe he can. He'll start looking as soon as he figures out who killed Little Hilly.

Harp leans closer to the old man. "Now I have to ask you something, mister old man. Do you know Little Hilly?"

The old man says, "No, who's he?"

Harp is happy to see the man isn't getting mad about being asked so many questions. He's beginning to think people might actually like being asked questions.

"Little Hilly is . . . was . . . a little guy, about this high." Harp holds out his hand to show how high. "Actually, about the same size as me. But I'm not looking for him. I know where he is. I'm looking for the bigger one, Big Hilly, who's usually with him. He has a big chest." Harp points to his own chest. "A lot bigger chest than mine."

The old man frowns. "Does he have long hair? Greasy like?"

Harp shakes his head. "No, he doesn't have very much hair left on his head at all."

The old man snaps his fingers. "Got it. Big bald guy, always hanging out with a little skinny guy."

"That's them," says Harp.

"Right over there." The old man turns to point. "Over there on the grass. That's where it happened. I was waiting for Teddy to finish pooping when your two friends came along. The little skinny one was eating a hot dog. He gave Teddy a bite of it."

"That's him," says Harp. "Little Hilly was like that. He was nice to people, sometimes, and dogs too . . . I guess."

The old man nods and sits back. "Well, if I see them, I'll tell them you're looking for them."

"Oh, they won't be . . . together. Just look for the big one."

"Uh oh, what happened? Did they have a falling out?"

"Uh, I'm not sure if they did or not. But if you see the big one, Big Hilly, tell him to come find me. My name is Harp. He knows me. Tell him don't talk to anyone else. Only me."

"Well, well. It all sounds rather mysterious. But if you'll look for

Teddy, I'll look for the big bald fellow. And I'll keep your secret." He puts his finger to his lips.

"Well, it's not exactly a secret. It's more like . . ."

It is a secret. No one must know.

Harp thinks about it. Maybe it should be a secret. Maybe no one should know why he's looking for Big Hilly. "Okay. Well . . . bye."

The old man tips his hat as Harp backs away. Harp wishes he still had a hat to tip back.

That was a waste of time, just like I said it would be.

"No, it wasn't. I'm investigating."

Investigating. What a hoot.

A little further on, still watching for things that are wrong, Harp spots something else that's wrong. Somebody has written in black paint on the white side wall of Betty's Bra Bar and Sex Shoppe.

Now this is a real clue.

He hurries closer to look, but he suspects it's probably just more of the crazy letters and pictures kids paint all over everything.

No, I'm telling you this is important.

Harp has seen those kids come late in the night with their spray cans to paint things on Betty's white wall. In the morning, Betty comes out with her paint roller on a long stick and paints white paint to cover it all up. She cusses like crazy while she does it, but sometimes the kids come back the very next night and do it again.

Are you listening to me? This is different.

And Harp has seen their odd paintings on other walls too. And sometimes they do pictures and words on places that aren't walls, like on the bus benches or on the stop signs. Harp has studied the things the kids paint for so long he just about knows them all by heart. Sometimes they just write bad words, but other times they do tall words, or long thin stretched-out words. Harp has seen big fat woozy words, and long wiggly wiggly words that go up and down like a roller coaster. And sometimes the pictures are scary, with strange-looking great big hands or scrunched-up faces that have wild eyes that watch you as you walk past, or moons that laugh at you, or stars with sad eyes that cry, or strange animals that if they exist anywhere Harp has never seen them. And then there was that one of the mean-looking flying man that flies over the top of the words and shoots lightning bolts out of his fingers. But the worst ones are the mouths with big red tongues that have words flying out. Harp doesn't like those pictures because the mouths yell things you're not supposed to say out loud, and they keep right on yelling those words at you until you can get far enough away so you can't see them anymore.

Yeah, yeah, we know about that, but I keep on telling you this one is different.

As Harp stares at the drawing he realizes she's right. This one isn't like anything he's ever seen the kids do before.

Finally he gets it.

This one is messy, hard to understand.

It's a message. Maybe it's a message for you.

This time it looks like somebody started to spray paint something, maybe a flying bird, but they didn't finish it. Instead, there's two great big words, "His Hand," painted in black spray paint. But the painter used too much paint so the words are all drippy and running down the white wall. And down below the two words there's something else, a sort of misshapen blob that's stretched out on both ends. Maybe it's some kind of . . . maybe an animal, because it has four legs and a tail. Maybe it's supposed to be . . .

It's a dog, stupid.

Harp stares at it. Well, it could be a dog. But it's not near as pretty as the dogs the kids usually paint. The kids usually use all different colors of paint, nice bright colors, and when they do a dog it's easy to tell it's supposed to be a dog. This time the painter only used black paint, and he was messy. The black paint is dripping down from the "His Hand" words right onto the dog.

Harp notices a can of black spray paint lying next to the wall under the painting. Harp picks it up and shakes it. It feel like it's empty, except for some kind of little marble-like thing that bounces around inside of it when you shake it. Why did they leave their paint can? They don't usually do that.

You said you were supposed to be looking for clues. This is a clue.

It's a clue? Harp stares at the painting. He backs away to see if it looks different from farther back. Those two words and all that drippy black paint on top of the dog make it look kind of scary, like the painter was mad at somebody when he did it. The more he looks at it, the more his eyes are drawn to what's in the middle of the dog. It's not the same as the rest of the dog, but it's hard to tell what it is because of all the dripping-down black paint.

Look closer. You know what it is.

It looks like an X, right in the middle of the dog.

No, it's not an X. Listen, 'Let them take up my cross and follow me.'

Suddenly, Harp sees what it is. It's a cross, a long cross with a point on the bottom of it, stuck right there in the middle of the dog. What a strange thing to put in the middle of a picture of a dog. Is it supposed to be a religious dog?

Some other people stop to see what Harp is looking at. They look at the painted wall, then they look at him.

Harp wonders why they are looking at him. He didn't do it.

All of a sudden, Harp realizes he still has the empty spray paint can in his hand.

They think you did it. Get out of here.

Harp drops the can, and it makes a loud sound when it hits the sidewalk. He hurries away, forcing himself not to look back. He knows he didn't do it, no matter what those people think. It's not his fault that somebody did a bad painting on Betty's nice white wall.

Think about that picture. It means something.

What?

Think.

Harp doesn't like thinking about that messy painting on the wall. It's not pretty, or even interesting. It's messy and it feels mean. Why did they write those two words, "His hand," and why did they draw a picture of a dog with a cross stuck in the middle of it? Did it have something to do with poor Little Hilly? It has to mean something.

It does. Look at the facts.

Facts. There are facts all over the place. But which ones mean something, and which ones don't? Harp knows one fact for sure: since Little Hilly got killed, things are changing. It's enough to make a person very nervous.

Think about this fact. It was night. It was dark.

That's right. It was foggy last night, and dark. In the dark somebody stabbed Little Hilly until he was dead.

You heard a dog howling.

That's right, a dog was howling. But then it stopped.

A dog howling in the night is a sign of death.

Yes, a sign of death. And then Little Hilly died. And during that same dark night, Little Teddy the dog disappeared, and somebody made a painting of a dog on Betty's white wall. And the painting has a pointed black cross, right in the middle of the dog.

A point at the end of it. That's not a normal cross.

Harp stops. The people on the sidewalk flow around him as he stands there thinking.

That's right. Now you get it, don't you?

Suddenly, it's all clear. Now he understands what the painting means. Poor Teddy. Poor little Teddy. It's not a pointed cross in the middle of the painting of Teddy, it's a knife, a great big cross knife.

Part 2
Shoeless Joe and the Usual Lady

This morning I was out of my cot and in line as soon as Mitch blew the whistle for prayer time. But Slow George was too slow. Little guys like me are fast but big guys like George are slow and Mitch doesn't like slow so today he got fed up and called for the Growler. The Growler came with the whipping belt in his teeth. The Growler got stuck in here on ward D-4 like the rest of us, but he helps Mitch. Mitch tied Slow George to his bed and the Growler started whipping on George's back. Mitch made us all line up and watch so we would learn a lesson about how God wants us to always act right. George screamed with every hit. I wished George would stop screaming so the Growler would stop hitting him. Finally George started crying. Big sobs into his pillow. George was broken. Mitch was satisfied. He untied George and then he went back to the aide station to read his Bible. The Growler sat at his feet with the whipping belt in his teeth. Our day began.

2-1

Disguises

*H*arp walks on down the strand, thinking. That bad picture on Betty's white wall makes him very nervous. He chews at the inside of his cheek, trying to understand what it could mean. Who would paint a bad picture of a dog with a big cross knife stuck in him?

Think about it. Little Hilly was stabbed with a knife. The dog was stabbed with a knife. On the same night.

The more he thinks about it, the more worried Harp is that Little Teddy the dog might be dead too. Somebody hated dogs and that person must have hated Little Hilly too. Now they're both dead. That painting is a clue, that's for sure. Does it mean the same person killed both of them?

He gets it. A miracle.

Harp goes on down the strand, lost in thought. Why would somebody kill a dog and a person too? Why would somebody kill anybody? Do you have to hate somebody to want to kill them?

Pay attention. People are watching you again. What did I tell you about that?

Harp looks up from his thinking and sees that he's almost back to the Sunnysidewalk Café. There's only one person sitting at the outdoor tables in front of the café. A woman, wearing a long red coat. She's drinking something out of a cup and she's watching him.

As Harp passes, the woman follows him with her eyes. What is she looking at? My jacket is all fixed up now so she can't be seeing any blood on me, can she?

Who will wear the bloody shroud?

Suddenly, he worries that maybe he has more blood on him

somewhere. He hurries past the café and goes behind a palm tree to look himself over. His brown pants are pretty dirty, but he doesn't see anything on them that looks like blood. And his old worn out brown shoes have some dark spots on them. Could that be blood? He wishes those bicycle cops hadn't come along before he could get his shoes washed up.

But he can't worry about that now. He has to get busy looking for suspects. Olivera said he had to ask the homeless beach people if they saw or heard anything last night.

Oh yeah? Have you seen any of them around here?

But wait a minute. Where are all the homeless people? He stops and looks around. He hasn't met one single homeless person on the strand all morning. How can he ask them questions if they aren't there?

And then he remembers. Oh no! All this thinking about poor Little Hilly made him forget. Today must be Sunday. All of the homeless people will have already gone up to the Unitarian Church for the free Sunday lunch. His stomach grumbles angrily at the thought that he might already be too late. He turns and runs back to the Sunnysidewalk Café. He goes right inside, not even caring if they get mad at him for crossing the homeless-keep-out white line. He turns to look up at their big clock above the door. Twenty 'til twelve. It's not too late. Thank goodness. He can still make it if he hurries.

He runs out of the café, and without even waiting for the light to turn green, he runs across the busy street and starts up the hill.

Slow down. People will think you're running away from something.

She's right. Even though he wants to get to the church fast, he has to walk normal because once you're away from the beach and going past people's houses they might look out their windows and see you. And if they get suspicious of you, they might call the police.

As he nears the church, Harp wishes he would have had time to wash out his shirt so it wouldn't be so smelly. But then it would be all wet. Better not go inside a church with a wet shirt. Harp knows a lot about how you're supposed to be when you're in a church. When he was little, Mother took him to church every Sunday. He never wanted to go there, so he'd hide under his bed, but that never worked. Mother would drag him out and make him put on his Sunday white shirt and his Sunday brown suit and his Sunday carefully polished brown shoes, and if he ever got his clothes even a little bit dirty on the way she'd get mad and hit him.

You deserved to be hit. Do you think rules are made to be broken?

Oh yes, Harp knows all about churches. You have to act a certain way in churches or people get really mad at you.

Harp is happy to see there's still a line outside the church. It means they haven't opened the doors yet. In fact, some of the homeless people are still lying on the grass inside their sleeping bags. They must have slept there all weekend just to make sure they didn't forget Sunday is free lunch day. Harp wonders if maybe he should have done that too. Then maybe he wouldn't have gone to the pier to sleep last night, and maybe Little Hilly would still be alive. Change one thing and everything else can change too.

As usual, the big strong men are at the front of the line. Harp knows his place, so he heads for the end of the line.

But as he passes Cowboy Tex, the big man reaches out and grabs his arm. "Hey, Harp, stay here and shoot the breeze with me."

Harp puts his head down and murmurs, "I'd better go to the end of the line."

"Naw, get in here by me." Tex pulls Harp into the line. A few of the others complain about butting in line, but Tex tells them to go to hell so they back off.

Harp tries to make himself small and is careful not to make eye contact with any of the other men in the line.

Tex pulls at the front of his big cowboy hat and smiles down at Harp. "Well, Harp my lad, how they hangin' today?"

Harp isn't sure how you're supposed to answer that kind of question, but he wants to be polite so he says, "I guess they're hanging all right, Tex."

"Well, that's good, son, that's mighty good." Tex pulls his little cloth bag of tobacco out of his shirt pocket and begins to make himself a cigarette. He concentrates on his cigarette making, hardly spilling any of the tobacco, and pretty soon he's got a little crooked cigarette made. He holds it out to Harp, but Harp shakes his head. Tex sticks the little cigarette into the corner of his wide mouth and turns away from the wind to light it with a silver lighter. He turns back and lets out a big cloud of smoke.

Harp waves it away from his face and tries not to cough out loud.

Tex leans back against the building and looks off at nothing.

Harp stares at Tex. Tex is really tall and skinny, and his face is all sunburned and cracked. A lot of the homeless beachers have faces like that. Harp's face got sunburned like that too when he first got to the beach, but Mother always said he should be careful about the sun so he got a floppy little hat from the Salvation Army and always wore it.

Oh yeah? Where's your hat now?

It's too bad Little Hilly borrowed that hat and never gave it back. It wasn't his fault that it got lost. Hilly lost it.

You'd better find that hat.

Harp doesn't want to think about where his hat is right now. He stares at Tex's big white cowboy hat. He's never seen Tex without that hat, so Harp decides his sunburned face must be from before he came to the beach, maybe when he was a cowboy out on the range. Harp is happy that Tex let him stand next to him up close to the front of the line. He hopes Tex will tell a cowboy story or two before they open up the doors. Tex tells really good stories about how he used to round up steers and brand heifers and all kinds of fun things like that.

He's no cowboy. He's a fake.

Really? A fake? How could that be?

Would a real cowboy like cows that much?

Harp has to admit that Tex has never mentioned being cold out on the range, or being lonely, or even what his horse's name was. As Harp watches Tex smoke his funny little cigarette, he decides it *is* possible that maybe Tex never really was a cowboy.

But then Harp turns away, surprised at himself. Where are those kinds of thoughts coming from? He's never doubted Tex before. Is he getting suspicious of everybody because of what happened to Little Hilly? He shakes his head to get rid of such doubts. Ever since he woke up and found Little Hilly lying dead on the sand, his head has been full of worrisome thoughts like that. And then seeing that painting on the wall of poor little Teddy with that cross-knife stuck in him made it even worse. Seeing things like that can make you suspicious of everybody, and pretty soon you start to wonder if anybody is telling you the truth. Harp doesn't want to be a doubting Thomas like that.

That's right. A curse on all non-believers.

Harp wants to believe people are nice. Most people, at least. Like Tex. Tex is one of the few homeless men who's ever been nice to him, or even talked to him. He decides he should have been friendly to Tex right away. Maybe it's not too late. He politely says, "Uh, how are yours hanging, Tex?"

Tex sticks the little cigarette in the corner of his mouth and squints at Harp through the smoke. "Well, jes fine, son, jes fine."

Now that the being friendly part has been taken care of, Harp decides he'd better get back to his main job of being Olivera's eyes and ears. "Uh, Tex, I have to ask you a question. Have you seen Big Hilly?"

Tex slowly turns his head and looks down at Harp. "Big Hilly? Hell, that's what everybody's askin'. Seems he up and disappeared soon as his little buddy got killed."

Careful. Don't say anything.

"Oh. Uh, does everybody already know about Little Hilly?"

Didn't I just say to keep your mouth shut? I don't know why I waste my time helping you.

"Yeah. That Mexican cop, Olivera, was here a while ago. His black cop car came pullin' up to the curb and Olivera gets out with two other cops. He goes up and down the line askin' if anybody knew anything about the killin'. Mostly he wanted to know if anybody'd seen Big Hilly."

"Has anybody? Seen Big Hilly, I mean?"

"Naw. But even if they did, nobody's gonna say nuthin to a lawman. After Olivera left, everybody started talkin' about what happened to Little Hilly. You know how people like to go on and on about somethin' they don't know nuthin' about. Some of 'em said they saw police down under the pier this morning, but nobody knows what happened. Then Speel comes sidelin' up. I know somethin', she says. You know Speel, she likes to pretend like she knows everything."

Harp stares at Tex. "Yes, I know, Speel. But can I ask you something, Tex? Why did you call Speel a she? Isn't Speel a he?"

Tex leans close to whisper. "Keep this under your hat, Harp. Everybody thinks Speel is a guy, but I can tell a steer from a heifer, and I know he's a she. She doesn't want anybody to know, so normally I don't say nuthin'. Guess it doesn't matter much which she is. Fat as she is, and dressed in those old overalls, who'd care one way or the other?"

"But . . . she doesn't look like a girl. She has short hair and . . . everything."

"Shaves her head. Every couple of months, I figure."

Disgusting. Think about it, which bathroom does she use?

Harp tries to remember if he's ever seen Speel in the men's bathroom. Maybe not. He's really surprised to find out Speel is a girl. Speel's voice isn't even high like a girl's. She talks kind of rough and acts like boys do. Harp wonders if anybody else on the beach knows. Everybody sees Speel just about every day when she goes up and down the strand sidewalk passing out his . . . her . . . little pieces of paper with handwritten sayings on them. She is pretty fat, like Tex said. In fact, she's the only homeless person on the beach who is fat. Now that Harp thinks about it, isn't that kind of suspicious? Why is Speel fat like that when nobody else on the beach is?

Tex takes his little cigarette out of his mouth and stares at it. "Anyhow, like I was sayin', Speel shows up actin' like a know it all and announces she was down at the pier this mornin' and she'd heard some fisherman say Little Hilly got strangled with his own belt."

Harp is confused by that. Little Hilly hadn't been strangled. He'd been stabbed. Why was Speel saying he'd been strangled?

Keep quiet. Let them think whatever they want.

"Uh, really? Strangled?"

"Yep. That's what Speel said. Little fella got strangled with his own belt."

Harp decides he'd better find Speel and ask her some questions. He's never talked to Speel before, but Olivera said he was supposed to talk to anybody who might know anything about what happened to Little Hilly.

How many times do I have to say it? Take my advice and stay out of it.

But he'll have to be careful not to give away any secrets to Speel. Maybe he could start by asking her something about the sayings she writes on her papers. Speel would like that. Then, after they'd talked about that for a while, he could ask her what she knew about what happened to Little Hilly.

Tex looks down at Harp. "Okay, son, I ask you this. Guy gets strangled with his own belt. What does that tell you?"

Harp tries to think what Tex means. "Uh, what does it tell you, Tex?"

"Well now, I'm not one to talk out of school, son, but if a man is always leading another man around, you know, arm-in-arm like . . . well, hell, it jes ain't natural. You wanna know what I think? I think there's somethin' downright unnatural about all them homos. If ya ask me, I think they oughtta be ex-ter-me-nated, the lot of 'em."

Harp nods and says, "Oh, I see what you mean." But he isn't quite sure exactly what Tex does mean.

Wake up. You do too know what he's talking about. Homosexuals. Immoral evildoers. Our Lord said, 'We are to hate the congregation of evildoers and never sit with the wicked.'

Harp does know that some of the men on the beach have partners, and he's seen some of them doing odd things to each other in the dark of the night. But whenever he sees that kind of thing, he tries not to look. Big Hilly and Little Hilly *did* pretty much stick together all the time, even at night. And Olivera seemed to think they were . . . that way too. But maybe people are just suspicious of men who stick together too much.

You pretend to wash your hands in innocency, but you know what's going on.

Tex stares at Harp. "And Speel said somethin' else. About *you*, son. She said she saw you down there on the pier early this mornin' talking to Olivera. Listen to me, Harp, you take my advice and watch your ass. You hear me?"

"Yes, I can hear you, Tex." Harp knows what watching your ass means; it means you have to watch out what's behind you.

That's what I keep telling you. But do you listen?

Tex reaches into his pocket and pulls out a pocket knife. It has a pretty white handle and a lot of different blades. Tex opens a long blade and begins to clean his fingernails.

Harp thinks about why Speel might have been talking about him. He sure hopes Speel doesn't tell anybody else he was talking to Olivera.

Then you'd be in for it.

But what's wrong with that? Olivera asks everybody questions.

Take my advice and get out of here right now.

But how can he leave before he gets something to eat? No, he's too hungry to leave. Besides, this time he's up close to the front of the line, so maybe he'll get a good seat close to the food for a change.

Suit yourself. It's your funeral.

But what if Olivera comes back and asks what I've found out so far? All I've found out is some people think Little Hilly got shot, or maybe strangled with his own belt, or that he froze even though it wasn't cold enough last night to freeze anybody. Olivera said I was supposed to be his eyes and ears and ask questions, but so far nobody is saying any good answers. It's not my fault if they don't have the right answers.

Harp watches Tex clean his fingernails. That sure is a pretty knife. Harp wonders why he didn't ever get to have a nice pocket knife like that when he was little?

Are you kidding? Give you a knife?

But wait a minute, Little Hilly got stabbed, didn't he? So wouldn't Detective Olivera be suspicious of anybody with a big knife like the one Tex has? Maybe he should be asking Tex a few more questions.

Stop asking questions. You want people to start wondering about you?

Harp changes his mind. What if people start asking *him* questions about why he's asking everybody else questions? That wouldn't be good.

Harp sits down on the sidewalk to think about it. He's got to get better at finding out things or he'll never figure out who killed Little Hilly. But what if people won't answer his questions? Does it mean they have something to hide? Harp is pretty sure a lot of the beachers do have something to hide, but it doesn't mean they killed Little Hilly, does it? For example, he hasn't told anybody on the beach about being in that bad place. What would they think of him if they knew that? Maybe they would think he was a crazy person. They might even think he was the one who killed Little Hilly.

Tex finishes cleaning his fingernails and puts away his knife. He takes his cigarette out of his mouth and looks at it. It's gone out. He drops it to the sidewalk and grinds it out under his fancy white boot.

Harp looks at those pretty white boots. Somehow Tex keeps them nice and clean, even though he lives on the beach.

Those are city boots. Didn't I tell he's not a real cowboy?

Harp wonders if a real cowboy would wear such fancy white boots. Wouldn't they get . . . cow stuff all over them? Uh oh, there it is again. He's starting to be suspicious of everybody. There's no reason to be suspicious of Tex. He isn't a bad outlaw or anything. Or is he? Harp glances back up at Tex. He doesn't look like a bad guy. He just looks . . . friendly, with his pale blue eyes and his long sunburned nose. But that long nose has a bend in it, up close to the top, like it got broke sometime in the past. How did that happen? Was he doing something bad and got hit on the nose like that time Mother hit him on the nose and made it bleed for a long time?

If a child gets hit, he deserved it.

Harp shakes his head to make those kinds of suspicious thoughts go away. See there, questions, leading to more questions, leading to suspicions. How could he be suspicious of Tex? Tex has always been nice to him.

Look out. Someone's coming.

Harp looks up from his thoughts and sees Speel coming. Uh oh.

Don't talk to that immoral person. The very idea, pretending to be a boy.

Speel is coming right for him, and there's something about the look in her eye that Harp doesn't like at all.

Disgraceful. The Bible says, A woman shall not wear that which pertaineth unto a man. To do so is an abomination before God.

Speel walks right up and grabs Harp's arm. She pulls him to his feet. "I need to have a little chitchat with you, Harp. Excuse us for a minute, Tex." She pulls Harp away.

Harp can feel that Speel's grip is very strong, especially for a girl. As they go, he stares at her. Can she really be a girl? She is kind of round under the top part of her overalls, but actually she's kind of round all over. Still, the more he looks at Speel's face, the more she does look a lot like a girl. Funny he never noticed before. Her nose is small and her brown eyes are small too. And she doesn't have any hair on her face. Maybe people think she's a boy because she's fat and because she has two chins and because she frowns all the time. Now that he thinks about it, Speel never has acted very much like the other homeless people. Homeless people are usually nervous and unhappy. Or else they're loud and drink a lot of booze and pretend to be happy. But no matter which type they are, they all have one thing in common: they have scared eyes. Speel doesn't have scared eyes. Her eyes are kind of . . . soft, like a girl.

She pulls Harp around the corner of the church away from the other people. She pins him up against the building and taps him on the chest. "Well, Harpy old lad, I got some important news for you. Hot off the presses, so to speak. You know that cop, Olivera? He was here earlier. I bet he was looking for you. Whattaya think of them apples?"

She's after something. Don't say a word.

Harp isn't quite sure what Speel means about apples, but he already knows Olivera was there because Tex already told him. So it's not really very hot off the presses.

"Well, let's have it, Harp. Man to man, no holds barred. Has Olivera got your number?"

Harp tries to think how to answer so many questions all at once. He's not even sure what Speel means, especially about the number part. And how can it be man to man if Speel isn't a man? "Well, Speel, I don't think anybody has my number. Actually, I don't think I even have one. So I guess what I mean is . . . uh, I don't know why Detective Olivera would be looking for me."

"Well, I know why, ol' lad. He's beatin' around your bush, boy. He's barkin' up your tree."

Harp tries to pull away. It must be just about time for them to open up the doors for the free lunch. If he doesn't get back there quick all the food might be gone.

But Speel has him pinned up against the brick wall. "Well? Out with it."

"Uh, I don't think I know what you mean, Speel."

That's it, just play dumb. That should be easy for you.

"What I'm trying to tell you is I think that Mexican cop Olivera is onto you. I saw him jawboning with you on the pier this morning. He was haulin' you over the coals, wasn't he? I'll bet he knows you sleep under the pier every night. He probably thinks you've got the real skinny on what happened to Little Hilly."

"I don't have any skinny, Speel. Besides, I don't sleep under the pier every night. Sometimes I stay with the Fearful Ones."

Speel pokes Harp with her finger again. "Oh yeah? Well, I happen to know you weren't within a country mile of the Fearful One's circle last night. Far be it from me to tell tales out of school, but it just so happens I know exactly where you were last night."

She's just fishing. Don't take the bait.

Harp shrugs and looks away.

"I bet you were under the pier last night, weren't you? I was up early this morning, and I saw you walking on the beach, walkin' away from the pier. You were walkin' fast, weren't you, makin' a beeline for parts unknown. What did you see under there Harpy, old Carpy? Something you didn't like? Maybe a stiff?"

Uh oh. Don't let on.

Harp shakes his head. "I have to go inside the church now, Speel. I'm hungry."

But Speel tightens the grip on his arm and leans closer. "It's all right, Harp. You can tell me. I'm on your side. I'm with ya all the way. What happened under there?"

"Nothing happened. I'm hungry now. We should go inside." Harp again tries to pull away, but Speel won't let go of his arm.

"Listen here, Harp. When the cops came here this morning and asked me if I saw anything, I kept my trap shut. I didn't have to do that, did I? You get my drift? I took a chance protecting you, didn't I? You wouldn't want me to go find Olivera and say maybe I did see something after all. Like maybe it was little Harp I saw comin' our from under the pier this morning?"

"No, don't do that, Speel. I didn't do it, honest. Little Hilly was already dead when I woke up."

Now you've done it. Didn't I say to keep your big fat mouth shut?

"Well, well, so you did find him. Hey, I'm not sayin' you did it, but when I saw you talking to Olivera this morning I figured he was on your case. Now tell me exactly what happened under there. The whole she-bang. Lay it on the line for me."

"There's nothing to tell, Speel. Little Hilly was already dead. I just woke up and there he was. His eyes were open, staring at nothing."

That's it. Just keep talking. You're getting yourself in deeper and deeper.

"Already dead, eh? Now hold your horses, Harpy my lad. You sayin' he got killed right where you were sleeping and you didn't see anything? And you didn't hear nuthin either, I suppose?"

"No, nothing. Honest, Speel. I just woke up and there he was."

"Well, if that don't take the cake. Somebody knocked off Little Hilly right next to you and you don't hear a thing. Mighty odd, if you ask me."

"It seemed very strange to me too, Speel. But maybe I was sleeping really hard. I was . . . tired."

"Sleeping hard. That's putting it mildly. Little Hilly gets killed right next to you and you don't hear nuthin'. But it's okay, if that's your story, I believe you, even if nobody else will. Now listen, Harp, for your own protection, you and me got to work together. Maybe we can figure a way to throw that cop off your trail. You scratch my back, and I'll scratch yours, so to speak."

You'd better not let me catch you scratching her back. You hear me?

Harp isn't so sure he wants to scratch Speel's back. There's still something about Speel that he doesn't trust. "Uh, you and me?"

"That's right, we got to work together, hand in hand, if we're gonna get you out of this sticky situation. You just leave it to me. I'll help you keep your head above water. Tell you what, I'll go talk to Olivera. Find out what he knows and what he doesn't. I'll get the lay of the land, so to speak, and report back."

Don't trust this weird person. Haven't we always done better by ourselves?

Harp is pretty sure he would rather just stay on his own, but he decides maybe he should play along, for the time being. "Well, if you think so."

"That's the ticket. Now don't you worry about a thing. Just screw up your courage and keep your chin up while I go find out which way the wind is blowing."

Harp isn't sure what all that means so he just shrugs.

"Good," says Speel, patting Harp on the front of his jacket.

Harp hopes she doesn't notice how dirty the front of his jacket is and start asking questions about what's under all that dirt.

But Speel doesn't seem to notice. She just starts tapping his chest again. "Oakie dokie, Harpie, old lad, now here's what we do. We just slip right back around and get in line like nuthin' happened, like we don't know each other from Adam, okay? Just act natural. I'll go first." Speel winks and heads back around to the front of the church.

Now you're in for it. She's probably going to go tell everybody what you said.

Harp stays where he is, wondering how a person is supposed to act natural. He decides to just act the way he usually does, not talking to anybody and looking at the ground whenever anybody looks at him.

If only you would learn to keep your mouth shut, you wouldn't be in this fix.

Harp knows maybe he shouldn't have said anything to Speel, but it's too late for blaming anybody now. Still, he'd better keep an eye on Speel to see if she's going to tell anybody else.

He hurries back around to the front of the church and sees that everybody has already gone inside. Oh no, the food will be all gone. He runs to the door and squeezes in just as they are closing it. That was a close one. Once they close that door nobody gets in. And if you don't get in by then, you don't get any food.

2-2

Belief

*I*nside the church, they've already got the chairs set up facing the stage. At the side of the room, the tables and chairs are being set up for eating, but like always, there's a rope strung in front of the eating area so nobody can go over there until the sermon is done.

Harp scans the crowd. The usual homeless people are there, plus a few new ones he doesn't know. He spots Speel talking to a group of the tougher homeless men up by the stage. Harp hopes she isn't saying anything about him.

If you would have listened to me, she wouldn't have anything to tell them. Remember, the Bible says, Foolish talking is akin to filthiness.

Harp ignores her and keeps his eyes on Speel. She soon leaves that group and goes up and down the rows passing out her little pieces of paper, as usual. But this time she's talking to everybody as she hands out her papers, and that worries Harp. Now he's sure he shouldn't have said anything to her.

Harp moves around the edges of the crowd, not making eye contact with anybody, pretending to be counting the boards in the floor. He catches enough of their words to know they're mostly talking about Little Hilly. At least he doesn't hear his name mentioned.

Good. Maybe they don't suspect anything.

He drifts from group to group, listening. He hears a lot of talk about Big Hilly, but nobody seems to have any idea where he is. A lot of them seem pretty sure Big Hilly did it.

Then the Usual Lady goes up on the stage clapping her hands. "All right, quiet down now and take your seats. We have a very interesting speaker for you today. I hope you appreciate his words of wisdom."

Harp goes to find a chair, but the only ones left are in the back, about as far from the food as you can get. But even from way back there, he can smell the food, and his stomach growls in anticipation. He tries to make it be quiet because he knows there's still a long sermon to get through before the eating time comes. The week before, the speaker was a Mormon who talked and talked and talked. He said anybody who converted to his religion would get to be baptized by dunking in a special magic tub to wash away their sins, and then they'd get to have a Holy Ghost to come sit on their shoulder to help them be good. Harp thought it might be a good idea to have a ghost sitting on your shoulder to protect you.

Evil blaspheme. Evil religion. Didn't I tell you not to listen to that man?

Harp hopes this week's speaker won't talk as long as that Mormon man did because his stomach is already really, really hungry.

The Usual Lady goes on talking about today's speaker, about how inspirational he is going to be, but Harp stops listening and looks around. He's always wondered why they have basketball hoops at both ends of the big room. It's the first church he's ever been in where you could play basketball if you wanted to. Maybe it's because it's a Unitarian Church. It sure is different from the church Mother took him to when he was little. Mother's church was in a basement and you wouldn't even know it was a church except it had words from the Bible written on big sheets of paper that were stuck to the walls. The main thing Harp remembers about that church is that the preacher kept on saying God was Jesus, and Jesus was the one who would save them. Harp was never quite sure what Jesus was going to save them from, but one time, they brought in poison snakes and played with them to prove they knew what they were talking about. From that, Harp learned Jesus was supposed to save them from the poison snakes.

To be safe from danger, you must believe. The Lord said, 'Behold, I give unto you power to tread on serpents and scorpions and nothing shall by any means hurt you.'

Harp remembers how one man with a really big stomach and a puffy red nose held his hands up toward the ceiling and said he believed Jesus would save him from the snake. But the snake bit him on the finger anyhow. Everybody got excited, and they took the man away to the hospital. Later, Mother said the man didn't die, so that proved Jesus was just giving him a little test.

He wouldn't have even got so sick from that snake bite if he hadn't have been such a boozer.

Harp doesn't remember a lot of things about when he was little, but he does remember those nighttime meetings in the basement church. And he remembers getting smacked real hard on the side of the face in that basement once when he asked the wrong question. The question was about who God was, exactly.

Children must not question God. They must be punished to learn respect for His name.

Harp learned real quick that you had to be careful not to say the wrong thing when you were in a church. It's better not to say anything at all.

Don't blame me. You had to be taught to fear His power.

Harp also remembers that the people in Mother's church were mad at people who went to other churches. Mother called them ignorant Catholic Wops and blood-sucking Jews. Harp doesn't ever remember meeting a Catholic Wop back then, or a blood-sucking Jew either, so he's not sure what was so bad about them.

They are cursed. As the Bible says, Let those who curse Thee Lord be cursed themselves.

The only Catholic Harp ever met was a nice fellow named Juan who said he was a Mexican. Harp isn't sure, but he doesn't think Mexicans are Wops. Mother said Mexicans were wetbacked spics. Can they be both?

But Juan was nice to him when he first came to the beach. Once, when it started to get cold outside, Juan said he was a Catholic so they could go to the big Catholic church in Santa Monica to get warm.

I told you not to go with him. Didn't I tell you?

Harp knows maybe he shouldn't have gone to that Catholic church, but Juan was nice. When they got there, they first had to kneel down and make a secret sign with their hands. But after that they got to sit down on a wooden bench to watch what was going on up front.

It was warm in that Catholic church, and Harp liked being in there.

An evil place.

Maybe it was an evil place, but it didn't seem like it. A lot of big white candles were lit all around the sides of the room, and they smelled nice. The preacher who was in charge wore a long white and red outfit and a tall white hat, and he spoke to them from up on a platform that was covered with a red carpet. Harp couldn't understand exactly what the sermon was about because a lot of it was in another language entirely, but while the man spoke, Harp got to look at all the nice things they had in that church. They had shiny gold candle holders and a big wooden cross up front with an almost naked man stuck to it. And they had colored pictures on the windows that showed angels with wings like big birds and men with long beards, and there were pretty flowers all around the edge. One window had a pretty white horse standing on its hind legs. Mother's basement church didn't have nice things in it like that.

Those riches are a sure sign of their evilness. All true believers are poor, like us. The Lord sayeth, Only those who forgo possessions of the rich can be my disciple.

It was nice in that church, and warm, so it was too bad that after a while a tall man in a black suit came and said they had to leave. Juan said the man was sort of like a guard who was paid to watch the homeless people to make sure they didn't take anything. The man shooed them out, walking behind them all the way up the aisle and out the big wooden doors. On the steps, he pushed Harp and shook his fist and said they weren't supposed to ever come back again. That man scared Harp so bad he never did go back there.

There, didn't I tell you? Evildoers, just like I said.

Harp's attention is brought back to the room when the Usual Lady says again how nice it is to have them all there and how they shouldn't steal anything because it belongs to God and he wouldn't like it.

One of the off-beach guys yells out, "If it belongs to God why doesn't he share it with us?"

Harp doesn't think that was a very nice thing to say to the Usual Lady when she's the one who gives them free food. Besides, those men shouldn't even be here because the food is for the homeless people and those men live in cars parked in the junk car lot so they do have a home, sort of.

A lot of the homeless laugh real loud at what the not-homeless man said, and that makes the Usual Lady frown. But she doesn't get mad like you'd expect her too. She never does get very mad. She says, "Now, now," and goes on for a while with her usual words about God's light and His benevolent touch.

Harp thinks she's probably a nice lady, even if she does stop the food servers from giving anybody extra scoops of potatoes. And she guards the little teeny pieces of white cake like they were made out of gold instead of just being cake. That makes a lot of the homeless mad at her. They say she's mean and stingy with the food, but Harp thinks maybe she's just trying to make sure there's enough to go around.

After the Usual Lady is done with her little speech, she says the speaker for this week is a man who's studied about religion in India. Then she goes off the stage clapping, trying to get everybody else to clap too. Harp claps, but hardly anybody else does.

A man wearing white pajamas gets up on the stage. The front part of his head is bald, but he has long white hair in the back. He bows toward the Usual , and then he turns and bows to everybody in the audience. Some of the men get up and bow back and that makes everybody laugh.

Instead of sitting on the folding chair the Usual Lady put out for him, the man sits down cross-legged by the edge of the stage. He doesn't have any shoes on, but the bottoms of his feet aren't near as dirty as the people on the beach who don't wear shoes.

Beware! This man is up to no good. You must not listen to his words.

Before the man can even begin speaking, Shoeless Joe jumps up and begins pacing and mumbling to himself like he always does. Harp thinks it could be because Joe saw the man wasn't wearing shoes, but maybe it was just a coincidence.

Harp quickly gets up and leads Shoeless Joe back to a chair next to his own.

Leave that dummy alone. People are looking at you.

Harp knows he's the only one who can make the huge black man mind. People are afraid of Joe because he's so big, but Harp knows Joe is as gentle as a baby in his heart.

Harp sits the big man down and shakes his finger in front of Joe's face. "Now listen, Joe," he whispers, "you have to be quiet and let the man talk or we'll never get anything to eat."

Joe looks at him with his sad doggy eyes, so Harp has to add, "I'm not mad at you, Joe, but you have to stay sitting down until it's time to eat, or else they'll make you go outside to do your pacing."

Joe must have only heard that last part about going outside because he jumps up and makes for the door. The man at the door lets Joe out, and that's too bad because Harp knows they won't let him back in until the eating is all over.

Good riddance.

He feels bad for Shoeless Joe. He'll be really hungry.

After Joe is gone, the speaker begins talking. "This is a time of disharmony," he says. "A time of disharmony and imbalance." The man isn't looking at anybody. He's looking up toward the ceiling.

Don't listen to this. Close your ears.

Then the man goes on to say a lot of other things like that, but Harp isn't listening very close. He's wondering if the man mentioned disharmony and imbalance because somebody told him about Little Hilly getting killed last night. Maybe they told him to put something in his sermon about it to convince the homeless people to be nicer to each other.

Harp sees a flash of sunlight from the back of the room, and he turns to see the door to the outside is opening. Detective Olivera is coming in, followed by the two beach bicycle cops. Harp is surprised to see the bicycle cops dressed like regular policemen instead of being dressed in their blue shorts and T-shirts that say "POLICE" on the back. They stand next to Olivera at the back of the room, looking everybody over.

Some of the homeless look around to see what's going on, but as soon as they see it's the cops, they turn back and pretend to listen to the speaker.

Harp remembers what Speel said about Olivera looking for him. Did Speel tell on him? Is that why the cops are here?

One of the bicycle cops pulls at Olivera's sleeve and points at Harp. He whispers something and Olivera nods.

Now you've done it. They're onto you. Didn't I warn you?

Harp turns away and tries to concentrate on what the man on the stage is saying. He's talking on and on about peace and benevolence and things like that. But Harp doesn't feel peaceful. In fact, his heart is beating so loud he worries that the other people might be able to hear it. *Why did those two bicycle cops have to come in and point at me? Why can't they just leave me alone?*

You know why.

Harp notices that some of the other homeless men saw the cops looking at him, and they turn around in their chairs to look at Harp too.

Harp continues to look at the speaker, pretending he doesn't even notice everybody is staring at him. The speaker sees that nobody is paying any attention to him so he makes his voice a lot louder. "These times are a test of us all, a test of our belief, of our faith."

Harp wonders if the man is talking to the cops at the back of the room. *Is he saying it's a test for them too?*

A lot of the men are still looking backwards at Harp, so the man stands up and claps his hands. He waves at two young boys who are standing next to the stage. The man points at the two boys and shouts, "Listen to me, everybody! Look at this!"

As the boys start up onto the stage, everybody turns back around to look at them. Harp suddenly realizes it's two of the Devil Boys from the beach.

Legions of the Devil! Avert your eyes.

Harp tries not to look, but it's the first time he's ever seen them so close up. They have on their usual yellowish-orange magic pajamas, but this time they're more friendly looking, smiling like regular people. *Would they really kill Little Hilly just to get his blood?*

They're just pretending to be friendly. You've got to get out of here before it's too late.

Harp knows he should probably leave, but how would be get past the police? Besides, his stomach is only thinking about the eating part. It is saying stay right where you are, wait for the food.

Stubborn, that's what you are. Stubborn and willful. It is better to let the body starve than to let the words of the Devil fill your mind.

Harp puts his fingers in his ears. *No, I'm going to stay right here* until it's time to eat.

You'll be sorry you didn't listen to me. Mark my words.

Harp tries to only focus on what is going on up on the stage. This close, the two Devil Boys look a lot like normal boys, except that they don't have any hair. They're holding onto the ends of a fancy yellow blanket that has words printed on it. The blanket has white fringes all around the edges and silver words in the middle that say, *Hare Krishna Hare Krishna Krishna Krishna Hare Hare.* The speaker points at the blanket. Harp takes his fingers out of his ears to hear what he's saying.

"The path to peace and harmony is to chant these words out loud. You should do it at least three times a day."

Harp doesn't understand how just saying a bunch of words will help bring peace and harmony, but the speaker immediately answers that question as if he's answering Harp's thoughts.

"God doesn't care if you know how to chant the words correctly because God understands all ways of saying it. He understands all languages, so it doesn't even matter if you know what the words mean, as long as you say them."

Devils can see inside your mind. Can't you see what he's trying to do to you?

Harp thinks about what the man said. If all you have to do is say magic words to make things better, that sounds like a pretty good deal. The man's magic words must be like the secret prayers Mother taught him when he was little. Mother taught him all of the secret words of the Lord. She said the words would protect him from those whose inward parts were wickedness, the people whose throats were like open sepulchers. He learned to say the magic words whenever he met evil people. Is now the time?

Yes, say the words I taught you. Say them right now!

He whispers the secret words really softly: "Destroy thou them, O God. Let the heathens be sunk down in the pit that they made themselves."

Good. Now you're getting it. Go on, go on. Upon the wicked he shall rain snares, fire and brimstone.

Harp whispers, "And a horrible tempest shall be the portion of their cup."

That's right. For the righteous Lord loveth righteousness.

"So it serves them right. Amen."

Good boy.

A man in front of Harp turns around to frown at him, but it doesn't matter because Harp has finished the prayer anyhow. The man shakes his head and turns back.

Now that he's warded off the evil, Harp decides it might be all right to listen to what the man on the stage has to say.

No! Are you trying to drive me crazy?

The man on the stage starts talking even louder, as if he's trying to get Harp to listen. "I will chant the words the right way, and then you will all get a chance to try it."

Do not let those words of evil pass your lips. I'm warning you.

The man begins to say the words, but Harp is surprised to hear that the man isn't talking them; it's more like he's singing them: "Hare Krishna Hare Krishna Krishna Krishna Hare Hare," he sings. Then he says, "All right now. Let's all try it together."

The man starts singing the words really loud and some of the homeless join in.

Harp knows he doesn't have a very good singing voice because Mother always told him not to sing in church. She said his singing voice was so bad, the other people wouldn't like it.

Children should be seen and not heard. Especially children who can't sing good.

Some of the other homeless people must think they are good singers because once they get the hang of it, they join in real loud. "Hare Krishna Hare Krishna Krishna Krishna Hare Hare." They sing it a lot of times, over and over, until Harp has all the words on the blanket memorized. He knows better than to say those evil words out loud, but he can't keep himself from singing the words in his mind.

Stop! Don't even think them! Those words are meant to hypnotize you.

Harp decides he mostly likes the song part so he stops thinking the words and just hums the tune. It's nice to do it with his eyes closed while he rocks back and forth in time with the singing.

The singing of the words turns out to be the best part of the sermon because after that the two Devil-worshiper boys take their fancy yellow blanket away and the man starts talking again, telling about how Krishna was born like a real baby, sort of like Jesus only different because Jesus was just a person, and Krishna was a God.

Blasphemy!

The man says Krishna wasn't really like any other baby before or after that because he didn't come out of his mother all red-colored and wet and wrinkled up like most babies. Instead, he came out like a grown-up person, only smaller, with wonderful gold bracelets and rings and jewels all over him. Harp remembers the scary pictures he saw in a book in the library about how babies come out of mothers, and he wonders why all those jewels wouldn't have hurt Krishna's mother when he came out.

Why are you listening to this nonsense? Think about something else.

Harp decides not to listen anymore. The smell of the food from the other side of the room keeps on reminding him of how long it's been since he's had anything to eat. Being so hungry makes it hard to concentrate on anything.

The speaker goes on and on, but finally he winds down, saying, "Now you understand that Krishna consciousness is not an artificial imposition on the mind. It is the original energy of the living entity."

Everybody can tell he is about to be done so they start clapping real loud. Even the cops at the back of the room are clapping, and it makes Harp wonder if they came for the food too. Some of the homeless are already on their feet hoping to be the first in line for the food, but then the man says, "Does anybody have any questions?"

There's a groan from everybody, and Harp knows nobody better ask any questions or they might get beat up later when they get back down to the beach.

But just because there aren't any questions, that doesn't stop the man. He asks himself his own question. "You may be asking how this can help you," he says. He starts answering his own question, and Harp is afraid he will just keep on asking himself even more questions. Harp tries to not let his stomach get too ready to eat just yet. He leans back and starts counting the bolts that hold the big steel beams up to the ceiling. Harp is making good progress in his counting when he hears a noise back by the door. He turns around and sees that the guard at the door is talking to some black boys who are trying to get in. One of them is bouncing a basketball. Olivera is still there, and he's talking to the boys too. It means the speaker has gone on so long that it's almost time for the homeless lunch to be over and the boy's basketball playing time to begin.

It makes the Usual Lady do something Harp has never seen her do before. She hurries up onto the stage and starts clapping her hands. "Very nice," she says, real loud. "Very inspirational. Let's all put our hands together to thank today's speaker, and then we'd better start eating."

The applause is very loud, almost like thunder. Harp joins in clapping too. The man on the stage raises both hands and tries to get everybody to sit back down, but it's too late; everybody is up and moving toward the food line.

2-3
Evidence

*H*arp jumps up and tries to get to the food line by cutting through one of the rows that's already emptied out, but he's cut off by the Blind Shrimp who blocks the way with his white cane. The Shrimp is a little guy, even littler than Harp, and he has a long white cane and very dark glasses to show people he's blind. Because of that, he does panhandling better than just about anybody else down at the beach. He even wears his dark glasses and taps his white cane all over the place even when he's not panhandling. Most of the homeless people on the beach don't think the Shrimp is really as blind as he lets on.

The Shrimp leans close to Harp's ear and whispers, "I need to talk to you." Then he goes on, tapping his way right up to the front of the line.

Harp goes to the end of the line, hoping there will be some food left by the time he gets up to the food servers. But then he sees Detective Olivera coming toward him.

Now you're in for it.

Uh oh, not again. Harp looks the other way, but it's no use; Olivera comes and gets ahold of his sleeve and pulls him right out of line. Harp's stomach complains loudly.

Olivera drags him into the corner and says, "Well, what have you found out?"

Harp thinks how to answer.

Just dummy up. Don't say anything.

He hasn't really learned anything much, but should he tell the detective that? Should he tell him about the Hare Krishna Devil boys who maybe wanted Little Hilly's blood?

He won't go for that.

But Harp worries that if he says anything at all, Olivera might keep him talking until all the food is gone. But if he doesn't say something, Olivera might get mad and not let him eat anyhow. Finally, he says, "Well, sir, I've been asking questions. A lot of questions. I talked to the old man who sits on the bench, and he told me about little Teddy being gone, and then I saw a bad painting on the wall of Betty's--"

"What the hell are you talking about? Old man? Bad painting? Listen, kid, never mind all that. What's the word with these guys?" Olivera nods toward the homeless men who are already at the tables eating.

Harp is really getting worried that there won't be any food left for him. He shrugs and says, "Uh, I haven't asked too many of them yet, sir. But I did ask Cowboy Tex. He said he didn't know anything."

Olivera shakes his head and looks down at his shoes. Then he looks back up at Harp with a frown on his face. "I'm really disappointed in you, boy. You haven't been doing your job like I asked you to." He jabs Harp in the chest with his finger, really hard. "Remember, you're supposed to be my eyes and ears with these guys. You help me and I'll help you. Otherwise . . ."

Tell him you're on his side. Tell him anything.

"Yes, sir. I understand, sir."

"Well, all right then." Olivera looks back at the tables and Harp looks too. The ones who already have their food are eating as fast as they can, occasionally glancing over at Harp and Olivera. That worries Harp. If the some of the mean homeless men think he's helping the police they might get real mad. Being Olivera's eyes and ears could turn out to be downright dangerous.

Olivera looks back at Harp. "What did Lemke want?"

Harp tries to think who he might be talking about. "Who?"

"Lemke. The little guy. The one who's always pretending to be blind."

Harp realizes he means the Blind Shrimp. So his name is Lemke. Nobody on the beach knows that. "Oh, I don't know. He just said he wants to talk to me later."

"He sleeps under the pier sometimes, doesn't he? Like you do."

Harp shrugs. "Uh, sometimes."

"Did you see him there last night?"

Harp shakes his head.

Olivera is staring at the Blind Shrimp who is eating really fast. Speel is sitting right next to him. She looks at Harp and Olivera, and then she leans close to the Shrimp and says something.

"Well, go ahead and eat," says Olivera. "But if Lemke or anybody else tells you anything, you call me right away. You still got my phone number?"

Harp nods.

"I bet you don't. Lemme see your hand."

Harp holds out his hand and the detective shakes his head. He takes out his ball point pen, but Harp pulls his hand away. "You don't have to write it again, sir. I know it."

Olivera looks at him like he doesn't believe him. "You tellin' me you got it memorized?"

Harp nods.

"Oh yeah, then tell it to me."

Harp recites the phone number.

The detective looks surprised. "Well, okay. Maybe you're smarter than you look. But don't forget what I said. I expect you to come up with something soon. You find out anything, you call me right away, right?"

"Yes, sir."

Harp starts to head for the food, but Olivera still has ahold of his sleeve. "And you'd better give me that coat," he says.

Now you've done it. I knew this would happen.

"My jacket?"

"Yeah, hand it over. Those two officers said they saw you washing it this morning." He points at the bicycle cops.

Whatever you do, don't give him your coat.

"You want to take my jacket? It's . . . it's kind of cold today."

"Yeah, I know," says Olivera. "Don't worry about it. It's just routine."

"Taking my jacket is routine?"

Olivera frowns at him. "Get it off, kid."

Don't do it.

Harp tries to think what else he can do, but Olivera is waiting and he might get mad if he stalls too long. The bicycle cops are waiting by the door, and they're also watching. Finally, Harp takes off his jacket and hands it to Olivera who walks away with it without another word.

Now Harp is really worried. What does Olivera want with my jacket?

Why do you think? Remember, you caught his blood.

Are they going to try to see if it has Little Hilly's blood on it? Can they tell blood was on it even though he got most of it washed off?

They can tell. Then they'll know.

Harp knows he'd better not stop to worry about that now. His stomach is telling him to get to the food quick, before it's all gone. He hurries to the food line, but he sees right away that the white desert cake is already gone. And there's no coffee cups left next to the big silver coffee thing. But that's okay because Harp doesn't like coffee anyhow. He's happy to see that at least there's some mashed potatoes left, and there's a little bit of whatever was in the big tray still stuck to the sides. It's yellow so maybe it used to be something with cheese on it. And there's a little bit of dry bread left too. Harp stuffs all of the remaining bread into his pockets and picks up two paper plates and two plastic forks. He holds the plates out to the serving lady, but the Usual Lady comes hurrying right over. "Now wait a minute, young man. Just because you waited to come up here until it's almost all gone, it doesn't mean you get two plates. You know the rules."

"It's for Shoeless Joe," says Harp. "He got restless and had to go outside to pace."

"Are you referring to that large black man who got up and disturbed the speaker? He knows the rules too. The sermon first, then the eating."

"Yes, ma'am. But Shoeless Joe gets restless sometimes, and he can only calm down if he paces back and forth. It's not his fault. He would have stayed and listened if he could."

The Usual Lady stares at Harp for a long time.

Harp waits, hoping he's right about her. He's almost sure she must to be a nice lady, in spite of her frowny face and her strict rules. Why else would she give them a meal every Sunday?

Finally she speaks, leaning close to Harp. "Tell me, young man, why did you call him Shoeless Joe? I noticed he was wearing shoes. In fact, they were quite nice black shoes."

"Yes, Ma'am, but those are only the tops. Joe, he gets restless and paces so much the bottoms are all worn away."

The Usual Lady straightens up and stares at Harp. "His shoes have no soles?"

"No, ma'am, they don't. But it's okay because his feet are so tough from walking all over the place, the bottoms of his feet are like leather. He likes the tops of his shoes to be nice so he takes good care of them. He doesn't know there are no bottoms anymore."

The Usual Lady shakes her head and walks away. As she passes the server lady she says something to her and the server lady divides what's left of the mashed potatoes and the dried yellow stuff between Harp's two plates.

Harp watches the Usual Lady go, feeling proud to be smart about people. He knew she had to be a nice lady. He knew her acting tough was only an act to keep everything under control. And while he was explaining about Shoeless Joe's shoes he saw her eyes fill up with tears. It proves she does care about people. She just tries to hide it.

Harp takes the two plates of food out through the exit doors, telling the guard that the extra plate is for Shoeless Joe and that the Usual Lady said it was okay.

You should eat it all yourself. You deserve it more than he does.

Harp finds Joe outside pacing back and forth, almost wearing a path right into the hot sidewalk. Joe is very happy to see Harp, and happy to see the plate of food too. Harp hands it to him, along with some of the bread.

Later when you're hungry you'll be sor-ry you gave away that food.

Before he lets Joe eat, Harp says the prayer he's heard some of the other homeless say: "Bless us sinners as we eat our dinners."

That's not the prayer I taught you.

Joe smiles happily and says, "Amen?"

Harp nods and pats Joe on the shoulder and leads the big man to the curb so they can sit down and eat the mashed potatoes and the dried-out yellow stuff.

While they eat, more and more of the basketball boys arrive. Harp likes watching those boys. They all seem so young and eager. A lot of them are wearing nice new-looking basketball shoes. Harp wishes they would ask him to play basketball with them, but he knows they won't. When he was in a school that one time, nobody ever wanted him on their team, so he never got the chance to learn how to play boy's games like basketball.

He hears the sound of even more bouncing basketballs coming up the sidewalk. But then he hears another sound, a clicking sound, coming up from behind. He doesn't even have to look around to know it's the sound of the Blind Shrimp's white cane, tapping its way toward him.

Oh no, not him again.

Part 3
The Blind Shrimp

Today we knew it was Sunday because on Sunday Mitch always leads us in a special Sunday prayer. And we get meat loaf. We only get a little teeny piece of meat loaf on Sundays with our usual mashed potatoes and gravy, but nobody cares because nobody likes the meat loaf anyhow. It's got something in it that tastes like sawdust. Carl the Older says it really is sawdust. He says they get it from the wood shop and use it to make the meat go farther. Carl knows things because he's the only one who ever gets to go off the ward to pick up supplies from the warehouse.

Today we also got fruit. It's still not summer yet so the fruit is only bananas and Mitch likes bananas so we have to leave them on our plates until after the food servers leave so Mitch can collect all the bananas and take them home with him in his big black briefcase.

The new guy took the banana off his plate and stuck it in his pants so it looked like a boner. Everybody laughed. The Snitch pointed it out to Mitch so Mitch said the Growler would have to be called. I told the Snitch to go tell Mitch that the new guy wasn't trying to steal his banana, he was only playing around. The Snitch ran right up and told Mitch what I said and Mitch got real mad and said "Who told you that?" For some reason the Snitch is afraid of me so when he said he didn't remember, Mitch said the Growler would have to whip both of them until he told. Mitch lined everybody up while he wrote "Thou shalt not steal" on his blackboard. Then he made us all watch the Growler whip the new guy and the Snitch so we would remember the lesson about stealing. But Mitch didn't make the Growler whip the new guy very many times because he was new and didn't know any better, and when it was the Snitch's turn he wouldn't take off his shirt and lie down on his bed like he's supposed to. He begged Mitch to have the Time-Out Closet this time. So Mitch put him in. Nobody chooses the Closet in the winter because there's no heat in there, but the Snitch is too weak to take the whippings so he chooses the Closet. Mitch yelled at him through the door to say if he played with himself in there God would know about it and punish him, and if God didn't punish him the Growler would be called to do it for Him. When Mitch called me to come line up the little paper cups for drug time. I could hear The Snitch crying in there. And there was another sound, a weird sound. I think was his teeth chattering. I went close to The TimeOOut Closet and whispered to the Snitch to stop crying because it was almost time for Mitch to go off shift so he would have to let him out. He thanked me and stopped crying for a while. I've been in that Time-Out Closet so I know what it's like. It's really small so you can't move at all and it's so cold it makes it really hard to keep track of the time. You have to say the same rhyme over and over and keep count of how many times you said it and even then the time seems to go really slow. Mitch better not try to put me in there again or he'll be sorry.

3-1

Seeing Beyond

*H*arp listens to the tapping of the Blind Shrimp's cane until it's right behind him. Then the tip of the white cane taps him on the shoulder. "C'mere, Harp, I got to talk to you."

Don't turn around. Ignore him and he'll go away.

Harp remembers that Detective Olivera said he should ask the Shrimp questions so maybe he'd better talk to him, just for a minute. Harp gets up. "What about?"

"C'mere away from that dummy. I got somethin' to tell you."

"Now, Shrimp, you shouldn't be calling Joe names. It makes him feel bad."

"Never mind about that, I got to talk to you alone."

The Blind Shrimp's dark glasses are so dark, Harp can't see his eyes behind them. He seems to be looking off into the distance.

Harp eats the last little bit of mashed potatoes and yellow stuff, and then he drops the paper plate and the plastic fork into the trash can. He turns back and touches Shoeless Joe on the shoulder. "See you later, Joe. I have to go talk to the Shrimp now."

Joe looks up and smiles, and then goes back to licking his plate.

The Blind Shrimp takes Harp's arm and leads him away. "Help me back down to the beach, Harp. We can talk on the way."

Tell him to get lost.

Harp decides he'd better go with the Shrimp even though he's not sure he wants to. If he's going to ask questions like Olivera said, he'd better play along for the time being.

They start down the hill towards the beach with the Shrimp leading the way, tapping his cane on the sidewalk.

This is going to lead to trouble. Remember, the Bible says, Thou shall not approach a blind man, or a lame man, or he that hath a flat nose.

Harp decides he doesn't want to be dragged along like that, so he stops. "What do you want, Shrimp?"

The Shrimp turns back and leans closer, looking off to the side. "Why was Olivera talking to you?"

"He was . . . asking me things."

"What kind of things?"

"Just . . . things."

"Not going to tell me, eh? Well come on, take my arm, I got places to go."

Harp doesn't especially want to help the Shrimp, but maybe he should be nice to a person who can't see very well.

He can see fine. Tell him to drop dead.

Harp isn't sure how well the Shrimp can see so he takes him by the arm and leads him back down toward the beach.

You never listen to me. I don't know why I waste my breath.

For a while, the Shrimp doesn't say anything. He lets Harp lead him, but he's still tapping away with his white cane. Finally, he says, "I'll bet Olivera was askin' you about Big Hilly, wasn't he? I bet he was askin' you if you knew where Big Hilly is. Am I right?"

Don't let on. You don't have to say anything.

Harp shrugs.

"Do you?"

"Do I what?"

"Do you know where Big Hilly is?"

"No."

"So why was Olivera asking you?"

"I don't know. Isn't he asking everybody?"

"Yeah, but nobody knows anything. The cops took Little Hilly's body away real early this morning so nobody saw nuthin'." The Shrimp stops and looks past Harp's shoulder. "But I bet you saw somethin', didn't you?"

Like the Bible says, A time to rend, and a time to sew, a time to keep silent!

Now Harp has to decide how to answer the Shrimp's question.

Olivera told him not to tell anybody about being his eyes and ears. Besides, isn't he supposed to be the one asking the questions?

The Shrimp is waiting for his answer. "I bet you did, didn't you? You saw something and that's why Olivera was talking to you."

Stall him. Then get away.

"Why would you think something like that, Shrimp?"

"Because Speel said why else would Olivera be talking to Harp and nobody else? And you know what else Speel said?"

Harp shakes his head.

"He said maybe you did it and not Big Hilly."

I was afraid of this.

"But I didn't do anything, Shrimp. Why would Speel say that about me?"

"He said why else would the cops take away your coat?"

Now you're in for it. If only you would have listened to me.

So Speel the Sayer was talking about him to the others, making them suspicious of him. But didn't Speel say he would help?

You never should have talked to that pervert

The Shrimp says, "So, I'll ask you again. Why did the cops take your coat?"

"I don't know, Shrimp. But let me ask you something. When Speel said that about Olivera taking my coat, did anybody say they had an extra coat I could wear? It's probably going to be cold and foggy again tonight, and I'll get really cold without a coat."

The Shrimp shrugs and goes back to pulling Harp along. "You can get another coat at the Salvation Army."

Harp stops, and even though the Shrimp tries to pull him onward, he won't budge. "Yes, I know that, Shrimp, but today's Sunday. They're not open today. And they don't give out the free clothes until Wednesday. And besides, they hardly ever have any good coats. What am I going to do until I get one?"

This time the Blind Shrimp seems to look straight at him from behind his dark glasses. "You've been asking a lot of questions, Harp. That's what Tex said about you too. Why is that? You don't normally ask people questions."

I told you not to ask so many questions. But, no, you had to do it your way, didn't you?

"Tex told you I was asking a lot of questions?"

"See there. Every time I ask you a question, you ask me one right back."

Harp shrugs and starts walking again. The Shrimp hurries to catch up, tapping his cane real fast. "Okay, fine. You don't want to answer my questions? Fine. Up to you. But listen, Harp, the reason I'm asking is because we got to help each other. Don't you know that? You help me and I'll help you. In fact, I might have a way for you to get some money, and then you can walk right into the Salvation Army store tomorrow and buy any coat you want. Hell, maybe we can get enough money so you can go into a regular store and buy a nice new coat. Whattaya think of that?"

"Really?"

"Sure, you just stick with me. I'll get you a coat. A brand new one. A warm one. Let's go." The Shrimp again pulls Harp along, tapping his way down the sidewalk.

He's trying to trick you. I can feel it.

Harp suspects the Shrimp is up to something, but he can't stop thinking about the chance to get enough money to buy a coat. He doesn't even know how much coats cost, but it would be really nice to have a good warm one. When he was little, his mother bought him a coat that was pretty warm. It was brown with silver buttons. But it already had a tear on the shoulder, so maybe she got it from someplace like the Salvation Army store. Now that he thinks about it, he realizes he's never once had a brand new coat. When he was on Ward D-4, he didn't need a coat because he never got to go outside. Nobody got to go outside, except Carl the Older and maybe the Growler sometimes. Mitch said they'd all been so bad before they got locked up they would never get to go outside again. Not ever. Carl the Older said it was because everybody who got put on Ward D-4 was considered too dangerous to go outside.

Then they closed down Ward D-4 and all the other wards and sent him to the Half-Way House. That's where he got the thin little coat with the broken front zipper Detective Olivera took away.

Harp never knew why they called that place the Half-Way House. It was just a regular house with a bunch of men who said they'd been let out of nut houses. The Half-Way House wasn't like Ward D-4 because they let you go outside and walk around during the daytime.

That was nice. Harp was happy to get out and see the grass and the trees and the cars going by. The people who ran the Half-Way House even gave him new underwear that wasn't too dirty, and a pair of brown pants that were real clean, and an almost-new checkered shirt with no holes in it at all. Harp wore those clothes every day until they closed down the Half-Way House, and he continued to wear them after that when he had to sleep outdoors on a bus bench.

After they closed down the Half-Way House there wasn't anybody gave him anything, not even food. That was hard and he got really, really hungry. But one morning a nice lady came by in a big white car and gave him a piece of paper. It had the name of a social services place printed on it, but Harp never went there because he didn't know why he was supposed to. The piece of paper didn't say if there was food there or anything else. And then came the bad night when the bad gang boys came and hit him and took everything he had in his pockets, including that piece of paper. Luckily it was dark and they didn't notice his little backpack under the bench or else he might have even lost his diary.

"What are you thinking about, Harp?" The Blind Shrimp is looking right at him again.

None of his business. Clam up.

Harp decides not to answer any more questions. He's thinking about how cold it's going to be that night without a coat. He sure hopes the Shrimp really does have a way to get money so he can buy a nice new coat.

What? Now you're going to fall for his tricks?

Harp knows some people on the beach say the Blind Shrimp isn't very honest, but Harp is really, really hoping maybe the Shrimp can get him a warm coat.

I give up. He who doth not listen to good advice shall be doomed to suffer from his mistakes.

"Listen, Harp. Just go along with me on this, and I'll get you the bestes, warmest coat you ever had. I got a good plan Take my word for it."

Don't trust him. I bet he's going to steal the money.

So, you gonna help me or not?"

Harp isn't sure if he should. "Are you going to steal something?"

"Steal? What would make you think something like that? There's just this one teeny little thing I have to do, and I need some help with it, that's all."

One teeny little thing. I bet. He's trying to use you, just like I said.

Harp suspects the Shrimp is going to do something that's not honest, but a warm coat would be so nice. Harp remembers a coat he saw in the window of the Timberline Sporting Goods store over in Santa Monica. It looked really warm, and it even had a hood on it with some kind of fur inside the hood. Fur like that would probably be really warm. He makes a decision. "Okay, what do you want me to do?"

That's it. You never learn, do you?

The Shrimp stops and leans closer. "First, I got to go set it up," he whispers. "Meet me on the pier when it gets dark."

"Set it up? Set what up?"

"I'll tell you later." The Blind Shrimp turns and goes tapping away up the sidewalk toward Santa Monica.

Harp realizes he got so worried about getting a coat he forgot to ask the Shrimp more questions about Little Hilly. Olivera said he was especially supposed to ask the Shrimp questions. But now it's too late. The Shrimp is moving away fast, tapping his way along with his white cane. Harp thinks about chasing after him, but decides against it. I can ask him later, when I meet him on the pier.

You won't be happy until you really get yourself in trouble, will you? All right, fine, go right ahead, but don't come crying to me later.

"I won't come crying. I know what I'm doing."

You know what you're doing? That's a laugh.

Harp hurries on down the hill. He feels like he should get back to the beach as fast as he can. Being away from the beach so long is making him very nervous.

Pay attention. Somebody's following you.

He does have the strange feeling he's being followed, but he doesn't dare look back in case it's the police.

When he gets to the corner, he pretends to cross the street, but he doesn't. Instead, he ducks behind a big brown delivery truck that's parked by the curb. He flattens himself against the side of the truck and waits, holding his breath. He hears footsteps. They stop. Then they come closer. They stop again, very close now.

Run!

3-2
Secret Stories

"*A*re you hiding, Harp?"

It's only the dummy.

Harp lets his breath out. It's only Shoeless Joe, peeking around the end of the truck. "No, I'm not hiding, Joe. Why are you following me?"

Joe looks down at the ground. "I'm sorry."

Harp stares at the big black man and wonders why Joe's eyes always seem so wet. It's like he's always about to start crying. Harp is sorry he got mad. It's not Joe's fault he's a dummy. "Are you going back to the beach, Joe?"

"I don't know."

"You don't know? Well, how did you get here?"

"I don't know."

"Don't you know how you got up to the church? Can't you just go back the same way you came?"

Joe looks confused. "Speel?"

"Speel? Oh, did Speel bring you to the church? Did she, I mean he, leave without you?"

Joe looks down at the ground. He looks really sad. His old worn-out clothes hang loose and floppy on him, like he used to be even bigger than he is now.

"Listen, Joe, I need to talk to . . . uh, him. Speel, I mean. Do you know where I can find Speel?"

Joe frowns, like he's trying to remember.

Harp wonders what it would be like to be lost all the time and not know where you are even when you get there.

Ha! As if you don't know.

But maybe poor old Joe doesn't care where he is. Trouble is, if he stays in this neighborhood where people live in houses, they'll probably call the police on him. People like Joe should always stay on the beach where nobody cares about them.

He takes Joe by the hand. "Oh, all right, Joe. Come with me. I'll take you back down to the beach."

Joe grins a big happy smile, and Harp sees that poor old Joe only has a few teeth left in his mouth. He has two, or maybe three, left on the top, but it looks like there's only one on the bottom. It makes Harp happy to remember he still has all of his teeth left. Except for the one Mother accidentally knocked out when she got mad that time. Mother only took him to the dentist once when he had a toothache, and he was glad he didn't have to go back because it hurt like the dickens when the dentist drilled on his tooth. Besides, Mother said it cost too much money that time so it wasn't worth doing it again.

God gave you all the teeth you need. They aren't supposed to last forever.

Harp tugs on Joe's hand to get him started, and they start down the sidewalk toward the beach. As they walk, Joe keeps on getting distracted by things like flowers and pretty leaves lying on the sidewalk. He keeps on stopping, and Harp has to get ahold of his arm and hurry Joe along. Then a squirrel runs across the road and almost gets hit by a car, and that really upsets Joe. It takes some strong pulling for Harp to get him going again.

Why are you wasting your time with this bird-brain?

A little farther along, a dog barks at them, and Joe gets scared. He hides behind Harp, but calms down when Harp points out the fact that the dog is safe behind a white fence. "See there," says Harp, "nothing to be scared of. C'mon, let's keep going."

Unless it's a black dog.

"That's right, unless it's a black dog. You have to watch out for black dogs, Joe."

"Black?"

"That's right. Now listen Joe, I'll tell you the thing about black dogs. If you hear a black dog howl just before the sun comes up, it means he sees the spirit of somebody who's already dead."

Joe raises his hand, like the kids at school did when they wanted to ask a question. "Dead? How did they die?"

"It's not important how they died, only that the black dog howls when it's the spirit of the dead person. Do you want me to tell you more about dogs? I know a lot of things about dogs."

Joe laughs. "Doggy."

"Uh huh. That's right. Doggies. Do you want to know what you should do if you get sick? I'll tell you. If you get sick, you pull a hair out of your head." Harp tugs at his own hair to show him.

Don't tell him about that. It's a secret.

I probably shouldn't tell you this, Joe. It's kind of a secret, so you have to promise not to tell anyone else."

Joe puts his hands over his mouth.

"That's right. It's a secret." Harp leans close to Joe and whispers, "You put your hair inside a piece of bread. Then you feed the bread to a dog."

Joe says, "Bread?"

"That's right. You put your hair in the bread, and then you feed it to the dog. It really works. You won't be sick anymore."

Joe slows almost to a stop while he thinks about that. Harp has to pull at this arm again to keep him going. Finally, Joe seems to decide something. He stops and pulls at Harp's sleeve. "You know . . . a lot of . . . things, Harp."

"Mother taught me things, Joe, lots of good things. Before she . . ."

Don't say it.

"Went away."

Joe's eyes fill up with tears. "She . . . ran away?"

Harp shakes his head. "No, I didn't mean she ran away. She went to . . . the other side."

"Other side?"

"Yes. That's what people said anyhow."

"Where is . . . other side?"

"Never mind." Harp knows Joe wouldn't understand even if he tried to explain it. Joe was always asking questions, but there wasn't any use telling him the answers because he never knew what you meant anyhow.

But thinking about questions makes Harp remember he's supposed to be asking the homeless people questions. Joe is a homeless person, isn't he, even if he is a dummy? "Listen, Joe, I have to ask you a question. Did you see anything funny last night? Or hear anything?"

Joe shrugs and gets distracted by a pretty flower again.

"Now listen to me, Joe. This is important. You walk on the strand sidewalk all the time. Did you see anybody there acting suspicious last night?"

Joe suddenly smiles and points at Harp's chest. "I saw you."

Harp stops walking and looks into Joe's eyes. "You saw me? Where did you see me?"

"You were mean."

He's loony. Pay no attention to him.

"You saw me last night? I didn't see you, did I? Where was I?"

"Walking."

He's off his rocker. Don't listen.

"Yes, you said that. But where?"

He's confused. He didn't see a thing.

Joe stares down at the ground. "I'm sorry."

Harp pats his hand. "It's all right, Joe. I'm not mad at you."

That makes Joe look up and smile his big toothless smile again.

"But if you remember where you saw me, you should tell me later. When you remember."

"All right."

Make sure he doesn't tell anybody else.

"But don't tell anybody else you saw me, okay?"

"Why not?"

"Because I said so, Joe."

"Okay."

They start walking again, and Joe seems to forget what they were talking about as he stares at a row of nice red and white and yellow flowers some people have planted along the sidewalk in front of their house. Joe stops to pick a bright yellow flower, and he plays with it as Harp hurries him along. He's pulling the petals off, leaving a trail on the sidewalk behind them.

He's distracted. Now's your chance to get rid of that birdbrain.

Harp knows he should probably go on alone, but he's a little worried about what Joe said about seeing him on the strand last night. Could that be possible? He doesn't remember being on the strand last night. Maybe I should ask him a few more questions.

A waste of time. He doesn't know anything.

Harp waits for Joe to catch up. "But what about hearing, Joe? Did you hear anything last night? Let's talk about dogs some more. Did you hear a dog howling last night?"

That makes Joe stop to think. He doesn't seem to be able to walk and think at the same time. He nods happily. "Doggy."

Harp pats him on the shoulder. "That's good, Joe. You heard a dog. Was it howling? If the dog was howling in the night it means somebody died. Do you remember where you were when you heard the dog?"

Joe screws up his face like he's thinking really hard.

Harp pats Joe's hand. "It's all right, Joe. You don't have to remember. I'll find somebody else who heard the dog last night."

He pulls on Joe's arm to get him moving again. "Hey, Joe, I know a story about God's dog. Do you want to hear it?"

Don't tell him that.

Joe starts nodding and nodding like he can't stop. He grabs Harp's hand, eager, like he's about to get fed.

"All right, here's the story."

I'm telling you, don't be giving away our secrets. The nitwit won't understand it anyhow.

"It's about God and how he liked all the animals so he kept them for himself."

All right, go right ahead. But I'll have no part of it.

"But the Devil wanted an animal too. Finally, God created a goat for the Devil so he wouldn't be so lonely. The Devil was happy to have his goat, but he decided to play a trick on God so he let his goat eat all of God's flowers."

That makes Joe look really sad. He still has the center part of the yellow flower in his big hand. He's hanging onto it even thought he's already pulled all of the yellow petal parts off. He looks at what's left of the flower and then back at Harp with a forlorn look on his face.

Harp sees Joe is about to start crying, so he quickly says, "It's okay, Joe, the flowers were special God flowers, so they all grew back."

That makes Joe happy again, and he lets Harp lead him on down the sidewalk as Harp continues the story. "But as soon as the new flowers grew up, the Devil's goat kept on eating them so God created a big bad dog and sent it out to eat the goat. Then guess what happened next, Joe? When the Devil found out his goat was dead and almost all eaten up, he got really mad and went to see God. He said it wasn't his fault about the goat eating all the flowers. Harp makes his voice real low, like a Devil does and growls, 'It's just the way a Devil goat is, just like I'm the way I am.'"

Joe stops. He looks scared and puts his hands over his eyes.

Harp takes Joe's big hands and pulls them away from his face. "Now don't go getting scared, Joe. I was just pretending to be the Devil."

"You look mean."

Harp tries to pull on Joe's hand to get him going again, but he won't budge.

"Like last night, Harp. Your eyes. Mean."

"Last night?"

"Mean eyes."

"Awe, Joe, now you're making things up. Don't you want me to go on with the story?"

"God make him another goat?"

"I'm getting to that part, Joe. You have to be patient or else I'm not going to tell you any more stories."

Joe's eyes fill up with tears again, and he has his hands together like he's praying. "Please, Harp. More story."

"Oh, all right. But you have to let me finish without interrupting all the time."

Joe uses both of his hands to squeeze his lips together to show he won't talk anymore.

"All right, now listen close. The Devil wanted God to make him a new goat, just like you said he should. But God didn't really want to make a new goat because he didn't want a goat around eating his flowers all the time. So he played a trick on the Devil. He said, 'I will make you another goat, but not until the season's change and my flowers are all dead anyhow. I'll make you a new goat as soon as the little leaves fall off of that tree there.' God pointed to a nearby tree. So the Devil went to sit under the tree to wait. But it was a pine tree, and as long as the Devil waited the little tiny pine needles didn't seem to want to fall off. He waited and waited and waited." Harp taps Joe on the chest. "And that's why you should stay away from pine trees, Joe. Because the Devil might still be there, sitting under that tree, waiting for the little pine leaves to fall off so he can get a new goat."

Joe looks confused, then concerned. "No new goat?"

See there. I told you he wouldn't get it.

"No, Joe, he didn't get to have a new goat. Pine leaves don't ever fall off so the Devil had to wait forever. God didn't want any goats around to eat up all of his nice flowers, and that's how he made sure it wouldn't ever happen again.."

Joe thinks about that. "Lonely."

Harp nods. "Yes, that's right, Joe. The Devil will be lonely for his goat."

"Bad dog."

"Well, I guess that part about the dog killing the goat was bad, Joe, but it's just the way God works. God works in mysterious ways sometimes."

That's for sure. Just look at the two of you.

Joe picks at what's left of his yellow flower as Harp leads him on down the hill. Joe keeps on dragging his feet, not paying any attention to where he's going. Harp thinks Joe looks very sad. He's trying to smell his torn-apart flower even though Harp is pretty sure there can't be any smell left in it. As he thinks about it, he doesn't understand why the story made Joe so sad. The Devil was the bad one to let his goat eat all of God's nice flowers in the first place so he deserved to be tricked, didn't he? But Harp is sorry the story made Joe unhappy. He decides to cheer him up. "Listen, Joe, tomorrow I'll tell you a happy story."

That brings Joe out of it. He grins and squeezes Harp's hand and says, "Tell me now. Tell me now."

No! Only one story a day. That's the rule.

"No, you have to wait until tomorrow, Joe. We only get to have one story a day."

"No, no, pleeeze, Harp. Now. Tell me now."

"I'm sorry, Joe. Only one story in one day, that's the rule. Rules are not made to be broken you know."

"Pleeeze, Harp. Pretty please."

"No, I'd better not. But listen here, I know a story about a fox and there's a poem in it. What if I tell you the poem that's inside the fox story?"

Joe smiles and pumps Harp's hand. "Tell me. Tell me."

"All right, it goes like this. Now listen careful, Joe. 'I'm not sleeping, I am waking, would you know what I am making? I am boiling beer and butter, would you like to stay for supper?'"

Joe laughs right out loud. It's the first time Harp has ever heard Joe laugh. Joe is so happy he squeezes Harp's small hands between his own great big hands and giggles like a little child would.

That makes Harp laugh out loud too. He wonders if Joe liked his story-telling so much, maybe other people would like to hear Mother's stories too. It might be a way to make some money so he wouldn't have to be hungry all the time.

No! You can't go around telling everybody our secret stories.

Harp thinks about Speel and how she tries to get people down at the beach to give her money when she passes out her little sayings to them. Maybe people would give him money too if he wrote down some of the stories Mother told him when he was little.

Didn't I just say no? What part of no don't you understand?

3-3
Justification

When they get close to the beach, Harp says, "Let's turn here, Joe. I want to go past the restaurants." Joe does as he's told and follows along close behind.

When they come to the first restaurant, Harp stops to put his face against the window. He sees a lot of people inside sitting at little tables and eating things.

He turns back to Joe. "They're all happy in there, Joe. That's good. It's like Little Hilly said, if you can't be happy, you might as well be dead."

Joe says, "Dead?"

Who'll make his shroud when he's buried in the ground? I, said the Beetle, with my thread and needle. I'll make the shroud.

Harp shakes his head to make the bad rhyme about being dead go away. "Never mind, Joe. Just don't think about it. That's what I do." He leads Joe away from the restaurant.

Two blocks further on, they come to a restaurant that has tables right out on the sidewalk. Harp draws Joe aside and points back at the people. "See there, Joe. The sun is out now, and it's nice and warm. That's why the people are eating their food outside."

Joe nods like he understands.

Get away from there. Don't attract attention to yourself.

Harp pulls Joe behind a light pole and whispers, "See that lady? She's dunking her bread into her soup. It looks good, doesn't it?"

Joe points. "Can I have some?"

Harp feels bad for Joe. "You didn't get enough to eat at the church, did you?"

Joe shakes his head.

Harp remembers he's got three dollars and three quarters and a dime too. Maybe they have something in that restaurant for three dollars. Then he and Joe could sit out in the sun with the other people and eat good food just like the regular people. "I'm still hungry too, Joe. Wait here. I'll see if I can get something for us."

Why are you doing this? Aren't we always better off staying alone?

He's not sure he wants to go where people might look at him, but his stomach says he should at least take a look. He goes back to the front of the restaurant where they have a menu on a little stand. As he's looking at everything on the menu, he hears a woman say, "And then they found the dead body."

Is she talking about Little Hilly? Harp leans closer to listen.

The woman is eating green lettuce out of a small glass bowl and she's stopping between bites to say excited things about the person who was killed. She leans across the table to her man friend who's eating a sandwich. "He was murdered during the night, and for a while it looked like the murderer was going to get away with it."

The man doesn't seem to be listening very carefully. He's just eating and nodding and saying, "Uh huh."

She says, "Are you listening to me?"

The man puts down his sandwich and wipes his mouth with a napkin and says, "Who starred in it?"

Who starred in it? They must not be talking about Little Hilly. Maybe they don't even know Little Hilly is dead. It makes Harp a little sad to think Little Hilly had to die and people don't even care.

He goes back to looking at the menu, but the only thing he can find for less than three dollars is coffee. He doesn't like coffee.

Somebody's watching you. Get out of here.

Harp looks up to see a man in a white apron coming toward him, so he quickly turns and walks away, pretending he didn't see any food on the menu that he liked.

Fancy food. That's the last thing we need.

Joe is still waiting for him, trying to hide his big body behind the light pole.

"They didn't have anything good, Joe. But maybe we can find something else." He pulls Joe along down the street until they get to where the alley cuts through back to the beach.

"Let's go over there, Joe." Harp points to the big white apartment building on the corner. "They've got some big garbage cans out back. Let's see if we can find something more for you to eat."

But when they get to the garbage cans, it's too late. A big blue garbage truck is already there and two black men are dumping everything into the back of it. "Don't say anything," whispers Harp. "Just keep walking." He takes Joe by the arm and leads him quickly past the garbage cans. One of the garbage men nods to Harp as he passes. Harp nods back and then puts his head down and hurries away, pulling Joe along.

Now that man is suspicious of you. Why can't you be more careful?

Why did that man nod to me like that? Harp looks back and sees the man is still watching him. Does the garbage man suspect me of being there to steal his garbage? Or is it because I'm with Joe whose skin is that same black color as his?

As he pulls Joe away, Harp wonders if maybe that garbage man saw something last night. Detective Olivera would probably want him to go back and ask that garbage man some questions.

You're just begging for trouble, aren't you?

"Well, I'm supposed to nose around and ask questions. Doesn't that mean I should ask everybody I see?"

Not if you know what's good for you.

Joe is staring at him.

"I wasn't talking to you, Joe. I was just . . . thinking out loud."

Joe is still staring at him.

Harp ignores him and looks back at the garbage man. Now that he thinks about it, Harp isn't sure if it's too good an idea to walk right up to a man emptying garbage cans and ask him questions about somebody getting killed. But now it's too late anyhow: the man has jumped back onto his big truck, and they're driving away leaving only a big cloud of black smoke behind.

Harp hurries on through the alley, pulling Joe along. Harp is beginning to think all this asking questions and looking for suspects could get to be a full time job. Maybe it's better just to look for clues. Looking for clues is better than asking questions because to look for clues all you have to do is look at things, not talk to people.

3-4

Sharp Things

When they make it back to the beach, Harp sees that there are even more people on the strand sidewalk than there were that morning. He turns to Joe and says, "Well, here we are. You can find your own way now, can't you?"

Joe looks around, frowning.

"Well, bye then, Joe." Harp pats Joe on the shoulder and heads away down the sidewalk. He doesn't have anywhere in particular to go because he isn't supposed to go to meet the Blind Shrimp until it gets dark. He'd better just walk around and look for clues.

Don't look now, but you-know-who is following you.

Harp stops and turns around. It's Joe, and he's still following, even though he's not supposed to.

Harp waves him away. "Go on now, Joe. I have to go by myself and look for clues."

Joe stops and looks at the ground.

"Go on now. I mean it!" Harp stamps his foot.

Joe pouts and turns back, but he doesn't go anywhere. He just stands there kicking at pebbles.

Harp goes on down the sidewalk, not looking back.

Good, you finally got rid of that moron.

Harp is sorry he had to speak harshly to Joe, but he can't have a big person like Joe following him all over the place while he looks for suspects. It might attract too much attention.

When he comes to the place where the old people feed the pigeons, he sees right way that there are no pigeons there. They must have already eaten up all the bread crumbs and flown away. And the old people are gone too. The only person there is The Amazing Cedric the Chainsaw Juggler, and he's not doing anything amazing, he's just sitting by himself on a little stool, and he's got one of his chainsaws on his lap. It looks like a brand new one. It's shiny bright green, much prettier than the old yellow one he had before. Cedric's big gold and black flag that says "The Amazing Cedric the Chainsaw Juggler" is already up and flapping in the breeze, but it doesn't look like Cedric is ready to start juggling yet.

Harp stops to watch anyhow and Cedric notices. He waves his hand and says, "Hey kid, come over here for a minute."

Ignore him. Just walk away.

Harp points to himself.

"Yeah, you. Come here and help me a minute."

Harp slowly walks over.

Why can't you just stay away from people? We don't need them.

Cedric points to the ground. "Sit down here and hold this thing for me while I file down the chain."

Harp sits down in front of Cedric who turns the chainsaw around and puts it into Harp's hands.

Don't do this. It's dangerous.

The chainsaw makes Harp nervous. What if it starts up by itself? It might cut his arms and legs off before Cedric can make it stop.

Cedric has a metal tool in his hand. "You hold it tight while I do the filing, okay?"

Harp holds onto the chainsaw really tight while Cedric begins to rub the metal tool against the saw's chain.

All right, fine. Don't listen to me then. I give you my best advice, but do you listen?

Cedric looks up from his task. "Ever catch my act, kid?"

Harp nods. "Yes, sir. It's very scary."

"Fraid I'm gonna cut my fingers off, eh?"

"Yes, sir."

Cedric laughs. "Well, now you know my secret, don't you? I file down the damn chain in case I miss. But you won't tell anybody, will you?"

"No, sir."

"Still plenty dangerous, even with a blunted chain, right?"

"Yes, sir."

Cedric works on his chainsaw chain for quite a while. When he finishes, he takes back the saw from Harp and puts it aside. He stands up and fishes a dollar out of his pocket and hands it to Harp with a wink.

Harp gets up and happily stuffs the dollar into his pocket, but then he changes his mind and takes it back out to look at it. It's nice and clean. No blood. Now he's got a good clean dollar that he can spend anywhere he wants to, even without washing it. Later on, as soon as his stomach gets a little more hungry, he can go to a store and buy something good. Maybe cookies.

Cedric pulls on his gold sweater with the big red "C" on the front and combs his hair with his fingers. Then he walks out into the middle of the sidewalk and starts yelling real loud: "All right, ladies and gentlemen, step right up. You've read about it in the newspapers. You've seen it on TV. Now you can see it with your very own eyes. That's right, it's time for Cedric, the amazing chainsaw juggler. Step right up." He comes back and picks up his nice new green chainsaw. He pulls the cord and it roars to life.

Get away from there. You know you don't like crowds.

As the people crowd in, Harp hurries to get out of their way. He likes seeing Cedric juggle things, but he likes to watch from a safe distance. It's too scary to be up close when the chainsaw is running. What if Cedric misses and he gets hurt real bad? There would be blood all over the place, and some people might think it's Harp's fault. Harp knows Cedric comes to the beach every weekend to flip sharp things up into the air. He always catches them, but you never know when things might change. Look at what happened to Little Hilly when he was least expecting it.

Cedric keeps on doing something to the chainsaw to make it roar louder. Harp knows he does it to draw the people in. Pretty soon people are coming from all directions. But Cedric doesn't start juggling his chainsaw right away. He never does. When there are a lot of people gathered around, he puts the chainsaw down on the ground, and it putts away there while he talks to the people. He says, "I'm going to toss some sharp things up in the air now. Anybody want to volunteer to catch them?" Some of the people laugh, and Cedric says, "No? Okay, I guess I'll have to do it myself."

Cedric starts flipping three shiny knives way up into the air. Harp has never seen Cedric flip knives up before. Usually he just flips up hatchets. So why is he doing knives today? It's another thing that's changing, and it's very suspicious. What if he misses and cuts himself?

Don't be such a scaredy-cat. He never misses.

Even though Harp knows Cedric never misses, he hopes Cedric fixed the sharp side of those knives so they aren't so sharp like he fixed the sharp part of the chainsaw.

But Cedric doesn't miss. He catches every one of the knives.

Told ya.

Harp can finally let out his breath.

Then Cedric starts flipping his usual shiny hatchets, keeping all three of them up in the air at the same time. A woman right in front of Harp says, "Oh my."

Then Cedric starts flipping up the knives *and* hatchets all together. Harp has never seen him do that before, so it makes him hold his breath again.

Scaredy cat. Scaredy cat.

But luckily Cedric doesn't drop any of them, so Harp can let out his breath again.

Then Cedric stops and looks around at all the people. He acts real serious, and the people quiet down. Cedric points at the chainsaw that's still putting away on the ground. He says, "Ready?"

Several of the people in the crowd say, "Yeah."

A boy with a pretty girl hanging onto his arm says, "Go for it."

Cedric picks up the chainsaw and does something to it that makes it run faster. White smoke comes out of it as he flips it up into the air, and when it comes down, he catches it by the handle. Some people gasp, and then everybody starts clapping.

But Cedric stops them by holding up his hand. He picks up one of the hatchets. Harp knows what's coming, and he can hardly look. He's never seen Cedric miss, but this time he has a bad feeling about it. He remembers what happened this morning when Bailey the balancing man tried to balance his cute little wife in that chair and dropped her. Things are changing.

Cedric flips the hatchet way up into the air, and with his other hand, he flips up the chainsaw. Harp knows Cedric is supposed to catch both of them, but he almost misses the hatchet, and that distracts him so much he misses the chainsaw completely. It lands right on top of his foot. He hops around, holding his foot and the young man with the girl on his arm laughs. Cedric stops hopping. He looks mad. He shakes his head and picks up his chainsaw again. It's still running. He holds it up so the crowd can see it and says, "New saw."

This time almost everybody laughs, and Cedric turns up the saw so it runs even faster. Oh no, he's going to try it again.

It's your fault. Everything goes wrong wherever you go.

Harp doesn't see how it can always be his fault, but he decides he'd better get out of there just in case. What if Cedric cuts all of his fingers off and can't make money juggling things anymore? Harp thinks maybe Cedric should have stayed home and practiced with his new chainsaw a lot more before he tried to juggle it in front of all those people. Whatever is going to happen, Harp doesn't want to be there to see it and maybe be the one who gets blamed for it.

Then get out of here.

As he walks away, Harp can hear the people back there clapping again. He hopes they aren't clapping because Cedric missed and cut some part of himself off.

It's your bad thoughts that does these things.

He puts his fingers in his ears so he doesn't have to hear the chainsaw's sound. He whispers the magic words Mother taught him: "Have mercy upon me, O Lord, for I am weak and you are supposed to protect the weak."

When he's far enough away, he decides it's safe to take his fingers out of his ears.

You are weak, but it's no use asking Him for help. It's still your fault.

Harp quickly puts his fingers back into his ears. It's not fair that I should get blamed for everything. I helped Cedric make it so his saw wasn't as sharp. That was good, wasn't it? Cedric even gave me a dollar. How can I help it if I accidentally had a few bad thoughts while I was watching Cedric do his juggling? He whispers, "It is not my fault, not really."

3-5

Cause and Effect

*H*arp goes on down the strand, thinking about the knives Cedric was flipping up into the air. They were very shiny, and they looked sharp. Cedric never had knives before. Why did he change to knives instead of just hatchets? Little Hilly was killed with a knife, so do those brand-new knives make Cedric a suspect?

This is a waste of time. Everybody can't be a suspect.

Harp slows down until he's barely moving. The people flow past him. He's thinking hard about sharp knives and shiny hatchets and how things can be changing all around you and you might not even know it. For example, Little Hilly was already dead before he knew about it. Maybe it's because he wasn't paying close enough attention. He wasn't paying attention last night and somehow got to the pier without even knowing it. And sure enough, a bad thing happened. Mother was always mad at him for not paying attention. She'd say, "Pay attention. Where is your mind today?"

Like now? Where is your mind now?

Harp looks up and sees he's almost made it to the volleyball courts. How did he get there so fast? Some of the people are passing very close to him, almost touching him.

Look out! If they touch you, their evil thoughts will pass into you.

A lady is coming right at him, pushing a covered cart with a baby inside. Harp quickly moves to the edge of the sidewalk. As the lady goes past, Harp sees that the baby inside the cart is eating something, and whatever it is, he's getting it all over his face. Maybe it's a piece of banana. Harp thinks a banana would taste good right now. Now he's even more sure he didn't get enough to eat at the church.

Complain, complain. You always were a whiner.

And here's another thing worth complaining about: it's going to be cold again tonight. Why did Detective Olivera have to take my jacket?

They'll use it against you. I told you not to give it to him. Remember the rhyme. Who caught his blood? I, said the fly, I caught his blood.

No, no, Harp doesn't want to think about that bad old rhyme right now. That rhyme makes him really nervous. Besides, there's no time for that anyhow. He has to pay attention. He has to see if any more clues have appeared while he was up at the church. Anything might be a clue. Even people might be clues. Like . . . like the weekend seller people who come on the weekends to try to sell things to the off-beachers. Those seller people are lined up all along the sidewalk. The fortune teller lady is there in her tall red hat that has the silver stars on it. When any of the off-beachers walk by, she holds up her glass ball and says, "Your future is in here. Learn your future from my magic crystal ball." Many times Harp has wished he could stop and ask that lady to tell his future, but he knows she wants money to do it.

Stuff and nonsense. UnGodly superstition.

Even if it is stuff and nonsense, Harp wishes he knew what his future was going to be.

Just ask me. I'll tell you. It's going to be a really bad. Isn't it always?

"Well, I'm not going to believe every bad thing I hear. And who's to say that fortune teller lady is stuff and nonsense? If I had enough money, maybe she could tell me who killed Little Hilly."

I could tell you, but you don't want to know.

"But I do want to know. Detective Olivera said I had to find out, or else. Olivera said he had to look for suspects, and any of the people walking on the sidewalk could be a suspect, even the off-beachers."

You're off your rocker. Why would they want to kill a useless little nobody?

Harp shakes his head, hard. He's sure he's not off his rocker, no matter who thinks so. "I'm looking for suspects, just like Detective Olivera said I had to." He stares at the lady with the shaved head and the little ring in her nose? She could be a suspect, couldn't she?

Her? Give me a break.

Harp knows that lady comes to the beach every weekend to sit there on her blanket all day long making strings of beads. Why does she do that? Almost nobody buys her beads. And why did she shave all of the hair off her head? And didn't it hurt when she stuck that little ring through the side of her nose?

Questions, questions. You're going to drive me crazy with all your questions.

Harp gets back on the sidewalk and starts walking, determined to look carefully at every person he sees. Mostly he'll look carefully at the ones trying to get money from people. They might be suspects. There's the young man with the slicked-down black hair doing card tricks, like he always does.

Yeah, maybe he's got something up his sleeve. Get it?

"I don't know what that means, but I do know he's wearing a black cape, and that's suspicious."

He always wears that black cape.

"Well, maybe he does, but it's still suspicious." Harp stops to watch as the young man holds up his usual big playing cards, all spread out. Every time somebody walks past, he taps the cards with his shiny black stick and the cards always fold up and go away. Harp has never seen him do any other trick besides that one.

Forget him. He's nothing.

Well, what about the other people? He goes to the side of the sidewalk to watch them go by. But they just look about the same as they always do. The more Harp looks, the more it seems like everything on the beach seems to be the way it always is. Nothing but the usual people, doing their usual things. "How am I supposed to find good suspects where there's nobody but the usual suspects?"

Like I said, a waste of time. Wise up, will you?

But Harp doesn't think it's a waste of time. Maybe things only look normal. Maybe that's the idea, everything might be trying to look normal so nobody will notice. The more he thinks about it, the more Harp is sure there must be clues all around. He just has to look closer if he's going to figure out what they are.

He moves on down the sidewalk, hurrying past the usual young music players who are playing their musical instruments as loud as they can. Harp wonders if they play that loud so people will give them money to make them stop.

He stops to watch Adelle, the sidewalk artist, draw her funny pictures of people. This time she's drawing a picture of a little boy who can't seem to sit still. His mother scolds him and tells him to stop wiggling around. She tells him she's paying good money for this picture, so if he wanted it so bad, why is he wiggling around so much? But Adelle doesn't seem to care if he wiggles. She just keeps drawing him. She's good at drawing people's pictures. Harp is impressed that she can even draw a wiggling little boy and make the drawing look like he's sitting still. She draws rosy cheeks on the boy, and gives him wide ears and a big smile—even though the little boy only smiles once, when his mother makes him do it.

Seeing that nice picture of a smiling rosy-cheeked boy makes Harp smile too. He wishes somebody would have drawn a nice picture of him when he was little.

Why? Who would want a picture of you?

Harp is pretty sure he never got to have any kind of picture, except for that one time when Mother took him to a booth that must have had a camera hidden in it because after she squeezed both of them in there, and put some money in a slot, a row of little pictures came out. It was the first time Harp had ever seen himself in a picture, and he thought he looked funny with his blonde hair almost all cut off and his ears sticking out and grinning really big like Mother said he was supposed to. But Mother didn't like how the picture made her look, so she tore up all of the pictures and threw them right down on the ground. Harp picked up all of the pieces, and later he taped them back together and hid them under his mattress. Sometimes he liked to take those pictures out and look at them, just to be sure who he really was.

Why think about dumb things like that? Pay attention. Don't you realize somebody's watching you?

Adelle is almost finished with the drawing of the little boy when Harp suddenly feels like he's being watched. He looks over his shoulder to see who it is. There's nobody close by, but there is a man wearing dark glasses over by the Strand and Sand Surf Shop. Harp realizes that behind those dark glasses, the man's eyes could be drilling right into him. The man is pretending to be a panhandler, holding out a paper cup, but he's not doing it right so nobody is giving him any money. Harp is sure the man is watching him, but he's not going to fall for that one. Without even changing his expression, Harp just turns and walks away. He'll pretend like he didn't even notice the man. He tries to walk normal, like he doesn't suspect a thing. He keeps right on going until he's exactly thirty steps away. Then he ducks behind the Rolling Rentals Skate place and peeks back through the tall rack of skates. The man is still standing next to the building, and he's still holding out his cup to the people as they go by.

He's up to something. Watch out for him.

Harp has never seen that man before. He's kind of tall, and he has a big nose, and a big stomach, way too big for a homeless person. Not only that, he's wearing clean-looking black pants. No homeless person could keep black pants looking that clean for very long. And besides, nobody is going to give the man any money because he's not panhandling right. He's not pretending to be crippled, and he's not playing any musical instrument, and he doesn't even have a sign saying he's a veteran. He's just holding out his cup like he thinks somebody is going to give him money for doing nothing.

I'm telling you, he was watching you.

Harp hurries away. Was that man really watching him from behind those dark glasses? Mother always said people who watch you are trying to do something bad to you. She said only God can protect you from them. She said you had to remember the magic words. Now, what were they?

Keep me as the apple of Thy eye and under the shadow of Thy wings. Protect me from the wicked that would oppress me.

That's it. "Keep me as the apple of Thy eye." Those are the magic words Mother taught him. She said God was always up there in heaven, always looking down, always watching. She said sometimes God even gets inside of you and looks out through your eyes. When Harp was very little, the idea of God hiding inside his head and looking out through his eyes was really scary. It meant God could see everything you did and see everything you were thinking. That's how he knew God must have been watching out through his eyes that time he found Mother's secret box of old pictures hidden in her closet. Some of them were pictures of people without any clothes on, and they were doing bad things to each other. When Mother found out, she hit him a lot of times and put him in the closet for the whole night and most of the next day. It must have been God that told on him. How else could she have found out?

God sees the wicked. They cannot hide from Him.

And what about that time on Ward D-4 when he wouldn't let the other men touch him in his private places during the night? God must have been looking out through his eyes that time too. How else could Mitch have found out? Or when he touched his own private parts under the covers? Only God could have known about that, but somehow Mitch found out, and Harp got punished. At least he thought that must be what Mitch was punishing him for.

Your unclean thoughts shall be found out. Beware my wrath sayeth the Lord!

Harp shakes his head to make those kinds of thoughts go away. He knows he's been bad sometimes, but he tries so hard not to be.

3-6
Even More Suspects

As he goes on down the strand sidewalk looking for suspects, Harp weaves his way through all the people. A tall man is walking with a short woman, and they both stare at Harp. The man leans down and whispers something in the woman's ear and she laughs.

"Why are they whispering like that? It's suspicious."

A lot of other people flow past, almost like a river going around him. Some of them have big smiles on their faces, and a lot of them are eating things like ice cream or hot dogs or cotton candy while they walk. Before Olivera said he had to look for suspects, Harp didn't pay much attention to the off-beachers. In his mind, they were only vague pictures of unknown people, like the old pictures of people Mother had on her dresser. But now he wonders if those off-beachers should be watched too.

More wasting time. Why can't you do something more productive?

"Like what?"

Like get some money.

"I thought you said money was the root of all evil."

That's only for rich people. Poor people like us deserve to have their money.

Harp is not so sure. From what he's seen, it still seems like money *is* the root of all evil. On the beach, the homeless people are always getting into fights over money. In fact, maybe somebody killed Little Hilly for his money. But no, that can't be right. Little Hilly still had money in his pocket. So why was he killed?

I told you why. But did you listen?

Thinking about money makes him think about the Blind Shrimp.

He wonders what he's going to do until it's time to meet the Shrimp on the pier when it gets dark.

Do what you always do, wander around and waste your life away.

He glances up at the sun and sees that it still has quite a ways to go before it goes down. Maybe he should go to the weight-lifter's pen and watch the big men with big muscles lift up the big weights.

More wasting time.

Or he could go out and listen to the waves. That isn't a waste of time. In fact, that's exactly what he should do. He hasn't listened to the waves since this morning. That's too long to go without listening.

He hikes out across the wide beach, and when he gets to the ocean, he sits down on the sand to watch the waves come in. The waves aren't very big today, but there are some surfer boys out there anyhow, sitting on their surfboards and talking to each other while they wait for a wave to come.

A killer is nearby looking for you, and this is what you do with your time?

Harp decides to listen to the waves and nothing else. It's like the waves are talking to him, trying to remind him of something he forgot to do. But he doesn't think he forgot anything. "It was just a normal day on the beach, wasn't it?"

You call this normal? This is the most unnormal day of your life.

"Well, it's normal except for waking up this morning and finding Little Hilly dead. And . . . well, maybe Bailey dropping his wife. And maybe Cedric missing his chainsaw and almost cutting of some of his parts. It was normal except for those things."

So that's your idea of normal?

"Well, maybe it isn't really such a normal day. So what?" It probably wasn't normal for Detective Olivera to tell him he had to find out who killed Little Hilly. But he's been looking hard all day, and asking people questions, and he's still not sure who did it.

You don't have a clue, do you?

"A clue? Hey, that gives me an idea. I should write down clues and suspects. Maybe I should make a list of everybody who might be a suspect."

About time you did something constructive.

Harp takes off his backpack and pulls out his diary. He rereads what he wrote that morning. It just says Little Hilly got stabbed a bunch of times, and it says Big Hilly wasn't there to protect his little buddy, so the police probably think he did it. Now, as he rereads it, he can see that the story isn't written very good. But he doesn't want to get distracted away from writing out his list of suspects. "I'll just have to rewrite yesterday's story later."

He licks the tip of his pencil. "Okay, who should be on my list of suspects? Maybe I should put Big Hilly on my list first because that's probably who Olivera thinks did it."

At the top of a fresh page, he writes:

LIST OF SUSPECTS

Big Hilly- Nobody knows where he is.

And what about the Devil worshippers in their magic clothes who maybe wanted Little Hilly's blood? "I'd better write that down."

The Devil worshippers. Maybe they wanted Little Hilly's blood.

"There. I've hardly started my list and I already have some good suspects on it."

You call those good suspects?

Harp throws down his pencil and it sticks into the sand, point first. "Well, what am I supposed to do? I've been asking everybody questions and nobody knows anything."

All right, I'll help you. Try this riddle: Here comes a candle to light you to bed, here comes a chopper to chop off your head.

"Chop off whose head? Little Hilly's?"

Think about it.

"I did think about it. I give up."

Do I have to tell you everything? A wee short child, that can't run on his own.

"Oh, I know that one. Wee Willie Winkie. I got it, didn't I?"

Finally.

"But wait a minute, what does that have to do with Little Hilly?"

Do I have to spell it out for you? That fake cowboy.

"Oh, that's right." Tex. Little Hilly got chopped up with a knife and Tex has a big knife with a white handle. And he said homos ought to be ex-ter-me-nated. "I'd better write him down."

Tex - Has knife with white handle - Doesn't like homos.

But then, as he rereads it, he's not so sure. Maybe Tex shouldn't be a suspect just because he has a knife. A cowboy out on the range might need a knife for cutting things like rope and . . . for whittling. Harp remembers a man with no legs who had a knife, and he used it to whittled things. The man sat in a wheelchair on the front porch of his house that was right across the street from their house. Harp remembers that sometimes he used to go over and watch that man whittle. One day the man was using his knife to whittle a long thin Santa Claus out of a stick. When he was done, he showed it to Harp. Harp wanted to have that whittled Santa Claus, but the man said no, it was for his grandson. Harp remembers how sad it made him feel not to get that carving. It made him realize he never got anything good like a whittled Santa Claus. He ran away and cried behind some bushes.

What a big baby. Crying over trifles.

Now that Harp is all grown up, he knows it was silly to cry about not having things like carved Santa Clauses, or toys.

If God wanted you to have toys, they would have rained down on you from the heavens.

"That's right. Who needs toys and things like that anyhow?"

Harp shakes off the bad old thoughts and goes back to looking at his list. A tear drops onto the paper. It blurs Big Hilly's name. Harp wipes his eyes with the back of his hands, trying to stop remembering bad old things.

Stop that sniveling. What do you have to be sad about? You could still be locked up.

That makes the tears stop. He realizes he doesn't really have anything to be sad about. "That's right. At least I'm free. At least I'm not locked up on Ward D-4 anymore." He looks at the paper. Big Hilly's name is now a blob of wet pencil dust. Harp wonders if his tear falling on that name could be a sign? Does it mean Big Hilly did it? Or does it mean he didn't do it. Harp blows on the wet spot until the paper dries, but the outline of it is still there and it makes it hard to read Big Hilly's name. Harp wonders if it means he should try harder to find out where Big Hilly went.

Harp chews on the end of his pencil, rereading what he's written so far. Only a few names. Who else? How do you tell who would make good suspects? Detective Olivera said to find out who had it in for Little Hilly. But how do you find that out?

More important is to think who had it in for you.

"What? Nobody had it in for me. Detective Olivera said to look for whoever had it in for Little Hilly."

A man and a woman walk by, holding hands. The woman glances at Harp.

Stop talking to me out loud when people are around. Do you want them to think you're crazy?

Harp watches the man and woman walk on down the beach. The woman turns slightly to look back at him and says something to the man who also looks back.

Harp turns away and pretends to be watching the surfer boys sitting on their surfboards out past the end of the pier. When he looks back, the man and the woman are far away.

That was a close one.

Harp looks back down at his diary. Still only a few names. Is that all the suspects? Is there anybody else he should put on his list? For a moment, he has the funny thought that he should write down his own name.

No! That's all. Nobody else. Stop writing now.

The police would probably want his name written down if they knew he was under the pier when Little Hilly was being killed.

No! Don't think about that.

No, she's right. That was a silly thought. His name doesn't belong on the list. He should only write down the names of people who really might have done it.

Nobody knows.

That's right, nobody knows anything.

Nobody suspects.

Nobody suspects anything.

If only you hadn't got that blood on you.

Little Hilly's blood could be a problem. The police have his jacket now, but even if they do find some blood on it, how could they know where that blood came from? It could be from a dog . . . or something.

They can tell.

Maybe they can tell the blood isn't from a dog, but if Olivera suspected him, he wouldn't have asked Harp to help find the killer, would he? He should concentrate on figuring out who the real killer is. "Like . . . hey, what about the Blind Shrimp?" People said the Shrimp wasn't very honest and only wore his dark glasses and carried his long white cane to fool people into giving him money. But no, he's probably too small and weak to stab anybody that many times.

He could have had help.

"That's right. Maybe more than one person did it." The Blind Shrimp might have got together with somebody else to do it. "I'd better write that down."

The Blind Shrimp - and maybe somebody else helped him.

Harp stares at the paper. There must be more suspects. He thinks about the people he sees on the beach all the time. How about The Amazing Cedric The Chainsaw Juggler? Cedric had those brand new knives.

What? Are you going to write down everybody on the beach?

"Well, Cedric had knives, didn't he? If he was brave enough to flip a chainsaw up into the air and catch it with his bare hands, he could be a killer, couldn't he? Besides, I have to have somebody on my list, don't I? What if Olivera comes and says, 'Who do you have on your list of suspects?' What am I supposed to say? Hardly anybody? No, it's better to have some extra names on the list, even if they aren't the top suspects."

A waste of time.

Harp decides to write down Cedric's name, no matter what anybody says. He writes:

The Amazing Cedric - has brand new knives.

You're forgetting the most important part. Which one of them would want to kill you?

Harp still feels like he's forgetting something.

The one who's after you.

No, that's not it." Somebody else. Then he remembers: Speel the Sayer. She said she would help him, but can she be trusted?

You can't trust that weird person any further than you could throw her. And as fat as she is, you couldn't throw her very far.

Speel said she saw something early this morning by the pier. But did she really? And where does she sleep at night? Not on the beach, that's for sure. And why does she pretend to be a boy? It's very suspicious. "Maybe Speel did do it. Maybe she snuck under the pier in the middle of the night and stabbed Little Hilly because . . . well, for some reason. I'd better write her down.

Speel the Sayer - Pretends to be a boy. Says she wants to help me.

What does she really want?

The same as what everybody wants. They want to hurt you.

"Who wants to hurt me?"

Shh. Not so loud.

"Well, who?" he whispers.

What about whoever drew that picture of a dog?

Harp thinks about it. A picture of the stabbed dog on Betty's white wall. "Somebody who hates dogs?"

You were afraid of dogs.

"Well, so what? Maybe a lot of people don't like dogs."

And what about that other picture, the dirty one that somebody drew on Sally's flag? Sally must have been really mad when she found it. And Betty was going to be mad too as soon as she saw what was painted on her nice white wall. But would either of them kill somebody for painting bad pictures?

No. Girls don't kill people. Forget that idea.

"Girls don't kill people? Well, maybe they do and maybe they don't. Harp decides maybe he doesn't have to put Sally and Betty on his list right now. If he finds out later Little Hilly was the one who did the bad drawings, then he can put Sally and Betty on his list.

He closes his diary. Enough writing for now. He has a good list of suspects, so it's time to start investigating them. "I'll use my eyes and ears, just like Olivera said I should. I'll eliminate each of his suspects, one by one, until there's only one left on the list. That will be the killer. Then Olivera will be happy and won't think I did it anymore."

Don't count on it.

Satisfied that he now has a good plan, Harp decides he can rest up a bit. He takes off his shoes and socks and wiggles his toes in the sand. The sand feels nice and warm. He looks around at the people on the beach. Some are lying on blankets in the sun. Most of the off-beachers come to either lie in the sun or to walk around on the strand sidewalk.

But that reminds him of the one off-beacher who wasn't lying in the sun or walking around: Big Nose, the man by the Sunnysidewalk Café, the one with the dark glasses who was panhandling but didn't know how to do it right. He must be an off-beacher. Maybe he should be a suspect.

Harp opens his diary again and adds one final name to his list:

Big Nose - man with dark glasses by Sunnysidewalk Café.

Doesn't know how to panhandle.

Harp slaps the diary closed. That's enough. All this thinking about suspects is making him sleepy.

It's because you wander around all night when every normal person is sleeping.

He puts his diary away and leans on his elbow to watch the waves.

Seagulls are circling over one spot way out past where the surfer boys are. What are they doing out there? Maybe they are looking for fish to eat. It reminds Harp of how hungry he is.

But at least he's not cold. The sun is finally warm enough, so not having a coat doesn't matter, at least not right now. He lies back on the sand and closes his eyes to listen to the waves. They slide in and out making their nice swooshing sound. In and out, in and out. Their nice sound makes him feel better. He decides he doesn't have it so bad. He may get a little hungry sometimes, but he's free. He can sit on the sand in the nice warm sun and watch the waves all day if he wants to. He doesn't have anywhere else to go, or anything else to do.

The Bible says, Slothfulness casteth thee into a deep sleep and an idle soul shall suffer hunger.

"I'm not so idle. Don't I walk around a lot? And so what if I do get a little hungry sometimes? I don't have much to be unhappy about. Even Little Hilly said I should try to be happy. If you aren't happy, you might as well be dead, like Little Hilly."

3-7

Story People

Catch her, catch her!

"But I can't catch her, Mother, she doesn't have any clothes on."

Just as I suspected. Dirty thoughts hiding in a filthy mind.

Harp opens his eyes. The sun is almost down to the ocean. The surfer boys are gone. Three dark-winged pelicans are out over the water, gliding along, hardly flapping at all, rising and falling just enough to stay above the waves. Harp watches them and thinks about how much fun it would be to be able to fly along like that. You could fly and fly and go anywhere you wanted and nobody could stop you.

You're trying not to think about your dream, aren't you? It's no use pretending. I know what you were up to.

"Dream? What was I dreaming about?"

Someone was falling.

That's right. Someone was falling from way up high. Was it Bailey's cute little wife? She seemed to have lost her little bikini swimming suit while she was falling.

Your dreams betray your dirty mind. You can't hide from God inside your dreams.

But the more Harp thinks about it, the more sure he is that there was somebody else in the dream. A man, hiding in the shadows. He was wearing an old floppy hat pulled down over his eyes. Did that man push her? Why did he want to hurt her?

Dream murderer!

Harp sits up. He suddenly realizes it must have been the killer he saw in his dream. "If only I could have seen the killer's face." The killer pushed her over the edge, and there wasn't anybody there to catch her so now she's dead too, just like Little Hilly, and just like that poor little dog.

The murderer was wearing your hat.

That's right. In the dream, the killer's hat was just like Harp's old floppy hat. Maybe having a hat in your dream means something important.

It means you were careless with your hat. You lost it.

"Well, maybe I shouldn't have let Little Hilly borrow my hat, but how could I know he would lose it?"

You always were a careless boy.

"Oh, so what? That's not important now. The important thing is to look for clues. Now, what clues could be hiding inside that dream?"

The killer is hiding in there.

Harp wonders if a person really could hide inside a dream. But maybe his dream means something else. Maybe something is hiding inside his own brain, waiting to come out whenever he falls asleep.

You'll never figure it out.

"Well, I know it means something. Otherwise, why would I have dreamed it?"

"Were you having a dream, Harp?"

Harp jumps to his feet, ready to run. But when he spins around, he sees that it's only Shoeless Joe, sitting there on the sand right behind him.

Calm down. It's only the dummy.

Harp waits for his heart to slow down a little, then he says, "You scared me, Joe. You shouldn't sneak up on a person like that."

Joe looks down at the ground and says, "I'm sorry."

Harp can see what Joe has been doing. He's made a little pile of sand, and he has his torn-up flower stuck in the middle of the pile, like a flag stuck in the top of the king's castle.

Harp sits back down next to Joe to put his shoes back on. "Now listen, Joe, I told you to stay back by the sidewalk. You can't be following me around all the time."

Joe grins. "You were talking. You said somebody didn't have their clothes on."

"Never mind about that, Joe. It was only a dream."

Joe nods, like he understands. "I dream too, I think."

Get rid of the moron. It's better for us to be alone.

Harp stands up and dusts the back of his pants off. "I don't have time to talk about dreams now, Joe. I've got to go. I have important things to do."

Joe stares at him with his mouth wide open like it's stuck in a yawn.

"Okay. Well, bye, Joe. I'll see you later." He pats Joe on top of his head and turns away. He heads across the sand away from the ocean. He doesn't want to be mean to Joe, but he needs to be by himself to think more about that dream. Could a killer really be hiding inside a dream?

"I go with you, Harp."

Harp stops and turns around. Joe is right there. He's faster than he looks. "Now Joe, I told you I had important things to do. You have to stay here."

"Time for story now?"

No! Only one story a day. That's the rule.

Harp shakes his head. "Like I told you, Joe. Only one story a day. You have to wait until tomorrow."

"But, Harp."

Harp hurries away, trying to walk fast despite the deep sand. What time is it? The Blind Shrimp said to meet him on the pier when it got dark. But did he mean when it's just starting to get dark, like now, or when it's really dark?

"Pleeeze, Harp."

It's him again.

Harp stops again and turns back. Somehow, Joe was able to keep up. Harp puts his hands on his hips and gets a stern look on his face. "Joe, now what did I tell you?"

You'd better not let him follow you. That's the last thing you need now.

"I'm not going to tell you again, Joe. I don't want you following me."

Joe's eyes immediately fill up with tears. He doesn't say anything, but his eyes are pleading. Harp realizes he must want a story really bad. Maybe Joe's mother didn't read enough stories to him when he was little. That makes Harp feel bad. He thinks, what would my life be like if I didn't have Mother's stories in my head? How would I know anything about the way things are. I wouldn't even know about the Lord our savior, or Cock Robin, or the old lady who swallowed the bird to catch the spider to catch the fly, or baby bunting gone a-hunting, or any of the other important things. Harp relents and takes Joe's hand. "It's all right, Joe. Don't cry."

Mark my words, sooner or later that halfwit's going to get you in trouble.

Harp doesn't see any reason why Joe can't just walk along with him. He isn't hurting anything. "You can come a little ways with me, Joe. But then you have to go away. I'll tell you part of a story while we walk to the strand sidewalk. I can't tell you the whole story right now because it's a rule, only one story a day. But I can tell you the rhyme in a story. All right?"

Joe nods happily.

He leads Joe along by the hand while he tries to remember the exact words of the rhyme the bird said. Joe liked the story about the goat. Maybe he'd like one about a little bird.

Why waste your time? He won't understand it.

"It doesn't matter if he understands it or not. He'll like the story because it has a helpful bird in it."

Joe says, "A bird?"

"I wasn't talking to you, Joe. Anyhow, here's the rhyme. Now listen careful."

Joe nods his big head, grinning like he's never been happier in his life. It makes Harp think again about what Little Hilly said about being happy. He wishes Little Hilly was still alive so he could talk to him about how hard it is to be happy, even if you try.

Not that again. I've about had it with this happy, happy nonsense. You want to know something it says in the Bible? It says, Happy shall she be that taketh and dasheth thy little ones against the stones.

Harp puts his fingers in his ears. The old stories are good, but some of them are just too scary, even if they are from the Bible.

Joe looks at him and puts his fingers in his ears too.

Harp takes his fingers out of his ears and Joe does too. He grins at

Harp, still waiting for his story.

"All right, Joe, this is it. In this story, the bird has an important rhyme, so pay attention. The bird says: 'To thy death art thou sped, until God's word is said. In the water white lilies bloom. This brave boy will mark thy tomb.'"

Joe grabs both of Harp's hands and pulls him to a stop. Harp tries to shake loose, but Joe is too strong. "Let me go, Joe. I have to go meet the Blind Shrimp."

Don't tell him that. He'll go blabbing it to everyone.

But Joe won't let go. He's staring with his eyes open really wide. "Tell . . . again."

"The rhyme? Why, didn't you hear it the first time?"

Joe won't let loose of his hands.

"If I tell it to you again, will you let loose of my hands?"

Joe nods.

"All right. Here it is again. Now you have to listen more careful this time. The little bird is up on a branch over the water. He looks down at the mean sisters who are drowning the little baby and says, 'To thy death art thou sped, until God's word is said. In the water white lilies bloom, this brave boy will mark thy tomb.'"

But Joe still won't let loose of Harp's hands. He looks scared. "The baby got drowned?"

I told you he wouldn't get it. He thinks the baby got drowned.

"No, not really. But that's what they tried to do. I don't have time to tell you all the things that happened after that, Joe. I have to go meet . . . somebody at the pier. You just think about the bird's rhyme and I'll tell you the rest of the story tomorrow."

Joe must be thinking really hard because he doesn't seem to notice when Harp pulls his hands free and hurries away.

Good riddance to bad rubbish.

Harp gets to the sidewalk and heads for the pier. He hopes he isn't too late. The Shrimp promised to get him a new coat, and when it gets cold later, he's really going to need that coat.

But Harp barely even makes it to the place where the Chinese boys fly their pretty kites before Joe catches up.

Oh, no, not him again. You weren't firm enough with him. You'd better hit him.

Joe falls into step next to Harp and says, "Why?"

Harp says, "Why what?"

"Why they try drown little baby?"

Harp tries to walk even faster to get away, but Joe is a good walker even if he doesn't have bottoms in his shoes.

Harp stops again. "Listen, Joe. I don't have time to tell you the whole story right now, but it's about a king who marries a common girl, and he helps the girl's two sisters by letting them marry important men in his castle. The trouble is they never have any babies of their own so when the king's wife has a baby, they're jealous. They take her baby away while she's sleeping and go to drown it in the river."

As they walk on, Joe is silent. Harp wonders what he's thinking. Did he understand now why the bird said his poem? It's hard to tell how much Joe understands. Maybe the poem just confused him.

Of course it confused him. He doesn't have a brain in his head.

Maybe Joe is like the man who used to deliver groceries to their house when Harp was little. That man was always smiling whenever he came with the groceries. He rode an old red bicycle with a big basket on the front. Mother always called the man "Dummy." She told Harp to stay away from the Dummy. But the Dummy was nice, and once he shared a bottle of pop with Harp. It was true that man didn't understand things very well, but why should that make Mother mad at him? Harp tried to ask her about that, but she said it didn't matter if she was mean to the Dummy because he didn't know the difference. But Harp remembers that the Dummy always looked sad when Mother said mean things to him, so maybe he did understand some things after all.

Joe is staring at the ground like he's thinking really hard. Sometimes Joe seems a lot like that Dummy man, but at other times he seems to catch on right away. Maybe Joe isn't a dummy, at least not like that man who delivered groceries. Maybe Joe only gets distracted, like he's thinking about other things and doesn't always hear what you say to him.

Harp hurries on, but Joe soon catches up and taps him on the shoulder. "Harp, they shouldn't drown poor little baby."

Harp glances over and sees a tear running down Joe's cheek.

Not again. What a cry baby.

Harp reaches up to pat the big man on the shoulder. "Listen, Joe, it's all right. The little baby boy didn't get drowned. The bird flew away and found a fisherman and told him there was a wonderful fish in the water and brought him back and showed him where to cast his line. The fisherman reeled in the little baby boy and liked him so much he took him home to his wife, and they raised him up like he was their own."

Joe laughs and claps his hands together.

A woman walking in front of them turns around and frowns.

Harp stops and takes ahold of both of Joe's big arms. "Okay, Joe, now you know what the little bird did so you don't have to worry about the baby anymore. You stay here now or I'm going to have to get really mad at you."

Joe acts like he didn't hear. He's staring off toward the ocean.

"Did you hear me, Joe? I have to go to the pier now."

Joe turns to look at him. His eyes are still wet, but he's smiling. "I like it baby not drown."

"Yes," agrees Harp, "it was lucky that little bird was there so he could go tell the fisherman about what he saw. But now you have to go back. You promised you'd go away if I told you the rhyme."

Joe takes ahold of Harps arm. "Tell later?"

Harp pries Joe's big hand off his arm. "Sure I will. I'll tell you the whole story later. I'll see you after I go find . . . the person I have to go find."

Joe nods like he understands, but as Harp starts out again toward the pier, he hears Joe's gruff voice calling after him: "I think something bad should happen to those sisters."

Harp doesn't look back. He just waves his hand and keeps on going.

Good, you finally got rid of that nitwit. He'd just get in your way.

Harp feels bad Joe never got to learn the good stories when he was little. Tomorrow he'll have to be sure to remember to tell Joe about how the bad sisters get what's coming to them when the king comes to the river to go fishing and the bird is there waiting for him to tell him what happened to the little boy.

But as he walks toward the pier, Harp wonders if tomorrow Joe will even remember what the story was about. Sometimes Joe can't seem to remember things, even if he tries really hard. Harp hurries on, wondering what it would be like not to be able to remember things. That would be bad.

3-8

Watchers

As he passes the grassy picnic area, Harp sees a man and a woman having a picnic on a blanket. They have a big basket and a tall bottle of something and a dark red drink in their two glasses. They both have red and white checkered napkins tucked under their chins, and they seem very happy. There are probably some really good things to eat in that basket. It would be nice to sit down and join them.

Are you crazy? One look at you and they'd call the police.

Harp decides he'd better just keep on going.

Just beyond the picnickers, he spots Worried Jack standing by a palm tree. Jack is watching the roller skaters do their trick skating around the little red cones they put out on the bike path. "Detective Olivera said I should as questions. Maybe I should go ask Jack some questions."

No. Don't even go near that nut case.

Harp knows Jack acts very strange sometimes, but Olivera said he was supposed to ask all the homeless people questions, and he's hardly asked anybody anything.

A waste of time, if you ask me.

But maybe he doesn't have time to stop and talk to Jack. The sun has just dropped into the ocean, and the sky out in that direction is already blazing red and purple. The Shrimp said to meet him when it gets dark, but it's not what you would call really, really dark yet, so maybe I have time.

Harp heads toward Jack, but Jack sees him coming and tries to shrink down and make himself real short.

Harp says, "Hi, Jack," but Jack just slides around to the other side of the tree. Harp moves around after him and gets ahold of Jack's arm, just like Detective Olivera did to him. Jack tries to pull his arm free, but Harp holds on tight. "Listen, Jack. Don't run away. I have to ask you something important."

Worried Jack looks worried. He chews at his upper lip and looks away.

Harp shakes his finger at Jack, just like Mother would. "Now don't you worry, Jack, I'm not going to do anything bad to you. But I have to ask you some questions. I'm trying to find out who killed Little Hilly. Do you know who did it?"

Jack turns his head away, but he answers: "It wasn't me, no matter what they say."

Harp looks around and lowers his voice. "I never said it was you, Jack. But I've got to find out who it really was."

Worried Jack still won't look at him. He's watching the roller skaters do their backward skating tricks, as if what they're doing is really important to him. But maybe he's only pretending to watch. Is he hiding something? Does he have some kind of secret?

His only secret is that he's got a screw loose.

"Listen, Jack. This is important. Did you see anybody unusual around here last night?"

Jack is looking up at the sky. Harp isn't sure he even heard the question. "Listen, Jack, we have to find out who killed Little Hilly. Otherwise the police will be coming around all the time. You don't want that do you?"

Jack turns to look at Harp. His eyes seem very sad. "It doesn't matter. They'll never leave me alone anyhow."

Like I said, bats in his belfry.

Harp has seen this kind of thing from Jack before. Jack always thinks people are after him, even if they really aren't. "Now, now, Jack, I don't think the police suspect you."

"Oh yes they do. It's me they're after."

Can that be true? Should he put Jack on his suspects list? Harp tries to remember if Worried Jack ever did anything mean to anybody. The only thing he can remember is the time Jack thought the fortune-teller lady was trying to get inside his head so he tipped over her card table and spilled her cards and her magic stones all over the sidewalk. She got really mad and said he'd cracked her crystal ball so it couldn't tell the future right anymore. Could Jack get afraid like that again and maybe hurt somebody. Or kill somebody?

Harp smiles to show Jack he doesn't mean him any harm. "Now listen, Jack. I don't think the police are after you. I just want to know if you saw or heard anything last night."

"Like what?"

"Now, Jack, just let me ask the questions, okay? Did you see or hear anything last night?"

Jack looks away again. "I see a lot of things."

"Like what, Jack? What did you see?"

"I saw you. Maybe you did it."

Don't listen to this. His brain has gone haywire.

Harp touches Jack on the sleeve to show him he's being friendly. "I didn't do it, Jack. Really. I liked Little Hilly. He gave me some pizza once when I was really hungry."

"Still doesn't mean you didn't do it. Maybe you did it, and now you're trying to pin it on me."

He's nuttier than a fruitcake.

Harp is about ready to give up. First Jack wants to turn things around to be the one asking the questions, and now he's even trying to turn things around about who killed Little Hilly. "Now listen here, Jack, I didn't do it, really. Even Detective Olivera doesn't think I did it."

"That's how they fool you. They get you when your guard is down. They're only giving you enough rope to hang yourself."

"Enough rope? Oh, you mean they're trying to trick me."

"You bet. They're settin' you up to take the fall. That's how they work. Believe me, I know."

Make him stop. Next he'll be telling other people about you.

"But Jack, I didn't do it. I wouldn't do anything like that. You know me."

"Maybe I know you, and maybe I don't. Maybe you're somebody else in disguise."

"Now listen here, Jack, I'm really me, honest. You know me. Here touch my hand. It's just the regular me."

Jack cautiously touches the back of Harp's hand and then looks into his eyes. "Well, if you didn't do it, then you'd better find out who did. Or else you've had it. Take my word for it."

Jack turns away again to watch the skaters. One of them falls down, and Jack takes in a big breath and claps his hands once. Harp wonders why Jack is so happy about a skater falling down.

Harp thinks about Jack's suspecting him. Would people really think he did it?

Don't pay any attention to him. He's loony.

Maybe he is loony, but couldn't he be right? Maybe the police are just giving me enough rope to hang myself.

Didn't I already tell you to stop thinking thoughts like that? Get away from this screwball.

Harp remembers there were men like Jack on Ward D-4, men who thought everybody was out to get them. Some of them even heard things and saw things in the air. Harp learned that those men might seem okay most of the time, but sometimes they got nervous and then you had to watch out. Maybe Jack was like that too. Maybe he could kill somebody if he got too nervous. Harp tries to think of something calming to say. "It's going to be a nice day, isn't it, Jack?"

Jack shrugs. "Maybe it is, maybe it isn't."

Can't you see this guy's lost all his marbles? Isn't there somewhere you're supposed to be?

Harp is ready to give up. "Listen, Jack, we have to find out where Big Hilly is. Otherwise Olivera said they might run us all in."

Jack shakes his head sadly. "They already know where he is."

"Why do you say that, Jack?"

"Cause they do. They know where everybody is."

Harp looks around to be sure nobody is listening. The usual Sunday off-beachers are going by, but nobody is close enough to hear anything. That's good.

"Listen, Jack. If they know where Big Hilly is, why don't they just go get him?"

"They have their reasons."

Harp is beginning to think this is a waste of time.

Finally he figures out it's a waste of time. Let's go.

But Olivera said I was supposed to talk to people. He said to ask around. If only he knew how hard it was.

Move it!

Harp starts to leave, but this time it's Jack that gets ahold of his sleeve and pulls him back. "Listen, Harp," he whispers, "can I trust you?"

"Uh, sure. Why not?"

Jack stares at him, and Harp can see how worried Jack really is. He's got big wrinkles across his forehead and a real worried look on his face. Harp wonders if maybe somebody hurt Jack real bad, sometime in the past maybe. It makes him feel bad for Jack, for anybody who's been hurt like that. Harp knows what it's like to be hurt.

Oh, so what? Whine, whine, whine. You were never hurt all that bad.

Jack leans closer and whispers, "They put a . . . special device in here." He taps the side of his head with his finger.

Now it's secret devices. What next?

Harp looks closely at the place Jack is pointing to. "Really?"

"Yes. It's very small, but I can feel it in there. They use it to listen to what I say."

Harp leans closer. "Are they listening to what we're saying right now?" Harp thinks if the police really could hear what they were saying at least it would prove to Detective Olivera that he was asking questions like he was supposed to.

You think the police can hear you through his head? You're getting as nutty as he is.

Harp is pretty sure Jack can't really have a device like that inside his head. He doesn't even have a scar where they put it in.

Suddenly, Jack grabs ahold of the front of Harp's shirt and pulls him close. He whispers, "Don't worry, Harp, I turned it off." He glances around, and then he lets go of Harp's shirt and taps on the side of his head again. "I know how to get my brain to work in advanced thought. That turns it off."

"You can turn it off?"

"It's not easy, but I learned how to do it. It makes them really mad, so I can't do it very often. If I do it too often they'll think it's broke and come looking for me so they can fix it."

What a dingbat.

Harp is pretty sure Jack isn't telling the truth. Even if they could do something like that, it would be really expensive. So why would they want to do something so expensive to a homeless person's head? Why would they bother? Harp doubts the police would even care about what homeless people talk about.

"I know what you're thinking, Harp."

"You do?"

"Yes, you're thinking why don't I just cut it out and throw it away. Well, I'll tell you. The device may be bad, but sometimes I can use it for good." He leans closer. "It lets me read other people's minds."

"So you're reading my mind? Right now?" Harp quickly starts thinking about good things to eat, like nice red apples, just to test him.

To test him? I can't decide which one of you is crazier.

Jack smiles, nodding his head. "Yep, I know exactly what you're thinking. You're wondering how they can track me? How do they know where I am? Well, I'll tell you. It's done with rockets."

"Rockets?"

"That's right. They use rockets to send a secret machine up into space. You know that rocket the Russians sent up with that dog in it? It's like that, except this time they sent up a machine that sits up there in the sky just to watch me."

Harp glances up at the sky. "It can see you from way up there?"

Look closer. Maybe you'll see the Easter Bunny up there.

Jack nods his head over and over again, getting more and more excited. "Yes, it really can. It has very powerful telescopes in it. Now you're thinking why don't I just hide under the pier so it can't see me, but they've got that figured out too." He put his hands over his ears. "Radio waves," he whispers. "The device gives out radio waves. It comes out of my ears. They do it that way so they can track people even when they're inside a house, or under the pier."

We've got better things to do than stand here listening to this nonsense. It's getting dark. The killer is out there somewhere looking for you.

Harp decides it's time to move on. Jack hadn't even guessed he was thinking about nice red apples. But thinking about food reminds Harp he's still hungry. "Maybe I should go back and check out the dumpsters on the pier again."

Here we go again. Always thinking of yourself.

"Dumpsters?"

"Never mind, Jack. I wasn't talking to you."

"Oh, do you do that too? Who do you talk to?"

Like I said, he's a basket case. Ignore him.

Harp pats Jack on the arm. "That's too bad about your head, Jack. But if you hear anything inside there about what happened to Little Hilly, you let me know, okay?"

Jack looks away. "Maybe. It depends."

Harp starts to ask him what it depends on, but decides that's probably what Jack wants him to ask. Sometimes when you finally got Jack going, it was hard to shut him off again. Besides, Harp knows he should be getting on to meet the Shrimp at the pier.

He leaves Worried Jack there by his tree and hurries toward the pier thinking about secret machines and radio waves. Worried Jack sure believes some strange things. Maybe he hears worrisome voices in his head, like some of the men on Ward D-4 did. But there is one thing Worried Jack said that really is worth worrying about, that part about Detective Olivera giving him enough rope. Was it possible? Could Olivera be trying to trick him?

Don't I always say you can't trust anybody? Trust only me and everything will be fine.

But wait a minute, the police don't have any reason to suspect him, not really. Detective Olivera even asked him to help solve the case. "If Olivera suspected me, he wouldn't have asked me to help find the killer, would he? No, Olivera can't suspect me. We're almost like . . . like partners, working together to find the real murderer."

Partners. Ha!

Harp thinks about what he's going to tell Olivera the next time he sees him. So far he hasn't even started to narrow down his list of suspects. Olivera won't like that. He'll want results. It means he's going to have to work harder. He'd better look at his list and really start to think like a smart person.

If only you could.

Harp stops and sits on a bench. Maybe he should add Worried Jack's name to his list. Then Olivera will see he really has been asking questions and getting new suspects all the time. He writes:

Worried Jack - Thinks he has device in head so they can watch him. But he probably doesn't.

While he's got his diary out, he looks at the list again. Big Hilly, the Devil worshippers, Tex, Speel, and Worried Jack. And Big Nose. Wait a minute. Everybody on the list has a real name except for Big Nose. Who is Big Nose? And why is he hanging around the beach? Is he still pretending to panhandle next to the Sunnysidewalk Café? Harp wonders if maybe he should go there and see.

You're supposed to be going to meet that Shrimp character.

"Yes, but not until after dark. It's dark, but not completely dark. Not yet. There's still time before I have to go meet the Shrimp."

I give up. I might as well be talking to myself.

Harp puts away his diary and starts up the strand toward the Sunnysidewalk Café. Now that it's getting dark, there aren't as many off-beachers on the strand, and the ones that are there are mostly teenagers. Harp has watched those young people many times. They come out after dark to look for partners, boys looking for girls, mostly. They seem to really enjoy it.

Pleasure seekers, time wasters, sex maniacs. The Devil take them all.

Harp decides not to look at those young people anymore, but he doesn't think they're sex maniacs. At least not all of them. Some of them are probably just looking for friends to be with.

Are you contradicting me?

He doesn't have time to think about sex maniacs right now. There's a killer on the loose, and Olivera expects him to find out who it is.

When he makes it back to the Rolling Skate Rental stand, Harp peeks through the racks of roller skates to see if Big Nose is still there next to the Sunnysidewalk Café. He is, and he's still wearing his dark sunglasses, even though it's getting really dark. Big Nose has moved back against the building, into the shadows. He's not even trying to panhandle anymore. He still has his paper cup in his hand, but he's not holding it out anymore. He seems to be talking to himself. Maybe standing there all day and not getting anybody to give him money has made him go crazy.

Look closer. Somebody else is there.

But wait. He *is* talking to somebody. There seems to be somebody there in the shadows with him.

Harp cuts across the sidewalk and goes out to the bike path. From there he might be able to see who's hiding in the shadows with Big Nose.

Careful, careful. Don't let them see you.

He darts across the bike path and a man on a bike almost hits him. The man calls him dirty names, like they always do, but Harp doesn't care about that; the important thing is to get to the nearest palm tree so he can hide.

He makes it and ducks behind the tree. He peeks out. There is somebody with Big Nose, but Harp can't see his face. Whoever he is, he's not very tall. He's kind of wide, and he's wearing a suit.

Is it a brown suit?

It is brown. A wide man wearing a brown suit.

Then you know who it is. Think.

That suit, that square face. Harp suddenly realizes who it is. It's Detective Olivera. But why is he hiding over there in the shadows? And why is he talking to Big Nose? Is Big Nose helping the Olivera too?

Harp decides he'd better get out of there before Olivera spots him and starts asking what he's found out. As he hurries away, he realizes that if Big Nose is working for the police he might as well cross him right off his suspects list. But wait. Just because Olivera was talking to Big Nose, does it mean for sure that he's not a suspect? Maybe he is a suspect and that's why Olivera is talking to him. It's hard to know these things for sure.

Harp notices a chill in the air. Uh oh. The sun is completely gone now, and the fog is starting to come in. That means it will be getting cold again. He hopes the Shrimp wasn't lying about getting him a warm coat.

He'd better not be lying. If he is, he'll answer to me.

As Harp passes the beachside parking lot, he notices Paddy's little wooden Poochmobile where he sells hot dogs to the people who pass by. Harp's stomach reminds him that he hasn't had anything to eat since he was at the Unitarian Church, and that was this morning. A long time ago.

Harp stops to stare at the funny painting of a dog Paddy put on the front of his Poochmobile. It reminds Harp of that bad painting of a dog that was on Betty's wall, but Paddy's dog painting is much nicer. It's silly looking, with long floppy ears and a big red tongue hanging out, and on the other end of the Poochmobile there's a big fake hot dog for a tail. It looks kind of dumb, but boy, that picture of the big fat hot dog in a bun above Paddy's window sure looks good. A person with money could walk right up there and buy one. But wait, I still have Little Hilly's dollars in my pocket. "Should I use one of my dollars to buy a hot dog?"

Go ahead. It's your money now.

Harp checks to make sure the dollar bills are still safe in his pocket. Sure enough, they are all there, the three he found in Little Hilly's pocket, and there's another dollar besides, the one The Amazing Cedric gave him to help him fix his chainsaw.

Harp goes closer and looks at Paddy's list of prices. A hot dog is only one dollar.

He makes a decision. He waits until there are no people around and then goes up to the window.

"Well, if it isn't little Harp," says Paddy. "What can I do you for?"

"I'd like a hot dog please."

"You bet. Coming right up. You want mustard and catchup on that?"

"Uh, does it cost extra?"

Paddy grins and wipes the back of his neck with a dirty towel. "For you, no extra charge."

Paddy puts the hot dog in a bun, squeezes out a lot of mustard and catchup on top of the hot dog, and holds it out to Harp.

But when Harp reaches for it, Paddy pulls it back. Harp wishes he would have grabbed the hot dog when he had the chance. He can't take his eyes off of it. His mouth is getting really wet inside just looking at it.

"That'll be one dollar, young feller. You do have a dollar, don't you?"

"Yes, I do, Paddy." Harp turns his back and takes the four

wadded-up dollars out of his pocket. He doesn't want Paddy to see the three dollars he got from Little Hilly because he's not sure if they have blood on them. He'd better use the one he got from The Amazing Cedric. But how do I tell which one that is? Can Paddy tell what blood on money looks like?

Harp chooses the cleanest looking dollar and turns back to hand it over to Paddy.

Paddy takes the dollar and looks at it. Is he looking for blood? He still doesn't hand over the hot dog. Harp's mouth is making so much water he has to swallow twice.

Paddy straightens out the dollar bill and puts it in his box. He turns back to Harp. "Well now, looks like you're in the chips today, son. How about a nice Coke to go with this here dog?"

"No, thank you, Paddy. I can get a drink of water at the fountain." Harp turns to point to the water fountain. But he quickly turns back to make sure Paddy hasn't taken the hot dog away.

Paddy hasn't taken it away, but he's still holding it back. "Too bad about what happened to your little pal last night. That Mexican cop, Olivera, came by today asking a lot of questions. He was asking about you. Any reason he was doing that, son?"

Keep your mouth shut.

Harp shakes his head and stares at the ground.

"So you don't know anything about it?"

Don't answer. Don't even look at him.

Harp shakes his head again. He doesn't want to look Paddy in the eye because he's not sure what Paddy would see in there. He wishes Paddy would just hand over his hot dog and let him go on his way.

"Well, it's no skin off my nose what you people do. I didn't say nuthin' to Olivera, if that's what you're worried about. I just sell hot dogs." He holds out the hot dog.

Get out of here. Fast!

Harp grabs the hot dog and hurries away. He heads toward the pier, thinking about what Paddy said. Why was Olivera asking questions about him? Was Olivera checking up on him, making sure he was asking everybody else questions? Harp hopes that's all it was.

As he walks, he holds the hot dog carefully, making sure it doesn't slip out of it's little paper holder. When he's far enough away from

Paddy's Poochmobile, he slows down and takes a bite off the end of the hot dog. He eats slowly, thoroughly chewing as mother always said he should, enjoying every bite before he swallows it down. He stops at the drinking fountain and takes a long drink. Mother always said he should drink water while eating, and that he should make sure he eats with his mouth closed.

But the hot dog is gone too soon. Now he wishes he would have eaten it even slower. He licks the paper clean and throws it away in one of the "Keep Our Beaches Clean" garbage cans.

You forgot to say your prayers before eating. You've been forgetting the important things today. What's the matter with you?

Uh, oh. I did forget to say the special before-eating prayer. She's right, I have been forgetting important things like that. It must be because of what happened to Little Hilly. Since then, the whole day has been messed up.

Then do it. Right now!

He stops right in the middle of the sidewalk and folds his hands. "Our Heavenly Father, kind and good, we thank Thee for this tasty food. Please clean from it the bad dirt and germs. In Jesus's name, this I pray. Amen."

That's better. From now on, I expect you to start doing things right.

Harp remembers how important Mother said the eating prayer was. And if he'd been bad, she'd add the other special words to the prayer: "I know you are present at this table watching us, dear Lord, and I know you will punish any child here who is not reverent while eating." But Harp knows he doesn't need to add that part because he isn't at a table, and besides maybe you didn't have to be as reverent if it was only a hot dog you were eating and you were already finished eating it anyhow.

Are you being a smart-Alec?

Harp hurries on, grinning slyly to himself.

3-9
Reward and Punishment

When Harp gets to the pier, he doesn't see the Shrimp anywhere. Maybe he's waiting farther out on the pier.

Don't go out there. People will be suspicious of you.

Harp decides he better not go farther out on the pier to where the fisherpeople are fishing. Maybe they'll remember me from this morning when Olivera was talking to me. "I'd better just wait by the stairs until the Shrimp comes."

Good boy. Now you've got your thinking cap on.

He puts one foot up on the lowest part of the old wooden railing and leans on his knee, looking out at the ocean. He wonders why the ocean gets so restless and moody right after the sun goes down. It's like it's afraid of the night coming on, like everybody else is.

But then he looks down and notices the dark spots on his shoes. "Uh oh, why didn't I wash them when I had the chance?"

The cops came. Remember, you always have to be on the lookout for cops.

"Oh, that's right. Those two bicycle cops came, and they saw me washing my coat. That was bad luck."

That wasn't just bad luck. They were watching you.

But maybe police-type people are always there, always watching. Mother warned me about staying away from people because they might be working for the police.

Harp uses his sleeve to try to wipe his shoes off, but the spots won't go away. Maybe he should go back to that drinking fountain and try to clean them.

You should have thought of that before. Why can't you do anything right?

Now that he looks at his shoes again, he notices the laces aren't quite right. He reties them twice, making sure they look exactly the same. That's better. But maybe he should retie them once more, just to be sure.

Stop that. Didn't I warn you about doing things over and over again?

Harp decides not to retie them again. He knows his little habit of wanting everything to be perfect used to irritate Mother. She always said it made him seem nutty when he'd do things over too many times. But why should she care if he wanted his bed made nice and neat without a single wrinkle and with the blanket hanging down just the perfect length from the floor on all sides? There *was* an exactly right way to do it, so why not do it until you got it exactly right? It was more relaxing when everything was done right. On Ward D-4, Mitch punished anybody who didn't make his bed exactly the right way every morning. And if they were too crazy to do it right, Mitch told Harp to do it for them. Pretty soon they all wanted Harp to make their beds because he knew how to make every bed perfect, every one of them exactly the same. The right way. The perfect way. What was wrong with that?

I'll tell you what's wrong with it. It makes you look like a nut.

He looks around. Nobody is watching him, so they can't think he's doing anything wrong. He decides to retie his shoes just one more time to be sure.

I give up. You are hopeless.

When he's finished with the retying, Harp forces himself to stop looking at his still-not-quite-perfect shoelaces. He looks around for the Shrimp. There's still no sign of him. "Maybe I *should* go farther out on the pier and look for him."

No! Don't attract attention to yourself.

Harp decides it would be better to stay where he is, out of sight. But he can hear the nice music coming from the merry-go-round. Maybe he should go see if the Shrimp is at the merry-go-round.

No! There will be people there. Stay away from people.

It would be fun to watch the kids go round and round sitting on the painted horses.

Didn't I just say no? Stay where you are and wait.

"But that merry-go-round music is really nice. I'll just go and watch for a minute and come right back."

Why do I waste my breath on you?

He heads slowly in the direction of the music, staying in the shadows to be sure nobody is noticing him.

But then he spots a quarter next to a trash can. He quickly moves to it and steps on it. He waits, looking around to see if anybody is acting like they lost a quarter. Some of the off-beachers are passing by, heading out onto the pier. Nobody seems to notice him, and nobody seems to be looking down at the ground like they've lost anything. When they've all gone by, he bends down and grabs the quarter.

"What'd you find? Money?"

Harp spins around. It's the Blind Shrimp, standing right behind him. Harp says, "Where did you come from, Shrimp?"

The Shrimp taps the pavement with his cane. It makes an irritated sound on the old wood of the pier. "I must have missed that money," he complains. "You good-eyes always get the money."

Harp feels sorry for the Shrimp. Nobody likes him, probably because he complains all the time. It must be hard tapping your way all over the place and not being able to see so good. Harp holds out the quarter. "Here, you can have it."

Don't give it to him. Finders keepers.

"Naw," says the Shrimp, waving it off. "I don't need it. I had a good day. Did you see that bus load of church people?"

Harp shakes his head.

"There was this yellow bus, see. Side of the bus had the name of some church on it. A woman off that bus gave me a reward for finding her camera."

"You found her camera?"

"Yep. It was on a bench with some other stuff."

He stole it.

"Did you steal it?"

"Naw, I didn't steal it. Not really. Anyhow, it was her own fault. She put it down on that bench while she fed the seagulls. If I hadn't found it, somebody would have stole it for real, and she'd of never got it back."

"So you gave it back to her."

"Sure, I'm an honest person, aren't I?" The Shrimp smiles and looks up toward the sky. Then he takes Harp's arm and leads him along the rail toward a more secluded spot. He leans closer and whispers, "You shoulda seen her, Harp. She had everybody on the bus looking all over the pier. She even called in the security guys who pretended to look in a few trash cans before they shrugged and gave up and went back to watching the pretty girls."

Behind the Shrimp, Harp watches three pelicans rise up and over the pier before they disappear back into the darkness out over the moody ocean. Pelicans are lucky. They can go anywhere they want to.

The Shrimp turns to see what Harp is looking at. "Birds," he says. He frowns and pulls at Harp's sleeve to get his attention back. "So here I come, tapping my cane on the sidewalk real loud like. 'Anybody here lose a camera?' I'm sayin'. 'Found this here camera.' The lady said she didn't have much money for a reward and tried to give me a lousy dollar, but when I acted real upset about it and told them how bad I needed money seeing as how my eyes are no good, and the doctors say it will cost a lot of money to fix them. I said I could have taken the camera to a pawn shop and got a lot of money for it. Finally, her friends managed to cough up some dough."

I le's a thief. Didn't I tell you? Watch yourself.

Harp knows taking that lady's camera wasn't a very nice thing to do, but at least she got her camera back. Still, it meant he'd better be careful around the Shrimp. "You said to meet you here, Shrimp. What was it you wanted me to help you do?"

"Just come along with me, old pal. I'll explain it on the way." The Shrimp takes Harp's arm and pulls him along.

Don't go with him. Remember what the Bible said about associating with evildoers.

Harp allows himself to be pulled along for a bit, but then he stops. "You said you had a way to get me a warm coat. Were you telling me a fib?"

The Shrimp looks like his feelings are hurt. He points to himself. "Me? Tell you a lie? Do I look like a liar?"

That's what we said, buster, a big fat liar.

Harp doesn't say anything. He knows it's another one of those questions people ask when they didn't really want an answer.

"I think you'd wanna come along with me, Harp. I got something important to tell ya."

"What?"

"Walk along with me and I'll tell ya."

He's trying to lead you astray.

Harp allows the Shrimp to lead him on for a ways, but he's determined not to walk very fast.

The Shrimp taps his cane back and forth on the sidewalk as they go. "You know, Harp, I heard you were goin' around asking people questions. Why is that?"

Harp shrugs. "No reason."

"Well, you asked me a question. Want to ask it again?"

"What question was it?"

"The question you were asking everybody. Didn't you want to ask me if I heard anything last night?"

"Oh, yes. Did you?"

"Maybe."

"What does that mean, Shrimp? Did you or not?"

"I hear lots of things. I get around, and I see things, in a manner of speaking. Did you know when a person loses one of his senses, like his eyesight, the other senses get a lot better?"

What a joke. He's no more blind than I am.

"Uh, no, I didn't know that, Shrimp. But are you saying you heard something last night?"

"I sure did. And I bet you wanna know what it was."

"Yes, I do, Shrimp. What did you hear?"

"Would you give me that quarter if I told you?"

Don't give it to him. It's yours.

Harp didn't even realize he was still holding the quarter. He looks down at it. It's only a quarter. He's got three more quarters in his pocket, Little Hilly's quarters, and three dollars and a dime besides. He hands the quarter to the Shrimp.

The Shrimp puts it in his pocket and says, "Okay, here's what I heard. I heard a dog howling."

Now Harp knows other people heard that dog howling. Detective Olivera would be proud of him for asking the right questions. "You heard a dog, Shrimp? Where were you?"

"Well, never mind where I was. What's important is where the dog was. He was on the beach, not too far from this very pier. And guess what else?"

"What?"

"The dog stopped howling. Real sudden like."

"Real sudden?"

"Yep. Like somebody made it stop. You know what I mean?"

Harp does know what he means. It's just like that bad picture of the dog on Betty's wall. Somebody must have stopped him from howling by stabbing him with a cross-knife. Poor little dog.

"That got your attention, didn't it?" says the Shrimp. "I heard you'd been asking a bunch of questions about what anybody saw or heard last night. I found out something good for you, didn't I?"

Harp nods. Maybe the Shrimp really did have especially good hearing. Nobody else had heard the howling dog, or at least they didn't say so. Shoeless Joe might have heard it too, but it was hard to tell what Joe might have heard and what he didn't.

"So now I done you a favor. You have to do one for me."

A favor he says. More likely he's looking for a patsy.

"Well, maybe. What do you want me to do?"

Have you gone deaf? What did I just say?

"Nuthin' much. Just go along with me for a little while."

"Well, okay. But where are we going? Is it to a place where you can get me a coat?"

"Damn, Harp, you sure ask a lot of questions. Just come along now, and we'll see about getting you a coat later."

Harp allows the Shrimp to take his arm and pull him along. The Shrimp taps his white cane really fast as they go over the bridge that leads off the pier to the busy city street.

Fine. So go then. If you're so bound and determined to get yourself in a jam, go.

Harp follows along as the Shrimp taps his way toward the downtown area. He's glad the Shrimp is going to help him get a coat. Now that it's dark and the fog is coming in off the ocean, it's starting to get really cold again. The wind cuts right through his thin little shirt.

The Shrimp pulls at his arm. "C'mon, Harp, quit dawdling."

Harp matches the Shrimp's pace, but he wonders why the Shrimp won't say where they're going.

Because he doesn't want you to know he's going to get you in big trouble.

Harp worries that the Shrimp is going to do something illegal. It wasn't very nice of the Shrimp to take that lady's camera, and maybe he's planning something else like that again. It makes Harp nervous. Just going away from the ocean into the city makes him nervous. He begins to count his steps so he knows how far they've gone. He already knows how many steps it takes to get most places, but it can't hurt to count them again. When you don't know where you're going, it's good to know exactly how many steps it will take to get back.

If you'd of listened to me, you wouldn't have got yourself into this situation in the first place.

"We got to stop at the Corner Market," says the Shrimp.

That cheers Harp up. "Are we going to get something to eat?"

"That's right, something to eat. But not for us." The Shrimp continues to pull Harp along, tapping loudly with his cane to move the people on the sidewalk out of his way.

Harp isn't sure what the Shrimp meant by getting food that wasn't for them, but his stomach is not happy about it. It's been a while since he finished that hot dog, and his stomach is beginning to say it's time for something else. He's still got that one old dry piece of bread stashed away in his pocket, but he hoped he could save that for a midnight snack. He can't help but wonder why the Shrimp would be going to the market to buy food for somebody else. It didn't make sense.

He doesn't make sense? What about you? Does anything you do make sense?

At the market, the Shrimp tells Harp to wait out front while he goes inside. Harp waits like he's told, but he doesn't like standing out there where everybody can see him. He tries pacing back and forth, and that helps, but only a little. At least the walking back and forth keeps him a little bit warmer. Now that the night has come it's getting colder and colder. He's really missing his jacket now, and he thinks about it hanging somewhere at the police station. "Will the police give it back to me when they're done with it?"

Fat chance. I told you, it's evidence. They're going to use it against you.

"What will they do if they find Little Hilly's blood on it?"

What do you think they'll do? They'll come after you.

The more he thinks about it, the more that blood on his jacket worries him. Maybe he should have thrown it away in that big pile of trash where the mice live.

About time you figured that out.

The Shrimp comes back out of the market holding a brown paper bag.

"Is that the food?" asks Harp.

"Never you mind about what's in the bag," says the Shrimp. "But wait 'til you see what this little bit of yummy treat can get us. Come on, let's go."

Harp still can't figure out what the Shrimp is up to. Yummy treat? But if it's so yummy, why don't they stop and eat it?

The Shrimp walks pretty fast for a little guy, and he keeps the pressure on Harp's arm to pull him along. When they get to the downtown area, they pass closed-up stores, and some of them have clothes in the window. Harp looks into every window, hoping one of them might be selling nice warm coats. But whenever he slows down to look, the Shrimp pulls him along faster.

Face it, he's not looking for a coat. He's up to something.

In the middle of a block, the Shrimp stops to wait for a man to pass. The man has a dog on the end of a long leash, and for some reason, the dog gets interested in what's in the Shrimp's paper bag. The Shrimp holds the bag up high and fends him off with his cane. "Control your dog, mister. Can't you see you got a handicapped person here?"

The man pulls his dog away, and the Shrimp waits until the man has gone on before he pulls Harp into an alley.

"Why are we going in here?" Harp whispers.

The Shrimp doesn't answer. He just goes on into the alley, pulling Harp along.

Harp doesn't like being in that alley one bit. The farther in they go the darker it gets.

Now see where he's taking you. I warned you.

Harp remembers being in an alley once. It was when he first came to the beach. He went into an alley looking for food, and there were men in there, sitting against a wall, passing around a bottle. They yelled for him to come join them, but Harp was afraid and ran away. From then on he stayed out of alleys.

Harp stops. "I don't like it in here, Shrimp."

"Keep quiet." The Shrimp says it so sharp and mean, it makes Harp worry even more. If they aren't going to do anything bad, then why is the Shrimp saying they have to be so quiet? It gives him that bad old tight feeling in his throat.

Well, you got yourself into this mess. There's no use getting all nervous now. Think about something else.

He tries to think of nicer things, but his throat is still too tight. He tries to clear it, and the Shrimp says, "Shh."

Harp tries to clear his throat again, and this time the Shrimp stops and looks at him. "What's the matter with you, Harp?" he whispers. "You got a frog in your throat?"

Harp shrugs and tries to not to think about having a frog inside his throat. It reminds him of a story Mother once told him about a frog that wanted to turn into a prince. When the poor little thing tried to crawl into bed with the king's daughter, she threw it against a wall. The princess said, 'You're cold and icky, even if you are a prince in disguise.'

Princess, princess, open the door for me. Dost thou not know what thou saidst to me yesterday by the cool waters of the fountain?

Harp thought it was only fair that the king made the selfish girl keep her promise to the frog and let it sleep in her bed. That way, once the frog was in bed with her, it could . . .

"Wake up, Harp. Are you listening to me?" The Shrimp is staring at him.

"No, I don't have a frog in my throat. I'd like to go back to the beach now."

"We'll head back there in a few minutes. I've got somethin' to do first." The Shrimp puts his white cane on his shoulder and pulls Harp deeper into the alley. It's so dark Harp can hardly see anything, but the Shrimp seems to know where he's going even without using his cane.

With what little light is coming from the streetlight at the end of the alley, Harp can see that all of the dumpsters in the alley are overflowing, and the whole place smells bad. The Shrimp finally stops, but it's right next to a really smelly dumpster. Harp holds his nose, but even with his nose pinched off, he can still tell the dumpster smells like rotten food. Not only that, but the whole area around it smells like dog poop.

"This is it," whispers the Shrimp.

He pulls Harp behind the smelly dumpster to look at a wooden door that has some letters printed on it, but it's too dark to read what the letters say.

Harp pulls at the Shrimp's arm. "Let's go, Shrimp. There's nobody here."

"That's the idea," whispers the Shrimp. "It's Sunday, remember?" Then he gets down on his knees in front of the door. "Look at this."

Harp stoops down next to him and sees there's another little door in the bottom of the big door. The Shrimp pushes at the bottom of the little door, and it swings in.

"A tiny little door," says Harp. He's never seen a cute little door like that before.

"Yeah, it's a doggy door. But be quiet." The Shrimp leans his cane up against the side of the brick wall and reaches into the paper bag. He pulls out a hot dog and hands it to Harp. "If the dog comes out, feed him this wiener so he won't start barking."

You're afraid of dogs. You hate dogs.

"A dog? What dog?"

"It's just an ordinary dog. No big deal. Anyhow, I'll take the rest of the hot dogs to keep him from coming out so you don't have to worry. I'm going inside, now. You wait here."

Before Harp can answer, the Shrimp pushes his head through the little door.

Harp touches the Shrimp's back. "Uh, how do you know the dog likes wieners?"

The Shrimp pulls his head back out. "Shh. He might be asleep." He sticks his head back inside.

Didn't I tell you? He's up to no good.

Harp remembers something Mother told him once: "Let sleeping dogs lie." He touches the Shrimp's back again. "Uh, Shrimp. I think we should let the dog keep on sleeping."

The Shrimp pulls his head back out. He looks angry. "Now don't go getting cold feet, Harp. I know what I'm doing." He sticks his head back in.

Harp does have cold feet. In fact, every part of him is cold. But he knows that's not what the Shrimp means. Having cold feet means being afraid, and he is afraid.

It's too late for regrets now. I warned you, but you wouldn't listen.

He taps the Shrimp on the back again. "I want to leave now, Shrimp."

The Shrimp pulls his head back out. This time he stands up and grabs the front of Harp's shirt. "Don't flake out on me now, damn it. I been scouting out this place for weeks. All you got to do is keep watch and let me know if anybody comes. And like I said, if the damn dog comes out, give him some of that wiener."

"But maybe he doesn't like wieners. What if he tries to bite me?"

The Shrimp lets loose of Harp's shirt and smoothes it down. He pats Harp on the chest. "Believe me, he likes wieners. I been giving him wieners for weeks to get him used to me. If he comes out, just give him little bites of it, and don't let him start barking."

"How should I keep him from barking?"

"Like I said, feed him the wiener."

Take my advice and run away. Right now!

Harp is pretty sure the best thing would be to leave right now, but he can't stop thinking about that warm coat. Are there warm coats in there? He's feeling very nervous, and his throat is feeling tight again. He tries not to think about frogs.

Right. Don't think about frogs, think about how much trouble you're going to be in if anybody sees you.

The Shrimp sits on the ground and flips over onto his back. He begins to slither in through the doggy door, head first. Harp watches, amazed that the Shrimp is able to wiggle through such a tiny little opening. Harp is small too, but he doesn't think he could ever get through a teeny little door like that.

The Shrimp's feet disappear, and the little door is left swinging. Harp feels very alone in that dark alley.

Hey! Are you listening to me? It's like I'm not even here.

Harp doesn't have time to listen to anything. What if the dog comes out? He bends over and holds the wiener out toward the little door. What if it's a big dog? Maybe it's a big mean dog.

Hark, hark the dogs do bark, the beggars are coming to town.

Not that old rhyme. Right now, any rhyme about the beggars coming to town and dogs barking at them seems scary. What if the dog thinks he's a beggar and comes out to bite him?

So, get out of here.

"But should I run away without waiting for the Shrimp?"

Forget him. Now's your chance to get away.

He looks down the dark alley back toward the main street. He really wants to go back out there, out of the dark and smelly alley, but it wouldn't be very nice to leave without telling the Shrimp.

What do you care what he thinks? He's the one who got you into this.

He looks at the Shrimp's white cane leaning up against the wall. It must be bad to have to tap your way everywhere with a cane like that. He picks up the cane and closes his eyes. He taps it on the pavement to see what it's like to be blind, but it makes too much noise so he puts it back where it was.

He peeks around the dumpster to make sure nobody heard. The alley is still quiet and empty. "What if somebody comes? What if a police car comes?"

Then you'd be in for it.

The Shrimp said I was supposed to let him know if anybody comes, but how can I do that?

Should I open the little door and yell for the Shrimp to come out? But what if the mean dog is waiting inside, ready to bite my nose?

Don't worry about your nose. Worry about getting locked up in jail.

He goes back and leans down by the little doggy door, holding out the wiener. He wishes the Shrimp would hurry up. What's he doing in there for so long?

What do you think he's doing? He's stealing something.

Now that he thinks about it, Harp is pretty sure the Shrimp isn't in there getting him a coat because the Shrimp said he'd been scouting this place out for weeks, before he even knew Harp needed a coat. The Shrimp said he'd get some money to buy Harp a new coat. It means the Shrimp is probably in there stealing money.

Finally he gets it.

"I should have never let the Shrimp talk me into this. It makes me feel dumb when people talk me into things."

It is dumb to let people take advantage of you. If I've told you that once, I've told you that a thousand times.

"Does the Shrimp think I'm dumb? Probably. Some other people probably do too."

Face it, my boy. Not everybody can be a genius.

"But I don't feel dumb. I got good grades that time I was in school, especially in story writing. The teacher said I was good at making up stories." The more Harp thinks about it, he wonders if maybe he could be like the boy in the story who shared his food with the little grey man. The other people thought that boy was dumb to share his food with a beggar, but he got rewarded for his kindness in the end when the little grey man knew where to find the golden goose.

If only you could have turned out more like that boy and made something of yourself.

Harp decides not to think about being smart anymore. A waste of time. And this whole thing of standing in an alley waiting for the Shrimp is a waste of time too. His arm is getting tired from holding out the wiener for so long. He wishes the Shrimp would hurry up. He's just about ready to take a chance and stick his head into the doggy door to see what's going on in there when the Shrimp's head pops out. "Give me your wiener. I ran out. The damn dog is starving."

"But what if the dog comes out? I won't have anything to give him."

"He's not coming out. He's happy in here, as long as I keep feeding him. Just give me the damn wiener."

Harp hands it to him, and the Shrimp's head disappears back inside.

Harp looks down the dark alley. He tries to tell himself there is nothing to be afraid of. If the police come, he can just run away. He's always been good at running, even when he was little. It's too bad he never got to go out and play with the other kids. He could have shown them how fast he could run.

Is it my fault that they didn't want to play with you? If you didn't always act so weird, maybe somebody would have chosen you for their team.

"Nuh-uh, it was because you never let me go out and play with the other kids so I never learned how to play their games."

Are you disagreeing with me?

"You were the one who made me stop going to school. You lied and told them I was going to a special school, but I wasn't. I wasn't going to any school at all."

So what? You were better off not going to that evil school.

"All I got to do was stay inside and cook for you and make sure you got all your medicines."

I'm not listening to this.

"Well, it's true."

Stop talking out loud to me. Someone will hear you.

Harp remembers that Mother took a lot of different kinds of medicine from doctors, and she also had her bottles of special medicine that Harp had to go pick up from the man at the liquor store. The man would put her medicine in a plain brown paper bag and say, "Here's your mother's special medicine, Harp, now don't you be taking any sips on your way home. Harp never once took a test sip on the way home, but one night she fell asleep in the bathtub while he was bathing her, and he had to take the glass out of her hand. That time he did try just a little teeny taste. It tasted so terrible he never did it again.

I should have known you'd be up to no good when I wasn't looking. I'm going to have to punish you for that.

The Shrimp's head pokes out of the doggy door. He pushes the brown paper bag out. It looks like it's full of something. "Here, grab this."

Look inside the bag. Maybe it's money.

Harp picks up the bag. Should he look inside?

But the Shrimp crawls out too fast and grabs it out of his hand.

Then he sits back down and puts both of his feet against the doggy door. "Go find something to block this door."

Harp can hear something scratching inside the door. It must be the dog, wanting more wieners. He goes down the alley a short ways and finds a milk crate. He brings it back, and the Shrimp wedges it against the little door. Harp isn't sure that's a very good idea. Won't it just show the owner of the store how the Shrimp got in?

Who cares? It's not your problem.

The Shrimp grabs his cane and says, "Let's get out of here." He hurries down the alley toward the street, almost running, not even bothering to tap his cane.

Harp follows, still wondering what's in that paper bag.

I'm telling you, it's money. Watch for a chance and grab it.

When the Shrimp gets back out onto the main street again, he slows to a walk and begins tapping his cane on the sidewalk again.

Harp is glad to be out of that alley, but he worries about what the Shrimp has gotten him into.

Never mind about that. Find out what's in that bag.

"What were you doing in there, Shrimp? Were you stealing something?"

"Naw, just lookin' around."

"If you were just looking around, then what's in that paper bag?"

"Oh, this? It's nothing, just something I picked up. I got something for you too. Want it?"

"What is it?"

"Hey, I went to a lot of trouble to get this for you. Do you want it or not?" The Shrimp stares at him, but Harp can't tell what the Shrimp's eyes are saying behind those dark glasses.

"Sure, I guess so."

The Shrimp stops walking and sticks his hand inside the bag. He feels around in there for a minute, then he says, "Now, don't look."

Harp looks away.

"Here it is."

Harp turns back.

The Shrimp is holding out a candy bar.

That's all? You risk your neck for him and all he gives you is a lousy candy bar?

The very sight of it makes Harp's mouth water. "What kind is it?"

"What does it look like? It's a Butterfinger."

He holds it out closer to Harp, but Harp doesn't take it. "Listen, Shrimp. That's nice of you to get me a candy bar. I like Butterfingers. But did you steal it?"

"Hey, what makes you think I stole it? How do you know I didn't buy it for you when I went into the store to buy the wieners?"

"Did you?"

"Of course I did. I was thinking about you all the time. I've just been waiting to give it to you when we were done. A reward like."

He's rewarding you like you're a good doggy.

Harp is pretty sure the Shrimp wasn't really thinking about him all that much, but he decides it might as well take the candy bar anyhow.

Oh, sure, now you're satisfied. You get one lousy candy bar while he gets to keep all the money for himself.

As soon as Harp takes the candy bar, the Shrimp hides the paper bag under his coat and starts walking again. Harp catches up, tearing open the candy bar's yellow wrapper. But then he wonders if maybe the candy bar is supposed to be for both of them. "Do you want some?" He holds it out toward the Shrimp.

I can't believe this. You're acting like he did you a favor.

The Shrimp waves it off.

"Thank you, Shrimp." Harp takes a bite. It tastes so good it makes his mouth hurt.

The Shrimp is walking so fast Harp can barely keep up. He seems distracted, constantly turning his head to watch the cars that pass by. He's tapping his cane so fast it sounds like he's beating out some kind of song.

Harp can see they're heading back toward the beach, and that makes him feel a little less nervous.

Ask him about the coat.

Concentrating on the candy bar, Harp has fallen behind, but when he sees the Shrimp is about to go over the bridge back to the pier, he hurries to catch up. "Uh, Shrimp, what about that coat you said you were going to get for me?"

"Coat?" The Shrimp keeps on walking. He won't look at Harp.

"Yes, my coat. You said if I helped you, you'd get me a nice warm coat. It's going to be cold again tonight."

The Shrimp looks at him. "Yeah, well, don't you worry about it. Tomorrow morning we'll go down to the Salvation Army store, and I'll buy you a damn coat if that's what you want."

"That's nice of you, Shrimp."

The Shrimp shrugs and says, "Hey, you helped me out, didn't you? Least I can do is help you out."

He promised you a new coat, not a dirty old used coat.

Harp tries not to show it, but he's thinking a worn out old coat from the Salvation Army isn't really the same as a nice new warm coat from a real store. The Shrimp promised to get him a nice new coat.

So now do you see? It's just like I told you. If you let them, they'll walk all over you.

Harp finishes the candy bar just as they reach the pier.

The Shrimp turns to Harp. "Well, I got to shove off now. See you later."

Harp watches him go down the steps to the beach.

You let him get away with the money. Why didn't you stop him? He didn't get you a new coat, and now you're going to be cold all night, and it's his fault.

Harp goes to the railing to look down to see where the Shrimp is going. Instead of heading for the sidewalk, he's heading down toward the water. Harp leans way out over the railing and sees the Shrimp duck under the pier. Is he going to sleep under there tonight? Or is he just going under there to hide something?

Go after him! Get the money.

Maybe he *should* go after the Shrimp and complain. Or something. He should have been firmer with the Shrimp. He should have demanded the Shrimp keep his promise about getting him a coat, or at least give him some money so he can go buy one himself. But now it's too late.

It's not too late. Go after him.

Harp knows he lets people get away with things. But what can he do?

You know what to do.

The fog is starting to come in. Soon, it closes around Harp like an icy hand making him realize it's going to be another cold night. How is he going to get through the long cold night without a warm coat? He leans against the railing and thinks about the Shrimp sitting nice and warm under the pier, maybe with a bunch of stolen money. It's not fair.

3-10

Night Fears

Wake up. You're not paying attention.

Harp has the strangest feeling he fell asleep while he was walking. Can I be that tired? He looks around to see where he is. He's on the beach, walking away from the pier. How did I get here?

Ahead he sees six small white birds nestled close together. They're all in a line, close to the surf line.

One's bad luck, two's good luck, three's health, four's wealth, five's sickness, six is death.

Oh no, six birds. Another sign of death, just like the dog that was howling the night Little Hilly got killed. He spits on his right thumb and rubs it into the palm of his left hand. He whispers the words Mother taught him: "Death go away from my door. Go and come back no more." He turns away from the birds. He won't look at them. He'll go somewhere else where there are no signs of death.

But where should I go? Through the dense fog he can see lights ahead. It must mean I'm almost to Venice Beach. How did I get to Venice Beach already? Is that where I want to go? It's going to be really cold tonight so I have to find a place to keep warm until the sun comes up, but where? "I can't go back to the pier, can I?"

No, stay away from there. No matter what, stay away from there.

He walks on, thinking about those six birds of death. It reminds him of the story about the poor boy who couldn't get warm.

That boy was a lot like you. He didn't understand the meaning of fear.

Right, in that story, the boy didn't understand the meaning of fear. A man who wanted to steal the boy's money came and said, "Look, there is the tree where the hangman teaches men to fly. You want to learn about fear? I'll teach you about fear. Just try sitting down below those seven men who got married to the ropemaker's daughter. Just sit under those hung men all through the long night, and I guarantee you'll soon learn about fear." Harp remembers that story well. Mother was sick the night she told it, and she couldn't get warm that night either.

You were no help. You couldn't cast the evil spirits out of me.

Harp remembers trying to make her warm by giving her hot baths all night. While he bathed her, she told him the story of the boy who wanted to learn about fear. Lying there in the bathtub, with a wet washrag over her face, she told how the boy started a big fire to get warm. But then the boy began to feel sorry for the seven hung men. It was such a cold night, the boy thought they must be cold too, dangling up there in the wind. So he cut them down and arranged them around the fire as if they were alive persons. But the fire was too hot and the seven men all caught fire and got all burned up. Oh yes, Harp remembers that story well. What a scary story.

It wasn't all that scary. Not for you anyhow. It wasn't you that got burned up, was it? You got out without singeing a single hair on your head, didn't you?

Harp decides he doesn't want to think about that part of the story. And now here I am, freezing to death, just like the poor little boy in the story. "Detective Olivera took away my coat so now I'm cold to the bone and nobody cares."

I care. Everything I do is for you. It's just you and me against them all.

"Well, maybe, but that doesn't help me get a coat, does it?"

It's not my fault. The Shrimp did you wrong, so it's his fault. He should have bought you a warm coat with all that money.

"That's right. He said he was going to get me a coat and he didn't. So now I'm going to be cold all night. Maybe I should go join the Fearful Ones' circle."

No. Let's just be alone.

Harp wishes he didn't have to be around people tonight, of all nights, but at least it would be a little warmer with the Fearful Ones.

He'd better go there, no matter what anybody says. He turns up the collar of his old shirt and heads for the strand.

When he gets to the strand sidewalk, all the shops are closed and dark. The cold wind is blowing, and there is nobody else on the sidewalk. It makes him feel lonely.

Why should you be lonely? I'm here aren't I? I'll always be here with you.

Harp decides he's too cold to listen. It's so cold even the stores are closed. The closed-up shops look very sad and worn-out. Harp wonders where the people go when they leave the beach. They probably go to nice warm houses. It reminds him of how nice and warm it was in the kitchen at home. Mother used to turn on the oven and leave the oven door open to make it nice and warm there. They'd sit in front of the stove, and she'd make him hot chocolate. She'd drink her special medicine, and after a while, she'd start telling him her wonderful stories about magical kings and beautiful princesses and birds that talked and smart little boys who learned how to understand what the animals were saying when they were barking or growling or croaking or meowing. That old memory brings tears to his eyes. He can almost feel how nice and warm that kitchen was. But that house with its nice kitchen is all gone now.

And whose fault is that?

Harp is still too cold to listen.

He finally gets to the paddleball court and sees the Fearful Ones under the bleachers, where they always are on cold nights. Tonight, they're sitting in an even tighter circle than usual, and they've got some pieces of cardboard wedged around themselves to help block out the cold wind.

Stay away from them.

"Be quiet. I have to get warm, don't I?"

Well, ex-cuse me. Fine, just pretend I'm not here.

Before he approaches, Harp knows he has to call out the usual words: "It's Harp. May I come in?"

"Are you alone?"

Harp isn't sure whose voice that was. Maybe Worried Jack.

"Yes, I'm alone."

"Come forward and be identified."

It *is* Worried Jack, and when he sees it's Harp he wiggles aside a little bit to make room between himself and Hippie. Hippie is sound asleep, hunched forward with his arms folded across this chest and his head resting on his chest. He's got dried-out flowers in his long blonde hair, like always, and his long blonde beard is as tangled as ever. Harp squeezes in and immediately smells Hippie's sour, damp smell. But Harp knows he shouldn't complain because Hippie is a big guy, and he will block quite a bit of the wind when it starts to blow strong off the ocean later in the night.

Harp settles in and tries to get comfortable. Worried Jack grunts some kind of complaint so Harp stops moving and looks around the circle. He recognizes them all; the usual group of Fearful Ones are all there. But where is Tex? He's not there.

Some of the men in the circle are already asleep, sitting slumped forward, or leaning up against their neighbor. The ones on the other side of the circle are passing around a bottle.

Harp suddenly realizes Shoeless Joe isn't there either. He nudges Worried Jack who is sitting perfectly still, watching the bottle make its way around the circle toward him. "Where's Joe?" he whispers.

Worried Jack doesn't look at him. He's still watching that bottle as it makes slow progress toward him. Finally, he answers, "He's over there. Inside the restroom. Pacing I guess."

That pacing is a good idea. If it gets too cold, I can go in there and join Shoeless Joe. We can pace in there until dawn, and then the sun will come up and it will get warm again.

Harp raises his hand like he used to do back in school when he wanted to ask a question. "Anybody got an extra blanket or anything? I lost my jacket."

The few men in the circle who are still awake stare at him for a moment, but then they look away.

Harp gives up. Nobody is going to help me. He leans up against Hippie and tries to get comfortable. It's been so long since he's had a good night's sleep, he feels like he might be able to sleep soundly tonight, even sitting up. He listens to the waves in the distance and tries not to smell Hippie. He tries counting the waves, timing his heartbeat to their rhythm. He thinks about the old days, about old rhymes that used to sound so nice when Mother would whisper them to him late at night.

Little drops of water, little grains of sand, make the mighty ocean home, and the pleasant land.

But this time her nice little rhyme doesn't work. He's not going to sleep, and he still feels nervous. So many new things have happened today, even the sound of the waves feels cold and gloomy. It makes him think about what it would be like to be pulled under the dark ocean, down, down into the dark depths, like a cold, cold grave.

Who'll dig his grave? I, said the Owl, with my pick and shovel, I'll dig his grave.

Harp tries not to think about death and graves and bad things like that. No bad owl is going to dig his grave, no way. He'll think about warmer things, like . . . like lying on his back on the nice dry sand, the warm sun on his face. It's a nice thought. So relaxing . . .

3-11

Dream Realities

"**W**ake up, Harp!"

Somebody talking. Maybe it's a dream. If it is, it must be a cold dream because I'm shivering. He snuggles up to Hippie and tries to go back to sleep. But somebody won't let him sleep. Somebody is shaking his shoulder.

Harp tries to hold onto the dream. What was it? There was a dog, a big black dog, with big sharp teeth. It wants something from me. What? A wiener? But I don't have any wieners left. The Blind Shrimp took them all.

That's right The Blind Shrimp took everything. It wasn't fair.

In the dream, the dog looked up at him with big, sad doggy eyes. They were just like Shoeless Joe's eyes. But there was something wrong. Oh, no, the poor dog had a knife stuck in his side, and I was trying to pull it out.

No! Don't touch the knife.

"It's not fair. Why do I always have to be the one to pull the knife out?"

"What? Don't talk nonsense, Harp. I'm telling you, you have to wake up now."

Harp opens his eyes. It's not completely light yet, but some of the Fearful Ones are already standing up and moving away. Why are they looking at me?

Harp shakes his head to try to wake up. Why is everybody leaving? They're all gathering up their blankets and leaving. Even Hippie jumps up and runs away without a word.

Harp blinks. "Where's everybody going? What's the matter?"

Somebody won't stop pulling at his shoulder.

It's that weird person who pretends to be a boy.

Harp turns around and sees she's right. It's Speel the Sayer. "Oh, hi, Speel. It's you."

Speel looks worried. It makes Harp wonder if he's still asleep and dreaming. Maybe this is just another dream and Speel is in it. Does Speel have a knife stuck in his side?

"Didn't you hear me?" yells Speel. "Have you got wax in your ears?"

Harp doesn't think he has any wax in his ears. Why is Speel yelling so awfully loud when the sun isn't even up yet? Maybe that's why the Fearful Ones are running away, because Speel is yelling so loud.

"Harp, I'm telling you you've got to make a break for it. The police are hot on your trail."

Uh oh. I was afraid of this.

"Hot on my trail?" Harp tries to get to his feet, but his legs feel like they're still asleep. He almost falls over, but Speel catches him and helps him stand up.

"They're onto you, Harp. You've got to make tracks before they get here. No time to lose."

"Tracks? Onto me?" Harp is confused. "Who is onto me?"

"The police, little buddy, the coppers. You gotta get your ass in gear before they nab you."

"But why? Olivera knows I didn't hurt Little Hilly."

"No, no," says Speel, pointing toward the pier. "This time it's not Little Hilly, it's the Blind Shrimp. They found him under the pier, deadern a doornail. And they say you did it."

Part 4

Speel and the Ghost

Yesterday was a special day. We didn't know why it was a special day but we knew it must be because Mitch blessed us with a special prayer at breakfast and then we got a little piece of ham on our plates. It had to be a really really special day because Mitch didn't take the ham away and keep it for himself. Maybe it was supposed to be our Christmas dinner even though Carl the Older said Christmas was already done and over with. After we ate our breakfast the day didn't seem special anymore because everybody just went back to doing what they always do. Shaky Sandy had a fit but I don't know why because I didn't see anything that got him excited. He flopped around on the floor until Mitch told the Growler to hold him down. After his fit was over it was pretty quiet on the ward except for the Big Black Cusser who was doing what he always does, pacing back and forth in the dorm cussing up a blue streak. He's the only one who gets to be in the dorm after the beds are all made up in the morning because he's too noisy to be with us in the Day Room. I guess the Big Black Cusser must have had a bad time with a woman named Jasmine because he's back there all day long cussing her out. Maybe she was the one who put him in here. The Big Black Cusser yells every bad thing he can think of about Jasmine. He starts whispering to her in the morning, but then he gets louder and louder til he's shouting so loud we're all happy he's back there in the dorm and not out here in the Day Room with us.

The trouble is yesterday the dorm window was open because Mitch said it stunk real bad from everybody farting all night. Pretty soon a doctor and two big aides came banging on the ward door. When Mitch went to let them in everybody ran and hid hoping it wasn't them they were coming for. The doctor asked Mitch who was that man who was yelling nasty insults out the window at his wife. I wanted to step right up and say it wasn't the doctor's wife he was cussing out, it was Jasmine. But when I saw the big shot needle the doctor had in his hand I was too afraid to say anything. Mitch took them back to the dorm and the two big aides got ahold of the Big Black Cusser and they threw him down on one of the cots while the doctor gave him a shot in the butt. Carl the Older told me it was probably Thorazine in that shot needle. He said that's what they give you if they want you to quiet down. It didn't take long for that Thorazine stuff to make the Big Black Cusser quiet down, and then they dragged him out and threw him into a chair in the day room. I watched him for a long time. He just sat there staring straight ahead. It was the first time I ever saw him not yelling and cussing and pacing.

After quite a while he started coming out of it. He started whispering again, real soft at first, still cussing out Jasmine, but gradually he got louder and louder until Mitch had to tell the Growler to take him back to the dorm again. Pretty soon he was back to his usual pacing and yelling and cussing. I was kind of glad to hear him back there shouting because the ward sounded almost too quiet when he wasn't doing it. The trouble was somebody must have been listening outside the window because here they came back again and they gave him another shot in the butt and put him right back in the same chair in the Day Room. But this time that shot must have had a lot more Thorazine in it because the Big Black Cusser fell out of the chair and Mitch had to tell the Growler to get the cloth strips to tie him back in. I watched the Big Black Cusser all day to see if he was going to come out of it, but he never did. When we got up this morning I went right out to the Day Room to see if he was back to his usual cussing, but he wasn't. He was still tied in his chair with his head down on his chest.

So far he hasn't moved or said anything. He just stares straight ahead and drool runs out of the side of his mouth. I would have offered to help him get to the bathroom, but he's too big for me to move so he just pees in his pants and I know pretty soon he'll get those ugly sores on the insides of his legs like the other men who don't move get. I tried putting some food and water in his mouth, but he won't swallow it. A big guy like him probably needs a lot of food and water so I think maybe he'll die soon.

4-1

Hiding Out

*H*arp stares at Speel. He can't believe what he's hearing. "You must be wrong, Speel. The Shrimp can't be dead. I was just with him last night and he wasn't dead."

Speel takes ahold of Harp's arm and leans close like she's going to say a secret. "Don't let out a peep about that," she whispers. "If you tell anybody you were with the Shrimp last night, the cops will pin the rap on you for sure."

Don't trust her. She's up to something.

Why is Speel whispering? There's nobody else around. Worried Jack and Hippie and all the others have already run off, and it's still dark so the whole beach is deserted.

"Listen to me, Harp. Don't tell 'em anything. If the cops nab you, take the fifth. Keep your trap shut, you hear me?"

Harp wants to be polite so he says, "All right, Speel. I'll keep my trap shut. And I'll take the fifth too, if they offer it to me. But why do the police think I would hurt the Shrimp?"

"Who knows, but that's what I heard 'em say. A bunch of cops were down under the pier this morning, and I saw them hauling away a stiff under a blanket. I followed 'em to the meat wagon, and they took off the blanket to put the stiff in a big bag. That's when I saw it was the Blind Shrimp."

"The Shrimp is dead? Really dead?"

"Yep. It's curtains for little old Shrimpy."

"Curtains?"

"Right. A gone goose. Pushing up daisies now, he is."

Harp always has a hard time understanding Speel's talking in sayings, but one thing was clear: she was saying the Shrimp was dead. Can it be true? He's dead? And under the pier, just like Little Hilly?

Don't look at me. I don't know any more about it than you do.

"Uh, Speel, can I ask you, was he *really* under the pier?"

"Now you're getting my drift, Harp. You bet. Under the pier and dead as a dead dodo, same as Little Hilly. And that's not all. That cop Olivera was there, and I heard him talking to the other cops about you. He said, 'That settles it. I'm gonna go find that Harp character.'"

"Find me?"

"That's right. Didn't I tell you to watch your ass? When we talked up at the church yesterday, didn't I tell you? Now they think you knocked both of 'em off."

Harp feels bad about the Shrimp being dead. The Shrimp wasn't a very honest person, but should he have to die just for that?

Forget him. You've got to worry about yourself now.

It's like what happened to Little Hilly all over again. Both dead, both killed under the pier in the dark of night. He touches Speel's sleeve. "Was he stabbed?"

You just had to keep on talking, didn't you? You never learn.

"Whoa now, Harp. Don't go shootin' your mouth off about the Shrimp getting stabbed. All I know is he had blood all over him when they zipped him up in that bag. If he was stabbed, nobody knows that except the cops and whoever killed him. Just keep mum about him being stabbed and nobody'll be the wiser."

Keep mum? What's a mum? There she goes again, saying odd things that don't mean anything. But he sees Speel's point. If the Shrimp was stabbed when he was under the pier, just like Little Hilly was, then the cops might think the same person did it. Do they know I was with the Shrimp last night?

They know. You've got to get away, far away.

Maybe I *will* have to run away from the beach, but where can I go?

Anywhere. Just go!

"You've got to fly the coop now, Harp. You'd better come with me." Speel pulls on his sleeve.

No, not with her.

Harp isn't so sure he wants to go with Speel. After all, he doesn't know her very well.

"Now don't hold back, Harp, if you want to stay free as the birds, you'd better just pull up stakes and come with me."

"Where are we going, Speel?"

Speel doesn't answer. She just gets ahold of his arm pulls him along, just like the Shrimp did. "C'mon, c'mon, I'm telling you they're hot on your trail. I got a place you can lay low. It's inside, where it's warm."

"Inside? You mean not . . . outside?"

"Didn't I just say that? Yes, inside, warm as toast. Now let's get a move on."

This is how they trick you, with promises and deception. She's just like that lying Shrimp character.

"Inside? You mean inside a house?"

"Sort of. Get your ass in gear. The cops could come rolling in here at any minute. If they catch you now, your name is mud."

It's been so long since Harp has had a place to sleep inside out of the weather he can hardly remember what that's like. Maybe he should go along with Speel.

Didn't I just say no?

"But wait a minute, Speel, maybe I should call Olivera and tell him I didn't do it. He said if anything happened I should call him."

Call that cop? Are you crazy?

Speel throws her hands up in the air. "Are you crazy? Detective Olivera is the one whose tryin' to pin the rap on you. They'll take you straight to the slammer, sure as hell."

"The Slammer?"

"Right. And you can bet your bottom dollar they'll toss you into that clink for a hell of a long time. Once you're in there, all the tea in China won't spring you."

Harp isn't sure what tea in China has to do with it, but he does know Speel is right. If they suspect him, he could get locked up in a jail. Mitch and the Growler got locked up in a jail. What if they were there in that same jail waiting to get back at him?

"Are you listening to me, Harp? Once they close those cold lockup doors, you'll play hell getting back out again. They might even toss you into the booby hatch."

Harp understands perfectly well what Speel means by the booby hatch. When he was on Ward D-4, Carl the Older always called it the booby hatch. Mother had another name for it. The Nut House. She always said, "Keep on like that and someday they'll lock you up in the nut house."

And I was right about that, wasn't I?

"Come on, come on, don't be draggin' your feet, Harp. We got to get off this beach before those coppers make the scene."

As Speel hurries him along, Harp thinks about poor little Shrimp being dead under the pier. He can almost see him lying there on the wet sand. The Shrimp's eyes would be wide open, staring at nothing, just like Little Hilly's were. Poor little Shrimp.

Forget him. It could be worse. It could have been you.

Harp hurries to keep up with Speel. It might be better to go along with Speel, just for a little while, until he can figure things out. Besides, if Speel really does have a warm inside place to go to, Harp shouldn't refuse her kindness, should he?

I'm telling you, it's a trap. She's just luring you in. I can feel it.

Harp puts his fingers in his ears. Mother used to say he shouldn't trust strangers, but Speel isn't a stranger, not really. Everybody on the beach knows Speel.

Speel turns to stare at him. "Why are you doing that?"

"Doing what?"

"Why do you have your fingers in your ears?"

Harp quickly puts his hands behind his back. "Oh, I don't know. No reason."

Speel frowns and shakes her head.

As they hurry away from the beach, Harp suddenly realizes that now he's got another murder to solve. First Little Hilly got killed, and now the Shrimp. Two killings, both under the pier. Why them and nobody else? Did they have something in common?

They were both small, like you. It was dark.

No, it can't be that. This is a brand new mystery, and Detective Olivera will probably want him to solve this one too. That's probably why Olivera said he wanted to find him. He wants me to solve the Shrimp's murder, just like he wanted me to solve Little Hilly's. Now I'll have to start asking people questions all over again. I'll have to look for new suspects. I'll have to find out who had it in for the Blind Shrimp. Hey, what about the owner of that store with the little doggy door? He might have got real mad when he found out the Shrimp crawled in and stole his money.

That isn't why he was killed. You know the real reason.

No, I don't. But maybe the store owner didn't do it. How would that store owner know it was the Shrimp who took his money? And how would he know where to find the Shrimp? Nobody knew he would be hiding under the pier but me.

Pay attention to where you're going.

Harp suddenly realizes he hasn't been paying attention to where Speel is leading him. They aren't on the beach anymore. In fact, they're a long ways from the beach.

Speel leads Harp on past a smelly old canal with almost no water in it. It stinks and Harp holds his nose as they go past it. Maybe there's dead fish in there where more water used to be. Why did they let almost all of the water get away?

As soon as they're past the dried-up canal, Harp unholds his nose and starts wondering how far Speel might take him away from the beach. The farther they go away from the beach the more nervous he gets.

I told you, it's a trap.

But no sooner has Harp had that thought when Speel turns into an alley that goes behind some little white houses. Speel is walking very fast, and Harp has to hurry to keep up.

All right, you're going to ignore me. Well, don't say I didn't warn you. From this point on I won't say another word. You're on your own now. In the end, you'll beg me to come back.

Harp stops. He suddenly feels very alone, and very nervous. Maybe he should go back to the beach.

Speel comes back for him and takes ahold of his arm again. "C'mon, Harp, keep up. You've got to make a clean getaway before the cops realize you flew the coop."

Harp isn't sure he should go any further from the beach. But he can't seem to decide what's best, so he just follows Speel on through the alley, trying not to think about how far away the beach is.

"Not far now," says Speel. "Just around the corner."

But they don't turn any corners. They keep on going straight up the alley. The sky is getting lighter, but it's still a little foggy, and it makes the alley feel spooky. He wishes Speel's house was somewhere on a regular street, not in a foggy alley. And for some reason, he's feeling very strange. His brain doesn't seem to be working right, but he doesn't know what to do except keep on following Speel. He's trying not to think about bad things, but he can't seem to keep some scary thoughts out of his head. What if Speel is taking him away for some bad reason? He remembers a scary story Mother once read to him about a mean mother and father who took their two little children into the deep, dark forest and left them there to die. Was Speel taking him somewhere like that? Would he be left there to die?

They go past some more little houses, and Harp hopes nobody is looking out of the windows. They might not like homeless people going behind their houses. They might call the police.

And another thing Harp doesn't like: there's nothing neat and orderly about the alley. There are garbage cans all over the place, not put out in neat rows like they do it back at the beachside apartments. Some of the cans are knocked over, and garbage is spilling out all over the ground. And behind some of the houses old cars are parked right on top of the grass where they don't belong. He looks back toward the beach. How far have they come? He can hardly even smell the sea air anymore. He tries not to think about it. Instead, he thinks about that smart boy who figured out he was going to be left in the forest to die. He left a trail of bread crumbs to lead himself back home. That was smart. But the birds came and ate up all of the bread crumbs so the boy and his little sister got lost in the woods anyhow, and then they almost got eaten by the mean witch who made her house out of cake with sugar windows to attract little children so she could eat them. So how did that little boy get away from the witch? He can't remember, and not remembering makes him even more nervous.

Even though Speel said she was in a hurry, she keeps on stopping to look inside the garbage cans. At first Harp thinks maybe Speel might be looking for food, but she never takes any food out. Instead, she takes out white envelopes.

"Speel, what are you looking for?"

Speel turns to show him an envelope she's just found. "White paper. I can use this." She puts the envelope in her pocket and goes on to the next garbage can.

When Speel comes to an old garage, she finally stops. Most of the paint is gone off of the garage, but of course the spray-painter kids have been there, drawing their crazy pictures and words all over the garage's big door. There's a picture of a great big hand with most of the fingers regular size but with the thumb really big and colored orange. The thumb has the words "V Boys" on it and some bad words are next to that. Harp is glad to see that at least there aren't any scary pictures like the picture of a knife stuck in poor little Teddy the dog. He's in no mood for seeing anything scary right now.

Speel doesn't even seem to notice the drawing. She puts her finger up to her lips and points to a little white house that's close to the other side of the garage. Harp waits while Speel turns the handle in the middle of the big door and pulls it upward to open it. Then she ducks under and disappears inside. After a few seconds Speel's head pops back out and she waves for him to come in. Harp isn't so sure he wants to go in there, but Speel grabs his sleeve and pulls him in.

The inside of the garage is pretty dark, but there is one light bulb hanging down on a wire from the ceiling. Speel must have just turned it on because it's swinging back and forth, flashing bright and dim and then bright again.

The place is really messy with newspapers and magazines stacked all over the place. And it doesn't smell very good either. Harp decides he'd rather be back outside so he heads for the door. But Speel gets ahold of his sleeve and won't let him go. She puts her fingers up to her lips again. "We have to be quiet."

"Why do we have to be so quiet?" whispers Harp. "Maybe we shouldn't be in here at all. I want to go back to the beach."

"Now don't get ants in your pants, Harp. This is my place. We just have to be a little quiet when we're in here."

Harp looks at Speel to see if she was making a joke when she said that part about having ants inside his pants, but Speel isn't smiling. It must be another one of her strange sayings. Harp wishes Mother would have taught him about sayings. They were almost like little nursery rhymes.

"It all right, Harp. Don't be scared."

Harp leans down to look back out under the big garage door. "But what if they catch us in here?"

"The cops don't know about my place. They'll be chasing wild geese down at the beach. The only person who knows I'm in here is my mother, and she hardly ever comes out here. Even if she does, you can hide back there." She points back toward the dark places where stacks and stacks of newspapers and magazines go almost up to the ceiling.

Harp thinks about how funny it would be to see the police chasing wild geese all over the beach, but then he gets worried about Speel's mother coming in and catching them. Was she a mean mother? Would she punish them?

"My mother threw me out of the house last year," says Speel. "Why? you might ask. Because of . . . well, because of how I am, I guess. She wants me to be . . . regular. But later she relented and said I could live back here in the garage if I was quiet and didn't play any music or recite my sayings too loud in the middle of the night. So we have to be quiet as mice."

That makes Harp think about the mice living under the big pile of garbage back at the beach. Are mice really all that quiet down in their tunnels at night? Probably not. The more he thinks about hiding in a garage and having to be quiet, the more sure he is that it would be better to go back to the beach.

But just as he's ready to duck right back out the door, Speel says. "Are you hungry? I've got food here."

Harp decides maybe he should be polite and stay for a while.

Speel pulls down on a rope that's tied to the garage door, and the door swings shut.

Being closed in makes Harp really nervous. He edges a little closer to the door in case he has to make a run for it.

"Come on, Harp, relax. Sit a spell."

Speel points at an old mattress lying next to the wall. It's a nice fat one, and not too dirty. Harp knows about mattresses. Whenever anyone on the beach finds a thrown-away mattress in a dumpster, everybody wants it, no matter how dirty and worn out it is. There's sure to be fighting over it every night until after a while it gets too soggy from the foggy air and smelly from so many men lying on it that it starts to fall apart. Then nobody wants it anymore.

Speel's mattress looks pretty clean, at least compared to the ones on the beach. Harp knows his pants are really dirty so he carefully sits only on the very edge.

"Now, how about that grub?" says Speel. "I could eat a horse."

Harp is getting used to Speel talking in funny sayings so he just says, "I might eat a horse too, Speel. All I had was a hot dog. And that was yesterday."

"Well, let's dig in then." Speel goes to a cardboard box and pulls out a paper sack that has stains all up the sides of it. She reaches in and pulls out a piece of brown cake. She holds it up and says, "Ta da."

Harp says, "Cake."

"You bet, chocolate cake. Let 'em eat cake, right?" Speel hands the piece of cake to Harp.

It looks really good, but Harp isn't sure if he's supposed to split it with Speel or not. He hopes not. Even though he had that hot dog with mustard and catchup on it, and the Butterfinger candy bar Shrimp gave him, he's still really hungry.

Speel pulls another piece of cake out of the sack and holds it up. "Uh, let's see. How about this? Man cannot live by bread alone." She tries to stuff the entire piece of cake into her mouth, but some of it crumbles out the sides and down the front of her overalls.

Harp takes a little nibble of his piece of cake, and the taste of it makes his stomach very happy. He closes his eyes as he chews it. He continues to eat with his eyes closes, taking only small bites, like Mother taught him. She'd say, "Never put more in your mouth than you can swallow in one lump. That's the way genteel people eat."

Harp finishes his cake and watches Speel who's already pulled another piece of the chocolate cake out of the sack and is quickly eating it. Harp wonders if there's any more cake in there.

Speel digs into the sack and pulls out yet another pierce. She holds it up and says, "Cake, better than steak. Right?" She hands it to Harp.

Harp takes it and says, "Thank you." But before he eats it, he asks, "Speel, how come you always talk like that, if you don't mind me asking?" Then he's sorry he said it. He doesn't want to hurt Speel's feelings after she gave him such tasty chocolate cake.

"Like what?" says Speel, concentrating on her cake eating.

"You know, like making up funny ways to say things, like when you said the Blind Shrimp was dead ern a doornail."

"You never heard that one? I didn't make that one up, not really. I wish I did. I found it in one of those." She points to the many tall stacks of magazines. "But I have some of my real made-up sayings here. You want to hear some?"

"Oh, well, I guess so." Harp knows all about Speel's sayings. Everybody on the beach knows about them. She hands out her handwritten sayings on little pieces of paper to anyone who'll take them.

Speel gets up and goes to a big cardboard box. She pulls out a handful of little pieces of paper and brings them back to the mattress. She takes out one and holds it up. "I just wrote this one yesterday. You wanna hear it?"

"All right."

"It goes like this: 'If you have a bee in your bonnet, you'll take it off at the drop of a hat.'" She stares at Harp, waiting for him to say something.

"Oh, yes. That was nice, Speel. Eighteen words, and only two of them were the same."

"Well," says Speel, "it doesn't matter if some of the words are the same."

"Oh, right. I knew that."

"Do you want to keep that one?" She holds it out to Harp.

"No, thank you, Speel. I already have some in my backpack."

Speel stares at Harp, her mouth open. "You kept them?"

"Yes. Don't you remember? You gave them to me a long time ago."

"Yes, but . . . well, I didn't think anybody kept them. People usually just throw them right into the nearest garbage can as soon as I hand them out. I try to get to the garbage cans fast to dig them out so I can give them to other people, but sometimes they get all dirty in there."

"I don't think that's very nice of them to throw your sayings away, Speel. If you wrote a saying for them, they should keep it."

She shrugs. "Oh well, a real writer is never appreciated in his own time. Sometimes nobody knows about the best writers until they're dead. Like me. Nobody knows me."

"Oh, that's not true, Speel. Everybody on the beach knows you."

"Only because I pester them. Sometimes I make them take my little sayings whether they want them or not. Maybe I shouldn't do that, but a writer needs readers, right?"

Harp feels like he should say something to make Speel feel better.

Maybe he should say something about how much people liked her sayings, but he's never actually heard anybody say they do. Maybe Speel is right about writers not being appreciated in their own time.

"Well, never mind about that," says Speel with a shrug. "We've got more important fish to fry. We've got to figure out how to save your bacon."

"That's a good one, Speel. I mean the part about frying fish and bacon. Both things to eat." Harp looks around the cluttered garage. "By the way, you don't seem to have a stove in here or anything. My mother had a stove in her kitchen, and sometimes she fried bacon for me. And eggs too, sometimes."

"Yeah, mothers can be nice. Even though they're always trying to make you be somebody you don't want to be. My mother bakes me things all the time. She leaves them inside my garage door. Like this chocolate cake here. She left it for me this morning." Speel pulls another piece of cake out of the sack. "More cake? Better than steak."

He wonders if maybe he should remind Speel that she already said that one, but he doesn't want to make her feel bad so he only says, "Yes, thank you."

Speel hands the piece of cake to Harp and stuffs her own piece into her mouth all at one time again. Then she starts talking again, even before she finishes chewing. "Here's my plan . . ." She holds her hand up to her chest while she stops to swallow. "You and me, Harp, we got to team up. To save your skin. You can't go outside, but I can. So here's the plan. I'll go down to the beach to see which way the wind is blowing. Then I'll come back here and tell you what I found out. How does that tickle your fancy?"

Harp stares at Speel. He's pretty sure Speel means she's going to go out and do something to help him, but he's not sure how seeing which way the wind is blowing or tickling something will help. It must be more of Speel's strange sayings. He's pretty sure Speel means well, even if her words are confusing. "Uh, okay, whatever you think is best, Speel."

"Okay, then it's settled. I'll be the bloodhound while you lay low here. I'll go nose around and report back when I turn up something."

Olivera said the same thing, that Harp was supposed to nose around and ask questions. Has Speel been talking to Detective Olivera?

"What's the matter, Harp? Cat got your tongue?"

There it is again, another strange saying, one that sort of sounds like an old nursery rhyme. "No, Speel, the cat hasn't got ahold of my tongue. But I have to ask you something. Have you been talking to Detective Olivera?"

Speel shakes her head. "Not since he was up at the church yesterday. I stayed out of sight when I saw him this morning at the pier. Why, have you been talking to him again?"

Harp thinks about how to answer Speel's question. Speel is being so nice, hiding him in her garage-house and giving him chocolate cake and reading her made-up sayings to him. Maybe he should tell her what Olivera said, about helping to find Little Hilly's killer. Harp stares at Speel, and suddenly he realizes he doesn't have another person in the whole world he can talk to. That never mattered too much before, but now that the police think he killed the Shrimp, it might be good to have somebody to talk to.

Speel leans closer. "Hello, earth to Harp. Are you in there?"

"Well, I did sort of talk to Olivera," says Harp quietly, staring at the floor. "A little bit anyhow. Yesterday, at the pier Olivera said he wanted me to help him find out who killed Little Hilly. I didn't want to, but I was afraid if I didn't he'd lock me up and throw away the key."

Speel lets out a low whistle. "So that's why you've been asking everybody questions. I told them it wasn't like you to go around quizzing everybody like that. But why did Olivera take your coat? That's what everybody up at the church was asking."

"Well, he didn't exactly say why he took it. I washed it up after I found Little Hilly, but I think the two bicycle cops saw me. Then Olivera took it away from me at the church. He said it was just routine."

Speel holds up a hand to stop him. "Evidence. That's what they're looking for. It means they already suspected you, even before you . . . I mean even before they found the Shrimp. Now let's run down the facts. Little Hilly's life gets snuffed out under the pier. Stabbed, you said. Let's say they guessed you were under the pier that night so they suspected you killed the little bastard, but they weren't sure."

"Excuse me, Speel, but why did you call Little Hilly . . . what you said?"

"A little bastard? Because that's what he was. Everybody knew that. He was out for whatever he could get. He tricked me out of some money my mother gave me, and when I asked her for more she said I shouldn't have lost it in the first place. I told her it was Little Hilly's fault, but she blamed it on me."

"I'm sorry he took your money, Speel. He did something like that to me too."

"He did? Like what?"

"Never mind. It doesn't matter now."

"Yeah, well, anyhow, like I was saying, first Little Hilly gets killed under the pier, and then the Blind Shrimp gets killed under there too. And you were the last one to see both of them alive." She holds out her hands. "So, there you have it."

Harp hold out his hands. "There you have what?"

"There you have why the police think you did it. You're the obvious suspect. At the scene of the crime both times."

"But, I didn't do it, Speel."

"Well, maybe you did and maybe you didn't. What counts is the police think you did. If they catch up with you, you're goose is cooked."

"Cooked?"

"That's right. It'll be the old ball game for you, if you get my drift."

"I'm not exactly sure I do get your drifting, Speel. Are you saying there's no hope for me?"

"I'm not saying that. Not at all. Not a bit of it. Couldn't be farther from the truth. Don't look so sad. We'll keep you out of their clutches, you and I together, right?"

"If you say so, Speel."

"Sure, I do say so. Now I'm going out to do my nosing around. You stay here and don't make any noise."

"Can't I go with you? I don't want to stay in here all alone."

"No way. They've probably got an APB out for you by now."

"An APB?"

"Yeah, an all-points bulletin. It means everybody's looking for you. You just lay low here. I'll leave you some of my sayings to read while I'm gone."

"All right. Thank you, Speel. Uh, how long will you be gone? Do you think?"

"Oh, not too long. You just sit tight. Say, while you wait maybe you could cut up some of these envelopes into sayings papers."

She goes behind some of her stacks of magazines and brings back a cardboard box and a little pair of scissors. The box is full of white envelopes.

"Cut them up like this one. She hands Harp one of the little strips of paper with a saying written on it. Harp reads it out loud. "If someone hits you below the belt, you'll know it was between a rock and a hard place."

"Pretty good, huh?"

That one completely baffles Harp, but he doesn't want to make Speel feel bad so he just says, "Oh, yes, pretty good."

Speel picks up the chocolate cake bag and pushes open the garage door. "Just hang loose here, Harp. Kick back and relax. I'll be back in a jiffy."

The door closes and Harp is left alone.

4-2

Speak Only When Spoken To

*H*arp tries to do what Speel said and relax. But he can't relax. He stares at the light bulb hanging from its wire and tries to tell himself about how much better it is to be in a nice safe place. But he's not used to being inside a house, even if it is only a garage-house. The walls feel so close.

For the first time in a long time, Harp starts to think about why bad things always had to happen to him. It doesn't seem fair that just because Little Hilly and the Shrimp got killed, the police have to think I did it. It wasn't fair that people always suspected him of things. When he was little, people were always accusing him of doing mean things he knew he didn't do. Even Mother suspected him of trying to burn her up. So they locked him up on Ward D-4. But I didn't do anything on purpose, so why did they have to put me on that ward where Mitch and the Growler did mean things to everybody? I didn't do anything to deserve that. And after Mitch and the Growler were taken away, why did they have to close down Ward D-4 and all the other wards just when things were getting better? And why did they have to close down the Half-Way House where it was nice and warm. It wasn't fair that I had to live on the streets where the mean gang boys can come and hurt you in the night. If I hadn't found my way to the beach, I could have died sleeping on that cold bus bench. Then it would be me dead instead of Little Hilly and the Blind Shrimp. And now to make things worse, the police are after me for no good reason, and I'm stuck here in Speel's garage-house with nothing to do and nobody to talk to.

He waits, listening.

It's very quiet in the garage-house.

He turns to look at the big garage door, and all of a sudden he has the worrisome thought that Speel might have locked him in. He jumps up and goes to the door. He pushes against it. It won't open. In a panic, he pushes harder, but it won't budge. He grabs the handle in the middle of the door and turns it. He hears something like a metal scraping sound, and this time when he pushes against, the door it swings up. He leans down to look from under the door into the bright sunlight. The fog is almost gone and it feels warm out there. Maybe he should try to sneak back down to the beach. But what if the police are waiting for him there? And what would Speel think if she came back and found him gone? That wouldn't be very polite after Speel has been so nice to let him hide in her garage-house. Besides, maybe Speel will bring back some more cake. It's so hard to know what to do.

He pulls the garage door back down, but he leaves it open a crack at the bottom, just in case somebody might try to lock him in.

He goes back and sits on the mattress and stares up at the hanging light bulb. He's all alone, like the poor little girl in the story that was cast down out of heaven, all alone with no one to help, unable to break through the tangle of thorns that are all around.

"I don't know what to do."

He holds his breath and listens.

Nothing.

He whispers, "Please, Mother, talk to me. What should I do?"

So, you're finally ready to listen to me?

"What should I do? I'm afraid.

Will it be just the two of us now, like it always should have been?

"Yes, Mother. Just the two of us."

Then there's no reason to be afraid, my son. I'm here with you. We don't need anyone else.

"But the police are after me."

All you have to do is listen to me. Now calm down.

"Should I run away, or stay here?"

Stay put for now. Wait until it's dark, when no one can see you, then we'll run away.

That makes Harp feel a little better. He'll just stay where he is for now. It's safe and it's warm. He'll wait until it's dark and then he'll make his getaway. He'll go away to somewhere where nobody knows him. But where? He has no money except for Little Hilly's three dollars and three quarters and a dime. That wouldn't get him far. Even if I had more money, how would I know which bus to take?

But then he has another thought. Maybe I should make a run for the border. That's what they did in the movies. Harp had only been to a movie theater twice in his life, once to see *The Robe* and once to see *Quo Vadis*. Mother didn't believe a good Christian boy should see any movies except the good old Bible movies. But the TV in the Ward D-4 Day Room sometimes had cowboy movies on it.

Cowboy movies. I might have known. The work of the Devil.

"In the cowboy movies, outlaws always made a run for the border. Should I do that?"

That's dumb.

"No, it's not. For some reason the sheriff can't go across that border after them so once the outlaws make it into Mexico, they're safe."

Ridiculous. You've lost it. I knew those movies would rot your brain.

But Harp is sure it's a good idea. He learned about the Mexican border in school. His teacher referred to the Mexicans as "our little brown neighbors to the south." That means the border is somewhere to the south. All he has to do is go in that direction until he gets there. Maybe there's a bus that goes there. If only he had some money.

You know where to get money. Think.

"What money?"

You know.

"Oh, that money. You mean the money the Blind Shrimp stole from that store by crawling through the little doggy door."

That's right. You know where that money is.

Harp thinks about it. She's right. The Shrimp probably buried the money under the pier. All he has to do is go dig up that money and get on the bus that makes a run for the border.

Forget that border nonsense. Just dig up the money and get away from here.

But which bus goes to the border?

You're not listening to me. I said forget that nonsense. Just get the money.

No, he's sure it's a good idea. He won't listen to any more arguments. When it gets dark, he'll go dig up the money and make a run for the border.

Now that he has a plan, he feels better. All he has to do is wait. He stands up and tries to relax by pacing. But he can only count off six steps before he runs into Speel's stacks of magazines. He goes back the other way until he gets to the door. He looks at the light coming under the door. Is it getting dimmer? No, it's still got to be morning. It will be a long time before it gets dark. But he doesn't want to think about that. Thinking about what it might be like outside will just make him feel more trapped. He turns and takes six paces back the other way. When he gets to the magazine stacks, he takes one off the top of a stack and looks at it. It's a *Time Magazine* and there's a picture of a man on the front. Big print above the man's head says "Reagan's Secret Dealings with Iran." Harp knows who Reagan is. He's the President of the United States. He was on the TV all the time back on Ward D-4. But he doesn't know who Iran is. Maybe he's a friend of President Reagan's.

Harp looks through some of Speel's other magazines, but they don't seem to have any stories in them. Harp likes stories the best. When he was little, the library had lots of books with stories in them.

Not that library nonsense again. Those kinds of stories will rot your brain, just like cowboy movies will.

Harp doesn't think stories can rot your brain. Or cowboy movies either, but he doesn't want to start any more arguments so he keeps quiet. He'll just keep quiet and not listen to any more of her criticism.

He takes out one of the pieces of envelope paper Speel left for him. He compares it with the sayings paper Speel left for him. He picks up the scissors and cuts a piece out of the envelope, making sure it's exactly the same size as Speel's. Then he does the same thing with the next one. Hours and hours go by, and Speel still hasn't come back. All of the envelopes have been cut up, which is good because Harp is tired of cutting out little strips of paper. He's cut out hundreds and hundreds of sayings papers, and has them all stacked up nice and neat back inside the box ready for Speel to write on them. He straightens up the stack and notices that two of them are just a teensy bit longer than the others. He carefully trims those two and puts them back into the stack. But one of them is now shorter than any of the others. Oh, darn, now he'll have to trim all the others to make sure they're just exactly as short as the short one.

By the time he finishes that job, he's getting worried because Speel still isn't back. Harp can see through the crack under the garage door that it's still light out there, but the sun seems to have moved a long ways back toward the beach. He's not sure what to do next. It's so quiet in Speel's garage-house, it makes him feel very alone. He stares at the door. Should he go out there? "Help me. I don't know what to do next."

So you're ready to listen to me again?

"Please talk to me. Tell me what I should do now."

Think. What do you usually do?

"I usually just wake up."

Then what?

"Then I write in my book. Oh, that's it! I forgot to write the story of yesterday." He opens his backpack and takes out his diary.

Always forgetting the important things.

"I know I shouldn't forget my morning duties, but it's not my fault. Speel woke me up so fast this morning I never got a chance to do it." He gets his pencil, licks the tip of it, and begins to write yesterday's story:

> Yesterday after I

Aren't you forgetting something?

"Am I?"

You know.

Oh, that's right. First the prayer. He writes:

> Thank you Lord for letting me live today. Let others
> die instead of me,
> this I pray.

That's better.

He writes:

Yesterday after I wrote down what happened to Little Hilly I felt hungry so I went back to the pier but there wasn't anything good to eat there.

The police were down under the pier with Little Hilly and the fisherpeople were up top talking about it. I wanted to go away to wash my jacket but Detective Olivera made me stop and he asked me a lot of questions. He said I had to

Harp stops writing and stares at the words. Had it only been one day? Only one day since I found Little Hilly? Only one day since Olivera told me I had to find out who killed Little Hilly? It seemed a lot longer than that. And what had he found out in that one day? Not much. He'd talked to a lot of people, but he still didn't know who killed Little Hilly.

He turns to the page with the list of suspects. Big Hilly is the first name on the list. What happened to him? Why wasn't he there to protect Little Hilly?

Below that are a bunch of other names of suspects.

This is a waste of time.

"It is not. I haven't eliminated anybody from my list yet, so maybe one of them did it."

Take my word for it, they didn't.

"Well, what about . . . " He runs his finger down the list. "Big Nose. What about him? The man who was pretending to be a panhandler?"

How can he be the killer? He's working for the police

"Oh, that's right." He runs his finger on down the list. "And what about The Amazing Cedric? He juggles sharp knives, doesn't he?"

Forget him.

"But how can I just cross somebody off if I haven't investigated them yet?"

Cross them all off. They didn't do it.

"Oh, what do you know? And look, here's the Blind Shrimp's name." Uh oh. He realizes the Blind Shrimp's name shouldn't be on there. He's dead. "Oh no, this is the wrong list. This is a list for who might have killed Little Hilly, not who might have killed the Shrimp."

I could have told you that.

"Well then, I'll just have to make a brand new list."

Here we go again.

He turns to a fresh page. Where to begin? Maybe I should start with my old list of suspects. I could put all of the same suspects on the new list, and then I could cross off the ones who aren't guilty.

That's dumb.

"All right, if you're so smart, who should I put on the new list?"

It's a waste of time to put anybody on it. You'll never figure it out.

"It is not a waste of time. I can write out a new list if I want to."

Suit yourself. A waste of time, I say.

Harp writes:

New suspect list for who maybe killed the Blind Shrimp

But he can't think of anybody to write except the ones who are already on the old list. If they were suspects on the who-killed-Little-Hilly list, should they also be on the who-killed-the-Shrimp list?

He stares at the names. It's a long list. All of a sudden, the task seems too big. How do you find out who killed someone if they won't tell you? The whole thing makes him sleepy. He lies back on the mattress to think about it. It was so cold last night in the Fearful One's circle he didn't get much sleep.

"Now wait a minute." He sits back up and snaps his fingers. "I know a clue. Why didn't I see it before? None of the Fearful Ones could have killed the Shrimp because they were all there in the circle all night."

A genius.

"Well, it's true. It's an important clue."

He writes:

People in the Fearful Ones circle who couldn't have done it:

Worried Jack
Hippie
Shoeless Joe - pacing in restroom

Now that's a start. He's finally eliminating some of the suspects.

Two of them weren't even on your other list.

"Oh, that's right. But it's a start, isn't it? Now all I've got to do is eliminate some more."

Aren't you forgetting somebody?

"What? Who?"

There's one more name on your list.

"No, that's all. There's nobody else on the list except for . . . " Harp runs his finger down to the bottom of the list. "Oh. Speel. But how can I put Speel on my list of suspects after she was so nice to me? She let me hide here in her garage-house and gave me chocolate cake and . . . everything."

Think about it.

Well, it was true that he doesn't know where Speel was last night. And he doesn't know where she was the night Little Hilly was killed either. "But Speel says she wants to help me."

Why would anybody want to help you?

Harp doesn't have an answer for that. Why is Speel being so nice to him? Before this, she'd never even talked to him.

Harp slaps the diary closed. The whole thing is just too hard to figure out.

It's especially hard when you don't know what you're doing.

"I know what I'm doing. It's just that I'm . . . sleepy. That's it, I'm not thinking quite right because I'm too sleepy."

Then take a nap. I'll stand guard.

That's a good idea. He'll just take a little nap. He lies back on the mattress and stares up at the dirty ceiling. Why *is* Speel being so nice to me?

4-3

The Price of Fame

*T*his time when Speel wakes him up, Harp knows it isn't a dream. Speel couldn't have been in the dream because in this dream he was alone, swimming in the ocean. The ocean was dark, and the water was awfully cold. Is that what it's like to drown? Is that what it's like to be dead? So cold.

"Wake up, Harp. I've got somebody here who wants to chew the fat with you."

Harp sits up and rubs his eyes with the backs of his hands. There's a tall man standing next to Speel. The man is wearing a white suit and he's smiling. He's holding a paper bag in his hand.

Watch out. He's here to do you harm. I can feel it.

"Hello there, Harp. My name is Underwood. Vince Underwood. Sorry to wake you." The man holds out his hand, but Harp knows better than to touch it. He glances toward the garage door. It's only about five steps away, but it's closed all the way down again.

"Now don't be scared, Harp," says Speel. "Mr. Underwood isn't a cop. He's a reporter. He just wants to ask you some questions."

Harp looks up at Speel and then back at the man. "A reporter? Like . . . a newspaper reporter?"

"That's right," says the man. "That's exactly right. I work for the newspaper, and I heard you were in a bit of trouble. Maybe I can help you."

"Help me?"

No! You need his kind of help like you need a hole in the head.

"Sure," says Speel. "We both want to help you. To prove it, Mr. Underwood brought you something good to eat."

The man takes a little round cake wrapped in plastic out of the paper bag. "That's right. This is for you, Harp. Speel said you might be hungry."

It's all wrapped up, but Harp can see that it's a yellow-colored cake inside the plastic. It looks good, but he wishes it could have been chocolate, like before. His stomach reminds him he is still a little hungry so he says, "Thank you," and takes the cake, being careful not to touch the man's hand.

"Sure, son, My treat. Speel here didn't tell me you were such a polite young fellow. You can just call me Vince. I've got something else for you." He pulls a big bottle of Coca Cola out of the paper bag and holds it out to Harp.

"Now, would you look at that," says Speel, "Vince brought you a king-size bottle of Coca Cola too. Wasn't that nice of him?"

Harp takes the Coca Cola and sets the glass bottle down on the dirty concrete floor. But he keeps the little round cake in his hand. If he has to make a run for it, at least he can take the cake with him.

The reporter looks around the cluttered garage. "Haven't you got anything to sit on, Speel?"

"Oh, sure." Speel scurries back into the darkness and brings back a big white bucket.

She hands it to the reporter who turns it upside down and puts it down right in front of Harp. The reporter sits down on the bucket and leans forward, smiling. "Now, Harp, Speel here tells me you were the one who found the murdered man. The first victim, I mean."

Harp glances at Speel. "You weren't supposed to tell anybody about that, Speel."

"I know, Harp, but this is different. Vince here is a reporter. He has to get the facts straight. Isn't that right?"

Vince smiles and nods. "Yes, Harp, that's right. I'm a newspaper reporter. Everybody talks to me. I can put you in the newspaper. I can make you famous. Everybody will read about you in the paper tomorrow morning. You'd like that, wouldn't you?"

No! That's the last thing you need.

Harp wonders what it would be like to be famous. Maybe if he was famous, people would pay more attention to him.

Are you crazy? Think what that would mean.

But no, then people might start asking questions about other things, like where he came from before he was on the beach. He shakes his head and begins to unwrap the yellow cake. He'd better eat it quick before the man gets mad about him not answering questions and takes it back.

"No? Come now, son. Everybody wants to be in the newspaper. And you know why? Because the newspaper prints the truth. Only the truth can help you now."

We don't need his help. Tell him to go away.

"I don't think I need any help right now, sir. But thank you, anyhow."

The man sits up straight. "Oh, no? I think you do need help, boy." He leans forward again and shakes his finger in Harp's face. "Listen here, son, you may not realize it, but you're in a heap of trouble."

"I am?" Harp looks up at the man, but he's staring right into his eyes so Harp quickly looks down at the floor. Maybe if he just agrees with whatever the man says, he'll go away. He shrugs and starts eating the cake.

"Yes, you are, son, big trouble." He takes out a little notebook and a pencil. "All right, now suppose you tell me your side of the story. Speel said you found the body under the pier yesterday morning. You sleep under there, right?"

Harp nods, focusing on the extra sweet taste of the yellow cake.

"So what happened? You found him there when you went under the pier to sleep?"

Harp starts to correct him, but Speel says, "No, Harp told me he just woke up, and bingo, there was the body. Isn't that what you told me, Harp?"

Harp nods. One more bite and he'll be finished with the yellow cake. Then maybe the man will give up and stop asking questions.

"And that's all you know about it? The guy was just lying there, already dead when you woke up?"

Harp swallows the last bite of yellow cake before answering. "His eyes were open."

What did I just tell you? Didn't I tell you to keep your trap shut?

Harp decides to just tell the man the facts, nothing else but the facts. Then maybe he'll be satisfied and go away.

"Yeah, well, I guess that's what dead people do. They open their eyes, when they're dead. But you didn't see anybody else around?"

Harp shakes his head. Although there wasn't anybody else around, I have my list of suspects. Should I tell the reporter man about that?

No! Listen to me, or did you stop listening to me again?

On the other hand, maybe I shouldn't say anything to him. Olivera said I was supposed to keep his talking to me a secret. I'd better just tell the reporter about how it was under the pier that morning, and nothing else. Just the facts. "There was a dog howling."

"A dog?" says Vince.

But then he doesn't say anything else.

Harp doesn't know what Vince is waiting for so he waits too.

"All right," says Vince, and now this other fellow is killed last night. Also under the pier. Did you see him there? Were his eyes open too?"

"No dog was howling."

The reporter frowns. "Right, right, I didn't mean that. I mean did you wake up and find this second man dead right next to you? Just like the first one?"

Harp shakes his head and keeps on shaking it to show the man he's saying it wrong. "No, no, I wasn't there."

"You didn't sleep under the pier last night?"

"No, I slept in the Fearful Ones circle."

"Fearful ones?" Vince looks at Speel.

Speel says, "A group of homeless men who sleep in a circle. For protection."

Vince looks back at Harp. "So you claim you weren't even there last night. Not under the pier, I mean."

Harp nods.

Vince looks puzzled. "Now wait a minute. Let me get this straight. Speel here told me this policeman named Olivera talked to you after the first man was murdered. And then he took your coat away for evidence, but he didn't arrest you. Then this second guy is killed, and now the police are saying you did it. Why do you think they're saying you did it if you weren't even at the pier last night?"

Harp raises his hand. "Uh, did they really say I did it?"

"Yes, Harp, I'm afraid they did. I saw it on the wire. The police bulletin said they were looking for a very short homeless man named

Harp, about eighteen years old, with close-cropped blonde hair. That's you, isn't it?"

Now you've done it. They're on to you for sure.

"I guess so," says Harp.

"How about that, Harp?" says Speel. "You might get to be famous after all. They might even put you on the most-wanted list. I've got a story about the most-wanted list right there in one of my magazines." She glances toward the stacks of magazines at the back of the garage. "Uh, somewhere." Speel turns to the reporter. "So they think Harp did both murders? Do you think they put out an APB on him? Will there be a reward?"

Vince shrugs. "I don't know about that. I came down here to the beach as soon as I picked it up off the wire. I'll have to go to the local police station here to see what they're saying now." Even though he's talking to Speel, Vince keeps on glancing at Harp. He turns back to Harp and leans close. "Listen, Harp, I covered the murder of the first man, this Hill fellow. He was stabbed a bunch of times. In the back. You didn't have an argument with him did you? Some kind of dispute?"

Don't admit anything.

Dispute? Harp isn't sure what Vince is getting at. Should he tell him about Little Hilly not giving him his share of the panhandling money?

No! Nobody can ever know about that.

"No, I liked Little Hilly. He was my friend. He gave me a piece of pizza once."

"So, this Hilly fellow was a friend of yours? And you claim there wasn't any bad blood between you."

"Bad blood?"

They know. Who caught his blood?

"No, it's not true. Really, Mr. Vince, I didn't catch his blood. I liked him. Why would I hurt him?"

Vince turns to Speel. "Is that right. They were friends?"

Speel shrugs. "I didn't know Little Hilly had any friends. He was kind of a . . . jerk, if you get my meaning. I thought his only friend was Big Hilly."

Vince turns back to Harp. "Big Hilly? Who's that?"

"He's the main suspect," says Harp. "Detective Olivera thinks he did it, but I know he didn't."

"You say he's the policeman's main suspect, but you know he didn't do it? How do you know that, Harp?"

"Well . . . I mean, I don't think he did it."

"Well, I'm sorry to be the one to tell you this, son, but I talked to your Detective Olivera on the phone before I came down here. He's saying you did it, both murders I mean. You're his main suspect, not some mysterious Big Hilly character. Detective Olivera says he knew it all along it was you, but he was giving you enough rope to hang yourself."

Harp can't believe his ears. Olivera is saying he did it? Giving him enough rope to hang himself? That's what Worried Jack said. Maybe Worried Jack did know something after all. But why would Olivera ask him to help find Little Hilly's killer if he thought he was the one that did it?

"Are you still with me, Harp? Did you hear what I said?"

Harp nods, but he doesn't feel like listening to the reporter man right now. He's got to think this through. He feels like crying.

Now don't start sniveling. You've got to think clearly.

Harp can hardly hold back the tears. It's not fair. First his only friend, Little Hilly, gets killed, and then his new friend Detective Olivera turns against him.

Then that leaves us alone, doesn't it? Just you and me, like I said all along.

Harp shakes his head hard to make the tears go away. He doesn't want the reporter to see him cry, or Speel either. Mother always said he shouldn't let anybody see what he was feeling. She always said people will let you down, and she was right. She said they would hurt you if they got the chance, if you didn't hurt them first. How right she was. So now he knows nobody is going to help him. He's on his own. All right. They'll be sorry, just wait and see.

That's better. We'll make them pay.

"Pay attention, kid. Just a few more questions. How about this second victim?" He glances at his notebook. "This Lemke guy. I haven't been to the police station yet, but Olivera told me on the phone he was also stabbed. A lot of times in the back, just like the first guy. No dispute with Lemke either?"

Just clam up.

Harp shakes his head, determined not to say anything more.

"Well, all right then. I'll go talk to the police now. See what I can find out. Can you think of anything else you need to tell me?"

Don't trust him. Don't trust anybody but me.

Harp shakes his head again. He's already said too much. This man isn't his friend. And Speel isn't either. Nobody is going to help him. If he's going to stay out of jail now, he'll have to help himself.

The reporter takes Speel's arm and leads her to the big garage door. They whisper there for a few moments before Speel turns to say, "You stay put here, Harp. I'll be back before you know it."

4-4

Mouse in a Trap

*H*arp jumps to his feet. "Wait, Speel, don't close the door."

But it's too late. They go out and the garage door closes. Harp is alone again. He hurries to the door and leans his ear against it. He can't hear anything out there. Did they go away?

He takes ahold of the handle and turns it very slowly, making sure it doesn't make any noise. But the handle only turns half way and stops. Feeling the panic rise up in his throat, he tries harder. The handle won't move. He starts to frantically bang on the door.

Stop that! Don't make so much noise.

Harp stops. She's right. What if Speel's mother hears me? She might call the police.

He turns away from the door and looks at the garage room. There's nothing there except stacks and stacks of old magazines back in the darkness. Now he knows what the poor miller's daughter felt like, locked forever in the kings tower until she could learn how to spin straw into gold.

She found a way out, didn't she?

"I know she found a way to escape. She was clever. But this is different. There's no little man to come in through the window to help me because . . . because there isn't any window."

Now don't start feeling sorry for yourself.

"But it isn't fair."

So life isn't fair. Get used to it.

Harp sits down on the mattress to think. Why did Speel have to lock him in?

It's obvious. They've gone for the police. They're going to turn you in.

That's right, the reporter said he was going to go talk to the police. Maybe he'll tell the police where I am. Maybe that's why Speel locked the door. They're trying to trap him.

You have to find a way out before they come back.

"But there isn't any way out."

Look around. You have to find a way out.

Maybe she's right. Maybe there is another way out. He gets up and quickly goes to the back of the garage. What is behind all these dusty old magazines?

A wall. Maybe there's a window.

He pushes aside the first few stacks, but there are more stacks behind. He begins to throw the magazines out into the middle of the floor, but every time he gets through a stack, there is another stack behind it. There are so many magazines, it seems like he'll never find the wall.

Keep going.

He keeps going, but when he finally breaks through the last stack, all he finds are some dirty old cardboard boxes, stacked all the way up to the ceiling.

The wall is behind them. Keep going.

She's right, the wall has to be behind these boxes. He reaches up as high as he can reach and pulls at the top box. The whole stack begins to lean toward him. He jumps out of the way, barely getting clear before it all comes crashing down. The box splits open and spills out its contents. More magazines, really old dirty ones, with yellowed pictures on their fronts. But now he can see that there is a wall behind the boxes. Finding new strength, he pulls down the rest of the boxes.

And there it is, the wall. It's dark so far back in the garage, but Harp can see a little bit of light coming in through cracks between the boards. That light gives him a little hope. He raps on the boards, but they feel more solid than they look.

"Oh, no, there's no way out."

Don't give up now. Try to pry one of the boards off.

He tears at the boards with his fingernails. Maybe one if them is a little bit loose. But despite their dirty old look, they all seem solid.

Harp puts his eye close to a crack between two boards. He can see some daylight out there, and he can see the white house a little ways away. The outside is so close, it makes his heart hurt. He wants the freedom of that outside. "I want to be out there, now Mother. Let me out."

What can I do about it? You have to fend for yourself this time. Keep looking. Find a way out.

Harp sits down on a box and puts his head in his hands. It's no use. There's no way out. He's trapped like a mouse in a cage.

Whining won't help. Keep looking.

Harp wipes his eyes with the back of his hands. "No, there's no use trying anymore. There's no way out of here."

You don't know that. You have to keep trying. Remember Benjamin, the youngest and weakest boy? The one who was named from the Bible. He escaped because he trusted his mother. Remember?

"Yes, but he was smart. Nothing ever works for me. I always do it wrong."

Now, now, don't be a quitter. Even though he was sentenced to die, little Benjamin lived. Don't you remember? The white flag, come home? The red flag run away? Think about the story. He trusted his mother, and he lived. You have to trust me.

"But he had a real mother to help him."

Are you saying I'm not real? How dare you?

"Well, I try to believe, don't I? I asked you for help, but did you give it to me? No. You never help me when I really need it."

I can only help you if you help yourself. Now get up off your lazy behind and keep looking for a way out of this mess you've got yourself into.

"It's no use. I'm tired."

I said now! Get up and get moving. Do you hear me, young man?

"Oh, all right. But it's no use. You always say I never do anything right anyhow."

This is different. This time you have to do it right. Get Busy. Try the other side.

Harp stands up and fights his way through the magazines that are strewn all over the floor. He makes it to the other side of the garage and begins to pull down the stacks of magazines. When all the stacks of magazines have been pulled down, there was still a stack of boxes against the wall. He pulls the top box off, and it crashes to the floor. He stops and listens to see if anybody heard the noise. But he hears nothing, so he tips over the rest of the boxes, one by one. He's finally to the wall, but it's just like the other wall: more old boards.

"See there. It's the same as the other wall." He kicks at a box. "I told you, there's no way out."

He waits, but there's only silence in the garage. This time it feels like he's trapped for good. It's like he's back in Mother's closet, and this time she's never going to let him out. She won't even talk to him. It's too much to bear.

He sits right down on a box and cries into his hands. This time he'll cry as hard as he wants to, and nobody can stop him. He lets the tears come out like he should have let them come a long time ago.

Cry baby, cry baby. Harp is a little cry baby.

He jumps to his feet. "So now you're back. And you're being mean again. Well, now I don't care what you say. I can cry if I damn well want to."

Don't you curse at me, young man.

"Why not? Why the hell not? Why shouldn't I curse? Nothing ever goes right, and everybody is mean to me, even you."

The Bible says, He that curseth his mother, shall surely be put to death.

"All right, all right. I've been bad, I know it." He sits back down on the box and begins to hit himself in the sides of his head with his fists.

Stop that! I told you to never do that.

Harp looks up at the dark ceiling. "I said I was bad, didn't I? What more do you want?"

Don't look at me. It's not my fault if you can't do anything right.

"Well, whose fault is it then? You said you'd always take care of me. You said you'd show me what to do. Then you let that judge lock me up in Ward D-4. Was that taking care of me? Is that how you protect me?"

What could I do? I . . . I wasn't there.

"That's what you always say. It's not your fault. But I'm the one who always has to pay for your mistakes. I trusted you, and look what happened."

Maybe I did make a few mistakes . . . in the past.

"A few mistakes? How about a lot of mistakes?"

Well, what about you? Do I have to remind you of what happened that night, of what you did to me? I was in bed, sound asleep. And what did you do? You crept in and . . .

"No, no, no, you can't hold that against me forever. I told you it was an accident."

All right, so we both made mistakes. But this time I'm right. This time I know what's best for you.

"That's what you always say. You know best. But I'm fed up."

Listen here, young man. Stop this sniveling and take some action for once in your life. You've got to get out of here.

"Don't you think I know that? I'm trying, aren't I? Why don't you help me?

I am helping.

"You only help by telling me what I'm doing wrong."

Listen, we've always done well together, haven't we? We've had a few minor problems, but it always works out in the end, doesn't it? You should just keep on doing whatever I tell you to do and everything will work out all right in the end. Trust me.

"I did trust you, but now Little Hilly is dead, and the Blind Shrimp is dead too, and the police think I did it. Haven't I always tried to do whatever you said? Haven't I always tried to be a good boy? And look what it got me. I'm in more trouble than ever."

So now you're blaming me?

"I'm not . . . blaming you. I just want to get out of here before they come and put me in jail, or back in a place like that Ward D-4."

Listen to me, get up and go look behind that last stack of boxes. If there is a way out, it's got to be there.

"Really? Do you really think so?" Harp turns to look at the last stack of cardboard boxes. "There might be a way out back there?

You're not just saying that?"

Stop sniveling and go see for yourself.

Harp dries his tears on his sleeve. "All right, all right. I'm going, aren't I?" He can see there's only one stack of boxes left. He might as well go see what's behind them.

He carefully climbs up on top of the stack of boxes and looks down behind them. This time he's sees something that gives him a little hope. There's a little more light coming through this wall than the other walls. He hurriedly tips over the whole stack of boxes and sees that this wall has some sideways boards that are on top of the regular wall boards. It looks like maybe it used to be . . .

A window.

"Yes, it does look like a window." He goes closer and peeks through the sideways boards. Light is coming through. "There is a window, but it's got these board nailed on top of it."

I told you there was a way out. Now do you believe me?

Harp begins to pull at the boards. If only he can get them to come loose. One of the boards creaks when he pulls on it. But it won't come loose, no matter how hard he pulls.

Pull harder. Don't be such a weakling.

"I am pulling hard. It's stuck."

Well, then get something to pry with. You've got to get through to that window.

Harp hops down off the box and looks around the garage. There must be something to pry those boards off with. But there doesn't seem to be anything in the garage but magazines and old newspapers and tipped over cardboard boxes. Nothing to pry with. He looks at the king-size bottle of Coca Cola that's sitting on the floor next to the mattress. Would that work? Can you pry with a pop bottle?

Try it.

He hurries to get it, and while he's there, he picks up his backpack and puts it on, just in case he gets out. He looks at the Coca Cola bottle. It feels pretty heavy, and the glass seems pretty thick. It's worth a try.

He wades back through the piles of magazines and climbs back up on top of the boxes. He puts the top of the bottle under the loosest board and begins to pry with it.

Be careful. Don't break the bottle.

He works at the board carefully, only prying a little bit at a time, making sure he doesn't break the Coke bottle. With every pry, the board squeaks, and gradually, very slowly, it begins to come loose. When he thinks it's loose enough, Harp gets ahold of the end of the board and puts his feet against the wall. He pulls and pulls until the nails finally come loose with a groaning sound. "I did it. I really did."

Don't break your arm patting yourself on the back. You're not free yet. Keep working.

Harp carefully puts the board out of the way and peeks through. The glass in the window is cracked.

Break it.

Should I?

Do it.

Harp pokes at the glass with the coke bottle and it shatters.

Be quiet. Do you want somebody to hear you?

Harp carefully picks at the glass, pulling the shards loose one at a time and placing them on top of the cardboard box. When he gets most of the glass taken out, he cautiously sticks his head out through the hole and looks around. It's getting dark, and the fog is coming in again. He picks up a whiff of sea air, and it makes him yearn to be back down at the beach. If only the hole was big enough to get out of.

Well, don't just stand there. Get the rest of those boards off.

He pulls his head back in and goes to work loosening the next board. He works hard, prying at it with the bottle. It's not as loose as the first board, but it's gradually coming loose. He stops to rest and looks back toward the garage door. What a mess he's made: there are magazines and newspapers and broken-open boxes all over the floor. Speel will be really mad when she comes back. But what if Speel comes back before he can get out? What if she brings the police ?

Then quit wasting time. Hurry!

He turns back to his task. The second board is stuck tight. He keeps on scraping his knuckles and they're bleeding. He stops to suck at the blood.

Don't be such a baby. What's a little blood to you? Keep working.

He goes back to work. If he can just get this one more board loose he'll be free. Then he'll make a run for the border and get away from everybody. He'll find a nice place where nobody knows him, and he'll act real normal so nobody suspects a thing.

That thought makes him feel better, and it makes him feel stronger. He pries harder, and the board suddenly comes loose. This time he doesn't worry about the sound: he pokes the glass out with the Coke bottle.

He stops to listen. Nothing. He peeks out. It's getting very dark out there. The fog is rolling in, like it does almost very night. Nobody is around. He carefully crawls out. But his hands can't find anything to grab. He begins to slip out the hole.

Be careful. You'll break your fool neck.

He slides down the side of the garage and hits the ground head first.

"Owe."

Shh.

"I hit my head."

So you fell down and hit your head. So what? You're not hurt bad. Get up and get away from here.

"But it hurts."

Shush, I said. And stop talking to me out loud. People will hear you. Can't you do anything right?

Harp lies there on the ground, staring up at the sky, wondering why he can't ever do anything right.

He sits up and rubs the back of his head. Nothing seems to be broken inside his head so he gets up and goes to the corner of the garage. He peeks around. Nobody's coming. He hurries down the alley, constantly looking back to make sure he's not being followed. He's glad it's getting dark now, and he's glad the fog is getting so thick. The police are probably out there somewhere looking for him, but they won't get him. He imagines himself slipping right past them in the fog. He's the silent avenger, unseen, but all knowing, creeping right past his evil pursuers.

Have you been reading those comic books again? What did I tell you about that?

4-5

Trust

*B*y the time Harp makes it back to the beach, it's completely dark, and the fog has rolled in again. He hides in the alley behind the Beachside Apartments building, waiting to catch his breath. Next to the parked cars there are four big garbage cans, all in a row. He wonders if there's anything good to eat in them.

He's about to look when he hears a siren in the distance. Is it coming his way? Are they coming to get him?

Calm down. Everything will be fine now that's it's just the two of us.

"Will it?" he whispers. "Will it ever get back to the way it was?"

Quit worrying so much. I said I'd take care of things and I will.

The siren goes on past and wails away into the distance.

See there? Nothing to worry about.

Harp leans against the side of the building and counts his breaths until they begin to slow down. He tries to tell himself that she's right, that everything will be all right. But he's not so sure. He feels different, like something inside himself changed when he was alone in Speel's garage-house. He chews at the inside of his cheek and worries that something has gone wrong inside his head. Maybe all this thinking and investigating and searching for clues has made his brain too hot. Maybe he's getting sick. When he was little and did things Mother didn't like, she always said he must be getting sick. She'd make him some nice hot chicken soup to make him feel better. How long since he'd had some nice hot chicken soup? They had soup sometimes on Ward D-4, but it didn't have anything in it that tasted like chicken, and it was never hot because Mitch wouldn't let them eat it until he finished his long before-eating prayer. If anybody tried to sneak something to eat before the prayer was done, the Growler was called, and nobody got to eat anything until the whipping was over and done with.

Harp peeks around the edge of the apartment building, trying to see through the fog. Is anybody over there on the beach? He doesn't see any movement, but the fog is so thick it's hard to tell. Somewhere, a long ways away, a car horn honks over and over again. It seems like it's going to go on forever, but then it stops. Then it's so quiet he can hear the cars on the freeway in the distance. That reminds him that he's been forgetting to listen to the sound of things. So many things have been going wrong, it's hard to think about things like sounds. He hasn't even had time to watch the white ocean birds that soar up in the sky all day, or go look for the funny little black crabs that scurry away when you peek under their rock hiding places. None of those things seem as important as they used to. He hopes this will all be over soon so things can get back to being normal.

Don't think about such nonsense. Remember what you're supposed to be doing. Go get the money.

"All right, all right, I'm going," he whispers. He hurries out onto the strand sidewalk, and as he passes Betty's Bra Bar and Sex Shoppe, he's happy to see that her white wall has been painted over. It's as if the bad painting of the stabbed dog had never been there.

Harp wonders why nobody is on the sidewalk tonight. Maybe the cold fog is keeping them away. He shivers. If only the Shrimp would have got him a new coat, then maybe none of this would be happening.

You brought this on yourself by getting mixed up with him in the first place. Didn't I tell you not to go with him?

"Yeah, well, if you would have helped me get a coat, I wouldn't have had to go with the Shrimp. It's your fault."

Is not.

"Is too."

Well, I'm helping you now, aren't I? Get moving. Go get the money.

"And that's another thing. How do I know there really is any money?"

It's there. Trust me.

"Well, if there really is money, how will I know where to find it?"

It's buried under the pier. Do I have to remind you of everything?

"Oh, right. Under the pier." But is the money really under the pier? If he already knew where it was, why did he forget it?

No time to think about that. The police are hot on your trail.

"But if the money is buried there, how did--"

Quiet! Listen.

Harp stops to listen. Was it a whistle? Is somebody whistling at him?

Hide!

Harp ducks behind the closed and shuttered hot-dog-on-a-stick stand, trying to see where the whistle came from. He can't see anything through the swirling fog.

Then he sees a shadowy figure moving slowly toward him. The low whistle comes again, then a sad voice: "Teddy, where are you? I want you to come home now, Teddy. I need you."

Harp realizes it must be the red-faced old man, still looking for his little dog. Harp wishes poor little Teddy hadn't had to die.

Don't think about that now. Get on with the task at hand.

He can't stop to think about poor little Teddy now. He has to make it back to the pier without being seen.

As soon as the shadowy figure goes past, Harp darts across the sidewalk and heads for the beach. When he passes the horseshoe-tossing pits, he realizes he's almost to the old brick restroom where the Ghost lives. "The Ghost knows a lot about what goes on at the beach. Maybe I should talk to him."

Now don't get distracted again. That weirdo doesn't know anything.

"Yes he does. He hears things. He knows things. I'm going in to ask him some questions."

Suit yourself, but I still say it's a waste of time.

Harp ducks around to the front of the little restroom building and goes inside.

The flap in the cardboard wall in front of the Ghost's stall opens, and two dark eyes peer out. "Oh, it's you, Harp." The ghost's voice sounds like it's coming from inside a deep cave. It makes Harp wonder how many layers of cardboard the Ghost has got built up inside that stall. The flap closes.

Harp goes into the stall next to the Ghost's and taps on the wall. "Listen, Ghost, I have to talk to you."

"Go away. I'm trying to get some sleep in here."

Harp sits down on the toilet and taps on the wall again. He sees that the Ghost now has his cardboard going all the way up to the ceiling. He's completely sealed off from the rest of the world. Harp wonders how the Ghost gets food in there. He can get water from the toilet, but how does he get food?

Hurry up and ask him your questions and get out of here.

Harp taps on the wall again. "Listen, Ghost, you see everybody who comes in here. Did you see anybody come in here the night before last night? Anybody you don't know?"

"Last night?"

"No, the night before last night."

"What time? Early or late?"

"It might have been real late."

"Nope."

"You didn't see anybody?"

See there. A waste of time.

"Nobody I didn't know. Last night, Shoeless Joe came in and paced for a while. Then he left. How's a person supposed to get any sleep with Shoeless Joe in here pacing all night?"

Harp tries to imagine how the Ghost sleeps in that little stall. Does he curl himself around next to the toilet?

The police are hot on his trail and he worries about how this weirdo sleeps.

"I'm sorry you couldn't sleep, Ghost. You didn't hear anything that night?"

"I didn't say that."

"So you did see something?"

"I didn't say that either."

Why is the Ghost being so troublesome? Maybe it's because he didn't get enough sleep. "Just tell me, Ghost, what did you see or hear?"

"I heard something."

"What was it?"

"A dog."

"You heard a dog?"

"Yep. I heard a dog howling. Down by the water, I think. Then it stopped."

"Did it stop real sudden, like somebody stopped him?"

"That's right. Did you hear it too?"

"Yes, I did. Shoeless Joe said he heard it too, and the Blind Shrimp."

Do you have to blab everything right out loud?

For a few moments the Ghost doesn't say anything. But then he says, "It's too bad about the Shrimp. Did you kill him?"

"No, of course I didn't. Why did you say that? Why would I want to hurt the Shrimp?"

"Everybody says you did it because you wanted his money."

"If I took his money I wouldn't be here on the beach, would I?"

The Ghost is silent for several seconds again. Then he says, "If you did have money, where would you go?"

Careful, careful.

Harp doesn't want to tell the Ghost about making a run for the border so he says, "Never mind about that. I've got to get going."

"All right. Watch out for that stranger."

That stops Harp. He feels his heart start to beat fast again. "What stranger? I thought you said you didn't see anybody you didn't know."

"You said the night before last night."

"I meant anytime. Are you saying a stranger came in here looking for me?"

"That's what I said, didn't I? He came in last night."

Uh oh. It's the killer. I warned you. Didn't I warn you?

"Well, what did he look like?"

"I couldn't see him very well. But I can tell you about his eyes. When he looked in through my hole, I saw his eyes. Real mean eyes, hateful eyes."

"Mean eyes. Okay, what did he say?"

"He said he was looking for you. How many times do I have to say it?"

Harp wonders if the man was from the police. Some of the police had mean eyes, but the Ghost probably knew all the police on the beach. "So, Ghost, if he looked at you, why couldn't you see his face?"

"It was dark."

"Well, the only reason it's dark in here at night is because you keep on taking the light bulbs out. If you'd leave them in, you could see better."

"How can I sleep with a light on? Besides I always leave one on, over by the door."

"All right. So the Stranger had mean eyes. Was he big or little?"

"Big guy."

Harp realizes he's getting pretty good at asking questions. He's asking one question right after the other, and the Ghost is answering every one of them. Olivera would be proud of him.

Are you forgetting that fat cop is the one who's after you?

"Could you see his nose?"

"He had a big nose. I think."

Aha, thinks Harp. Big Nose. The man who was pretending to panhandle by the Sunnysidewalk Café. "Listen, Ghost, was his nose crooked at the top? And did he have a big stomach? And clean black pants?"

"No, that's a cop. That cop came in here tonight with Olivera. Watch out for that Olivera, Harp. He threatened to tear down my house here if I didn't tell him where you were."

"But you didn't tell him, did you?"

"I didn't know, or I would have. Where would I live if they tore down my house?"

See. He'll turn on you. Give them a chance and they'll all turn on you.

Harp thinks about the Ghost's words. Would he really tell on him? Maybe everybody was like that. Maybe they could all be broken down by the police if they had some information the police wanted bad enough. *I'll have to be careful not to tell the Ghost any secrets.*

Now you're using your noodle.

"So it was a big man, with mean eyes and a big nose. That's all you know?"

"He was crazy."

"Crazy. Why do you say that, Ghost?"

"I can tell."

"Like what? Crazy like Hippie? Or afraid of everything, like Worried Jack?"

"Naw, everybody around here is crazy like that. This guy was *real* crazy."

"Real crazy?"

"Right. I can tell."

A crazy person is after you. Get out of here, quick!

Harp suddenly feels trapped. What if the crazy stranger with the mean eyes comes back? He hurries out of the stall and taps on the Ghost's cardboard front door. "I'm leaving now, Ghost. You be sure to tell me if you see that man again, won't you?"

The little flap opens. "I'm not coming out to find you, if that's what you mean."

"I know you're not coming out, Ghost. You never come out. But maybe I'll come back and ask you later."

"All right, but I won't answer if I'm asleep. I need my sleep."

"I understand, Ghost. Thank you for telling me what you saw and heard."

"You sure you don't have any money?"

"No, I'm sorry, Ghost. I don't have any."

"If you get some money, would you bring me some Pepsi Colas and some French fries?"

"All right, if I get some money and . . . if I'm still here."

"Are you going somewhere?"

Harp shakes his head. "I didn't say I was going anywhere, did I?"

"All right. Bye, Harp. I hope you find him and get your hat back."

Your hat!

That stops Harp again. He turns back. "What did you say, Ghost? About my hat, I mean."

"I said I hope you find him so you can get your hat back."

"Are you talking about the Stranger?"

"Yeah. He was wearing your hat. Had it pulled down over his face. He said, 'I'm looking for a little guy named Harp. He wears this hat.'"

"Are you sure it was my hat?"

"Yeah. That little floppy brown one you always wear."

Harp is suddenly overcome with a feeling that the world is closing in on him. Why would the Stranger have his hat?

You know why. Because he's the killer. Run, before it's too late!

He tries to think clearly, but his heart is beating so hard it's making his ears ring.

Why are you just standing there? Run away! Now!

Harp can't move. His head hurts, like somebody is pulling on it from both sides. His hat. The stranger has his hat. What does it mean?

It means what I've been trying to tell you all along. He's after you. He's trying to kill you.

But how did the stranger get his hat? Little Hilly borrowed that hat to do some panhandling. And then the mysterious stranger with mean eyes ends up wearing it. Does it mean the Stranger killed Little Hilly and took his hat?

Didn't I just say that? Are you listening to me or not?

But why would a stranger want to kill Little Hilly?

This is the last time I'm going to say this. He meant to kill you.

Could it be true? Could it mean the killer wasn't after Little Hilly at all. It could mean the killer was after . . . me?

He finally gets it. About time.

"I've got to get out of here, Ghost. Did the Stranger say anything else?"

"Nope. But I'll tell you something else, if you ask me nice."

"What?"

"Ask me nice."

"Please."

"As he went out the door he took off your hat. And guess what he was doing with it."

"What?"

"He was smelling it."

"Smelling it? You mean like holding it up to his nose and sniffing it?"

"Yep. He went out the door smelling your hat. Like I said, he was crazy."

Crazy is right. This is worse than I thought.

"All right, Ghost. I'm leaving now."

"About time. I need to get to sleep."

"If Detective Olivera comes again, don't tell him I was here, okay?

"Okay, Harp, I won't if you promise to bring me that Pepsi Cola. And don't forget the French fries."

"I will if I can, Ghost, but I've got to go now." Harp slips out the door and hurries across the sand toward the shore. He tries to think who the Stranger could be. A man with mean eyes. Asking about him. And wearing his hat. What could it mean?

It means you're in big trouble. You've got to go somewhere else, somewhere where he can't find you.

He should stop and put that man right at the top of his suspects list. In fact, the Stranger might be the only one that needs to be on his suspects list now.

There's no time for that. Keep going.

"Well, what should I do? Maybe I should tell Olivera about the Stranger."

He won't believe you. He'll lock you up and throw away the key.

Suddenly, someone looms up out of the fog, right in front of him.

It's him! Run!

He's ready to run, but then he sees that it's not a real person. It's only a little man made out of sand with sticks for arms and a red plastic beach bucket for a head. The kids must have made it and left it there to scare him. It's just one more thing to make him feel bad. Everybody is against him. First Speel locks him in her garage-house, and now the police think he's been going around killing people. And to top it all off, a crazy stranger with mean eyes is after him. It's too much. "Why do bad things always have to happen to me?"

Quit feeling sorry for yourself. I'll get you out of this mess. Haven't I always got you out of trouble?

Harp is confused about what to do. Here he's practically figured out who the real killer is, and he can't even tell anybody about it. And why doesn't anybody else except the Ghost know about the Stranger? Why hasn't anybody else seen him? "Maybe he's a ghost. Not like the Ghost, but a real ghost."

A ghost that kills people? Get serious.

"Well, why hasn't anybody else seen him?"

Maybe he only comes out at night. Did you ever think about that?

A killer who only comes out at night? Yes, maybe he's like Beelzebub, only appearing when the magician calls him out of the darkness. Suddenly Harp has a brilliant thought. What if he could be like the magician who had a magic book that locked with a magic key? He could look up the answer about how to catch the killer.

You? Catch him yourself? If I had that magician's book, I'd look up in it why you're so dumb.

"No, really, Mother, I may not have a magic book, but what if I can find out who the Stranger is and . . . I don't know . . . lead the police to him. Or something."

Lead the police to him? Now I know you're nuts. Lead the police to yourself is what you'd do.

Harp knows it would probably be better to just run away. But if he could just catch the killer himself, maybe everything would go back to normal. Then he could just go back to walking on the beach and listening to the waves and watching the sea birds dive for fish and seeing the little crabs scramble away between the rocks.

Forget it. That's all in the past now.

Harp hurries on, suddenly very sad. It seems like the good times never last. But then, it's been so long since he's had any good times maybe he's forgotten which times the good times are.

When he makes it to the water's edge, he stops. He watches the waves slide in and out. The air is cold and wet, but the smell of the sea is a good smell. It reminds him he's been away from the ocean all day, and he missed it. It's like coming home. For a moment he thinks about sitting down to listen to the waves lick the shore.

Are you crazy? Go get the money and get away from here.

"I know, I know. I'm going, aren't I?" It's just too bad when a person can't even stop for a few teensy little minutes to listen to the waves, or watch Bailey lift up his cute wife, or even take the time to be amazed when the amazing Cedric flips his chainsaw up into the air and catches it without cutting any of his parts off. Since people started getting killed, he never seems to have time for anything fun anymore. And now he has to go to the pier and dig up the money, and then he has to make a run for the border, and it doesn't seem like that's going to be very much fun either.

He starts walking again, but then he stops. "Wait a minute. What if whoever killed the Shrimp already got the money?"

It's still there. Trust me.

"Well, maybe, but it seems like the killer would have took it."

No, just keep going.

He starts walking again, but all of a sudden his plan to make a run for the border seems too complicated. Maybe there isn't really any money buried under the pier. And maybe there isn't any bus that goes to the border, wherever the border is. Maybe everything is all wrong and nothing will ever be right again.

Just shut up and keep going. I'll do the thinking around here.

He keeps going, but when he sees the pier ahead, it looks dark and old and scary in the fog. He stops dead in his tracks. What was he thinking? Why should be go back to the pier? It's a bad place, it's where Little Hilly and the Shrimp were killed.

Don't you trust me?

"But what if the killer is there waiting for me?"

There won't be anybody there. Don't I always know what I'm doing?

"But how do you know? Why should I believe you?"

You have to trust my voice. Just listen to my voice. Don't I always know what's best for you?

"But you didn't know about the Stranger. And the Ghost said the Stranger had my hat. You didn't know about that either. He might be under the pier waiting to kill me. The pier is the last place I should be going." He turns around and hurries away from the pier.

No, stop! You have to go to the pier and get that money. We need money.

Harp stops and looks back at the dark shape of the pier. "Are you sure? What about that old Cock Robin rhyme you keep reminding me of? Nobody helped Cock Robin. They all knew about it, but nobody did anything about it, not even you."

They mourned him, that's all that's important. The rhyme says, 'And who'll be chief mourner?' Me. I'll be the chief mourner. When you die, I'll be there with you. It will just be you and me again.

"But I don't want to die. Not yet."

There's nothing to be afraid of. I'll be there with you every step of the way.

"Well, if you're sure."

I am sure. Now turn around and go get that money!

"All right, all right, you don't have to shout." Harp puts his fingers in his ears and heads for the pier. As he gets close to it, he slows down, watching for any movement. The pier really did seem different, dark and cold in the fog, dead and lifeless.

Harp shivers. He feels afraid. But why should he? He knows that pier so well. It's his secret place, like the secret cupboard the boy hid in when the wolf pretended to be his mother and came to eat him. How many nights has he slept under that pier? Too many to remember. His hiding place way up under the pier is small and dark and safe.

When he gets to the pier, he takes his fingers out of his ears and stands next to one of the big wooden columns. He stares into the darkness, listening for any sound. He doesn't hear anything, but just to be sure, he takes out his little flashlight and shines it all around. Nobody. He turns to shine the light on the spot where he found Little Hilly's body. There's no sign anybody was every lying there. Was that where the Shrimp got killed too? Or was it up under the pier? He turns to shine his light up toward his secret place. "Should I go up there?"

Shh. Stop talking out loud to me. Just go up and get the money.

"All right," he whispers. "But I'm not so sure about this." He tries to tell himself there's nothing to be afraid of. It's only the wooden old pier, same as always. All he has to do is find where the Shrimp buried the money, dig it up, and make a run for it.

He crawls up toward his secret place, looking for signs of dug-up sand. But he can't see anyplace where it looks like money might be buried. He stops. "Well, where is it?"

It's up in your secret place. Go up there.

He crawls up to his secret hiding place. Thank goodness, it doesn't look like anybody has been there. His sand wall is just like he left it, all pushed up against the pier so no one would ever suspect there's a little hidden cave behind there.

Quit wasting time. Go in and get the money.

Harp begins to dig the sand away with both hands. But then he stops. A smell comes out. It's mostly the usual strong tarry smell of the underside of the pier, but there's another smell in there too, like nothing he's ever smelled before.

Look inside.

He turns on his little flashlight and pokes it through the hole. Something touches his hand, and before he can pull it back out, something gets ahold of his wrist and keeps ahold of it, really tight. He cries out, "Ouch! You're hurting me. Let go!"

But whatever is in there won't let go. The last thing Harp sees before the flashlight goes out is a great big hand holding onto his wrist, and the hand has a black tattoo of a cross on it. The big tattooed hand begins to pull him in.

Part 5

The South Mountain Indian

The ward is all upset again today because of what happened to Bacon Benny last night. Yesterday Benny got mad because Mitch wouldn't let him play in the pinochle game. Benny started yelling "Mitch has got a girl friend, Mitch has got a girl friend." That made Mitch real mad. We all knew about Mitch's cute little girl friend who works in the recreational therapy department but Mitch didn't know we knew. Benny carried on about it so long Mitch said Benny must have spit out his morning meds and then Mitch said he had a hangover and needed some peace and quiet so he told the Growler to hold Benny down while he put a double dose of meds in Benny's mouth. Then he held Benny's nose while he poured water down his throat to make sure he swallowed all the pills. Carl the Older told me Mitch already got in trouble once for giving patients meds the doctor didn't write out, but I guess he had such a bad hangover he didn't care if he got in trouble again. I knew Benny really had taken his normal morning dose so I was worried about what all those extra pills would do to him. The Growler tied Benny to a chair in front of the TV, but when a TV show about a magic witch came on Benny couldn't stand it and started yelling again. Mitch threw down his pinochle cards and told the Growler to tie Benny up and throw him into the Time-Out Closet. I think Mitch must have fed Benny even more pills before he threw him into the Time-Out Closet because Benny stopped yelling and was real quiet in there. I felt bad for Benny because ever since he got put in the Closet for stealing bacon off the crazy guys plates he was real scared of being inside it. I walked by there to listen because I hoped Benny was throwing up all those pills, but I didn't hear anything. Mitch told me to stay the hell away from there so I had to go out into the Day Room and write my little stories all day to keep from worrying about it.

Before Mitch went off shift, he sent The Growler to let Benny out but Benny was still knocked out cold so Mitch and the Growler carried him back and put him on his cot. During the night I woke up and saw Benny's eyes were open so I crawled over to try to talk to him. But he wouldn't wake up even when I shook him. I went out and got Mr. Taylor the night aide and told him Benny wouldn't wake up. Mr. Taylor came back to look but when he shined a flashlight on Benny's eyes he said it was too late. He made me help him drag Benny out into the dining room so the others wouldn't wake up in the middle of the night and get all riled up when they saw Benny dead. We left him lying there on that cold cement floor while Mr. Taylor went to call the morgue guy. He made me go back to bed so I don't know how long it took them to come and get Benny but he was gone when we went in for breakfast this morning.

5-1

Empathy

*A*s soon as the big hand pulls him through the sand wall, Harp is pretty sure he's about to be dead. It's completely dark inside his hideout hole so he can't even see who it is that has ahold of his wrist. That tattoo of a cross on the hand was a lot like the picture of the big cross knife on Betty's wall, so Harp figures this must be the same thing that happened to Little Hilly and the Shrimp. The last thing they probably ever saw was that tattoo. Harp waits for the feel of the knife to stick in his back.

No! Don't give up. Fight back!

Harp wishes he could fight back, but he can feel that the big hand is too strong. He just hopes it won't hurt too much when the knife goes in. He doesn't even mind the idea of dying so much; at least he won't be cold and hungry anymore, but he wishes he could have said goodbye to Speel and the Ghost and Worried Jack and Tex and the others. He says a special little whispered goodbye to Shoeless Joe: "Bye, Joe. I hope somebody will tell you stories and bring you food if you forget to eat."

"Who's Joe?" The voice is deep and scratchy, like it's coming out of a throat that's made of old rough wood. The voice comes from only a few inches away from Harp's face.

"Shoeless Joe. He's my friend. Yesterday he was too nervous to stay inside the church until it was time for the food."

There's silence inside the blackness of the hole. Harp doesn't feel any knife sticking him.

You're not out of the woods yet.

Harp takes a deep breath, happy that he's not dead yet. He can smell the man's breath. Harp knows that smell: whiskey. A lot of homeless people have that kind of breath from drinking whiskey.

"Why do you call him that?" says the woody voice.

"Shoeless? Well, it's because he thinks he has shoes on, but really he's only got the tops. The bottoms are all worn off from him pacing so much."

Another silence. Then, "He doesn't know it?"

"No, he keeps the tops nice and clean, and he doesn't ever look at the bottoms." Harp is thinking fast. The big hand still has a strong grip on his wrist, but the man hasn't tried to stab him yet. It can't be anybody from the beach. Everybody on the beach knows about Shoeless Joe's shoes. Is it the Stranger with the mean eyes?

Harp listens to the man's breathing and waits, but the man doesn't say anything else so Harp asks, "Aren't you going to kill me?"

There's a funny kind of sound, like a cough. "Why would I want to kill you?"

The hand lets go of Harp's wrist.

This is your chance. Run for it!

Harp wonders if he really should run away, but wouldn't the man just grab him again before he could get out?

All right, don't listen to me. Just wait around to see if he's going to kill you.

"Because you . . . I mean . . . because somebody killed Little Hilly, and the Blind Shrimp too."

"Is that right? Somebody got snuffed?" The voice clears its throat. "Where?"

"Right close to here. Under this pier. Down by the water."

For a while the voice doesn't say anything. Then it says, "When?"

"Just last night. I mean the Shrimp was last night. After I saw him go under here. But Little Hilly was the night before, the same night little Teddy got lost."

"So you're telling me a couple of guys got killed here?"

"Yes, under this very pier. Didn't you do it?"

"Not me."

"Oh, sorry. I only said that because I don't know who did it. The police think I did it because I sleep under here sometimes. And now you're under here too so I thought maybe you did it."

"I get it. Well, they'll probably try to pin it on me. They usually do."

"That's what Worried Jack said."

"What, that they'd blame it on me?"

"No, I mean Worried Jack thought they'd try to pin it on him. But they didn't, they blamed it on me."

"On you, eh?"

Harp nods, but then he realizes it's so dark inside his secret place the man can't see him nodding. "Yes. Speel said the police are after me."

"But you didn't do it?"

"No. I liked Little Hilly. He was my friend . . . sort of."

"And this other guy, this blind guy? He got killed too."

"Yes, but he wasn't really very blind. He had a white cane and dark glasses, but he could see pretty well, I think."

"So it was a con."

"Well, I'm not sure what con means, but I think he could see pretty well. For a blind person anyhow."

"Hmm. Sounds like I rolled into the wrong place at the wrong time, as usual."

"Uh, so you're not from around here?"

"Naw. I just hitched in from . . . well, from somewhere else."

"How did you find my secret hideout, if you don't mind my asking?"

"Hideout?"

"Yes, inside here. Where we are."

"I just stumbled onto it. I was lookin' for a place to get some shuteye and crawled in here. Next thing I know you're shinin' a damn light in my eyes."

"Oh, I'm sorry. I didn't know you were in here. I was looking for the . . . well, I thought the Shrimp might have been in here. Before he got killed I mean." Harp wishes he could see the man's face. Did he have mean eyes like the Ghost said? Or maybe this isn't even the same stranger the Ghost saw. "Uh, did you go in and ask the Ghost about me? I mean last night?"

"Who's the Ghost?"

"Never mind."

Silence.

"Uh, do you think I could have my flashlight back now?"

"Oh sure. But if somebody got killed around here we don't want to go shining any lights in the dark, do we?"

Harp shakes his head. Then he remembers again that it's too dark to see a head shaking. "No, I guess not."

He feels the flashlight in his hand.

The voice says, "Let's get the hell out of here. I need a smoke."

Harp feels the man's big body push past him and out of the hole. Harp follows. They sit on the sand next to his hideout hole, and the man strikes a match to light his cigarette.

While the match burns, Harp can see that the man not only has that cross tattoo on the back of his hand, but he has other tattoos on the back of his other hand.

I can't stand this anymore. Can't you see he's a bad person? Run!

Harp can see the man even has tattoos on his neck. He's never seen tattoos on a neck before. But that doesn't necessarily mean he's a bad person, does it? Harp looks closer. The man's face is very dark, and so is his hair. But he's not a black person, he's something else. "You're not a black person, are you?"

The man shakes his head just before the match goes out. "Black? Naw. Haven't you ever seen anybody like me?"

Didn't I tell you to get away from . . .

"Be quiet!"

The man turns to look at him. "What?"

Are you telling me to shut up?

"Oh, I didn't mean you. I mean I . . . was just thinking. There was a man in . . . I mean, in this place where I was before. He looked like you. His name was Indian Dan."

"Yeah? What tribe?"

"I don't know. I'm sorry."

How dare you talk to me that way?

Harp puts his fingers in his ears.

"No need to be sorry. But why do you have your fingers in your ears?"

Harp puts his hands in his lap. "Oh, no reason."

"Yeah, well, my name's Ax. Some call me South Mountain Ax"

What kind of name is that for a person? Evil name, evil person. Just like I expected.

"Uh, like an ax? For chopping?

"Yeah, I guess so. Short for Axel, what they called me when I was little."

"Nice to meet you, Ax. My name is Harp. So, uh, Ax, are you . . . an Indian?"

I'm not going to waste one more breath on you. If you won't mind me, you're on your own, buster.

"You could say that. My Momma was anyhow. Full-blooded Apache, or so they tell me. Never met the lady personally."

"You never met your mother, Ax?"

"Fraid not."

"Even when she . . . uh, had you?"

Ax laughs. "Well, I spose I did meet her then. But I don't remember that. First lady I can remember was a Mexican lady who tied me to a doorknob. That's about all I remember of her though. There were a lot of other ladies after that. And some men too. Some real sonsabitches."

"Sons-a-bitches?"

"That's for sure." The end of Ax's cigarette glows in the dark.

Harp starts to relax a little. The man may be an Indian, and he may have tattoos all over himself, but he has a nice voice. He must be a nice man, probably not a man who would kill people.

The end of the cigarette glows again. "So, Harp, if you didn't off those guys, who did?"

"Does off mean . . . stab, Ax?"

"Yeah, or kill just about any old way. Stabbing usually works, or shooting. So if you didn't do it, who do you think did?"

There's something about Ax's deep scratchy voice that's very calming. And Ax is asking him questions like he really wants to know the answers, like he'll listen and think about what you say to him. "Well, Ax, that's what I've been wondering too. I've asked just about everybody on the beach, and I don't think anybody else knows either. I have a list of suspects in my book, but I can't figure out which one of them did it. Not for sure. There's a stranger who has my hat though. Maybe he did it. At first the police thought Big Hilly did it because he was always with Little Hilly and then he disappeared. But now they don't think so anymore. Like I said, now they think it was me."

"Big Hilly? Don't know that name. Has he ever been inside?"

Harp shrugs. "I don't think he hardly ever goes inside. He sleeps on the beach. Or at least he used to. Now he's gone away somewhere. Since Little Hilly got stabbed, nobody has seen him at all."

"Well, he's probably your man then. When you off somebody, you don't hang around to discuss it."

"Oh, I see. Er, Ax, have you ever offed anybody? If you don't mind my asking, that is."

"Nobody that didn't deserve it. But let me ask you another thing, Harp. Was this Big Hilly guy around when the blind character got it?"

"I don't think so. I was looking for him all over the beach and the police were too and nobody saw him anywhere. I think he left the beach and went somewhere else. Besides, he didn't have anything against the Blind Shrimp. I don't think he even ever talked to him, at least not when I was looking."

Ax smokes his cigarette until it's all gone, then he sticks it into the sand. "Well, Harp, I'd say you're up shit crick without a paddle, less you can find out who really did it."

"Well, I don't have a paddle, but that's what Detective Olivera said too, about finding who did it, I mean. He said if I didn't he might lock me up and throw away the key."

"Olivera? Who's that, a cop?"

That makes Harp know for sure that Ax isn't from around there. Everybody on the beach knows Olivera. "Yes. A policeman. He made me hold out my hand while he wrote his phone number on it, and then later he took my jacket. For evidence. At least that's what Speel said. I washed his number off my hand, and I washed my jacket too, before he took it, and then the Shrimp said he'd get me a new one if I helped him do something. And I did, but then he got killed too so now I don't have a coat and the police are after me and I don't know what to do."

Ax lights up another cigarette, and Harp watches his face while the match burns. Ax seems to be thinking really hard. After the match goes out, Ax says, "Sounds like you need somebody on your side, little buddy. Wish I could stick around here and help you, but I got troubles of my own."

"I'm really sorry you have troubles, Ax. Can I help?"

Ax smokes his cigarette for a while and doesn't say anything. Finally, he lets out a big breath with smoke in it and says, "You seem like a nice kid, Harp. But I'm afraid my troubles are too big for you to worry about. Hey, least I can do is hike out and get us something to eat. Bet you don't get to eat regular food so often, do you?"

"Well, I had some cake at Speel's. But that was . . . quite a while ago." Harp is trying to remember when that was. That morning? So many things had been happening it was getting hard to remember things.

"Well, a bit of cake isn't enough for a grown up fellow like you, now is it? You wait here, my friend, and I'll hike out to a store and get us some grub. How about that?"

"That would be very nice, Ax. Thank you." Harp reaches into his pants pocket. "Uh, I have some dollars."

Ax chuckles. "Sounds like you had some good upbringin', old buddy. Can't remember anybody bein' so polite and all since, well, since never. Anyhow, this one's on me. Where's the nearest store?"

"The Corner Market is the only store that's open all night. It's ninety seven steps across the bridge that goes from the pier to the street. Then two hundred and six steps--"

Ax laughs. "Never mind the number of steps, Harp. If it's nearby I'll find it. Okay if I take your flashlight? I'll get you some fresh batteries."

"That would be very nice of you, Ax." Harp hands him the little flashlight.

"I'll be back as quick as I can" whispers Ax. Then he slides down the sand and disappears into the darkness.

Thank goodness he's gone. You'll never see him again.

"So you're back. See, I told you he was a nice man."

A nice man. Don't make me laugh. Didn't you hear that part about offing people?

"Well, only if they deserved it. Besides, he's going to get me something to eat."

Oh, sure. You're so gullible. He stole your flashlight and ran away.

"I don't believe that." But it does make Harp remember that Speel said she'd be back in a jiffy, and then she didn't come back for a long time. She brought that reporter man who told the police on me. "Ax is different. He'll be back. I'm sure of it."

Fat chance.

But what if the police catch Ax so he can't come back? That thought makes Harp feel very nervous. He suddenly realizes he's under the pier all alone, just like the Shrimp and Little Hilly were when they died.

You'd better be nervous. We'd better get out of here.

"But where should I go?"

Anywhere, as long as it's not here. Dig up the money now and go.

"But what about Ax? He went to get us some food. Shouldn't I wait for him?"

I ask myself why I bother with you. I give you the best I have to give, but do you pay the slightest bit of attention? No.

Harp has to make a decision. Maybe she's right. Maybe Ax won't come back. Maybe he should just dig up the money and make a run for the border. He looks back inside his secret hideout. Should he crawl back in there and look for the money?

But then he hears a sound. It came from down by the water. He tries to see through the fog. Suddenly, there's a light shinning in his eyes.

Somebody says, "There's one of 'em."

Harp holds his hand up to block the light. Is it the police? He holds up both hands. "I didn't do it, honest."

5-2

A Question of Turf

Harp hears a laugh. And then another one. It means there's more than one person. They're standing down by the waterline.

I told you to get away before it was too late. Now you'll be sorry you didn't listen.

"Look at that. They hide like rats up under the pier."

Harp can't see anything because of the bright light in his eyes. If it's the police why would they be talking about rats?

A cigarette glows next to the bright light, and Harp can smell it. It's one of the strange-smelling little cigarettes he's seen people smoke as they walk along the beach. It smells like burning weeds.

"Hey, watcha ya doin' up there, asshole?"

Harp doesn't move. The voice sounds young, but it also sounds kind of mean. Suddenly, he knows who it is. It must be the gang boys. Everybody on the beach knows about the gang boys. They only come to the beach to cause trouble, and sometimes they're mean to the homeless people. Harp remembers the night two of those gang boys caught him when he was looking for food in the dumpsters behind the Beachside apartment building. Those boys knocked him down and then they kicked him. It was lucky that when he got up to run away they didn't chase him. Some of the other homeless hadn't been so lucky and had ended up in the emergency room. It reminds Harp of the plastic emergency room bracelet he found in Little Hilly's pocket. Is that what happened to him? Did he get kicked by the mean gang boys?

"Hey, asshole. I'm talking to you." It's the same mean voice.

Run. It's your only chance.

Another voice says, "I bet he's one of them queers. Hey, queer, you got somebody else up there with you?" The light moves away from Harp to search under the pier. Then the light comes back to shine in Harp's eyes again. Harp worries about how many gang boys there are down there. This time if he runs he might not be able to get away.

"Okay, queer. Get your ass down here." It's the mean-sounding one again.

What's the matter with you? Are you listening to me or not? Run!

Harp remembers when he was little he could almost always run fast enough to get away from the mean kids. But this time his legs feel heavy, like they are made of cement. He doesn't think he would be able to run even if he tried.

I should have known. You're such a scaredy cat you can't even run when it's your only chance.

"Hey, he's got a little backpack on," says another voice. "Let's see what's in it."

That scares Harp more than anything. Losing his backpack would be even worse than getting hurt. His diary is in there with all of his daily stories in it. When all the trouble happened back at Ward D-4, the police took away his diary, and it was a long time before they brought it back. He doesn't want to lose it again. They can have anything else that's in his backpack, but not his diary. He stands up. Time to run, no matter how tired his legs feel.

Then Harp hears a different voice, "Hello, boys." Harp recognizes that deep rough-wood voice. It's Ax. He's come back.

The light swings away from Harp and shines on Ax who's standing very close behind the gang boys. Ax is holding Harp's little flashlight. He clicks it on and shines it on the boys. It's like Harp thought, there are three gang boys. One of them, the one in front, is bigger than the others. That must be the leader, the one with the mean voice. He's wearing a black leather jacket that has chains hanging all over it, and he has a shiny earring in one ear. The others are wearing the same kind of black leather jackets. The gang boys that hurt him out by the dumpsters that night were dressed just like that, but he's not sure if these are the same ones.

"Well, now looky here," says the leader. "Another one. Come back to do your little pal again, queer?"

Harp is amazed to see that Ax isn't getting mad at all. He just smiles at them and says, "A little past your bedtime, isn't it, boys."

One of the other gang boys steps forward. "Oh yeah, we'll do whatever the hell we--"

But the leader stops him by holding up his hand. "You got any money, asshole? How 'bout you just hand it over."

Ax stops smiling, but he still doesn't look scared. He keeps Harp's little flashlight pointed at the boy, and the boy keeps his light pointed at Ax. Neither one of them says anything for a while, but then the boy quickly reaches into his pocket and pulls something out. Harp hears a click and a knife blade pops out. Oh no, is he going to stick Ax?

Good. Now's your chance to sneak away while they're hurting him.

Harp is even more scared for Ax than he was for himself. The mean gang boy has a knife and Ax doesn't. That knife might even be the very same knife that killed Little Hilly and the Shrimp. Maybe the gang boys came to the beach in the middle of the night to smoke their strange little cigarettes, and they found Little Hilly under the pier and stabbed him to death. And then they came back and did the same thing to the Shrimp.

You know that's not it. Are you forgetting about the Stranger?

Well, even if the gang boys didn't stab Little Hilly and the Shrimp, they might stab Ax.

So? That's his problem. Save yourself.

Harp knows he should run away while the gang boys are all gathered around Ax. But why isn't Ax running away? Doesn't he realize their leader is about to stab him with that knife? Harp wishes he was brave enough to go down and try to help Ax.

You? Brave? Don't make me laugh.

He whispers, "But Ax needs my help."

Just stay out of it. It's not your problem.

"But . . ."

Quit talking out loud to me. Don't remind them you're still here.

Harp doesn't know what to do. He wants to run, but shouldn't he stay to help Ax?

What can you do against them? They're big and strong. You're little and weak.

She's right. What can he do against big strong boys like that? He's so small, and maybe the other boys have knives too.

Ax shines the flashlight at the back of the boy's hand. "Nice tattoo you've got there. You want to see mine?"

One of the other boys takes a step toward Ax. "Shut your face, queer. Just do like he said and hand over your money."

Ax shines his light on that boy, and then back on the leader. Then he calmly rolls up his right sleeve and shows them the tattoos on his arm. The leader shines his light on Ax's arm. There is a clock, and a spider web, and a number, and other tattoos that run all the way up his arm. Harp also sees that Ax has very big muscles on his arm.

The boy behind the leader steps back a little and says, "Jesus! He's from the One Hundreds Family."

"So, he's a Family," says the leader. "He's got no business being down here. This is our turf."

"Just passing through, boys," says Ax. "No harm done. Hey, wanna see a few more?" Ax is smiling again as he pulls up the front of his shirt.

The leader leans forward to see. Then he straightens up again. "So, you've been in Soledad. Is that supposed to scare us?"

"Naw, I wouldn't want to scare you boys. Just thought maybe I recognized you." He shines the light on the face of the leader. "But I guess you fellows are too young to have been inside."

The leader boy still has the knife in his hand, but Harp notices he's lowered it a little. "I been places," he says. He seems to be trying to decide what else to say when one of the other boys says, "Aw, let's forget these queers. C'mon, let's go."

"Yeah, we got places to go," says the leader. "But remember what I said, "This is our turf. Go back to Watts where you belong." He folds the knife in half and puts it in his pocket. "And we'd better not catch you here again."

The boys turn and walk away slowly, laughing and slapping each other on the back. Harp is pretty sure they're just pretending not to be scared of Ax.

You got lucky that time. Now get out of here before they come back.

Harp whispers, "No, I've got to thank Ax. He saved me."

Fine, just ignore me. Wait and see what happens to you without my help.

Harp slides down the sand to join Ax. "You scared them away, Ax. You showed them your tattoos and they went away."

Ax hands the flashlight to Harp and begins to roll down his sleeve. "Yeah, well, I hadn't got very far when I saw 'em coming this way. I figured I'd better hang around to see what kinda shit they were up to."

"I'm glad you did, Ax. I was afraid."

"Aw, no need to be afraid of that type. All bark and no bite."

"I'm glad they didn't start biting, Ax. But why were they afraid of your tattoos?"

"I guess my old tattoos still get some respect, at least from those kinds."

"You have a spider web on your elbow, Ax. I saw it."

"Yeah, I got that one . . . a long time ago."

"Can I see some more?"

"Aw, they don't mean anything now, Harp. They're just from when I was a crazy kid."

"I saw a clock on your stomach, Ax, and a number on your arm, 187."

Ax touches his arm and nods. "Oh yeah, that. Very observant, pal. Yeah, I guess I should get that number covered up. Maybe I could get it turned into some other number. Hey, we'd better turn that light off. It'll show up a long ways away out here, even if it is a little foggy."

Harp snaps off the light.

"Now, how about that food? Shall I get goin' to that store?"

"I'm still a little scared, Ax. What if they come back?"

"Aw, they won't be back, at least not without reinforcements. Those damns kids don't have the balls to get into anything serious. But they can get a little troublesome if they get dissed in front of their buddies, so maybe I'd better wait until it gets light before I run get us some grub."

"Okay," says Harp. "Can we go back up to the hideout under the pier? I'm kind of cold."

"Sure, let's go." But then Ax stops. "It's kind of close quarters up there. Those boys called you a queer. You're not like that are you?"

Harp knows what queer means. It's when you like boys better than girls. He's seen some of the homeless men go off into the dark with each other, and that's when the other homeless people call them names like queers. "I don't think so, Ax. I'm just cold."

"Well, here, take my coat." Ax takes off his coat and hands it to Harp.

"No, no, I couldn't take it. Then you'll get cold."

"Naw, I got my own heater." Ax pulls a little bottle out of his pocket. "You want some?"

"No thanks," says Harp. He takes off his backpack and puts Ax's coat on. It's kind of old and ragged, made out of the same kind of cloth Levi pants are made out of. Once Harp has it on, he can feel it's not a very warm coat, but it's a lot better than not having one at all. It's so big Harp can wrap it around double in front, and that makes it a little warmer. Harp knows it's really nice of Ax to give up his jacket on such a cold night, even if he does have his little bottle of heat. He doesn't know one homeless person on the beach who would give up his coat like that. Even Speel, who was really nice to him, didn't offer him a coat.

Back up at the secret hideout, they crawl inside and work together to push up the sand wall to block out the wind. Then there's nothing to do but sit back to wait for the dawn to come. It's close quarters, just like Ax said it would be, but Harp is able to at least sit up without his head knocking against the smelly old wood of the pier ceiling. It's too dark to see, but Harp worries that Ax is so tall he might be bumping his head.

It's very quiet inside the little hideout, except for the footsteps of the late-night fisherpeople on the pier above them. Harp feels the old pier creak and move a little bit every time a big wave comes in. "Are you asleep, Ax?" he whispers.

"No. Just thinkin'. You've got me thinkin' about those murders."

"Are you thinking those bad gang boys did it?"

"Them? Naw. If they did it you wouldn't see hide nor hair of 'em around here. They'd lay low, at least for a while."

That seems logical to Harp. But why did Little Hilly's killer come back to kill the Blind Shrimp, if it was the same person?

As if he's thinking the same thing, Ax says, "Seems to me after the killer offed your pal, he'd be long gone. So why would he come back to do in that blind guy?"

"He wasn't really very blind, Ax. He just had a white cane."

"Right, I get it. But why would the killer come back?"

"I don't know, Ax. What do you think?"

"I can't figure it. You'd think he'd expect the murdered guy's pals to be around."

"I don't think Little Hilly had any pals, Ax. Only Big Hilly. And if it was Big Hilly, why would he want to hurt the Shrimp too?"

"Yeah. Good thinking. Seems to me that's what you got to find out, what the killer had against the two dead guys. What they had in common."

Harp feels proud that Ax said he had done good thinking. "Listen, Ax, what if Big Hilly went away before Little Hilly got killed? Maybe that's why it happened, because Big Hilly wasn't there to protect him."

"That's an idea. Both of the guys that got killed were alone, right?"

"Yes. Is that a clue?"

"You bet it is. The first guy might have got killed in an argument with his friend, you know, some kind of beef between them, but if the second guy was a loner, then . . ."

"Hey, queers. You up there?"

"Oh, no," whispers Harp. "They're back."

Ax makes a little sound that might have been a low laugh, or it might have been a groan. "Yeah, sounds like it. Damn it. Why the hell couldn't they just walk away?" He begins to crawl out.

"No," whispers Harp. "Don't go out there. Maybe they don't know where we are."

"I'm not gonna hide like some mouse in a hole," says Ax pushing away the sand wall. "If they want trouble, I got some to give 'em."

Ax looks out and a light comes shining on his face.

Harp ducks back, afraid to move.

"What do you punks want now?" yells Ax. "I'm trying to get some shuteye up here."

"We told you to get off our turf. Now we--"

"Yeah, yeah," yells Ax. "Save your breath. I'm comin." He crawls out.

Harp feels very frightened. His mouth is so dry he can't swallow. Is he supposed to go out too?

No! Don't go out there, no matter what.

"Oh, you're back. Then what should I do?"

"Don't do anything," says Ax. "Just stay put." He pushes some of the sand back up to close the hole, and Harp hears him go away.

Harp waits, wondering what's going to happen. Then he has an idea. If the bad gang boys think Ax isn't supposed to be on the beach because it's their turf, maybe he should go down and tell them Ax is his guest.

You? Brave enough to talk to them? Don't make me laugh.

She's right. He'd probably be too afraid to go say anything to them. If only he could be brave, like the brave boys in Mother's stories.

Just stay out of it. You can't help it that you're not the brave type.

"But what if they hurt him?"

So what. What is he to you?

Suddenly, Harp feels very cold, so cold he can hardly move.

That's better. Just do what you always do. Hide. Hide like a little mouse in a hole.

"But I don't want to be a mouse anymore. I'm going to see what's going on." He gets up on his knees and pushes away some of the sand. He pokes his head out and sees there are even more gang boys this time, all dressed in black leather, and they're all gathering around Ax. Several of them have flashlights, and they're pointing them at Ax. The leader has his big knife out again and two of the others have big knives too. But nobody is sticking Ax, at least not yet. They're just crouched down, moving around him, like lions or tigers all gathering around something they want to eat. Why doesn't Ax run?

He'll be fine. Now's your chance to get away while they're busy with him.

Harp looks out toward the ocean. It's still foggy and dark. He could probably slip out the other side of the pier without the gang boys even noticing him.

That's my boy. Now you're thinking good.

After all, Ax said he didn't need any help.

That's right. We have other important things to do.

Maybe he should just go farther up the beach and watch the waves. It's been a long time since he had time to just sit and watch the waves. He imagines the nice sound of the waves lapping up on the shore. He could go there and be by himself and not think about anything. He doesn't want to leave Ax alone with the gang boys, but what can he do? He's so little and they're all so big. He'd probably just get in Ax's way.

Good thinking. Now go!

Harp puts his little flashlight in his pocket and slips out of the hole. He carefully crawls to the other side of the pier, trying not to make a sound. He stops to listen. The loud voices down there are still going on. He crawls down to the flat part of the sand, and when he's far enough away, he gets up and starts to run. His legs feel shaky, but he keeps moving, stumbling away into the darkness.

That's it. Keep going.

Suddenly, he's happy to be free and not stabbed to death like Little Hilly and the Shrimp were. It feels good to be out in the cold night air.

Yes! Let's go away, far away. Let's run.

He runs and runs, and keeps on running until he's completely out of breath and can't run anymore. He stops to catch his breath. He puts his hands on his knees. He can feel that his legs are trembling.

Calm down. You're safe now.

He straightens up and looks back. He's come so far he can't even see the pier back there in the fog anymore. His throat feels really tight, almost as bad as it was when he was little, like his throat was too small to let the air in.

Don't think about that. Just listen to my voice. Breathe. One in, two out.

His heart is pounding so loud it sounds like a drum is beating inside his head. Even though he's pretty sure he got away without the gang boys spotting him, his whole body feels shaky, like something is still wrong.

Everything is fine. Just sit down and relax. Listen to the nice waves.

It's very quiet except for the familiar swoosh of the waves as they slide up onto the shore. He sits down to listen. The fog surrounds him, hiding him. The waves are comforting, the same rhythm, over and over, like lying on Mother's lap and listening to her heartbeats.

That's my good boy. Stay here with me and everything will be fine.

But no matter how nice the waves are, he can't stop thinking about what might be happening to Ax back there.

Now, now, no reason to even think about that. He doesn't matter to us. Let's just stay here together. Nothing matters except that we are together.

He tries not to think what might be happening to Ax, but it's hard. Sometimes when things got very bad on Ward D-4, he used to go out to the Day Room and write his stories. If he concentrated really hard on writing, he could hardly hear the screams.

Now, now. No need to think about bad things like that. Don't think about anything except the sound of my voice.

But he can't seem to relax. It's too dark and too foggy, and too cold, and he's afraid for Ax. He looks back toward the pier. Was that a sound? Was that somebody yelling for help?

No, you didn't hear anything. You should take a nice nap now. Listen to the waves.

She's right, the waves are nice. They repeat their sound, over and over, like whispering. What are they saying? It sounds like . . . "Fraidy cat, fraidy cat, Harp is a fraidy cat."

No! That's not what they're saying. They're telling you to stop thinking bad thoughts. They're telling you to listen to my voice.

But the waves are not whispering nice things. They're saying mean things at him, just like the kids at school used to yell mean things and laugh at him. At recess they'd make a circle around him: "Little Loony Harpy, little Daffy Dilly."

Harp jumps up and shouts, "No!" It's not true. I'm not little Daffy Dilly anymore. I'm all grown up now. I don't have to be afraid anymore."

Yes you do. People will hurt you. You're small and weak.

"No! I don't want to be afraid all the time. That's what the waves are really saying. They're saying I'm all grown up now. I'm not Little Loony Harpy."

The waves are not saying any such thing. They're saying you're in danger. They're saying someone is trying to kill you. They're saying, listen to your Mother.

"No they're not. They're saying I have to be brave, like the brave boys in your stories. And they're saying I shouldn't listen to anybody who says different."

Are you defying me again? You know what happens when you try to defy me.

Harp decides not to listen anymore. He should be listening to see if Ax is calling for help. He begins to worry that the waves are so loud he won't be able to hear if Ax needs him. He jumps up and listens harder. Was that a shout? Is Ax calling for help? Maybe he's too far away to hear. Maybe he should go back a little closer.

Oh no you don't, young man. I didn't give you permission to go.

Harp starts to run. "I have to go help Ax. He needs me."

He runs faster and faster, but all of a sudden he trips over something and falls down. "Owe. I hurt my knee."

Didn't I tell you not to run? Now will you listen when I tell you something?

Harp feels around in the darkness until he figures out what he fell over. It's a pile of sticks, next to one of the beach firepits. "Hey, that's what I need. A stick."

A stick? What do you need a stick for?

"If I had a big stick, I could use it to help Ax. If the mean gang boys are still there, I can smack them with a stick."

You? Smack them? That'll be the day.

"No, really. I could smack them. They'd be afraid of me if I had a big stick."

Oh sure. A stick won't help you. What you really need is a magic wand. You could be like the boy who stole the witch's magic wand and used the dead girl's head to make a trail of blood on the ground to fool the witch.

Harp doesn't want to think about that right now. He picks up one of the sticks and shakes it in the air. But wouldn't it be wonderful if it was a magic stick? Then he'd show those gang boys. He could be just like the boy in the story. He could use the magic stick to make them all dance, just like when that boy made the wicked witch dance inside the thorn patch until the thorns tore her clothes off her body and pricked her and stuck into her until she was bleeding so hard she bled to death.

That's right. Find a magic stick and let's go away. We'll make gold and jewels and good things to eat.

Harp feels the weight of the stick in his hand. It seems thin and weak, just an ordinary stick, not magic at all. But it makes him realize he doesn't really need a magic stick. "I just need a regular stick, a heavy one to hit the gang boys with."

Getting awfully big for our britches, aren't we? You'll wish you'd listened to me. Mark my words.

He throws the skinny stick down and feels around for a better one. He'll need a big fat stick if he's going to help Ax. But the sticks are all too small. He feels inside the firepit. Aha! There's a bigger one. He picks it up and shakes it. It feels all gritty, like it got burned on one end, but it seems pretty strong. He tests it by hitting one of the big rocks that surround the firepit. Whack! The sound seems really loud in the night. He hopes nobody heard it. But the stick didn't break. That's good. And the sound of his stick hitting that rock was good too. Maybe he should do it again. He looks around, but he can't see anything through the fog. He lifts the stick up high and smacks the rock again, as hard as he can. Whack! This time the sound is really loud, almost like a firecracker going off. Wow, that would hurt. If he hit one of the gang boys on top of the head like that it might knock him right out cold.

Oh sure, big brave Harp, hitting the bullies with his mighty stick. This I have to see.

But is he brave enough to do it? Could he be a brave Harp, like the brave boy in the story, or would he only be the usual little scaredy cat Harp? He swings the stick at the darkness. It feels good in his hands, heavy and strong. He'll take it and go help Ax. He's got a stick now so they'd better watch out. He starts walking, then faster and faster, until he's running.

I can't believe this. All right, fine. Don't listen to me. Go ahead and get yourself hurt. See if I care.

He stops running to catch his breath, but he keeps walking toward the pier. He jabs the fog with his stick, as if it was a mighty sword. He'll be like the boy with no name who killed the mighty giant.

More likely you'll be his double who got his brains dashed out on the rock.

"Yeah, well, remember what happened to the mother who tried to stop him by putting a spell on him."

Are your threatening me? You keep this up and I'll . . .

"Shh!" Harp stops listening to her. He can see the outline of the dark pier in the fog ahead. The sight of it means he has to decide if he really wants to go there. He stops. He suddenly remembers how scary those big boys looked. And they have knives too.

That's my boy. I knew you'd come to your senses.

Now he's not so sure he should go back there. Maybe he isn't as brave as that boy who killed the giant. Maybe Mother is right. Maybe he will get his brains dashed out.

Finally, he gets it. Face it, son, you're just not made for this kind of thing.

There's no sound except for the swooshing of the waves. Nobody is yelling or anything. Is it all over?

He slowly creeps a little closer and stops again to listen. It's very quiet. Maybe the gang boys already ran away. But if they did, where is Ax? Did he go away too?

When he gets to the edge of the pier, Harp hides behind one of the big moss-covered columns and whispers, "Ax, are you here?"

There's no answer.

5-3

Loyalty is as Loyalty Does

"**A**x where are you?"

Harp hears nothing except the soft sound of the waves washing in and washing out.

He takes his flashlight out of his pocket and shines it all around under the pier. The light soon finds Ax. He's lying on his back.

He's dead, just like the others. Get away from here quick before you get blamed for this one too.

The sight of Ax lying there on the sand takes Harp's breath away. Is he really dead like Little Hilly and the Blind Shrimp?

He hurries to Ax's side, and when he shines the light, he's happy to see Ax's eyes aren't open and staring like dead people's do. They're closed, like he's sleeping. He shakes his friend's shoulder. "Ax, wake up. Are you sleeping?"

Ax opens his eyes and blinks. His face is all puffed up, and one of his eyes is all bloody and doesn't want to open very far. He turns his head toward Harp and smiles. "You came back, little buddy." His voice is as deep and rough as always, but now it's barely a whisper.

Harp blinks back his tears. "I ran away, Ax. I'm sorry. I got scared."

Ax's eyes close, and he lets out a big sigh. "But you came back. That was brave of you."

"But I should have come back quicker, Ax. Did they hurt you?"

"Maybe a little. Too many of 'em."

There's nothing you can do for him. He's done for.

Harp can't think of what to say. If only he would have come back sooner. He feels the weight of the stick in his hand and wishes he could hit every single person in the world who liked to hurt people. "I brought a stick to hit them with, but they were already gone."

Ax opens his one good eye to look at the stick. He smiles a little. "Looks like a good one, Harp. Too bad you didn't get a chance to use it." He closes his eyes again.

Yeah, too bad. Then you could be lying there dying just like him.

"I've never hit anybody with a stick, Ax. Mother said I shouldn't . . . even though sometimes she hit me. But that was different. I deserved it."

Ax can't seem to open his eyes anymore, but he says, "Better not to get started. Your mother was right."

See there, even he agrees. I was always right, wasn't I?

Harp wishes he could put his fingers in his ears to shut her out, but he has to keep the flashlight pointed on Ax. But then he worries that Ax is keeping his eyes shut because the flashlight's too bright. He turns it off. The fog is very close, and the city lights look all orange and glowy against the mist. It might mean morning is coming soon.

"Do you want to go back up to my hideout, Ax? I can help you."

"Naw. Just let me lie here for a minute, Harp. Those punks stuck me . . . a little."

"Oh, no." Harp turns his flashlight back on. "Should I look?"

Ax doesn't answer, and his eyes are still closed. Harp decides he'd better take a quick look. He pulls up Ax's shirt. There's some blood on Ax's stomach, but what looks the worst are three places that look like what hamburger looks like before it gets cooked.

Can't you see it's too late for him? There's nothing you can do except get out of there while you still can.

Ax takes a big breath and lets it out again. "I laid out a few of them, but they got me from behind. Their leader did most of the cutting. I think he was trying to cut off my tattoos."

Harp shines the light on Ax's cut-up places. He still has lots of other tattoos on his stomach that they didn't cut off. Harp has never seen so many tattoos. Some of the homeless men on the beach had tattoos, but the ones on Ax's stomach are different from any of them. There's a big one that looks like a cross with two extra arms with some little letters between the arms.

At least he's a religious man.

Next to the cross are some stick people that look kind of silly. But under the stick people there are pictures of knives and bad words that are not silly at all.

What kind of a person would put all those bad words on his body? Think about it. It's the work of the Devil. You should leave him where he lies and get out of here before anything else bad happens.

"I'm not leaving him, and that's final."

Ax opens one eye. "What?"

"Oh, I just . . . wanted to say I'm not going to leave you, Ax. Those gang boys made a lot of cuts on your stomach, but they're not bleeding too much now."

Ax closes his eye and doesn't say anything.

Harp is happy the gang boys didn't kill Ax. He remembers all the blood that was on Little Hilly's back, and how his eyes were open and staring. He shines the light on Ax's face again to make sure his eyes are not open. They're not, and that's good.

He shines the light back on Ax's stomach, worried that the cuts might keep on bleeding. "You know, Ax, one time when I was little, some bad boys at school hit me on my head with a rock, and I had to go to the doctor and get stitches. Maybe you need some of those kinds of stitches."

Ax doesn't open his eyes, but he pulls his shirt down. "Naw, nothin' to worry about. I've had worse. Those little pig stickers can't do much damage. Hell, I had a bigger knife when I was ten years old. Just let me get a little sleep. I'll be fine."

Harp turns off his flashlight and takes off Ax's jacket. He puts the jacket over Ax's chest, being very careful not to hurt his cuts.

Harp pulls his knees up to his chest and sits very still, trying to think good thoughts about Ax getting better. But it's so cold it's hard to concentrate. He turns on his flashlight and looks at Ax. It looks like he's fallen asleep. That's good.

Harp turns off the light and stares into the fog. He tries to think of warm thoughts, but the wind picks up and the fog starts to blow in under the pier, and that makes him start to shiver again. Maybe he should get up and walk to get warm.

So go. Take a nice long walk on the beach. It'll warm you right up.

"No," he whispers, "you're trying to trick me into leaving Ax."

Fine, then stay here until the killer comes for you. It's your funeral.

"You always say things like that. It's my funeral, or that I've got blood on my hands, or that I'm like the boy who got his brains dashed out. Why can't you ever be on my side?"

I am on your side. I'm trying to help you. I only have your best interests at heart.

"Well, then help me get through this. I want to sit here with my new friend until the dawn comes, until the warm sun comes up. Then Ax will wake up feeling much better."

Oh yeah, and what if those gang boys come back?

"If the bad gang boys come back, I'll . . . I'll hold them off with my stick."

Oh sure, you?

"There you go again. Saying bad things about me. All right, fine, then I'm not going to listen to you anymore."

No, wait! You're in trouble. You need my help.

Harp puts his fingers in his ears. If she's going to be like that, he doesn't have to listen to her. But she's right about one thing, trouble *does* seem to follow him wherever he goes. It's been happening since he was little. And now here it is again. Trouble followed him to Ward D-4, and people died. Now it's followed him to the beach, and more people got killed. First it was Bacon Benny and the Big Black Cusser, and now it's Little Hilly and the Blind Shrimp.

He takes his fingers out of his ears. "What does it mean?"

What does what mean?

"You know. Why does trouble follow me?"

Who knows? It just does.

"Will it ever end?"

You know when it ends. It ends when you're in your grave, like Cock Robin.

"No, don't tell me that."

Suit yourself, but it's true.

Harp thinks about what it would be like to be in the grave and not be alive anymore. So many people he's known are in their graves. Maybe things *are* his fault, like Mother is always saying. Maybe if he was a braver person they would all still be alive.

What would you know about being brave?

"The trouble is, I never learned how. You never let me go out to play with the other kids so I never got to learn what that was all about."

It was better for you to stay inside with me. It wasn't safe out there.

"But it made it so I never learned how to take care of things myself. Whenever there was trouble you took care of it. And I didn't get to learn about being brave on Ward D-4 either. Why couldn't I be the one who stood up to Mitch? If I would have stood up to him, then maybe some of the bad things that happened on Ward D-4 wouldn't have happened."

You? Stand up to Mitch? Look what happened to Bacon Benny when he stood up to Mitch.

"Well, if I would have done something, maybe Bacon Benny wouldn't have had to die."

What could you do? You're too weak. Why if it hadn't been for me, Mitch would have . . .

Harp puts his fingers in his ears. It's all in the past anyhow. Over and done with. No use even thinking about it. Mitch is in prison now so none of that Ward D-4 stuff matters anymore. But it makes him realize that despite all he's been through, he's still afraid of being hurt. Just because you get hurt a lot, it doesn't make you less afraid. When Ax was in trouble, he didn't stay to help him. He ran away. It must mean he's still afraid of dying. Carl the Older would say anybody who's afraid of dying is afraid of the Morgue Man. On Ward D-4, when somebody died, the Morgue Man came to take the body away. The Morgue Man was old and skinny, and he had a sour face with no teeth. Mitch always made Harp and the Growler and Carl the Older pick the dead person up and put him on the metal cart to be wheeled away. The Morgue Man would never help pick them up. He just stood there watching. From picking up those dead people, Harp learned that it's very hard to pick up a dead person, especially if the dead person was even a little bit fat. Dead people are so loose and floppy, it's hard to get ahold of anything. And nobody else on the ward would help. Every time the Morgue Man came, they all ran away screaming because they thought he'd come for them. Mitch always laughed about that. After the Morgue Man went away, Mitch liked to tell the really crazy ones if they didn't straighten up and fly right the old Morgue Man with no teeth would soon be coming for them. He said the old Morgue Man would take them away to Hell where the Devil would burn them up forever.

He takes his fingers out of his ears. "I suppose you have a comment about that."

Who'll carry the coffin? I, said the Kite, if it's not through the night, I'll carry the coffin.

"I knew you'd say something like that. All right, if that's the way you're going to be, I won't listen anymore."

Harp tries to sit very still and not think. He doesn't have to think about bad old things if he doesn't want to. He won't even think about the cold or the fog. He'll only think warm thoughts.

But it is cold. You can't deny that. You're freezing.

That starts Harp's teeth chattering, and he can't stop them. He tries to remember what it felt like to be hot. Was it ever hot when he was little? He can't remember a single hot day. He was always cold. But it had to get hot sometimes, didn't it? He worries that something must be going wrong with his memory. Usually little tiny details about things fill up his head, but so many things have been happening in the last few days, it makes it hard to think about anything else but the bad things. Back on Ward D-4, nothing ever changed so it was easy to keep track of memories. Mitch didn't like things to change, so they didn't. That was good. That was relaxing. If Mitch just wasn't so mean, it would have been a nice place to be, with food every day and some nice friends like Bacon Benny and Carl the Older. And the Big Black Cusser wasn't a bad fellow either. Now that Harp thinks about it, the Big Black Cusser was a lot like Shoeless Joe. Big and black, and a pretty nice fellow, all in all. Except Joe is quiet and the Big Black Cusser was noisy, yelling about that Jasmine lady all day. Too bad his brain got fried when they gave him so much Thorazine. He didn't deserve to die just for cussing, even if God didn't like those bad words.

Better him than you. Nothing like that happened to you, did it? Didn't I always protect you?

"All right, all right. Stop it." Harp knows none of that matters now.

Now the important thing is to keep watch in case the gang boys come back. He still has his stick, and he'll use it to protect Ax if he has to.

I'll tell you what you should do. You should lie back and sleep. Let me take care of things here.

"No, I've got to stay awake and protect Ax. You won't take care of him, just like you didn't take care of Bacon Benny, or the Big Black Cusser, or Little Hilly, or the Shrimp or . . . any of the others."

Well, if you ask me, you should . . .

"I'm not asking you. So just be quiet. I'm going to sit right here and protect Ax."

So this is the thanks I get? After all I've done for you?

Harp stares into the darkness and tries not to think about the bad things that happened on Ward D-4. He's got to think about what's happening now. Like the Stranger. He's out there somewhere. What if he comes out of the fog right now and tries to kill him?

No, no, he doesn't want to think about that either. He only wants to think about good things like . . . like the good old stories Mother used to tell him, stories about kings and witches and giants and elfs and wise boys who go out into the world to make amazing things happen. Those stories had secret little cottages in the deepest enchanted forest where you could go and hide from the witches and the dragons. Nobody would ever find you there. And not only that, there were beautiful princesses who got to marry the heroic boy because he'd saved her from the witches and the dragons, or from the evil stepmothers. In those stories, the heroic boy got to . . .

Listen! Somebody is coming.

Harp is suddenly wide awake. Was that a sound?

It's the killer. He's come for you.

Harp strains his ears to listen. Is somebody really there? Where is his flashlight? He must have gotten sleepy and dropped it. He feels around on the sand, but it doesn't seem to be there.

There it is again. A sound. There's somebody there, hiding in the dark.

Harp tries to listen, but his heart is beating so loud he can't hear anything else. He whispers. "Help me, Mother."

I tried to help you. I told you to run away, but you wouldn't listen.

Now it's too late. Now he's come for you. He's there, hiding in the dark. Very close now. You can almost hear him breathing.

Harp doesn't know what to do. If it's the killer, he'll have a knife. What chance does he have against a killer with a knife? "What should I do?"

Run away.

"But I can't leave Ax, can I?" Every part of him wants to jump up and run away, but he ran away before and look what happened. Ax got hurt.

He feels around on the ground, but he can't find his flashlight. But then his hand finds his stick. Maybe he doesn't have to run. What if he could hit the killer with his stick? Then he'd be the hero and everyone would know how brave he was.

But you must run away. You always run.

"No!" He slaps his hand over his mouth. He hadn't meant to yell like that. But it makes him feel better that he did. It was a really loud yell. Maybe it scared the killer away.

Fat chance.

Ax moans and Harp reaches out to touch him. "Don't worry, Ax. I'm not running away this time. I've got my stick, and I'll stay right here with you."

There it is again. That sound. The killer is coming closer.

Harp jumps to his feet, but the fog is so thick he can't see the killer. He must be hiding inside the fog.

Harp shouts, "Stay back, you killer. I'm here with my friend, Ax, and I've got a big stick." He swings the stick out into the night and hears a loud Whack! as it hits one of the big wooden columns. Harp likes how loud that sound was so he does it again. He swings as hard as he can. Whack! It was even louder this time. "I'm warning you, killer. Me and Ax are here, and we'll hurt you if you come any closer."

Ax moans again.

"See there? Ax says he'll hurt you real bad if you don't get out of here." He holds his breath, listening.

He's going away. He's running.

Harp grins and shakes his stick in the air. "And don't come back."

He's gone.

Harp laughs out loud. There. He did it. He scared the killer away. He's just like the boy who killed the monster with the magic spear, except he didn't even have a magic spear, only a regular stick.

Yeah, you're some hero. Lucky is more like it.

"Shh. I'm trying to listen." Has the killer really gone away? He doesn't hear anything. He's almost sure it really was the killer. And he chased him away, all by himself.

He'll be back. He'll wait to catch you alone.

All of a sudden, Harp's legs seem very tired and shaky. He quickly sits back down next to Ax. Was there really somebody out there in the darkness? Was it the Stranger? He frantically feels around in the sand until he finds his little flashlight. He snaps it on and uses the light to search up under every part of the pier. There's no one there. Good. He shines the light on Ax and sees that he's still asleep. That's good too. He carefully pulls the front of Ax's shirt up. The bleeding has stopped, but for some reason Ax looks kind of fat, like he just finished eating a big meal. They never did get anything to eat last night, so why is Ax's stomach all puffed up like that? Ax couldn't have snuck out to get something to eat. The more he looks at Ax's stomach, the more he's sure something just isn't right. A puffed-up stomach when you haven't had anything to eat doesn't make sense. Maybe he'd better wake Ax up to ask him.

He leans over close to Ax's face. "Wake up, Ax. I have to ask you something."

But Ax doesn't wake up. Harp gently shakes his shoulder. "Ax, wake up. Just for a minute."

But Ax still doesn't wake up. He doesn't even moan and try to turn away the way sleepy people do when they don't want to wake up.

I told you before, he's a goner. Time to get out of here.

Harp begins to worry that something really bad is wrong with Ax. Maybe those boys stuck Ax worse than he thought with their little pig stickers. He shakes Ax harder, but he still doesn't wake up. He touches Ax's forehead. It's cold, but Harp doesn't think it's cold enough to be dead. The floppy dead people on Ward D-4 were really cold. But if you're as cold as Ax is, maybe it meant you were on your way to being dead. Maybe you gradually get colder and colder until you're completely dead.

Harp jumps up. He has to do something before Ax is completely dead. He leans down close to Ax's ear and says, "If you can hear me, Ax, I'm going to go get help for you." He pats Ax's head and hurries out from under the pier. He makes his way across the sand toward the stairs that go up onto the pier.

No! Don't go up there. The police are up there.

"Oh, that's right. Where should I go?"

Go for a walk. Go watch the seagulls.

Harp ignores her. Not this time. This time he'll be brave. He'll go get help for Ax. He'll . . . he'll call up the telephone operator. That's it. Like that time when the house caught on fire. All you have to do is call the operator and she'll send help.

He goes up the stairs to the pier. Now, where's the nearest pay phone? I know, it's over by the Penny Arcade. He sneaks past the merry-go-round. It isn't open yet, and neither is the Taco Shack, or any of the other places. The sky is maybe getting a little bit lighter, but the real morning must still be a ways off.

He spots the phone and runs to it. He dials O for operator.

"Operator."

Don't talk to her. You'll get yourself in a mess again. I can feel it.

"No. Be quiet."

"What?"

"No, not you, ma'am. I was talking to . . . somebody else. Please, ma'am, my friend Ax is hurt. He's down under the pier."

"Which pier, sir? Do you need an ambulance?"

"Yes, ma'am, Ax is maybe dying because his stomach is too big."

"His stomach is too big?"

"Yes, but it's not because he ate too much. It's maybe because the mean gang boys stabbed him with their pig stickers."

"He's been stabbed? Is that what you're trying to say?"

"Yes, ma'am. I think maybe they hurt him more than he thinks."

"Sir, if you'll just tell me which pier, I'll dispatch an ambulance immediately."

"Well, it's by Santa Monica. There's a merry-go-round on it, and it's exactly eighty-three steps to get over the bridge from the street."

"Eighty-three steps? What are you saying? Do you mean the Santa Monica pier?"

"Yes. Under the pier, same as where Little Hilly and the Blind Shrimp got killed, except Ax isn't dead. Not yet."

"I understand, sir. I'll dispatch an ambulance to your location. Will you wait there to meet it?"

"Uh, I guess so."

Harp waits for her to say something else, but she doesn't so he hangs up and hurries back down to the beach to tell Ax. He just hopes Ax isn't dead yet.

When he gets back down under the pier, he's really happy to see that Ax looks the same as when he left him. But he still won't wake up. This time when Harp shakes him, Ax turns his head from side to side and moans.

Harp waits by Ax's side, holding his hand. The sky is getting lighter all the time. Then a man and woman walk past with a brown dog on a leash. They stop to look.

Harp stands up and yells, "My friend is hurt. Can you help?" But they hurry on, looking in the other direction.

Now those people know you're here. They'll call the police.

"But I have to wait for the ambulance. I told the operator lady I would." Harp stays close to Ax, and after a few minutes he hears a siren coming. He jumps up and runs back to the street as fast as he can.

When the ambulance stops, two men jump out. One of them is wearing a white coat.

Don't talk to them. Just walk on like you don't know anything about it.

"No. Be quiet."

The men stare at him. The man in the white coats says, "What did you say? Are you the one who called an ambulance?"

"It's for my friend, Ax." Harp points back toward the beach. "He's under the pier."

The man opens the back of the ambulance and takes out a red box. He turns back to Harp and says, "Is your friend drunk?"

"No, no. He maybe had a little whiskey to drink last night, but only to stay warm. He's really hurt. I'll show you."

The ambulance man follows Harp across the sand, but he's not going very fast.

"We have to hurry. His stomach is real big."

But the man won't walk any faster. "You sure your friend isn't just a little too drunk?"

"No, no. The mean gang boys stabbed him with their pig sticker. It's real bad."

"Stabbed?" The man speeds up.

When they make it down to where Ax is, the ambulance man kneels down and pulls open one of Ax's eyes and shines a little silver flashlight in. Then he pulls up Ax's shirt and looks at his puffed-up stomach. He doesn't say anything, but when the other ambulance man arrives with a folded up stretcher he looks up and says, "Multiple stab wounds. Looks bad."

They make Harp get out of the way while they put Ax on the stretcher. Harp follows them as they head back for the ambulance, but they're having trouble carrying Ax because he's so big. They stop and put the stretcher down on the sand while they rest, and when they get ready to pick him back up again, Harp grabs onto one of the stretcher handles to help. With three of them carrying Ax, they make it back to the ambulance pretty quick. They put Ax into the back of the ambulance, and one of the men climbs in with him. The other one tries to slam the door, but Harp grabs it and asks, "Can't I go with him?"

Are you crazy? What do you think you're doing?

The man says, "Get in," and they're soon underway with the siren going. Harp is trying to remember how long it's been since he was inside a car of any kind. Not since they took him from Ward D-4 to the Half-Way House, and that was in a bus. Being in a car makes him very nervous, but there's nothing he can do about it. He has to stay with Ax.

I've just about had it with all this helping Ax crap. You're digging your own grave, mark my words.

Harp doesn't listen. The ambulance man quickly cuts away Ax's shirt, and then he sticks a needle with a hose attached to it into Ax's arm. Pretty soon some kind of liquid is coming down out of a bottle and going into Ax. Harp has seen that kind of thing before when his mother was in the hospital, but that time Mother was awake and complaining about everything. This time it's Ax, and he still won't wake up. Harp holds onto Ax's hand. It feels cold, but maybe it's not quite as cold as before. Harp is surprised when Ax's eyes blink twice. Then they open. He smiles and tries to say something, but nothing comes out of his mouth.

"We're taking you to the hospital, Ax. They'll fix you up there."

Ax closes his eyes and says, "Too bad."

Harp wonders why Ax said that. Doesn't he understand that they'll help him at the hospital?

Ax opens his eyes again and whispers, "I had . . . a dream."

Harp pats his hand. "Did you? Was it a nice dream?"

Ax shakes his head. He blinks and looks up at the ceiling of the ambulance. "It was . . . a message. For you."

"For me?"

Don't listen to this nonsense.

Ax nods. His eyes close again. "You're going to have to be . . . very brave, Harp."

"Me? Was I in your dream?"

"Yes, and there was . . . a bird."

Ax stops talking. Did he go back to sleep?

But then Ax opens his eyes again. "A vulture . . . watching . . . circling."

"A vulture? What does it mean, Ax? Is it bad?"

Ax turns his head to look right at Harp. "You have to be very brave, Harp. You have to go back to . . . the scene of the crime. Under the pier. You have to wait . . . for the killer there."

Is he nuts? Do what he says and you're a goner too.

Harp doesn't understand. If the killer was going to come to the pier again, why would he want to be there? "You don't have to tell me anything now, Ax. You can tell me later, when you're feeling better."

"No. You . . . won't ever . . . see me again. Here, take . . . my pouch. It will help you. Take it off . . . my neck." Ax tries to lift his hand, but the hose that's attached to his wrist won't let him.

Harp sees what Ax is talking about. He has a little leather bag tied around his neck on a leather string. "Your little bag?"

"Yes, take it off."

Harp looks at the ambulance man, but he's busy fiddling with a machine on the wall of the ambulance. Harp scoots forward and carefully unties the leather string. As he takes the little bag away from

Ax's neck it makes a soft rattling sound. "It made a sound, Ax."

Ax says, "Yeah . . . rattlesnake tail . . in there. Other things . . . too. Don't look inside . . . magic."

It's black magic. Drop it before it gets inside you.

Harp ignores her, but he carefully holds the little bag only by the strings, being careful not to touch the leather.

Ax whispers, "Put it on."

"Me?"

"Yes. You have to . . . wear it around your neck for the magic . . . to work."

Whatever you do, don't put that thing around your neck. It's got evil in it.

"But Ax says it will help me."

The ambulance man looks at Harp. "Did you say something?"

Harp shakes his head and waits until the man looks away again. Then he carefully ties the strings around his neck. The little leather bag feels warm against his chest, like it's got it's own heat inside.

Now you've done it. You'll probably be cursed forever.

"Don't ever take it off, Harp. It'll . . . protect you."

Harp leans down very close to Ax's ear. "What do you mean, Ax? What will it protect me from?"

Ax whispers, "From him. From . . . the killer. Wait for him under the pier. He will come . . . for you." Ax closes his eyes.

Harp sits back up, but he's not sure what Ax means. He said to wait for the killer under the pier. But why would he want to do that?

Harp waits for more, but it looks like Ax has gone back to sleep. His face seems very tired, and it has a thin scar that runs from his nose almost out to his ear. Harp wonders what a long scar like that means. Did it happen a long time ago, maybe when Ax was little? Harp remembers the time Mother threw a glass at him. It cut his forehead and bled a lot, but it only left a little bit of a scar.

Harp notices Ax's jacket is lying on the floor of the ambulance. He picks it up and would have put it back over Ax, but the ambulance man has started to dab at Ax's stomach with a little piece of cotton with reddish-orange stuff on it. Harp watches the man as he does it. He seems like a nice man, like he's trying not to hurt Ax too much as he tries to help him.

The ambulance turns a sharp corner and stops. The siren winds down. Another man in a white coat opens the ambulance's back door and says, "Out of the way, bud."

Harp hops out. "Can't I help you carry him? I helped at the beach."

"We'll take care of him."

Stop interfering. Can't you see they don't want you here? Go away now.

Two more men come out of the hospital with a tall table with wheels on it, and they work together to put Ax on it. They wheel him into the hospital really fast, and Harp hurries to keep up. But they take Ax away through some swinging double doors that say "NO ENTRY." Harp is left standing there, holding Ax's jacket.

After a few minutes, the woman behind the counter gets Harp's attention by saying, "Psst, you."

Harp points to himself.

"Yes, you. You can't stand there. You're in the way." She leans over the counter and points toward the front of the big room. "You can wait over there, in the waiting area." She's pointing toward the front window where there are two rows of lined-up chairs.

Now's your chance to get away.

Harp moves toward one of the chairs, but then he stops. Being inside a hospital makes him nervous, even though this hospital is bright and clean-looking and not at all like it was when he was on Ward D-4. He decides he might feel better if he waits outside while they fix Ax up. Then he and Ax can go together back down to the beach where it's safe.

That's right. Go outside and keep right on going.

Harp starts toward the door, but just then two cops come in. They're on both sides of a black man, and they have ahold of his arms. The man has blood coming out of his nose, and he's limping like his leg is hurt. One of the policemen says, "Quit actin', you're not hurt."

Don't let them see you.

Harp quickly turns away so the policemen can't see his face. He sits down in the last chair in the row and picks up a magazine. He holds it up in front of his face and peeks over it to watch. One of the policemen says something to the woman behind the counter, then they take the man down the hall and out of sight.

Harp is about ready to get the heck out of there when the man next to him leans over and says," Hey, pal, you waitin' for somebody?" He's a very large man with a red face, and a big bumpy nose, and friendly brown eyes. He has grayish black hair that sticks up in the air like he forgot to comb it.

"Uh, yes, sir. I'm waiting for my friend Ax to get fixed up."

The man glances toward the double doors where they took Ax in. "Me too. I'm waitin' for my wife. She had a bad belly ache, and it was too early in the mornin' to go to the doc so I brought her in here. Don't know what's takin' 'em so long. Was that your friend they just wheeled in there?"

"Yes, that was Ax. He's hurt real bad."

"Oh yeah, what happened to him?"

"Some bad gang boys stabbed him with their pig stickers. After that, his stomach swelled up real big."

"No kiddin'. Stabbed. That's bad. Hey, did you hear about those two homeless guys that got stabbed to death down under the Santa Monica pier? It was in the morning paper."

Harp shakes his head.

There, didn't I tell you? I told you not to say anything to that newspaper person.

"No, I haven't seen any newspaper. What did--"

"Yeah. Two of 'em killed, last couple of days. Deadern yesterday's fish. Paper said it was about damn time the police did something about what goes on down there at the beach. Bunch of drug addicts and homos livin' all over the place down there. Homeless people sleepin' under the pier and such. The paper said a kid named Harp did it. Nobody knows his real name or where he came from. Probably a serial killer. That's what the paper said. Who knows how many other people he's already killed."

"Really? It said . . . uh, that he was a --"

"Yep. Front page story. Wish I'd thought to bring the paper with me." The man stands up. "Maybe I can find one around here somewhere."

No! Stop him!

"No, that's all right," says Harp quickly. "Uh, I'll read it later."

The man sits back down again. "Well, you should read it when you get a chance. Interesting story. It said they had this Harp kid locked up in a garage, but he broke out and got away. Probably a thousand miles away by now. The newspaper is puttin' up a big reward for him so you ought to get that paper and read about it. They had a drawing of what the kid looked like. Mean lookin' guy."

Harp can hardly believe his ears. The newspaper said he killed a lot of people? How could they think that? And there was a picture in the paper?

It means you have to get out of here. Now!

The man turns in his chair to look back toward the double doors. "Guess my old lady musta ate somethin' bad last night. She gets belly aches like that sometimes. Me, I've had two heart attacks, but I can eat just about any damn thing." He turns back to Harp. "Your friend isn't gonna die, is he?"

Harp also glances back toward the big doors. "I sure hope not. He's an Indian."

"No, shit? What tribe? From Arizona? Someplace like that?"

"I'm not sure about what tribe. His name is Ax. He's from the South Mountain."

"South Mountain? Jesus H. Christ! It's been a long time since I heard that name. But the South Mountain I know about isn't an Indian place. It's a real bad place over in Watts. There's only one little hill down there, and the locals used to call it South Mountain. Some kind of dumb joke I guess. Hell of a tough place. When I was on the force and we had to drive through there, the damn place was so scary we used to get our guns out and put 'em on the seat 'til we got through it."

Harp looks at the man. It must mean he was a policeman. But he doesn't look like a policeman. He just looks like a nice old man. "You were a policeman?"

"Yep, thirty-seven years on the force. Just retired last year. Then I got a little bit too weighty around the middle, from sittin' around eatin' and watchin' TV I guess. Had two heart attacks right away. Had bypass surgery, so I'm all right now." The man looks back toward the counter. Then he stands up. "Come on, let's go find out what's goin' on."

No! Don't attract attention to yourself.

"Oh, that's all right, sir. I'd better wait until they call me."

But the man reaches down and gets ahold of Harp's sleeve. "You can't wait for these people to come get you. You'll wait 'til the cows come home. Come on, let's find out what's going on."

He drags Harp up to the counter and raps on it to get the lady's attention. "What's going on in there, nursey? My old lady's been in there for hours. What the hell are ya doing to her? It's only a belly ache."

"I keep telling you, sir. They'll let you know when they finish examining her. You'll just have to wait along with everybody else."

"Well damn, I'll be here all day. And what about this guy's friend? The one they brought in on the cart."

"He's an Indian," says Harp.

"The big guy with all the tattoos?" asks the nurse.

"Yes, that's him."

She points toward the double doors. "He's in surgery. You might as well go home. We won't know anything until much later. And then he'll have to be under observation for some time after he wakes up."

The old policeman turns back to Harp. "Well, sounds like your friend hasn't died yet anyhow. At least you can go home and wait where it's comfortable. Me, I got to sit here and wait for the old lady. Don't know why this stomach thing keeps happenin' to her. Worries me."

Harp nods to show the man he understands, and then he quickly hurries out the door. It's still foggy outside, but the sun is starting to come up. He goes to the corner and looks both ways. Which way is back to the beach?

You can't go back there.

Or maybe he shouldn't go back to the beach if the police are looking for him there. He can't decide what to do. Maybe he should wait until he's sure Ax is going to be all right. He feels the warmth of Ax's little leather bag inside his shirt.

Throw that thing away. Right now.

"But maybe it's not evil magic. Maybe it really will protect me."

It's black magic. Trust me, I know about these things.

"Well, Ax gave it to me, so I'm not throwing it away."

A woman sitting in a car rolls down her window and looks at him.

Don't you dare defy me. And stop talking to me out loud. How many times do I have to tell you that?

Harp smiles at the lady to show he's a nice person, but she rolls her window back up and looks away.

Harp hurries on down the sidewalk until he gets a ways away from the hospital. Then he slows down as he walks past a whole row of little houses. They look nice, like friendly people might live inside them. Each little house has a little yard with nice a white fence in front. But then an old man looks out a window at him so he hurries away.

He reaches inside his shirt to touch the leather bag. Does it really have magic in it? Maybe Ax should have kept it to protect him during his surgery. But maybe whatever is inside the bag is still protecting Ax even now. Harp thinks about looking inside it to see what kind of magic is in there.

No! Whatever you do, don't let the evil magic out.

That's right, better not take the chance. Who knows what might be in there?

He shivers. It's still really cold. He looks up at the sky. The sun is up, but it's still too weak to get through the last of the fog.

He realizes he still has Ax's jacket in his hand. He puts it on, but as soon as he feels its warmth, it makes him feel guilty. Here he is, outside and walking around free and not hurt, wearing a nice warm jacket while Ax is inside the hospital, hurt bad. It again makes him wonder again why bad things always seemed to follow him.

Stop thinking like that. What's the matter with your thinking lately?

"Nothing's the matter with my thinking. I'm thinking good, real good." He gets to the corner and stops to wait for a response. Cars go by but there's nothing but silence. "Well?"

If you're going to be so dumb, I have nothing to say.

"That's right, you don't. From now on, I'm going to be brave, and I'm going to think good, and that's final." But thinking about being brave makes him wonder what he did with the stick he was going to use on the gang boys. It was all black and partly burned in the fire, but it was strong enough to teach those gang boys a lesson. At least it would have, if they hadn't run away like scaredy cats. He looks down at his hands. They are all black. He was so worried about Ax he didn't even realize the stick was getting black stuff all over his hands.

He spots a sprinkler going in a front yard so he goes through the gate to wash his hands in the water. He washes them really well, wondering how he could have walked around so long with hands that were that dirty and not even notice it.

But before he can get them as clean as he wants to, a woman comes out onto the front porch and stands there watching him with her hands on her hips. He hurries away, not looking back. He hopes she doesn't recognize him from the drawing in the newspaper. She might call the police to get the reward for turning him in. He touches Ax's little leather bag. "If you're still alive Ax, I hope your little bag really can protect me."

Didn't I tell you to throw that thing away? The Bible says, Thou shalt not bow down to their gods, nor serve them, nor do after their works.

"Oh yeah, well what about the time you made that little man out of cloth that was supposed to be my father? You stuck pins in it and burned its arms and legs off with your magic candle."

Don't you sass me, young man. That was . . . necessary. And didn't I warn you about talking to me out loud?

Harp mumbles, "Sorry," but he grins to himself. He's going to keep Ax's magic bag of stuff, no matter what she says.

What's that? Do you want me to punish you?

Harp puts his fingers in his ears and hurries on. He's a block away from the house with the sprinkler, and he still doesn't hear any sirens. That's good. Maybe Ax's little bag is working.

When he gets to the next corner, he takes his fingers out of his ears and looks down the street. He has to decide if he should head back for the beach or wait for Ax. Why did they have to take Ax into surgery? Did they have to take something out of him? He remembers the time Mother thought she was going to have to go to surgery to have something taken out of her. She told the doctors she was sure she had something bad inside her stomach. She said they had to cut it out of her quick, before it was too late. The doctors put her into the hospital for a while, but they never did take out whatever bad thing was inside of her. They just sent her home again. She always swore they didn't find anything inside her because they knew she didn't have enough money to pay them to take it out. She said the pain inside her stomach was probably because of her ungrateful son, but Harp didn't see how it could be his fault. More likely it was because of her special medicine that made her talk funny and fall down.

Are you saying I was a drunk? I'll teach you to be disrespectful to your mother.

"Never mind. I was just remembering things."

Well, watch it. Remember, the Bible says, respect your mother or . . . or else.

Which way to go? Back to the hospital or back to the beach?

Neither. Go somewhere else.

He touches the little bag. It feels like it's telling him to go back to the hospital to wait for Ax.

What? Didn't I just say to stay away from there? I don't know why I even bother to talk to you.

Harp hurries back toward the hospital. He's proud he did something to help Ax, even if certain people don't think he should have. Sometimes you just have to do something, even if it is harder than just not doing anything.

Back at the hospital, he peeks in through the glass emergency room doors to make sure no police are in there. Then he slips inside and looks into the waiting area to see if the old policeman is gone. He's not there, so Harp goes to the counter and clears his throat to get the lady's attention.

She glances up from some papers she's reading. "Oh, it's you again. Well, you'll be happy to know your friend came through the surgery all right. They took him up to the prison ward."

"The prison ward?"

"Sure. You didn't know?"

"Know what?"

"They had a warrant out on him. Been lookin' for him for quite a while, I guess. That's what the cops said anyhow. Didn't you see those tattoos all over him? All the cops came in to look. That spider web, for example. Supposed to mean something about being in prison. Guess he's proud of it. And that murder number tattooed on his arm? One eighty-seven? Tipped the cops off right away. They called downtown, and it didn't take them long to find out who he was."

I told you he was no good. Didn't I tell you?

Harp doesn't know what to say. His friend, Ax, a bad person? Is she saying that 187 number means he's a murderer? But he's not the one who killed Little Hilly and the Shrimp. He couldn't be.

The lady puts down her papers and leans across the counter toward him. She lowers her voice and says, "Listen, young man, you look like a nice boy. How could you fall in with that type?"

Because he's dumb.

"Uh, I didn't fall in, ma'am. I just met him last night. The gang boys came and stuck him with their pig stickers and then . . ."

"Oh, I get it. You just came by and found him." She smiles at him. "Well, that was really nice of you to call for an ambulance and come in here with him. He'd of died if you hadn't."

"Can I go see him now?"

"Naw. They don't let anybody up there. Besides, you'd best just go on home and forget about him. They'll send him back to prison as soon as he gets well. He won't see the light of day again for a long time."

That makes Harp feel sad. He knows what it's like to be kept inside a place without getting to see the light of day. He wishes he could see Ax at least once more, but he knows he should probably go right back to the beach before the police spot him and take him to jail too. But then he remembers the plastic bracelet that has the name of this hospital on it. He takes it out of his pocket.

No! You're not supposed to let anybody know you have that.

He ignores her and shows it to the lady. "My friend Little Hilly was in here a few days ago. See, it says February eleventh. Do you remember him?"

"John Doe. Means he wouldn't give us his real name." She shrugs. "You have any idea how many John Does we get in here every day? Drunks, dopers, crazies, and none of them with a name."

"I'm sorry he didn't give you his name, ma'am. The only name I know is Little Hilly. He may have come in with his pal, Big Hilly. They used to never go anywhere without each other."

The lady looks like that makes her remember something. "Little tiny guy? About your size? And a big guy? Big chest?"

Harp grins at her. "That's them."

The lady is smiling right back at him, almost laughing. "How could I forget those two? They were in here last Saturday night. Kicked up quite a row. The little one comes in screaming he's been accosted. The big one comes right in after him yelling that he didn't hurt a hair on the little one's head. He claims it was only a little slap. But the little one keeps on screaming he's been beaten. He demands somebody call the cops. Says he wants the big guy arrested."

"Oh, no. They didn't arrest him, did they?"

The lady nods her head. "They sure did. The cops were bringing in a woman with some burns on her arms, and the little guy ran right up to them. Started yelling he wanted the big guy arrested. Nobody could talk him out of it, even though we examined him and found out he wasn't hurt at all. The cops thought it was all pretty funny. Some kind of lover's quarrel, that's what they said. But the big guy pushed one of the cops and started yelling, 'Go ahead and arrest me. See if I care.' So they dragged him out of here, and he was yelling all the way that the little guy would be sorry. 'You'll live to regret this.' That's what he said. I think the cops took him away mostly just to shut him up."

"So Big Hilly is in jail?"

"I guess so. All I know is they hauled him out of here."

Harp says, "Thank you, ma'am," and heads for the door. Now he understands. Big Hilly couldn't have killed Little Hilly. He was in jail. But why didn't Detective Olivera know that? Maybe Big Hilly never did tell them his name. Or maybe Big Hilly isn't his real name. But it explains why he wasn't there under the pier that night to protect his little buddy. Poor Little Hilly. If he would have only known how much he would need his big pal that night.

5-4

What is Within

*O*utside, Harp stands in front of the hospital trying to decide what to do. The sun is almost straight up in the middle of the sky so he can't tell for sure which way the beach is. He starts walking, hoping he's going in the right direction.

He keeps walking, and after a while, the neighborhoods of nice little houses turn into neighborhoods of tall apartment buildings, but he still doesn't recognize anything. Maybe he's getting farther from the beach instead of closer.

You're doing fine. Just keep walking in this direction.

He goes on and on, but he still doesn't recognize anything. He glances up at the sky and sees that the sun isn't there anymore. He turns around and sees that it's low in the sky in the other direction. Oh no, he should be walking toward the sun. The sun always goes down out over the ocean. All this time he's been going in the wrong direction. "You told me the wrong way."

So what? You shouldn't be going back to the beach anyhow. You're in danger there.

"But I have to go back there. I don't know anywhere else to go."

Fine, don't listen to me then. You never listen when I tell you the right thing to do.

Harp hurries toward the setting sun. How did the sun get so low in the sky? Have I been walking that long? Why don't I remember? I might be a long way from the beach by now. It makes him feel very nervous to be so far from the beach.

That's right. It's too far. You might as well go the other way.

"No, quit trying to trick me.. Now that I know Big Hilly has been in jail all this time, I should . . I don't know, go back to the beach and tell somebody, or something. I should tell Detective Olivera that Big Hilly couldn't have done it. Or maybe I should go to the jail and tell Big Hilly. I bet he doesn't even know his little buddy is dead."

Are you crazy. Go to the jail? They'll lock you up and throw away the key.

Okay, then I'll go back to the beach and tell Detective Olivera. That way, he can let Big Hilly out of jail.

What? That's just as crazy. How many times do I have to tell you, it's not your problem?

"Well, I should at least cross Big Hilly off of my suspects list." Harp stops. :But wait, where is my suspects list?" He suddenly realizes he doesn't have his backpack on. "Oh my gosh, my diary is still in my backpack. I was so worried about Ax, I left it back in my hideout under the pier."

So what? You don't need it.

"But I do need it. It has all my stories in it. It has everything that happened to me. All my days on Ward D-4, and at the Half-Way House, and when I came to the beach. All my stories are in it.

Forget it.

"No, no, you don't understand. It has what happened on Ward D-4. The police said they needed it to know what happened there. They took it and didn't give it back to me until after the trial. I've never let it out of my sight since. It still has all the evidence in it. What if somebody takes it? I've got to go back to the pier and get it."

You go back to that pier and it's the end of you.

Harp puts his fingers in his ears and hurries back toward the beach. If he can only get there before somebody finds his diary.

He walks fast, almost running. After blocks and blocks, he still doesn't recognize any of the streets. How could I have gotten so far from the beach?

When he comes to a Safeway store, he sees a lot of people coming out of the store pushing carts full of all kinds of food. It makes his stomach very unhappy to see all that food when it's been so long since he had anything to eat at all.

You have money in your pocket. Go in and buy something.

"Should I?"

Why not? It's your money now.

He heads for the door, but hesitates. "What if somebody inside the store recognizes me from the picture in the newspaper? They'll turn me in for the big reward." He stays near the edge of the parking lot, watching the people come out with their food. His brain says to run away, but his stomach says, "Go in, get food." He decides to take a chance.

He goes into the store, keeping his head down, not looking at anybody. He goes down an aisle that has glass cases on both sides. He puts his nose against the glass and sees lots of different kinds of ice cream in there. His stomach says, "Yes! Ice cream!" But the sign says "$1.98" for the smallest little containers. He tells his stomach to be quiet and goes to the next aisle. It's all cookies and crackers, stacks and stacks of them, so many different kinds of good things that his stomach wants it all. It makes his mouth water, and he can't seem to make it stop. The cookies look the best, but he remembers Mother would never let him have cookies. She said they weren't good for him. And if they ever got cookies on Ward D-4, Mitch always took them home with him. Mitch said he was doing them a favor because cookies weren't good for them.

That was one thing he was right about.

Harp goes on to another aisle, looking for some kind of more healthy food. The next aisle has open cases with cold things in it. He picks up a package of frozen peas. Peas are healthy, but they're frozen. He puts them down and heads back for the cookie aisle. Maybe cookies are only bad for you when you're little.

I'm not even going to bother to comment on that.

He grabs the biggest bag of cookies he sees and goes to the front where a young girl says, "A dollar eighty-nine," without even looking at him. Harp hands her two dollar bills, hoping she doesn't look too closely at them. She doesn't. She gives him back a penny and a dime and turns to the next customer in line.

Harp hurries back out to the street and heads for the beach. As he walks, he munches happily on the chocolate chip cookies. Nobody in the store acted like they recognized him. That's good. He's happy he was able to get a great big bag of cookies for only two of his dollars, and he even got a penny and a dime back. It makes him happy to still have money in his pocket. His stomach is happy too.

How many times have I told you, cookies will rot your teeth.

Harp ignores her and stops to sit down on a bus bench. He lays out all of the cookies in two long rows. He looks at them for a while, then rearranges them into four equal rows. He decides to eat only one row at a time. He'll save the rest for later, for the long hungry night ahead.

He gulps down row number one, and then he puts the rest of the cookies back into the bag. As he hurries on down the street, he stuffs the bag down inside the front of his shirt so nobody can steal his cookies. Now, if only he can make it back to the pier without anybody recognizing him and calling the police.

That pier is the one place on this earth you shouldn't--

"I have to get my diary, and that's final?"

No, I'm telling you . . .

Harp quickly puts his fingers in his ears. He'll go to the pier and get his diary, no matter what anybody says. Then he'll dig up the money, and . . . run away . . . or something. It's a good plan. It really is, even if certain people don't think so.

Part 6

The Merry-Go-Round Girl

For two days Mitch was gone and nobody knew where. A new man came in as the daytime aide and he didn't say anything to us about why Mitch was gone. The Growler hid under his bed back in the dorm and nobody could make him come out not even to eat. Carl the Older came back from a trip to the warehouse and said everybody was saying Mitch got in trouble because Bacon Benny died. Important people suspected it was because Mitch had given him extra meds.

And then today Mitch came back. He came and stood in front of me and looked at me for a long time, and then he went and sat in his regular chair to read his Bible. He was whispering to himself and he wouldn't say anything to anybody. The Growler crawled out from under his bed and came running out of the dorm to sit by his feet. After a little while everything seemed back to normal. But it wasn't. In the afternoon a man in a suit came and I could tell Mitch was scared of him. The Growler growled at the man and the man started yelling for Mitch to call him off or else he'd have the Growler sent up for shock therapy. Mitch sent the Growler back to the dorm and after that the man sat in a chair in the lunch room and had us all come in one at a time so he could ask us questions. Mitch grabbed everybody before they went in and said if anybody talked he'd have the Growler kill us in our beds that night. The man asked us questions about Mitch, but I didn't tell because I didn't want to get killed at night in the dorm and I don't think anybody else told on Mitch either because after a while the man went away. After that Mitch made me stand up against the wall all day right next to his desk while he read his Bible and mumbled to himself.

6-1

Magic

After walking for a long time, Harp begins to wonder if he'll ever get back to the beach. The sun is getting lower and lower in the sky, and it's starting to get cold again. He pulls Ax's jacket tighter around himself and walks even faster.

Suddenly, he gets a little whiff of the ocean. It's a smell so familiar he didn't even realize he'd been missing it. That smell seems to turn his brain back on. He begins to recognize some of the streets. Now he's pretty sure he knows where he is. If he just keeps on going toward the setting sun, he'll soon be back to the beach.

May I say something now?

"Only if you're nice."

You can't go to the pier until it gets dark.

Why not?

Because it's not safe there.

"Well, I know that, don't I? But it'll be dark soon. Then I'll go get my diary."

An old lady in a red coat sitting on a bus bench is staring at him. She pulls her big red purse close to her chest.

Harp smiles at her, but she doesn't smile back. Instead, she looks away.

See there. People are afraid of you. Why can't you just act like a normal person?

"I am acting normal. I'm just walking down the street. What's wrong with that?"

You think it's normal to talk out loud to me?

"All right, all right, but I can act normal if I want to." He puts his hands in his pockets and frowns to try to look like everybody else.

A few blocks later, as he approaches a busy street, Harp hears brakes squeal and sees somebody standing out in the middle of the street. It's Worried Jack. Oh, no, did Jack almost get run over?

Not that nut case again. That's exactly what we don't need.

Jack is standing in front of a little red car, and a man is getting out of it.

Harp hurries out into the street to see if he can help, but before he can get there, Jack starts pounding on the front of the man's car. He's yelling something Harp can't quite make out. He's hitting the car really hard with both of this fists. Some of the other cars behind the red car start honking.

The man comes around to the front of his car and starts yelling at Jack. "What the hell do you think you're doing, asshole? Keep your dirty hands off my car." He pushes against Jack's chest, but Jack sticks out his chin and refuses to move.

Harp gets there just in time and takes ahold of Jack's arm, but Jack pulls loose and starts yelling back at the man. "I know what you're up to," yells Jack. "But it won't work. Not this time."

The man gets a surprised look on his face. "What the hell are you talking about, buddy?"

Jack takes a step toward the man. "I'm on to you now. I know where you're hiding your transmitters."

Harp pulls at Jack's arm. "Come on, Jack. Let's go back to the beach."

Jack turns to look at him, blinking. "Oh, hi, Harp. What are you doing here?"

"Never mind that, Jack. We have to go now." He tries to pull Jack away, but he only gets him a few steps toward the curb when Jack pulls free and goes right back to face the man again. "I'm on to your little game. You might as well tell them they'll have to try something else."

Oh brother. This guy is waaay round the bend.

The man holds his fist up in Jack's face, but he's looking at Harp. "Get your loony friend off this Goddamned street before I punch his stupid lights out."

"Oh, his lights aren't stupid, sir. He just gets worried about things, and sometimes it makes it so he doesn't know what he's saying."

"What?" says Worried Jack, turning to Harp. "Whose side are you on?"

"What the hell are you talking about?" says the man. "You want some of this too?" He shakes his fist in Harp's face.

"No, thank you, sir. We're going now." He pulls Jack away.

Oh, great. Now they think you're a nut too, just like he is.

Jack comes along, but he's shaking his head and mumbling to himself as he stumbles toward the sidewalk. When they reach the curb, he turns to look back at the red car. "I finally got it figured out, Harp. It's the cars. I shoulda known it."

Harp keeps a tight hold on Jack's arm to make sure he doesn't run back out into the street. Cars are lined up honking. The man shakes his fist at them just like he shook it at Jack and Harp. Then he gets back into his car and drives away.

"It's true, Harp. Think about it. What's all around us, all the time, day and night? Cars, that's what. We don't even notice them. That's what they're counting on. That's how they do it."

Are you going to stand there and listen to this nonsense?

Harp gently pulls Jack along. Jack is bigger and stronger than he is, but Harp hopes he can get him back to the beach where there aren't very many cars, and nobody cares if you act a little crazy sometimes.

But Jack suddenly stops and stares at him. "Harp, is it really you? I though you were in jail."

"No, I'm not in jail, Jack. Why did you think that?"

"Because Speel said you probably were. He said you probably got nabbed for the reward. He was really mad because he said he was the one who captured you and by rights he should have got the reward."

"Speel said that?"

I told you not to trust her. Didn't I tell you?

But the more Harp thinks about it, the more it makes sense. He had a feeling Speel was up to something.

Why else would she have been so nice to you? Has anyone ever been nice to you?

She's right. All that nice talk. That nice chocolate cake. But all the time Speel was just trying to get the reward.

I could have told you that. But would you listen to reason? No.

"Be quiet. I listened. I knew all the time Speel was up to something."

Jack is staring at him. "Why should I be quiet? I was just trying to tell you what Speel said."

Harp shakes his head. "No, I didn't mean you, Jack. I meant . . . Oh, never mind. I was just thinking out loud."

Jack nods. "Oh, yeah. I do that sometimes too." But then he sees another red car going past, and he runs back out into the street again to yell, "I'm on to you!"

Harp runs out and gets ahold of Jack's sleeve again. "Now, Jack, don't be looking at the cars anymore. We've got to get you back to the beach."

"But, Harp, that's one of them." He points. "I can feel the radiation when it goes by. It's sending out radio waves to track me. I knew it had to be more than Russian rockets. They had to have a way to track me at ground level."

Jack lets Harp pull him along, but he's still mumbling to himself.

When they get close to the beach, Harp decides against going over the busy bridge that goes back to the pier. Instead, he leads Jack down a side street until they can cut back to the beach through the apartment house's parking lot. After making sure there aren't any red cars in the parking lot, Harp brings Jack to a stop behind a big truck. "Listen, Jack, I've got to go now. Can you make it by yourself now?"

Jack stares at Harp as if he'd forgotten he was even there. "Oh, hi, Harp. Hey, you'd better hide. Speel said the police wanna throw you in jail."

"I know, Jack. But I didn't do it. You believe me, don't you?"

Jack shrugs. "Sure, I believe you. Uh, do what?"

"Never mind, just believe I didn't do anything."

Jack smiles. "Okay. That's what Tex said too."

Jack starts to turn away, but Harp catches his arm. "Wait a minute. What did Tex say?"

"He said you didn't do it. When Speel said it was you that probably stabbed Little Hilly and the Shrimp too, Tex stepped right up and said you didn't. He said it was a homo love triangle. Tex said Big Hilly killed both of them, and they both got what they deserved."

That's good. At least somebody still thinks Big Hilly did it.

"But it's not fair. He couldn't have done it."

"He didn't? How do you know?"

"What I meant, Jack, is that Big Hilly couldn't have done it. He was in jail the night Little Hilly got killed. Maybe he's still in jail."

Why did you tell him that? Can't you ever keep a secret?

"Okay with me," says Jack. "I've got to go find some lead shielding. Do you know if dumpsters are made out of lead?"

"No, I don't know about that, Jack. You be careful now. And stay out of the street."

Jack starts to put out his hand to shake Harp's hand, but changes his mind and just shrugs. "Bye, Harp. I hope they don't catch you." He wanders away and disappears into the gathering fog.

Harp stays in the parking lot between the cars, thinking. So Tex is still saying Big Hilly did it. "But I know Big Hilly couldn't have killed Little Hilly because he was in jail."

The police don't know that. They still think you did it.

"That's right. I should tell them I didn't. I should tell Olivera about the Stranger."

He won't believe you.

"Maybe he will. I'm going to call him."

Here we go again. See what happens when you think for yourself?

"You always say that, but sometimes I have good ideas of my own."

That'll be the day.

Harp hurries to the strand. It's getting darker by the minute, and the fog is so thick now the few people he sees on the strand are only shadows, like ghosts who seem to appear and then disappear again into the mist.

He keeps going until he comes to a pay phone, but somebody has stolen the part you hold up to your ear.

He hurries on, looking down at the sidewalk whenever he passes anybody. The few people he meets seem to be in so much of a hurry to get out of the wet fog they hardly notice him.

The next phone he comes to is working okay so he puts in one of his quarters and dials Olivera's number. A man answers, but it's not Olivera. Harp says, "I'd like to talk to Detective Olivera please."

"Hang on."

Then, after a minute, "Yeah, Olivera here."

"Detective Olivera? This is Harp. You know, the person you wanted to be your eyes and ears."

"Where are you, son? We need to talk."

For heaven's sake don't tell him that.

"I'm . . . well, that doesn't matter. You said I should call you if I found out anything. Well, I found out who killed poor Little Hilly. And probably the Shrimp too."

"Really? Well, that's . . . that's good. Now listen, son, you tell me where you are and I'll come right over. Then you can tell me all about it."

"I can tell you right now, sir. It's a stranger, he's wearing my floppy old brown hat."

"A floppy hat."

"That's right. A stranger. And he has mean eyes. That's what the Ghost said anyway."

"Mean eyes."

"That's right. If he's still on the beach you shouldn't have any trouble finding him."

There was a silence on the phone, and Harp thinks he hears Olivera talking to somebody else.

"Listen, Harp. I really need to talk to you about this. You just tell me where I can find you and I'll come there. Or I can just meet you on the pier. How about that? I'll meet you on the pier in ten minutes."

Tell him you're gone away.

"No, I'm . . . not there . . . anymore."

"Not where? Not at the beach?"

"No, sir. I'm . . . uh, a long ways from there now. Ax the South Mountain Indian got hurt, and I had to get him to the hospital and then I . . . ran away. I've gone far, far away now, just like the boy who sat on the hare's back and rode far away to his secret little hut in the forest."

"What? What's that about a secret hut?"

"Well, never mind about that. I just meant I went a long ways away, and I won't be back again so there's no use looking for me on the beach anymore. Just look for the Stranger. He has mean eyes, and he's wearing my old hat."

"Now wait a minute, son."

"I'm telling you he's the one who did it, not me. Cross my heart and hope to die. Bye now."

"Wait! Harp! Don't hang up!"

Harp hangs up the phone, but he stays next to it, staring at it.

He didn't believe you.

"Yes he did. He'll catch the Stranger, and then everything will go back to normal.

You wish.

"Yes, I do wish. Why can't my wishes ever come true? Why can't I be like the poor boy who the Lord gave three wishes to?"

More likely you'd end up like the rich boy who squandered away his wishes on nonsense.

"Would not."

Would too.

"All right, if I can't have three wishes, and if Detective Olivera doesn't believe me, then I'll go catch the killer myself."

That's a laugh.

"It is not a laugh. I can do it. Ax said if I waited under the pier, the killer would come to me."

He'll come to you all right. He'll come to you and kill you.

Harp decides not to say another word. He'll go to the pier, no matter what anybody says, and he'll wait there for the killer. Ax said he should go back to the scene of the crime and wait. He said the magic bag with its rattlesnake rattles and other magic things would protect him. So that's what he'll do, and he won't listen to any arguments about it.

No, I'm telling you for the last time--

"No, I'm not going to listen now." He heads for the pier, walking fast. He can feel the warmth of Ax's magic bag against his chest.

Stop! Listen to me.

"I'm not lis-en-ing."

Headstrong and ungrateful I should have known you'd end up like this. Sunday's child is full of grace, Monday's child is full of woe.

Guess what day you were born on?

"Oh yeah, well how about this one? Bye, baby bumpkin, where's Tony Lumpkin? Mother's on her deathbed from eating half a pumpkin."

How dare you talk to your mother like that? You're nothing without me. Why if it wasn't for me, you'd . . .

Harp puts his fingers in his ears and hurries on. It's getting dark, and as he gets closer to the waterline, the fog thickens, and he feels the same kind of cold chill in the air that he felt the night Little Hilly got killed. This time it feels like the chill is coming from somewhere deep inside himself. He pulls Ax's jacket tighter around himself and keeps going. He's not going to stop for anything until he gets his dairy. Then he'll catch the killer.

Suddenly, he sees the pier ahead. In the dense fog it doesn't look like the nice old pier he knows so well. Instead it looks like a lonely old pile of dark wood, cold and scary. "Maybe you're right. Maybe I shouldn't go there."

She doesn't answer, and that worries him. Sometimes he did things she said not to, and sometimes it turned out she was right. He doesn't want to make a mistake this time. It could be like when the king's son made the mistake of going to the witch's house in the deep dark woods. "Do you remember that one?"

Nothing but silence.

"I guess you told me that story to teach me to be wary of strangers, didn't you?"

Still only silence.

"Luckily, the king's son didn't drink the witch's brew, did he? So it was only the horse that died, and when thieves who wanted to rob him ate the poisoned bird, they were the ones that died, not him. Right?"

He waits, but there still is no response.

"Maybe you're right, maybe I shouldn't be here. But how do I know if I went somewhere else the killer wouldn't just follow me?"

There's no sound except for the gentle sound of the waves sliding up onto the shore.

"All right, don't talk then. See if I care. I'll show you. I'll go under the pier to get my diary. If the killer is there, then . . . well, it's just too bad. If I get killed, you'll be sorry you didn't help me."

He starts walking again, but slower than before. Even before he gets to the pier, he can smell it. The whole area smells wet and fishy. The fishermen must have been throwing their dead fish guts under the pier again. But that doesn't matter, I'm not afraid of bad smells. I'm brave.

When he gets to the pier, he hides behind one of the big columns to listen. The waves are very soft, sliding up onto the shore, whispering to him. It feels like they are saying, "Go away. Go away," but he's not going to go away, not this time. He'll show her he is *too* brave.

He pulls Ax's little leather bag out of his shirt, hoping it will protect him. He wonders again what could be in it. Maybe he should look inside.

No! Don't let the magic out.

"Ah ha!. So you're talking to me again. About time."

Throw that evil thing away.

"Is that all you can say? Throw it away? No, I'm keeping it." He smells the top of the bag, but quickly pulls his nose away. It smells icky. Can a bag of smelly old things really protect him against a killer with a knife?

Not a chance. That bag won't help you, nothing will help you if you stay here. Your only chance is to get out of here, and fast.

Maybe she's right. Maybe he should run away. But Ax said he should go back to the scene of the crime and wait for the killer. He said he saw it in a dream.

Are you going to believe me, or some stupid dream?

Harp can't decide what to do. If he waits for the killer to come like Ax said, he might get killed. Then who would tell the story? But wait, all of my stories are in my diary, and it's still in my secret place, up under the pier. Without my stories, nothing matters anyhow. "I have to go get it." He touches Ax's magic bag one more time and whispers a prayer: "Hearken unto the voice of my cry, magic bag, unto thee I pray. Please keep me safe, magic bag. If the killer is there, don't let him stab me like he did Little Hilly and the Blind Shrimp. Let me be brave and catch him instead."

I've never heard such blaspheme. Praying to a magic bag. All right, go ahead. Get yourself killed. See if I care.

Harp begins to crawl up the steep sand toward his secret hideout under the pier. But then he stops. He listens. Nothing but silence. The fog swirls around him. It makes him shiver.

He looks up toward his secret hiding place. First I'll go up there and get my backpack. I'll make sure my diary is safe. Then I'll . . . then I'll decide what to do next.

But what if the killer is waiting for him? He remembers how scared he was when Ax pulled him inside with his strong hand that had the tattoo of the cross on it. The killer could be hiding up there and pull him in just like Ax did. But this time the cross might not only be a tattoo. This time it could be real, the same cross-knife that was on that bad picture of the stabbed doggie on Betty's wall. But he has to get his diary. He whispers, "Here I go, Ax. I'm doing like you said."

He begins to crawl up the steep sand. When he gets close to his secret hideout, he again stops to listen. Was that a sound from inside? Is somebody in there?

Run!

He turns and slides down the sand. He tries to run, but his feet get tangled up and he falls forward, losing his flashlight. He tries to feel for it, but it's not there.

Never mind that. Run!

He knows he should run away, but he doesn't want to lose his little flashlight. Without it, he won't be able to see at night. He won't even be able to write in his diary at night.

Are you crazy? Are you willing to die for a flashlight?

But then his searching fingers feel something. It's not his flashlight, it's . . . his stick, the stick he was going to use to hit the gang boys with. It's just what he needs. If the killer tries to get him, he'll hit him with his stick.

He jumps to his feet and turns to face whoever is coming. He holds his stick up high and waits.

But no one comes.

Maybe it wasn't the killer. He searches around on the ground for his flashlight and when he finds it, he shines it back up under the pier. There's no one up there.

He's hiding up there, waiting for you.

"Then I'll go up and get him."

What? Are you out of your mind? Do what you always do, run away.

"But Little Hilly was stabbed in the back. He was probably trying to run away. I'm not running."

Oh, now I get it. You're going to be the brave one again.

"That's right. I'll be like Brave Hans."

Oh, so you think you're ready for that, do you?

"Yes, I'm ready. I have my club now, just like Little Hans did. And I'll use it too. Just you wait and see."

But don't you remember? When little Hans tried to defeat the robbers, he failed. He got hurt. Real bad.

"Yes, but after that Hans learned from the old tales his mother told him from the secret book. From those tales, he learned how to be brave. He got stronger, and then he beat them all up."

This is not a story from a book. This time the killer is real.

"You can't stop me. I'm going back up there. Ax said I should."

It's your funeral. Like it says in the rhyme, 'Who'll carry the coffin? I, said the Kite, if it's not through the night.'

"There you go again with that funeral stuff. Well, maybe it's better to have my funeral and be buried in the ground than to always be running away. Little Hilly said it was better to be dead than unhappy all the time."

Who'll dig his grave? I, said the Owl, with my pick and shovel.

"Quit that. You're supposed to be helping me."

All right, Brave Hans. If you won't listen to reason, I guess I will have to help you. Let's go.

Harp holds his stick in one hand and the flashlight in the other. He struggles back up the steep sand to his hideout. He stops to listens. There it is again. That sound. It's like . . . scratching. Is the killer in there? Why is he scratching?

Well, don't just stand there, Brave Hans, look inside.

Harp takes a deep breath and digs the sand away from the entrance. He peers in, but it's too dark to see anything. It's just like when Ax was hiding in there, but this time he's ready. He's got his stick so the killer better watch out. He gets a good grip on his stick and snaps on the flashlight. He shines it inside the hole. Nothing.

"There's nobody in here."

But then something moves. Two little red eyes stare back at him.

It's a rat! A big one.

"Aw, it's only a rat. I'm not afraid of a measily little rat. You were the one who was afraid of rats, not me." Harp pokes his stick at it, and the rat scurries farther back under the pier. Harp shines his light all around inside the sand hole until he's sure there's nothing else in there. He sees his backpack lying on the sand and that's a relief. Nobody stole it.

He quickly crawls inside and pushes some sand up to close off the entrance. Now nobody will know I'm inside. I'm safe.

He sits down and lets out a big breath. Yes, I'm safe, for the time being anyhow.

You were brave.

"I was, wasn't I?"

You sure were. You scared that big bad rat just about half to death with that big stick of yours.

"Well, how was I supposed to know it was only a rat? It could have been the killer."

All right, Brave Hans. We'll see how brave you are when the real killer comes.

Harp snaps off his flashlight and sits still in the darkness. He feels very tired. How long has it been since he slept? It's a little warmer inside his hideout, but it's still very cold, and he knows it will only get colder as the night goes on.

He feels hungry. Maybe it's time to eat a few more cookies. He pulls the bag of cookies out of this shirt. But then he scolds himself. "I know, I know, I said I would save them for a midnight snack."

I didn't say anything. Did you hear me say anything?

Okay, then I'm having a cookie.

Better not. You'll spoil your supper.

"Aw, heck. I never get to do anything I want to." He puts the bag down and lies back to rest, but he keeps his stick in his hand, just in case.

Now that he has his dairy again, he can write down the story of today. And what about my suspects list? Now that I know who the killer is, I should change my list of suspects. Now there's only one main suspect, the Stranger, so I guess I should cross everybody else off.

He opens his backpack and reaches in, but he can't feel his diary in there. He frantically feels around. He can't find it. In a panic, he quickly finds his flashlight, and shines it inside the backpack. He doesn't seem to be there. He dumps everything out. The torn-out pictures from magazines are still there, the one of the lady in the hat that reminds him of Mother, and the one of the little boy with the blond hair and the blue sailor suit that reminds him of what he might have looked like when he was little, if only he would have ever got to have a nice sailor suit like that. The pretty little rocks are in there, and the nice silvery safety pins, and the plastic hair clip, and the worn-out batteries, and the two pencils that he uses to write in his diary with. But no diary. "Oh, no. It's gone. What could have happened to it?"

You know what happened to it. The killer came and took it. Now he knows everything about you.

"No, no, it can't be. The killer couldn't know about my secret hideout."

Oh yes he does. He knows where you're hiding, and now he has your diary.

"But why would he want my diary? He didn't take anything else."

He has his reasons. What's important is to get out of here before he comes back.

Harp knows she's right. He should run away. But he's so upset about losing his diary that he can't even think about leaving without it. "Maybe he'll bring it back. I have to wait here."

He'll bring it back all right. He'll bring it back when he comes to kill you.

Harp throws down the empty backpack and picks up his stick. "All right, let him come. I'm mad, and I don't care who knows it." He's really, really mad this time. Steaming mad. This is too much. The killer came and took the only thing he really cares about, the only thing he can say is his own. That diary has all his stories in it, his whole life about when he was locked up on Ward D-4, and about everything that happened since he came to the beach.

Now he's really going to hit the killer with his stick. He deserves it. Nobody can take away my stories and get away with it. When the killer comes I'll smack him with my stick and make him give the diary back. Or else.

Calm down. You're getting over excited.

"Well, I'm mad. Wouldn't you be?"

I'd be getting the heck out of here.

"Well, I'm not. I'm not leaving until I get my diary back." He tries to calm down, but then he thinks about the Stranger reading his diary, and it makes him even more upset. "Those are my stories. Nobody should be reading them but me."

Calm down. Breathe. One in, two out.

Harp tries to calm down. He stays very still, listening to his own breathing. His breaths seem very loud inside the closed-in space. He counts as he breathes: one, two, one two. Gradually his breathing slows down, but for some reason his cheeks are wet.

It's only a diary. Nothing to cry about.

"No, don't say that! It's important. If it's important to me, it should be important to you too."

All right, all right, calm down. I didn't mean it.

Harp wipes away the tears and reaches up to touch the boards of the pier. They feel damp and cold. The smell of the old tar is strong. It's a familiar smell. How many nights has he slept inside his hideout? "How long have I been on the beach?"

A long time. Since it was warm.

"That's right, it was summer." Remembering the warm summer nights makes him feel all tired out. It seems so long ago. Since winter came, the nights are always cold and foggy. And there aren't as many people on the beach in the daytime, so it's getting harder and harder to find food. And being hungry all the time makes it hard to sleep. When did he last sleep? Maybe he slept a little when he was in the Fearful Ones circle, but probably only for a few hours.

So take a nap now. What's to stop you?

"No, I've got to stay awake and wait for the killer."

Ex-cuse me. If you won't do what I tell you, then do as you please. Just pretend like I'm not even here.

Harp ignores her and lies back to think. What could the killer want with his diary? And why didn't he take anything else? It's a mystery.

Through the crack in the old boards overhead, he hears the music coming from the merry-go-round up there. It's a nice song, even if it does repeat over and over. It's a little bit like that song Mother used to sing to herself late at night when she'd had too much of her special medicine.

Don't be snotty. I needed that medicine for my rheumatism.

"You'd sit there in your chair with your Bible on your lap, watching your little TV, drinking more and more of your special medicine, singing that song to yourself."

Well, what was I supposed to do? You were--

"Shh." He hears people walking above him on the pier. The footsteps come closer and closer. They stop right above him.

"That Harp character said he was a long ways from the beach, but I got a feeling he's still around here somewhere."

Harp recognizes that voice. It's Detective Olivera. He's up on top of the pier, right over him. He imagines Olivera up there leaning against the railing, looking out over the water. Harp holds his breath, afraid to even move.

"Aw, hell, boss, he'll be hundreds of miles from here by now. Why would he stick around the beach after what he did?"

"Just a hunch. I got the feeling he's close, maybe real close. Could be he's a real nut case. Ever think about that? Maybe he was . . . I don't know, driven to kill those guys."

"Whatta ya mean, like voices in his head tellin' him what to do?"

"Somethin' like that. You get all types down here on the beach. Half of 'em oughta be locked up in the nut house."

"Yeah, I guess you're right. But he'd have to be pretty crazy to stick around here after doin' in his two pals. He's got to know you're after him."

"Maybe so, but I've still got this feeling he's around somewhere. You sure you looked good under this pier?"

"Ya. I checked several times. Nuthin down there."

"Okay. Let's drive on down to Venice Beach and see if the plainclothes boys down there've heard any talk about where he might have gone."

"Two to one says he's long gone and we never see him again. That type may look dumb but . . ."

They walk away, and that's all Harp can hear. He listens to their footsteps as they go farther and farther away until he can't hear them anymore.

Those were cops. They were talking about you.

"I know. They think I went away and--"

Shh. Quit talking out loud to me.

Harp lies still, trying to decide what to do. Olivera didn't believe him about the Stranger. He didn't even mention his floppy hat. Why doesn't anybody ever believe him? What did I ever do to deserve this?

You know what you did.

He whispers. "No I don't. I didn't do anything."

Yes you do. You know. And quit talking out loud.

Harp stares up into the darkness wondering what Olivera would think if he knew he was hiding right under his feet. That other policeman thought he was hundreds of miles away.

And he's right. You should be long gone from here by now.

Well, it's good that they think that because I'm not going anywhere. Brave Little Hans wouldn't run away. He'd wait for the killer and get his diary back, and then he'd catch that killer and show him to Olivera, and then everybody would know he didn't do it.

Harp closes his eyes and imagines he's not under the smelly old pier, not cold and hungry. Instead, he's safe, hiding with Mother in the secret forest and she's reading to him from the magic book about knights with swords and brave boys who always win, and everybody has to do whatever he tells them to.

6-2

Secret Places

Smoke. A big bird is sitting on the roof. The house is burning. Fire is coming out of all the windows, its fingers reaching up to the sky. Mother is still inside the house, singing: "Sing a song of sixpence, pocket full of rye, four and twenty naughty boys, baked in a pie."

Why doesn't she get out of there? What is she waiting for? Run, Mother, run!

Wake up.

But then Harp smells the stinky old wood of the pier. He's not at the burning house. He's still under the pier in his secret place. It was only a dream. I must have fallen asleep.

He lies still and listens. Did anybody sneak up on me while I was asleep? All he can hear is his own breathing. The merry-go-round music has stopped. There are no people walking around up there on top of the pier anymore. It must be late. Is this the time of the night when the killer comes? What time was it when he heard that dog howling the night Little Hilly died?

Somebody's coming.

She's right. Somebody is out there. Harp can hear him moving around down below. Is it the killer? Harp feels Ax's leather bag against his chest. He reaches down to touch it. He hopes it's as lucky as Ax said it was.

There it is again. A sound. Somebody is under the pier.

It's the killer. He's come for you.

Harp turns over onto his stomach and pushes away a little bit of the sand wall. He peeks out. It is a person, like a shadow moving around down there under the pier.

This is it. You're trapped

Harp *does* feel trapped, like a mouse hiding in his hole. But the dark figure doesn't seem to be coming up to get him. He's just sitting down there. Then there's another sound. It's like . . . water.

He's peeing.

She's right, the person just came under the pier to pee. Harp smiles to himself. That's a relief. It's not the killer come to kill me; it's only a person peeing. It happens all the time. Probably one of the runners, or a dog walker. They always slip under the pier to pee when it's dark. If the person only knew somebody was hiding under the pier, watching. He giggles.

The person stands up and turns around. "Who's there?"

Harp ducks his head and holds his breath. Did he make a sound? He didn't mean to.

"I said, who's up there?" The person comes up a little closer. "Is that what gives you your kicks, asshole? Hiding up there watching me take a leak?"

It's a girl. Harp doesn't even dare breathe. She sounds mad.

Don't say a word. She'll go away.

"So, aren't you gonna say anything? You want me to go get a cop? I saw some cops up on the pier just now. If I yell real loud they'll come down here. Is that what you want?"

"No," whispers Harp.

"What was that? Did you say something, or was that a little tiny mouse squeaking up there?"

"I'm sorry. I was . . . asleep."

"Oh, I get it."

Her voice doesn't sound as mad anymore.

"You're one of the homeless dudes. Sleepin' off the booze, eh? Hey, you wouldn't happen to have any left, would you?"

Harp peeks out. "I . . . don't have anything. Except . . . some cookies. You want a cookie?"

She laughs. "A cookie? Well, all right. Matter of fact, I haven't had a damn thing to eat since lunch."

What are you doing? You know how nervous you get around girls.

"Well, are you comin' down from there or not?"

Stay right where you are, mister. I've got a feeling this one is trouble with a capital T.

"I have to go down," Harp whispers. "She'll call the police if I don't."

Well, it's her funeral then. A girl shouldn't be out in the dark. All alone like that.

"I'm not going to hurt her. I'm going down."

You'll be sorry.

"Hey, up there, what are you doin', talkin' to yourself?"

Harp grabs his bag of cookies and squeezes out of the hideout. "No, I'm coming." He scoots down the sand bank until he's right next to her. It's a girl all right, with long dark hair and a white T-shirt that has printing on the front of it, but it's too dark to see what the printing says. It's also too dark to see what her face looks like. But he can see she's a big girl, a lot taller than he is, and bigger around too.

He holds out the bag of cookies.

She takes the bag and looks inside. "What kind you got?"

"Just . . . regular cookies."

She takes one out and stuffs it into her mouth. "Ah, chocolate chip. Not bad."

She takes out another one, and then another. She keeps on putting them into her mouth like she's starving. Harp doesn't think she's even had time to swallow the first one, but she keeps on eating more. He hopes she won't eat all of them.

She sits down and shakes the bag, looking into it. "Didn't realize I was that hungry. That bastard I work for wouldn't even let me go get a decent meal at lunchtime. Brought me one lousy taco. I'm gonna complain to the temp agency tomorrow. They're supposed to give you time off for lunch." She turns to Harp. "Hey, relax a bit. Sit down here next to me."

Harp sits down and watches her eat. He wonders where she works. It must be somewhere nearby. Has he seen her before? She seems nice. He wishes it wasn't so dark. Her face is all in shadow.

She seems nice? So now you're an expert on girls? Georgie Porgie, puddin' and pie, kissed the girls and made them cry.

She stops eating for a second and looks around. "Damn. It's dark under here. And that fog. Did ya ever see anything like this fog? Hey, you stay under here all the time?'

"No, not . . . always."

"Well, I hope not. Too damn dark for my taste. And it stinks under here. Don't know how you stand it." She eats a few more cookies, but then she stops and holds the bag out. "Hey, sorry, dude. I'm eatin' up all your cookies. You want one?"

Harp takes a cookie. "Thank you."

She laughs again. "Hey, don't thank me. They're your cookies, aren't they?"

Harp thinks she has a nice laugh. He really wishes he could see her better. "Do you work on the beach?" he asks politely "I mean . . . around here?"

"Yeah, up on the pier. My first day. The temp agency sent me out this mornin' to work on the merry-go-round. But I may not be back. Don't think the guy liked me. Spect he was hoping for a little cutey, if you know what I mean." She laughs a short laugh that sounds like, "Huh, huh." Then she eats another cookie and says, "Cutey. That's not me, that's for sure. Don't get me wrong, bein' how it's so dark under here you can't say for sure, but I'll just tell ya right out I'm not ugly or anything, just not what you'd call . . . cute. My Aunt Peggy says I got to lose some weight. Maybe so, but I think I'm just naturally big. Raw-boned, you might say. Got it from my father. And he was, in spades. Raw-boned, I mean. If anybody ever was." She laughs again.

Harp likes to hear her laugh.

I bet you do. Next you'll be wanting to go for a roll in the hay with her.

"Not only does the jerk not give me any lunch, but he makes me stay late and clean up. Made me miss the last local bus. Now I'll have to walk all the way up to the main bus terminal in Santa Monica. Hey, you wouldn't know what time the express bus leaves for the valley, would you?"

Harp shakes his head.

"Was that a yes or no?"

"Uh, I don't know."

Georgie porgie, puddin' and pie, kissed the girls and made them cry.

"That's okay. I'll find it. Uh, thanks for the cookies. Guess I mostly ate 'em all."

She hands Harp the bag. He can feel that it's empty, and that makes his stomach complain.

"Guess I'll have a smoke and shove off." She takes out a pack of cigarettes. "Want one?'

"No, thank you."

When the match flares, Harp can see her face for just a moment. She has a large face, kind of reddish, and a large nose. But it's not a bad face. It's kind of . . . friendly looking. And she has nice hair, maybe red, like her face. It's long, down to her shoulders. He feels less nervous now that he can see how nice and friendly she looks. He knows he should say something friendly to her, but he can't think of anything.

How would you know what to say to a girl?

When he was little, Mother never let him talk to girls. So how was he supposed to know what to say?

Then don't say anything. Make her go away.

But that was when I was little. Now I'm grown up, and I can talk to a girl if I want to.

I'm warning you. Make her go away before it's too late.

She sucks at her cigarette. It glows red in the darkness. Harp can see that her eyes are looking at him, It reminds him of the glass eyes the merry-go-round horses have. They seem to look at you no matter where you stand.

She blows out the smoke and says, "The boss did the ticket takin'. Me, my job was to help the little kids get up onto the horses. And if they're real little, I had to make sure they put the belt on before the thing starts moving. Then I was supposed to walk between the horses and make sure everybody was doin' all right. You know what? The hardest part of the job was figurin' out how to walk around while the platform was movin'. At first I had to hold on to even take a step, but after a while you get used to it. All in all, it wasn't a bad job. I liked seein' those little kids on the horses. Cute. Some of 'em were so scared, I had to stick right next to 'em until they got used to it. Not a bad job. I've had worse."

"I almost got to go on a merry-go-round once."

"Almost?"

"Yes. It was when I was . . . little."

"You never been on one ? Hey, tell you what, if the guy wants me back tomorrow, you come up there, and I'll see if I can get you on for a free ride."

Harp thinks that would be fun. But even if it doesn't happen, he hopes she does come back so he can talk to her more.

Aren't you forgetting something? What about the police? And what about the killer who is probably going to come and stab you to death this very night?

Harp shakes off the worrisome thoughts and tries to remember how long it's been since he's talked to a girl.

You talked to a girl? When was that? And why didn't I know about it?

There was that girl who lived next door.

Oh, her. That little bitch. She doesn't count.

That little girl next door was mean. Once she threw mud on him. And she was always making fun of him. What happened to her? Maybe she moved away.

"Hey, you don't say much, do you? What's your name?"

"Harp."

"Harp? Like the kind an angel plays?"

"I . . . guess so."

"Well, okay, Harp. My name's Sandra. Put 'er there, Harp." She puts her cigarette in the side of her mouth and sticks out her hand.

Don't touch her.

Harp puts his hand out, and she shakes it up and down, real hard. Her big hand feels warm, and a little sweaty.

"You got a job, Harp?"

"Uh, no. Not really."

"I guess not, seein's how you're sleepin' under this pier and all. Well, I probably won't have a job tomorrow either. Don't think the dude liked the way I dress. Boy's clothes, he called 'em. 'Don't you have anything but boy's clothes?' he said. I told him I did, but actually I don't. Guess if he wants me back tomorrow I could borrow some girl's clothes from my aunt. But what the hell, he probably won't want me back anyhow."

Harp likes listening to her talk. She has a deep voice, like maybe she smokes too many cigarettes. Some of the men on the beach have voices like that from smoking too many cigarettes. But her voice is nicer than theirs. It's friendly, like her.

"Hey, listen to this. First thing the guy says to me when I got there this morning was, 'Hope you like kids.' I said, 'Sure I do, I was one once.' The dude didn't even crack a smile. Turns out he's got no sense of humor at all. Not too bright either. But I do like kids. Maybe I'll have some of my own some day. It was fun seein' them all scared and excited at the same time. Hey, Harp, don't you ever talk?"

"I . . . like . . . listening to you."

"Well that's pretty rare. For a guy anyhow. Too bad you don't have a place around here. We could go there, you know, maybe get to know each other better."

Don't you dare even think about it. I'm warning you.

"My place is . . . " Harp points up into the darkness. "Up there."

She looks up under the pier. "Up there? Whataya mean?"

"I mean . . . I sleep up there . . . sometimes. It's warm. Sort of."

She looks up toward his hideout and doesn't say anything for a few moments. Then she turns back to smile at him. "So you got yourself a little hideout up there. Show me."

No! I'm putting a stop to this right now.

She stands up and takes his hand. "Come on."

Didn't I just say no? Are you listening to me?

Harp hesitates. What could it hurt to show her his hideout? Besides, if the killer comes it would be safer up there. He stands up and leads her up the steep sand bank. When he gets there, he digs away some of the sand and clicks on his flashlight to show her.

She leans forward to see. "In there?

"Yes. It's . . . it's warmer in there. Uh, the wind can't get in."

"Okay by me." She crawls right in.

Harp crawls in after her and pushes up some of the sand to block the wind.

"Hey, it's kind of stinky in here, isn't it? What is that smell?"

"The boards." He points up at the pier, but then he realizes she can't see him. "The boards the pier is made out of."

He hears her rap on the wood. "Oh, I get it. Some kind of oil or something they put on. To preserve the wood. Well, I guess you must get used to it. Not that I have a big problem with bad smells. My old man was pretty stinky himself, what with working outdoors with the hogs all day. You can imagine what it was like when he came in at night. Sometimes I'd already be asleep, and he'd wake me up when he'd crawl into bed. Whew. Talk about stinky."

Her father got into bed with her? This is a sinful person. You must get rid of her.

"Your father . . . got into bed with you?"

"Ya, but don't go gettin' the wrong idea. It's just because it was cold. He touched me sometimes, you know where, but he never went too far with it, if you know what I mean. He was just missin' my mother, I guess. Then one day when I was at school, they told me he fell off the tractor and got sucked up into the hay bailer. After his funeral they sent me out here to live with my Aunt Peggy. She's all right. I got no complaints."

I'm not going to tell you again. Get rid of her or I will.

"No!"

"No what?"

"No . . . uh, complaints?"

"Not really. My life isn't so bad. I get three squares every day, and Aunt Peggy don't bother me much. She mostly just watches TV all day and half the night."

"My mother . . . watched TV too."

Now what? Now you're going to tell her our secrets?

"Is that right?"

"Yes. She liked to stay in her chair and watch TV. And she liked to take baths. I took care of her."

"Oh yeah? Was she some kind of invalid or something?"

"Sort of. She needed . . . taking care of."

"Yeah, well, my mother did too. At the end anyhow. I was pretty young then so I don't remember too much of it. Some kind of cancer, I guess. That's what my Aunt Peggy says."

For the first time, Sandra stops talking. Harp tries to think what to say. What do you say to a girl?

Nothing. You're supposed to send her away. Right now!

Harp doesn't want to send her away. What's the harm in talking to her for a while? "My mother used to read me stories. Do you like stories?"

"Stories? You mean . . . like what? Old fairy tales or something?"

"Yes. She read me a lot of good stories. Like . . . do you know the one about the king who wouldn't let anybody eat the apples from his favorite tree?"

"No, tell me that one."

Her voice came from down lower, so Harp realizes she must be lying down. What is she doing down there? Then he feels her hand touch his knee.

Either you get rid of her or I will.

"No, I'm going to tell the story now, and you have to be quiet."

Sandra laughs. "Is that a rule? I have to be quiet while you tell the story?"

"Yes, I mean no, not you. I mean I was just . . . thinking of . . . something else. I'm going to tell the story now. It's about this king who says if anybody eats an apple from his favorite tree they shall be cast down into the earth. I think down in the earth means like in a cave, real deep, or . . . something. Anyhow, the king's daughter, she's really pretty, but maybe not too smart, she decides she wants an apple. She thinks the rule about being cast down into the earth doesn't include her because, well, because she's the king's daughter. See?"

"Sure, I get it. Rich people never think they have to follow the rules. So I bet she picks an apple, doesn't she?"

"That's right, Sandra, she does. But as soon as the king's beautiful daughter eats the apple, she's cast down under the earth where there's a ferocious dragon who won't ever let her come out again."

"But I bet in the end a handsome young man comes to rescue her, doesn't he?"

"You've . . . heard this story?"

"No, no, go on. I'm all ears."

Harp thinks that was an odd thing to say about her ears, but he decides he'd better not mention it. "All right. Here's how it goes. When the king can't find her, he let's everybody know that if any young man can find her and bring her back, he gets to marry her. And have all kinds of riches besides. So these two brothers set out to find her. Along the way the youngest one meets an elf who says the daughter is down in a really deep well. The older brother says he doesn't believe it, but he'll lower the young one down into the well in a basket, if he's crazy enough to want to try it."

"Uh, oh. I don't trust that older brother."

"You're right not to trust him, Sandra. After the young brother goes down and defeats the dragon and rescues the princess, he puts her into the basket and the older brother pulls her up. But he runs off with her and doesn't let the basket go back down so the younger brother can get out too. He's trapped down there with the dragons and . . . whatever else is hiding down there. It's a really bad place."

"Sounds like it. So what happens? Does the older brother get to marry the beautiful princess even though he doesn't deserve her?"

"He sure does. But luckily the younger brother finds a flute in the cave, and he plays on it, and lots and lots of elves come, and they grab him by every hair on his head and fly him right out of the well."

"Hooray."

"Yes, it's like God's miracle. He runs right to the castle and tells the king what happened, and the king has the older brother put to death so the younger brother can marry the princess and live happily ever after that."

"Well now, that's quite a story, Harp. And you told it really good."

"I did?"

"Yes, you did. You're quite a guy, Harp. I don't think I've ever met anyone quite like you."

"You haven't?"

"No, why don't you lie down here next to me so we can get to . . . you know, get to know each other a little better."

Don't you dare even think about . . .

Harp stops listening. And this time he doesn't even have to put his fingers in his ears.

He lies down on his back, and pretty soon he feels Sandra's hand touch his hip. She wiggles closer. He can tell her face is very close to his face because he can smell her breath. It smells like . . . well, he's not sure what it smells like. He hasn't smelled anything like that before. A girl's breath must just smell different than a boy's.

"You know, Harp, this reminds me of something."

Her voice has changed. Now it's softer, not exactly whispering, but very quiet and nice.

"Once, when I was just starting to get boobs, I used to have a secret place sort of like this. Back then I used to hang out with this boy named Limp. That wasn't his real name, but that's what everybody called him because somethin' was wrong with his legs. And he always held his arm up across his chest, like this. Well, it's too dark in here for you to see me, but his arm was like, you know, kind of stuck up against his chest. He was all twisted up. But it wasn't his fault. It was some kind of disease he was born with."

Harp closes his eyes. He likes hearing her talk. He likes the feel of her breath on his face. He's never been so close to a girl, never been so close to anybody really. It's a feeling like . . .

Stop that right now! I won't have this.

"No. I'm not listening."

"You're not listening? What, you don't like this story?"

Harp feels her hand go away from his hip. "Oh, no, Sandra, I wasn't . . . I mean, I really like listening to you talk. What I meant was . . . I don't want to listen to anything else."

"Well, it doesn't matter. Just a dumb old story."

"No, really, I want to hear it. I do. I was just . . . thinking about something else. I do that sometimes. Please keep talking."

"Yeah? Well anyhow, basically what I was saying was old Limp was a good kid. Me and him got along fine. Did I say he couldn't hardly talk? At least not so's anybody could understand him. But I could. After a while I got so I could understand almost everything he said."

She stops talking and puts her hand on his hip again. Harp lies very still and listens to her breathing. He wishes he had known somebody like her when he was little. To have had even one friend might have made everything . . . different, especially if it was a nice friend like her. That little boy, Limp, was some lucky guy.

"But what I was trying to tell you was that we had a hideout, a little like yours here. We found it one day when me and Limp were out in the woods. We found this dug-out hole that was under a great big old oak tree. Some kind of critter had been living under there I guess, and it'd drug in sticks and weeds and old bones and such. We went back to my house and got shovels and we dug it out more. Later, we got some boards to cover up the top to keep the rain out. It was pretty neat, our own secret place."

She stops talking, and Harp feels her hand move up along his hip until it rests against his chest. "You know what we did in there?" she whispers.

"No," whispers Harp, "what?"

"We played . . . games."

"Games?"

"Yeah, made up games. Like we had one called 'You Tell.' Know what that is?"

Harp shakes his head, but then he remembers she can't see him so he whispers, "No. What is it?"

"It was like you had to tell the worst thing you'd ever done. Or the worst thing that had ever happened to you."

Harp is pretty sure it isn't the kind of game he'd like to play. He usually tries not to think about all the bad things that have happened to him. He hopes she doesn't want to play that game.

"Wanna play it?"

"I don't think so, Sandra."

"Com'on. Don't be a scaredy cat. You probably never did any bad things anyhow. I'll start so you'll see how it works. Okay, I told this one to Limp. It's about how I hid this smartypants girl's book so she couldn't study for the big test. I really wanted to do better than her, that one time at least. She thought she was so smart. But it didn't work. She borrowed somebody else's book and did better than me anyhow." She lets out her funny kind of quiet laugh again. Then she taps Harp on the chest. "Now you."

Harp tries to remember his school days. Mostly it was the other kids being mean to him. Did he ever do anything to get back at them? Only once. But he doesn't want to tell her about that.

"C'mon now, it's your turn. You have to tell something."

"I don't have any good school stories. I . . . didn't get to go to school for very long. Mother kept me . . . home."

"She kept you out of school? Why?"

"Oh, it wasn't her fault. She was sick . . . a lot."

"So you never got to go to school? That counts as a bad thing."

"I didn't mind. I stayed home and read. I read a lot . . . back then."

"Okay, but if you didn't mind doin' it, then it doesn't count as a bad thing. You have to think up another one."

Harp thinks about when that truant office came to their house, and they had to move to another house, a worse one. But maybe that didn't count because it wasn't all that bad being alone in that old falling-down house. "Mother hit me with a bottle. Does that count?"

"You bet it counts. Why did she do that?"

"I don't know."

"Well, I think it's a real bad thing. My father never hit me with any bottle, so you win that one. Now it's my turn." She's quiet for a few seconds, then she says, "One time, my father made me sleep in the barn for two days just because I'd forgot to lock the gate, and the cow got out into the field to eat alfalfa. The vet had to come and stab the cow in the stomach with a butcher knife to let all the bad air out. But then the vet sewed her up and she got better. Okay, your turn."

Harp feels bad about the cow getting stabbed. But he's glad the cow didn't have to die like Little Hilly and the Shrimp. It's very quiet and he knows she's waiting for him to tell something bad. Maybe he should tell her about how Mother used to lock him in the closet all night. And how he got locked up in Mitch's cold little closet. But he doesn't want to tell her about that because then she'd want to know how he'd got locked up on Ward D-4 in the first place. Then he remembers a really terrible thing. "One bad thing was when the house burned down and Mother got burned up. Does that count?"

At first she doesn't say anything and Harp isn't sure if she heard him. Then she whispers, "You're saying your mother got burned up?"

"She just . . . didn't come out. It was . . . an accident. After that they told me she'd gone to the other side."

"Gosh, Harp, that's terrible. Good thing you didn't get burned up too. You weren't in the house, were you?"

"No, I wasn't . . . inside that night. But I watched. The firemen were chopping at the windows and squirting water inside, but she didn't come out."

"Man, that is some really sad story, Harp. Really sad. To get burned up like that. Bad deal all the way around." She doesn't say anything for a while, then she says, "Well, okay, I guess you won that one too." But then, after she's quiet again for a while, she puts her hand on his arm and says, "Listen, Harp, me and Limp learned another game down there in our secret hideout. It's a game we called Parts. You wanna play that one?"

"Sure." Harp hopes the Parts game doesn't make him have to remember such bad things.

"Okay, here's how it works. Pretty simple really. We just show each other our parts, and then we name every funny thing they could be used for. Wanna try it?"

"What kind of parts?"

"Com'on, Harp, quit stalling. You know what kind of parts. Private parts."

He feels her fingers jab into his ribs. It sort of tickles, and he giggles and grabs onto her hand to make her stop. She doesn't pull it away so he keeps ahold of it.

She whispers in his ear. "Maybe we should just skip the first part of the Parts game and get to the good part."

Harp feels her hand move down his chest, down the front of his stomach. She seems to be trying to wiggle her hand inside the front of his pants. She scoots closer until she's right up against him.

"And I'll tell you something else," she whispers, "ol' Limp was a little guy, skinny, and all twisted up, but he had a big one."

"A big one?"

"Yeah, he had the biggest one I ever saw, up to that time anyhow. Can you believe it? A twisted up little guy like that? I'll bet you do too, don't you?"

"Uh, I'm not sure," whispers Harp.

"Okay, let's take a little look-see. I'll tell you how you measure up."

He feels her hand slide down inside the front of his pants, and then she touches him down there, and it takes his breath away.

"Not bad, not bad. Okay, let's get those pants off you and see what you can do with it."

He lets her pull his pants down, and then she's quickly on top of him. She's doing all the work so all he has to do is lie there and feel everything happening. There are so many feelings coming all at once, he has trouble keeping them all straight. He's not sure he's supposed to have feelings like that. It feels warm and wet and really nice, so he wants to just think about that and not about whether he's doing anything wrong. Besides, it's her doing everything and not him. He's just lying there, so how could anybody say he did anything wrong?

After a while she starts moving faster and faster, and all of a sudden that feeling happens down in his private parts that tells him he did what Mother said he's never ever supposed to do. Sandra goes on moving a little longer, but then she makes a funny sound, like, "Uh uh uh," and stops moving. Then he feels her weight go off of him, and he hears a bump, and she says, "Damn."

He realizes she must have bumped her head on the boards of the pier. He hopes it didn't hurt her too much.

He lies still, listening to her hard breathing. He can feel her sweat on himself. It feels cool in the night.

Gradually her breathing slows down, and then Harp feels her hand on his chest. He can smell her breath again, that same strange girl smell.

"Damn, Harp, that was nice," she whispers. "You liked it too, didn't you? I mean it wasn't all me, was it?"

"I liked it very much. Thank you."

"You don't have to thank me. It was great for me. Even though you don't have a really big one, like Limp."

"I don't?"

He feels her hand touch his cheek. "Just kidding, Harp old buddy. You did fine. But, hey, I gotta go. My aunt will be wondering what hole I fell into."

"You can . . . stay here. I mean . . . if you want to."

"Naw, I shoulda been home hours ago."

She starts moving around so he pulls his pants back up. He can feel there's a lot of sand inside them, but he doesn't mind. He'll shake it out later.

"Damn, Harp, this sand sure sticks to ya, doesn't it? Let's get out of here so I can stand up and brush it off."

Harp helps her dig out of his hiding place, and they slide down to the level part of the sand. It's still very dark and foggy, but he can see her, a little. She's busy trying to brush the sand off so he gets to watch her all he wants. He's never seen a naked girl before, except for Mother.

"Hey, how about brushin' my back off?"

"Uh, can I turn my flashlight on?"

"Sure, why not? You think I'm shy?"

Harp takes out his flashlight and shines it on her.

She turns her back to him, and he carefully brushes as much of the sand off as he can. Then she turns around to let him do the front. As he wipes off her shoulders and her chest, she looks down at herself. "Kinda big boobs, eh? Guess I need to lose a little weight, like my aunt says."

"I think they're fine, Sandra, not even as big as my mother's."

She looks up at him. "No need to be nice, dude. I know what I am. Just a fat farm girl from Iowa. But I do all right." She finishes wiping away the sand and puts her shirt back on. Then she leans up against him, and he helps hold her up while she puts her pants on.

When she's dressed, she pats him on the chest and says, "Well, I'll shove off now. Thanks again for . . . everything."

Harp snaps off the flashlight. "Will I . . . see you again?"

She puts her hands on his shoulders and gives him a quick kiss, right on the mouth. "Sure you will. Now that I know where you live." She points up under the pier and does her funny little, "Huh, huh," laugh. She pats him on the top of his head and says, "You hang in there, Harp. You're a good guy. I won't forget you."

Harp wishes he could think of something to do to make her not go away, but it's too late: she's already starting up toward the strand sidewalk. He wonders if he should follow her. Maybe he could walk with her to the bus stop. Maybe they could talk more about when she was little and lived on that farm.

Stay right where you are, young man. I want to talk to you.

Harp turns to look out over the water. "Oh, you're back. Well, I don't want to talk right now. I'm going to sit down here and listen to the waves."

Oh no you're not. You're going to listen to me. How dare you ignore me for all that time? How dare you do that. . . that sort of thing with that nasty girl? Explain your disgusting behavior, right this minute.

"No, I don't have to explain myself. She was nice. I liked her."

I guess you would. You're just like your father. All you care about is . . . that sort of thing, getting what you want, whenever you want it. Driven by your base instincts, like all men.

"It wasn't disgusting. It was . . . nice. And if you keep saying things like that, I'm not going to listen to you anymore."

No, wait! Don't turn me off again. I'm just trying to do what's best for you, son. Don't you realize that?

Then quit saying mean things about Sandra. She's nice. I hope she comes back again . . . someday."

If she does, she'll have to deal with me the next time. I'll . . .

"No you won't. If I like her, and if I want to be with her, you have to go away whenever she's here. Or . . . anytime I say so."

Getting mighty big for your britches, aren't you, buster?

"Yes. From now on I get to decide when--"

But his words are cut off because there's an arm around his throat. He can't breathe.

"Still as loony as ever, Harp? What did I tell you about that talking to yourself?"

That voice. It can't be.

It's him. This is the end of us.

Harp tries desperately to wriggle loose, but the arm around his throat just squeezes tighter, cutting off all of his air.

"Hold still, or I'll kill you right now. See this? It's God's instrument of punishment."

Even in the dim light, Harp can see the shine of the knife. It's a bright silver cross knife with a very sharp point on the end of it.

Part 7
The Stranger

When the man in the suit came back to ask us more questions, Mitch pulled me back and whispered that I had to go take a note to his girl friend in their secret place in the basement of the boiler building. The note was to tell her he couldn't come. But I was too scared because I'd never been off of Ward D-4, and besides I didn't know where the boiler building was. When I wouldn't go Mitch got mad and pushed me down onto the floor. Then he went and told the Growler to do it. I didn't think the Growler had ever been off the ward either, but Mitch sent him out. He was gone for a long time and when he came back he ran right past Mitch and went and hid under the desk. We all ran to look under there. The Growler was licking blood off of his hands and arms.

After that they came and took the Growler away and they took Mitch away too. Carl the Older said the Growler had killed the girl because he thought that was what Mitch wanted him to do. For the rest of the day they made us all sit in the chairs in the Day Room with the TV turned off. Three policemen came and they stood by the wall watching us, and after a while two doctors came in and lined us all up and gave us all a shot that made us sleepy. The man in the suit came back and we all had to go in one at a time to talk to him. This time somebody must have been telling them things about how it was on Ward D-4 because when it was my turn to go in they asked my name and looked at their paper and said they knew I'd been writing a secret diary. I wouldn't say anything but they sent one of the policemen back to the dorm and they found it inside my mattress. They took my diary away and I didn't know if I would ever get it back.

Then nothing happened for three days until the man in the suit came back with two policemen. They put handcuffs on my wrists and took me in a car for a long ride. It was the first time since I'd come to Ward D-4 that I got to see what it was like outside. There was green grass and tall trees and a lot of houses and other kinds of buildings too. We went for a long ways until the buildings got bigger and there were lots of people walking on the sidewalks. They stopped the car and took me into a big gray building made out of stone. I had to wait in a chair next to the two policemen in a room. I was there for a long time until they took me into a big room that had a lot of people in it that I didn't know. There was a judge up high who was dressed in a black robe. They made me stand up in front of that judge and say whether or not the things I wrote in my diary were true. They made me put my hand on a Bible so I had to tell the truth. A man in a gray suit jumped up and said I couldn't be depended on to know what the truth was because I was mentally incompetent. I don't know if they decided I could be depended on or not because after that they led me out and drove me back to Ward D-4 and I've been here ever since. Carl the Older said they put the Growler in a prison and Mitch too. That's all I know about it except one day the new aide gave me back my diary and that's how I'm writing in it now.

7-1

God's Messenger

"*I* am the destroying angel come to avenge myself against your lies, Harp. God hath sent me as his holy instrument of revenge."

The big arm is so tight against his throat Harp can hardly get any air to breathe. He feels dizzy and confused, but he knows that voice. It's Mitch.

You should have known he would come. If only you would have let me take care of him when I wanted to.

Harp suddenly realizes Mitch must be the Stranger that the Ghost saw, the crazy man with the mean eyes. But didn't Carl the Older say they'd put Mitch in a prison? How did he get out?

What does it matter how he got out? You've got to do something quick, or you're a goner.

"Surprised to see me, aren't you, Harp? It took me a long time to find you, but finally God showed me the way. Don't have your nasty little Devil dog to protect you now, do you?"

He's gone crazy. Think of something.

Harp gets his fingers up inside Mitch's arm so he can get some air to talk. "Oh, hi, Mitch. What are you doing here? I thought they put you in a prison."

"They?" The arm tightens again. "It wasn't *they* that put me in that place, it was you. It was your lies that got me locked up with those loonies. Me, God's servant, sent to take care of you deranged freaks, locked up like I was the lunatic."

Careful. Careful. He's off his rocker. Speak the Lord's words to him. Say, 'The Lord saith thou shall not kill lest ye be taken possession.'

"I didn't tell any lies about you, Mitch. Didn't I always do what you told me to?"

"Oh, yes, you pretended to be so sweet, so simple minded, always doing exactly what you were told to do. But I finally found out who the viper in my midst was. It was you, the evil little snake, one day crawling around the ward acting scared, and then the next day angry and threatening, scaring everybody half to death with your stories of Hell and damnfire. Even the Growler was afraid of you. But now I know you for who you really are, Satan's poisonous little disciple, sent to do me evil."

Tell him what I said The Bible is your only hope.

"No, really, Mitch. It wasn't my fault. They put handcuffs on me and took me to a big building and made me say what I wrote in my diary was true."

Mitch pulls so hard against Harp's throat it practically lifts him off the ground.

"You mean this here diary?" He shakes it in front of Harp's face. "I found it up in your stinking little hole up there where you take your whores to engage in your sinful lust. This book is all lies. Bacon Benny got what he deserved, and so did those other grotesque aberrations of humanity. Affronts to God's order, every one of them."

Listen to what I'm telling you. Say the words I told you to say.

"But, Mitch, you don't want to kill me. Uh, the Lord sayeth, ' thou shall not kill lest ye be taken possession.'"

"Don't you dare start your preaching to me again, you little Satan. I'm onto your tricks. It wasn't me that was made crazy by God, it was those lunatics on the ward. Every one of them was guilty of breaking God's laws, and they were delivered into madness for it. They had to be punished. God commanded me to do it. The Bible says, 'The Lord shall smite thee with madness and astonishment of heart for your sins.' Those men had to suffer for their sins through God's wrath. Now it's your turn."

Tell him the Lord forbids it.

"But, Mitch, I think the Lord wouldn't like you killing me, not really."

"Oh no, you can't fool me this time. You fooled me once with that kind of talk, but you won't fool me again. I am the Lord's messenger, not you. The Bible says, 'Your transgressions shall bringeth the punishments of the sword.' Now you will know its judgment."

"No, wait, Mitch, it wasn't my fault. The Bible says the child shall not be put to death for the sins of the Mother."

Me? Now you blame me?

"Are you not the vessel of her sin? Are you not the embodiment of her evil? The Lord's magic sword of punishment knows what is right and true. It shall now taste your blood."

Harp feels the point of the knife dig into his back, and he knows this is the end. He whispers, "Goodbye, Mother. I'm sorry."

Goodbye, my son. No matter what you may think of me, remember, I did it all for you. I always loved you.

Harp clenches his teeth and waits for death to come. He hopes it won't hurt too much.

He feels the sharpness of the knife start to go in, but then it's gone.

"Drop the knife, asshole, or I'll tear your Goddamned head off."

Harp feels the pressure of the big arm go away. He ducks under it and pushes away just as a very bright light comes on. He turns back to see Big Hilly with his arm around Mitch's neck.

"Hold on, Hill. No need to strangle him. I've got him covered."

Harp can't see who's talking because the light is so bright, but he knows that voice: it's Detective Olivera. The light is pointed at Mitch and Big Hilly. Mitch isn't struggling at all. He's making a sound like . . . like . . . crying. Mitch is crying, making big sobbing sounds. Harp has never seen Mitch cry before. And he's wiping his face with a floppy hat.

It's your hat. See there, if you'd have kept better track of that hat, none of this would have happened.

Seeing Mitch crying like a little baby makes Harp feel sorry for him. It's sad to see a grown-up man cry so hard like that.

Now you feel sorry for him? He was about to kill you.

"I've got him, Mr. Olivera," says Big Hilly. "You want me to beat the shit out of him?"

"No, just hold him. One of you pick up that knife."

Somebody hurries out into the beam of light and picks up the big silver knife. It's Speel. She holds it up. "I've got it, Detective Olivera." She uses the knife to point at Mitch. "We did it, didn't we? We brought the culprit to ground, just like we said we would. Hey, it means we get the reward, doesn't it? We get the whole kit and caboodle, right?"

"There isn't any reward for this guy. The reward was for Harp."

Speel frowns and shakes the knife toward Olivera. "But you already knew Harp didn't do it. The Ghost told you it was a stranger wearing Harp's hat."

A tall, skinny fellow steps forward. "Yeah, I oughta get the reward because I was the one who told you who the killer really was."

Harp can hardly believe it. That's the Ghost's voice. He's come out of his stall. And he really does look a lot like a ghost, with really white skin that's never been out in the sun. Harp is amazed so see how tall he is. How does a tall person like that sleep in that little tiny toilet stall?

"Yeah, well, we couldn't be sure of that until we caught the guy, could we?" says Olivera. "Besides, it was that prisoner over at the hospital, that Ax guy, who told us somebody was tryin' to kill Harp."

Harp is happy to hear that Ax told Detective Olivera something. It means he's still alive, even if he does have to go back to prison.

So now you're happy he's alive? He was the one who told you to come back here to wait for the killer. He's the one who almost got you killed tonight.

"Now hold on there, partner." It's another voice, coming from somewhere behind Olivera's bright light. "We were the ones who told you about Harp's secret hiding place up under the pier. We should get something for finding him for you."

Harp recognizes that voice too. It's Tex. Is everybody here?

Olivera shines his light on Tex. "Yeah, well, the only reward any of you are gonna get is the reward of saving Harp's ass. Now help me get this guy up to my car and you can go back to . . . whatever you people do down here at night."

"It's not fair," says Speel. "Here we help you out, and when it's all over but the shoutin' what do we get? We don't get squat."

"Yeah," agrees Tex. He takes off his cowboy hat and scratches his head. "We help you catch the homo killer and we don't get nuthin' for it."

Detective Olivera ignores them and takes ahold of Mitch's arm. Big Hilly grabs Mitch's other arm and they drag him away. As they head up toward the strand sidewalk, Harp hears Mitch's pleading voice:

"But I didn't kill anybody, honest I didn't. I was just after Harp. Harp let his Mother's craziness get out of his head and she got into mine, and now she's stuck in there. I had to kill him to make her stop."

Me? Now he blames me? After all I did for him?

The last thing Harp hears as they disappear into the fog is Detective Olivera's voice: "Yeah, well, you can tell it to the judge. You're goin' straight back to whatever nut house you escaped from, and this time we'll make sure you stay put."

That leaves Harp and Speel and Tex and the Ghost standing there in the dark. Harp takes his little flashlight out of his pocket and shines it on them. "Gosh, thanks, fellas. Mitch was about to stab me with his big cross-knife. You all got here just in time."

"Oh yeah, just in time for you," says Speel. "What about us? If we coulda nabbed you before Olivera found out about the real killer, we coulda split that big reward."

"Yeah," agrees Tex. "Bunch of homos killin' each other off, and for some reason they put up a big reward for you. We almost had it in the bag until you had to go and spoil it by almost gettin' yourself stabbed by the real killer. Oh well, we could stand her jawin' about it til the cows come home and it wouldn't do us a lick of good. I'm shovin' off." He jams his cowboy hat back onto his head and heads for the strand sidewalk.

"Jeez," says Speel, "you try to help a person and look what it gets you. I'm going home too." She starts to go, but turns back to shake her finger at Harp. "And you might as well know I'm never going to forgive you for messing up my garage, even if you are innocent." She walks away into the fog, shaking her head.

"Well, shit," says the Ghost. "This wasn't even worth coming outside for. I'm going back to my stall." He turns and stomps away.

That leaves Harp all alone again. He snaps off his flashlight and stares into the night. "Why is everybody mad at me? I didn't do anything, did I?"

Of course you didn't. Forget them. What do we care about them? Bunch of nobodies.

"I don't see why they have to be mad at me. I was the one who almost got killed, wasn't I? Mitch was going to stick his big cross-knife in my back."

That's right. You've had a hard night, haven't you, my boy? Why don't you lie down and sleep for awhile. I can take care of things here.

7-2
Endings and Beginnings

*T*he cold fog swirls around him, as if it's mad at him too. "I feel cold, Mother."

Then lie down and think warm thoughts. Think about how I used to make you hot chocolate by the kitchen stove. Think about how I always took good care of you.

Harp lies down on the sand, but there's something under him. He sits up and feels for it. It's his diary. Thank goodness. At least he's still got his diary. He holds it close to his heart and looks out into the fog. "It's not fair, Mother. I'm cold and I'm tired and I'm hungry. I don't even have any cookies left because Sandra ate them all. I might just as well lie here until I die. Nobody likes me anyhow."

"I like you."

Harp jumps up and tries to see through the darkness. "Who said that? Who's there? His heart is racing so fast he thinks it might jump right out of his chest. He's sure it was a real voice. Somebody's there, somebody hiding in the dark. Did Mitch get away and come back to kill him? Or is it another killer, the real killer? Where is his flashlight? He falls to his hands and knees, frantically searching all over the sand for it.

"What are you looking for, Harp?"

It's that same voice again. Very close now. Wait a minute, doesn't he know that voice?

"Is it time for my story yet, Harp?"

"Oh, for Chripe's sake, it's only Shoeless Joe." Harp sits back down on the sand and puts his hand against his chest. He's breathing so fast he must sound like a dog panting.

Calm down. It's only the dummy. Why are you always such a scaredy cat?

Harp waits for his heart to slow down a little. Then he says, "Listen, Joe, I told you before not to sneak up on me like that. You scared me again."

"I'm sorry."

"Well, don't do it anymore."

Joe doesn't say anything so Harp counts his breaths for a while to calm down. He feels around until he finally finds his flashlight. He turns it on and sees that Joe is sitting in the sand cross-legged. He's sniffing the remnants of his torn-apart flower that's hardly more than a bedraggled stem now. Harp is sure there can't be any smell left in that flower.

Joe looks up into the light beam and smiles his big toothless smile. "Is it time for my story now, Harp?"

This is too much. Get rid of this lamebrain. It isn't the next day yet and you know the rule, only one story a day.

"No, Joe, like I said before. Only one story a day. You have to wait until morning."

"But it's morning now, Harp." Joe points up toward the sky.

Harp looks toward the city and sees that Joe is right: there is a little bit of morning glow in the sky over that way. "Hey, it does look like the sun's coming up. How did you do that?"

Joe shrugs.

It doesn't seem like it should be morning already. Did he lose track of time again? "Shall I tell him a story? Is it time?"

All right, one story. Then you have to get rid of him. I want to be alone.

"Which one shall I tell him?"

Tell him the rhyme about Cock Robin.

"No, I don't like that one."

Who'll sing a psalm? I, said the Thrush, as she sat on a bush. I'll sing a psalm.

"No. Stop it! I said I didn't want to hear that one."

Who'll toll the bell? I, said the bull, because I can pull, I'll toll the bell.

"Who are you talking to, Harp?"

All the birds of the air fell a-sighing and a-sobbing when they heard the bell toll for poor Cock Robin.

"All right, all right. I'll tell it. But later I get to tell him a story that has a happier ending. Okay?"

Suit yourself.

He turns back to Joe. "This isn't a very happy story, Joe. But I have to tell it to you before you get to hear another really good story. This one is about poor little Cock Robin. It starts out with Cock Robin already lying there dead, and then as the story goes on, you have to guess all the people who might have done it. Okay?

Joe nods and smiles, almost as if he already knows what's coming.